M. A. CASTLE was born in Hampshire in 1939 [...] her family after the War. She failed the gramm[...] passed the thirteen plus to attend a commercial s[chool. Due to poor health,] she missed some schooling, and to amuse herself, made up stories and wrote them down in a green covered exercise book. After school she worked for a bank, married and started a family. Later she became the only female DIY rep in the West. She now lives in Somerset.

Writing was part of her life, but she had no particular goal in mind. Then, in 2014 she joined her current writing group. Her tutor, Sue Purkiss, noticed that she tended to overload short stories with too much information, and suggested that a longer story might prove more satisfying. This resulted in a breakthrough. Armed with a list of characters, she gradually developed the story over the next few years, with the enthusiastic support of the group. The result is *Keeper's*, her first novel, which she completed in her eighty-first year.

Keeper's

M. A. Castle

SilverWood

Published in 2020 by SilverWood Books

SilverWood Books Ltd
14 Small Street, Bristol, BS1 1DE, United Kingdom
www.silverwoodbooks.co.uk

Copyright © M. A. Castle 2020

The right of M. A. Castle to be identified as the author of this
work has been asserted in accordance with the Copyright,
Designs and Patents Act 1988 Sections 77 and 78.

All rights reserved. No part of this publication may be reproduced,
stored in a retrieval system, or transmitted in any form or by any means,
electronic, mechanical, photocopying, recording or otherwise,
without prior permission of the copyright holder.

This is a work of fiction. Names, characters, places and incidents either
are products of the author's imagination or are used fictitiously.
Any resemblance to actual events or locales or persons,
living or dead, is entirely coincidental.

ISBN 978-1-80042-001-4 (paperback)
ISBN 978-1-80042-002-1 (ebook)

British Library Cataloguing in Publication Data
A CIP catalogue record for this book is
available from the British Library

Page design and typesetting by SilverWood Books

KEEPER'S

Acknowledgements

Firstly, my very great thanks to Sue Purkiss, our creative writing class tutor, and the class members who offered support, encouragement and suggestions. I wrote short stories more like book synopses. Sue understood my problem and suggested I write longer stories, so I made up a list of characters and began to write homework with these characters. Gradually over the years I got to know my characters and a story emerged, and now I have a book.

Thanks to Glenys, Mel, and Shirley, who kindly spent their precious time reading early drafts, giving me constructive feedback. Then Sue, very kindly, passed her expert eye across the now more or less finished book, which produced more adjustments. Lastly, and very importantly, my thanks to the editor, without whom I would not have reached this far. Mistakes are all mine.

Chapter One

Here he was, uprooted from Suffolk, and not sure about the new life he'd found himself a part of. He saw that the plate-glass window reflected his expression of uncertainty and immediately pulled himself up to his full height, squaring his shoulders in attempt to, well, what exactly? These windows were the only generous aspect of the flat. He guessed them to be three metres across, almost the width of the room. Looking round, it was hardly any bigger than a very exclusive tool shed but fine for one person and, he had to admit, the décor was very smart.

He'd have to find something more suitable for family visits if they couldn't decide what to do permanently. For now, he'd Skyped a Frederico Jones in New York after seeing a discounted offer found through the bank magazine, and arranged a six-month lease. Frederico had had problems letting and Justin was in a hurry. It was a start, but a big stretch financially. Even so, he wanted, needed, a decision on where the family would live. It would have to be somewhere within reach of the city now that he was based in Canary Wharf.

His Scandinavian wife of eight years, and their six-year-old twins, showed no sign of thinking of moving anywhere. Well, that was unfair. Clara showed no interest in moving – Zoe and Carl were excited at the idea of exploring London. As he thought these unsettling thoughts, his view here was through the shifting branches of plane trees. The cool autumn wind blew a carrier bag across the road. That was him, that empty carrier bag, blowing about in this new environment, not knowing where it might take him.

Justin was preoccupied by his inner vision of geese across the marshes; their calls and then the silences. Foolishly, he thought, and wasn't even certain how much he meant it, he yearned for the big open skies of Suffolk, but the view in Soho only gave him a messy roofscape of satellite dishes. He'd been spoilt, for even when he was a child in Wimbledon Village, home had faced the common and the woods there, where he had enjoyed considerable freedom.

He'd been at Canary Wharf for two months now and almost everything remained strange to him. Absentmindedly, he pushed a hand through his dark hair, then stood sideways to reassure himself in the reflection of the window that he still had a flat belly. He made the effort to run each day in the autumn pre-dawn; at thirty-eight he considered that he needed to keep on top of fitness. It wasn't as satisfying as running along Suffolk's remote country lanes, teaching himself languages through his earphones, to the rhythm of his footfall; but, always hungry to learn and still with enthusiasm to keep fit, he had maintained the habit.

He thought of his previously settled life as a bank manager in Bury St Edmunds, living out in the countryside. He consoled himself that he still saw wildlife in London. Sometimes on his run he would see a grey squirrel scamper along a wall, up early for breakfast. There were foxes on occasion, skulking away, or they might pause from scavenging through a bin bag and just stare as he ran past.

Justin considered the new small team he was working with, all urban. He'd overheard someone referring to him as the "country boy" and instead of burying his head behind his screen, he'd turned and grinned, 'That's me, then!' and, looking around, joined in with the banter on the East Asia Trading Desk. After all, there was no future in being sensitive. He needed to toughen up to survive here and he didn't want to look an idiot, trying not to be an outsider. He thought that he'd been contented, enjoying a relatively low-key working life so recently in the backwater that was Suffolk.

He had been saved from redundancy, certain his degree in Mandarin was a factor. His previous experience in running a domestic bank must have counted for something. He'd always liked studying, and when he'd joined the bank after university, he had taken advantage of courses the bank had offered, first in accountancy, then later, a part-financed MBA degree, all part of his CV. Now, years later, he found himself gearing up, gaining an appetite for the new, here in Canary Wharf, much to Clara's annoyance. Clara had expected him to take a different, local path. Everything in the building was geared to international finance in comparison to what had been familiar – everything he'd known had been small scale, provincial. In spite of his wife's lack of enthusiasm, he was profoundly relieved that he was coping in his new position.

He still wondered about those souls now cast adrift in Bury St Edmunds when their, his, bank closed. He leaned forward, pressed against the glass to feel cold on his forehead, and wondered if he could adjust sufficiently to really fit in.

Clara's recent visit to this tiny flat with the twins had not been entirely successful, but he couldn't help smiling at the memory of Zoe and Carl's faces when he'd caught them having a pillow fight. That visit was partly meant to celebrate Clara's birthday, which was on the Saturday. He looked around now, still smiling, at the bijou sitting room. There was one bedroom and a sofa bed in the sitting room for the children to share. They'd had DVDs to watch, and tablet games for the Saturday morning if they woke up early, and were instructed to wait until they were called for breakfast.

Justin's plan was to have champagne, give Clara the perfume he'd bought her and an expensive propelling pencil with a leather-covered notebook he'd seen in Regent Street. She was always sketching something. This would fit in her bag. Chocolates were planned for the twins to give her at breakfast. Justin took the precaution of placing these in the bedroom chest of drawers in case temptation overtook them before the handover.

It began well. He met them at St Pancras Station. The twins were excited and Clara was beaming. He'd taken them to the flat by taxi. They had a light supper, starting with flaky cheese straws, as they watched Justin make omelettes. For dessert they had ice cream with little biscuits he'd bought in Soho.

Once they'd settled the twins and closed their door, promising to leave the hall light on, they retired to bed themselves. Suddenly, and after several weeks apart, they found themselves alone. It was a tender moment. Justin helped Clara undress as she moved slowly to allow him. She let her sweep of hair fall as it may down her back. He leaned in behind her, burying his face in the perfume. They slept little, waking early on Saturday morning, fully intending to enjoy this short respite from separation, safely tucked away, as they thought, across the small hall from the children.

His plan almost worked until there was a sudden loud crash. Gathering himself somewhat reluctantly, as Clara fell back on the bed groaning in dismay, Justin strode into the sitting room to find the culprits heavily engaged in a pillow fight. Six-year-old Zoe and Carl had broken a very classy lamp.

Somehow, the broken lamp seemed to represent something more than itself. Clara and Justin's moment was spoilt. He made breakfast and, over a strong coffee, they huddled around the kitchen table, deciding what to do about the lamp.

'We've got to replace it,' Clara said. 'We can't just apologise. So, what if you take Zoe and Carl to St James's Park and feed the ducks or something and we can meet back here for lunch?'

It was agreed. They had a look online to see where to find a similar lamp. Selfridges looked a possible source but Heal's was nearer, as was Liberty's in Regent Street. The twins spent time with considerable exuberance throwing an old frisbee they came across under a park seat. They were not particularly contrite, Justin noticed. Then, of course, they had to relay everything back to Clara when they met up again at the flat.

Clara had not had a good time. A similar lampshade and base hadn't been easy to find. Once purchased, Clara decided a taxi was essential to return her purchase and herself to Soho, exhausted. She emphasised a little petulantly that, after all, it was her birthday.

They eventually made it to Regent's Park and the zoo, Clara's mood still a little deflated. Justin had booked them all in for an early meal in a small restaurant off Brewer Street, but Clara declared somewhat snippily that she was too exhausted from the excitement of London to venture out again.

Justin tried to chivvy her, saying it would be fun, but she was adamant she was too tired. So, reluctantly, Justin cancelled their booking and offered to take the twins to buy fish and chips from a chippie he knew in Poland Street. The twins were tired, so he went alone. He bought a bottle of wine from an off-licence, but on the way back, regretted it. He should have got cider for fish and chips. Clara pretended wine was fine. But of course it really wasn't. There was something brittle about her. He was nervous of a showdown when she was returning to Suffolk at teatime the next day, so he delayed trying to discuss house-hunting, the one thing really concerning him.

Having partly recovered from Saturday's setbacks, the highlight and, to Justin's relief, the success for them all was on the Sunday. He'd bought tickets for the family day upstairs at a jazz club. Clara loved jazz and there was the chance to try some of the instruments. The band was great and both children were encouraged to try. Clara was in a better mood and he relaxed. Everything would be fine after all. They could discuss moving when he Skyped or they Snapchatted, or whatever.

He went with them to the railway station and saw them off. He was momentarily upset when Carl pleaded almost tearfully, 'Daddy, Daddy, you will come home soon, won't you?' followed by Zoe, always the more outgoing of the two, who literally jumped on him so he had to clutch her to avoid an accident. 'Daddy, Daddy. You will come. I'll make you!'

'Of course, of course. Very soon!' Thus, suitably mollified, more kisses were exchanged and he hugged Clara, then watched them get on the crowded train. They disappeared somewhere inside. He couldn't find them again. Even so, he found himself standing on the platform until the train had pulled out, with the lingering anxiety that Clara might blank him when he eventually tried to discuss what they would do about where to live.

Some days later, walking along Brewer Street, he decided to be more positive. He was working alongside Ling Chow. Ling – helpful, calm in manner, yet outgoing, and in his mid-twenties – had moved from the Hong Kong office. His grandmother had left years earlier with her late husband and lived in Chinatown where he was sharing along with his cousin, Linda.

Ling and Linda had invited Justin for supper. Justin, after initially being hesitant to accept this invitation, was now approaching Chinatown Arch. Their flat was located somewhere beyond. The emptiness he felt, nothing to do with hunger, was partly eased by the cheerful noise, bustle and racket of his surroundings. In this colourful chaos he doubted he'd find the address given to him. He resorted to his phone. The block of flats was actually halfway along, fronted by red doors. He pressed the number given to him. Cantonese sounded from the entryphone. After a moment he gathered himself and announced his name. There was a loud cackle of laughter and the door clicked open. Ling had prepared him for this welcome. This was Grandma then.

Clara, shuddering from the cold, took rinsed-off wellies through the porch into the utility room to dry them on old newspaper. The field was partly frosted from several days of low temperatures, but somehow there was always debris needing a hosing off. Once in the warmth of the kitchen, her view out through the window was partly steamed up. She wiped off some condensation, pausing to look across to the oaks around the field's perimeter, bare of leaves now, grand in stature, permanent. She wondered how old they might be, what changes they may have seen.

Their cottage was named Keeper's Cottage. They understood it had belonged to an estate in the past, the tenant gamekeeper's residence probably. What was left of the estate was over the other side of the village, owned by friends, Alice and Edie. She shivered – she needed a hot drink. Zoe and Carl, high from their scarper across the field with Arthur, their Irish wolfhound, and still tingling from the cold, chased each other around the kitchen table. Arthur, in his loping clumsiness, crashed into a chair, knocking it over and halting their game. Knowing he was now in trouble, he slunk beneath the safety of the table.

Autumn had been cold and now winter had them in its grip, with Christmas imminent. Justin had been home several times since their visit to his flat. But he wasn't dependably home each weekend. She'd begun to try not to expect him, but it wasn't easy.

Suddenly they were into the middle of December and Justin was expected home for Christmas. She'd originally thought they'd wait until he was home to get the tree. They'd always gone together to the forest to buy one at Christmas. It signified that they were a family and was a time to celebrate together, particularly since they'd had the twins. To her annoyance, their plans had had to change when Justin had let her know, apologetically, that there was some high-flown embassy function that he apparently couldn't avoid, which also meant a later date to come home and a shorter Christmas break. There was now an artificial tree in the sitting room needing some attention. It still listed. She heaved a sigh.

'Zoe, pick up the chair, darling, please.'

Zoe obliged, secretly tickling Arthur under his tummy in solidarity.

'I'll get the bread, Mummy!' Carl, just tall enough, reached up to get the bread from the bin. Toast and honey was expected, their favourite mid-morning snack. Clara, preoccupied, thinking of the imminent Christmas break and what it might bring, cut the first slices too thick to fit into the toaster. She now had Zoe and Carl's attention from across the table and, as they watched in silence, saw her second attempt was successful. Handing the children their slices of toast, she then sat with her coffee, fiddling with an unused teaspoon, chasing a few crumbs around, as the twins made sticky soldiers of their toast, each trying to prove they were superior in their efforts and expertise. Absentmindedly, Clara passed them a damp cloth to wipe their fingers.

This table wouldn't even fit into Justin's temporary flat, she mused, let alone Arthur who was now licking her other hand. Wellington boots would seem like something from another planet amongst its minimal sparseness and extreme modern style. Anyway, all that was irrelevant; his lease was up in the spring, when he'd have to decide on somewhere else to live. She wondered if he might cave in and return to Suffolk to work. She'd brought up the possibility more than once, convinced he could work as a translator, perhaps teach as well here at home. Justin had looked at her with a disbelieving expression, explaining, as if to a child, that what they had now was some sort of certainty of income, whilst what she suggested was not. But she'd still work on the idea.

Zoe and Carl had taken to pinging the remaining crumbs over the edge of the table for Arthur to catch. Clara decided to direct them to a more productive occupation. She wiped the table down and covered it with an old plastic cloth. They had card, craft scissors, glue, glitter and felt tips to play with and make hanging decorations for this disappointing tree, forlorn in the sitting room. Then she braved the depths of the hall cupboard to drag out the Christmas decorations in various boxes from the back.

Clara sat back on her heels, suddenly remembering supper and the casserole. Casserole! She needed to prepare it and give it time to cook through for the evening meal so, pushing the boxes against the side of the stairs, she followed the sounds of a small riot towards the kitchen where an argument was under way between the twins over the red felt-tip pens. Clara rummaged in a dresser drawer to find another with colour still in its tip and handed it over to Carl, who grumbled that Zoe always got her own way and the best pens. Instead of trying to reassure him that it wasn't so, she let Carl's comment sit in the air, unanswered, and made a face at the work surface where the vegetables she had to peel were lined up.

That chore completed, she filled the fruit bowl with clementines. Fresh clementines from the box, with their leaves still attached, gave her a quiet thrill. From time to time she returned to check on the twins and the casserole, encouraging their efforts and poking at the casserole listlessly.

There was probably more glitter than she'd realised. Perhaps, she thought, she should have rationed the glitter, as Arthur would take some time to be free of it. Taking another look at supper, she'd be the first to admit that cooking was not something that she had embraced entirely successfully. She leaned over the pan, sniffing its aromas. She thought it smelt okay so she turned the heat down and returned it to the oven to simmer.

Darkness fell mid-afternoon. She checked the kitchen clock. Another hour or so and Justin would ring. She busied herself with bringing in some logs and fed Arthur. At last, the landline rang and she leapt to answer it. 'Hi, darling. Yes, half an hour? Yes, we're on our way.' They would be, she thought, although it was easier said than done. It was dark, the children were tired and Arthur was in the back of the Land Rover behind his grating before she could stop him.

'Yes, come on, Arfy!' Carl yelled in support.

She sighed and closed the back then the side doors. He'd leapt in the rear section when Clara had pulled out her coat and it was easier to give in than the alternative, and quicker. Driving in, the twins argued and Arthur refused to sit. Resigned, she sighed and drove on, feeling tired and stressed. Still, she thought grudgingly, it was important to try to make this a special Christmas, to forget the fact she'd had to buy an artificial tree. She did miss the wonderful aroma of pine. Justin would have to look at it. Somehow it was a bit lopsided.

Since he'd been transferred – saved from redundancy, if she were honest – she couldn't imagine how their lives were going to settle, but Christmas would give them a space to relax. They'd see friends, walk on the fens and have some moments on their own. Yes, it would be good; had to be. She forced herself to relax her jaw. Why had she been gritting her teeth? The twins were batting each other now with their teddies. Hmm, she thought, that was enough to make anyone grit their teeth. They were quite a handful to manage without regular support from Justin. In his excitement, Arthur still wouldn't sit down so she had to use wing mirrors. Enormous Arthur, whom Justin had chosen, was another thorn in her side. She did like him but that was when she and Justin were living together, not in this new fractured miserable existence they were now enduring. It was difficult not to feel resentful.

Justin saw her through the crowd. A moment of clear joy swept over him and stopped him in his tracks. God, how he'd missed her, missed the kids. She straightened up, caught his gaze and grinned. She'd been bending down, separating the twins from sparring. Nothing new there then, he thought fondly. Clara's white-blonde hair was bundled into a Fair Isle beanie. Her Scandi skin, as he called it, much to her embarrassment, always glowing and golden, was almost completely hidden. In those few seconds he resolved to do his very best to make Christmas special. Though the thought was not new, it was quickly reinforced as they all rushed towards him. That evening, the twins stayed up as they celebrated with pizza, after Clara had second thoughts about the casserole. She quietly put it to one side to cool on the slab in the larder to reassess in the morning, and quickly heated the pizzas. Arthur settled happily on Justin's feet under the table.

Later, the twins helped decorate the lower branches of the tree with their newly-made decorations, Justin having dealt with the base, levelling it up. Then Clara lit candles along the mantelpiece and in the windows. For a while Zoe and Carl stood mesmerised, watching the flickering flames reflected in the glass. Justin then led them off to bed just before they became fractious with excitement and exhaustion, kissing Clara briefly as he passed.

Clara, mellowed by wine, his recent proximity and the thought of their evening to come, began to clear up. She remembered with a flush of guilt the prang she'd had in the station car park when she'd backed into a post. Luckily, there wasn't any real damage. In their excitement to see Justin, the twins had quickly forgotten about it. Anyway it wasn't as bad as she'd feared. She was certain that vehicle had blind spots. She paused from loading the dishwasher, straightened and gazed at her reflection in the window above the now-flickering candles. She smiled and pulled her hair over one shoulder, remembering how Justin had looked at her at the station.

Later, as they sat leaning against the sofa, their glasses refilled, the fire glowing before them, flames licking the walls of the fireplace, Justin relaxed. Relaxed enough to broach to Clara the subject preoccupying his thoughts, but recently avoided.

'Darling?' he ventured.

She turned towards him smiling, almost sleepy.

He continued, 'I wonder if you've thought any more about where to live, what to do?'

She sat bolt upright, now no sign of incipient sleepiness evident.

He'd hoped she might have considered an alternative to their current separate living and made a decision. He'd already looked at several areas within a commute of Canary Wharf. This wasn't at all what she'd expected to hear tonight. She leapt from her position by the fire. For a second he thought, nervously, that her drink was coming his way.

'What d'you mean?' she cried. 'Can't you put that to one side – all the upheaval, your bloody job – for our first evening?'

Then, to his consternation he saw tears welling. He stood and took her to him, gently removing her glass, placing it carefully on the coffee table, speaking in a conciliatory tone, 'Sorry, darling, sorry. It was insensitive of me tonight. It's just that, well,' – he searched around, feeling miserable – 'I miss you all so much.' He left out his obvious worry: their need to do something, anything, and make some plans.

'Well, the dog's on your side,' she muttered, through her tears, and hiccupped as Arthur licked one of Justin's hands. 'Then, he would be. He knows it was you who chose him at the rescue centre.' Clara sniffed, searching for a tissue up her sleeve, and blew her nose loudly. She took a deep breath. 'Well, I'm sorry too. Really, I am. But this is all I've ever wanted – to be settled, secure. Except of course we aren't, not any more, are we?' There was a shudder, then a very small concession to reality as, almost in a whisper, now she was prepared to lean into his shoulder, she muttered, 'Don't want to change, I suppose.'

Don't see how I can, she thought, sadly.

'If you can't see us all together in London, I'm home for holidays and long weekends,' Justin suggested, though this was clearly not what she wanted. It could have been so much easier. There were people he'd met at work who lived in Hampshire, Dorset and other counties and one who came from Devon. Suffolk was just another county. All of them with good rail links. It was common to have a small pad of some sort in the city too. It was true that he was adjusting much more easily than he'd thought possible a few months ago. He would quite like the family to live right in London, the East End perhaps. Though it would mean a terrace about a quarter of the size of where they lived now. Then, schooling would be another very different kettle of fish. Sooner or later they'd have to make these decisions. He thought briefly of Ling and where he lived in Chinatown – single without responsibilities – and his beautiful cousin, Linda, who had drifted in and out of their grandmother's flat on that memorable evening a few weeks ago; both young, both free.

Over the Christmas break, Justin tried to summon what had become an elusive mood of joyful relaxation. He thought back longingly to a year ago, before the thunderbolt of the branch closure, when life was simple. He'd even taken on other people's duties in November so that he might stretch leave into the New Year now, just to be at home. Their previous easy life, closeness, was somewhere out there in the ether. They hadn't discussed what he considered the inevitable move since Clara's outburst on his first evening home. Sitting back now, the dog leaning against his legs, everyone overfed and sleepy, he reflected that there had been some really good moments, particularly on Christmas morning when the presents were unwrapped.

Later, he'd made scrambled eggs with smoked salmon and they drank schnapps, the children grumbling about orange juice. They'd all wrapped up to traipse across the frozen fields, leaving Christmas dinner on a low heat to be finished when they got back, red-faced and glowing from the cold.

The grand finale had been the New Year's party with Alice and Edie and other friends. Continuing ice and snow meant that once they'd arrived at Alice and Edie's old mansion, they stayed overnight.

Justin's time at home was running short. He was beginning to worry about getting back to work and leaving the family behind. Clara's refusal to discuss their new life together was beginning to fill him with dread and a certain irritation. All these thoughts he'd determined to put aside until another day.

Alice and Edie, their hostesses, had decided – to Justin's relief – not to insist on fancy dress. They, however, wore vintage Zandra Rhodes. Alice was obviously uncomfortable. Floaty outfits were not the best for her large frame, whereas Edie, giggling and giving them a twirl in her outfit, looked amazing.

The twins loved to visit. There were games for the children in the big hall organised by Alice's parents, then their sleeping bags were lined up near the radiators for later. The rest of the party hit the cocktail bar and music got them dancing. Supper was served in a casual manner from trestles. Everyone contributed in some way, but Justin was annually surprised and impressed by the hospitality shown to them and the other guests, many of them friends from nearby villages.

'You see, Jussy,' Clara muttered, 'how impossible London would be for the children? There would be none of this now, would there?'

Justin glanced down at Clara, momentarily annoyed. Hardly Outer Mongolia, was it? Still, he didn't want to cause an argument right now, determined as he was for it to be a happy evening.

At midnight they all trooped outside wearing coats slung over shoulders, the children wrapped up to watch the fireworks from across the lake. The lake was frozen, so this year the reflection of the display was less stunning, but even so the show was spectacular. Once over, the children were ushered inside for hot drinks.

Adults lingered and to celebrate the New Year there was much kissing of neighbours. Clara had disappeared. Then he saw her kissing Jeff, a friend from their nearby village of Swayle. Justin turned, smiling at Jeff's wife Josie who stood next to him.

Josie had followed his gaze. 'Well, it would be rude not to now, wouldn't it?' She pulled him gently down towards her.

The kiss was on the lips and marginally too long to be comfortable. Justin felt pink as he drew away. 'Well, Happy New Year, Josie!' He knew he sounded awkward. She smiled; an eyebrow lifted as she moved away.

Weeks later, walking in St James's Park on a Sunday afternoon, he felt in his pocket for a mint. Out came a pearl earring attached to the packet. He had to stop to think. Clara didn't wear earrings. Then he remembered New Year's Eve and Josie. Had she been wearing earrings? If so, how could one have got into his pocket? He'd have to tell Clara to ask Josie if she'd mislaid an earring. He could leave it at home next time. Then he sat down on one of the many benches by the lake. No, perhaps he should give it some thought first. Things had continued to be difficult. It struck him then that he recalled Ling's cousin, Linda, whom he'd met briefly before Christmas, wearing small pearl-drop earrings. They had shifted merrily against her short, raven hair as she chatted to him. That was a ridiculous thought. Even worse, was it warped, wishful thinking? She was at least fifteen years younger than him, and she would have had to put the earring in his pocket. He shook his head in disgust at himself. That was what happened when normal life was put on hold. He'd begun to fantasise.

Clara hadn't settled easily, finally dropping off. Then the phone rang, disturbing her. She checked the alarm clock. It wasn't six yet. Grabbing the landline, she checked the screen. She'd guessed correctly – it was Dad. She gave a silent sigh. Since he'd retired, Dad was always up and about and didn't consider other people's need for sleep as a reason to wait to ring. He'd already been out and attacked the woodpile, he'd been quick to boast. Mama would be taking cookies round to the neighbours, apologising later. Clara turned on her side to make herself more comfortable, pulling the duvet over her shoulders.

'Mama said to ring you, darling. You already up, I expect?' Before she could gather herself to lie, he continued, 'Slipped my mind yesterday. Just to say we're coming over.'

Clara was wide awake now and sat up, leaning on an elbow. 'Dad, is everything okay?'

'Yes, yes. Never better, but we'd like to, well, talk,' he stumbled. Then, trying to cover the slip, he rushed on, 'I mean a treat. We didn't see you over Christmas. We'd like to have a long weekend. See you both and the children.'

Her heart sank. Obviously they were coming over to renew their efforts to convince her she should pack up and move to London. She had talked to herself enough times but between the stern talk and action, something happened and she stalled. Her mother had been particularly earnest and had rung her on numerous occasions during the school day when Clara wasn't helping at the twins' school in the village.

'Chicken, it's Mama.'

Chicken? She hadn't been called "chicken" since she was tiny. It didn't augur well for what was to come.

In no uncertain terms Clara's mother made clear that a wife's place was with her husband, wherever her husband's work took him, and where the money was, she added briskly. Something would happen sooner or later if she didn't pull herself together. He'd find someone else. She would lose him – and think of the children.

Privately, Clara thought her mother was being biased. She and Dad had been the extreme opposite of how she herself felt. As a result she'd been shunted around throughout her childhood and not with her parents, but so that her parents could work together as peripatetic doctors. She had only really loved the holidays when she'd been sent to Finland to Mama's parents. There she slipped in comfortably with the farming life, playing and sometimes working with her cousins.

Her father was still talking. She explained that Justin was on a course and would be away.

Her father sighed as if it was her fault. 'Oh well, give him our love, darling, but we may see him before he goes, briefly. We're off on a mini Art Society break to London tomorrow, before we come on up to you. We've got his address somewhere.'

'Dad, was there something special you wanted to talk about?'

But there was nothing more forthcoming, other than another sigh.

'We'll bring pastries from Fortnum's. See you Friday evening.' Then he rang off.

The For Sale sign was now planted firmly by the drive in the front garden. The bank, which provided the mortgage and was helping with Justin's rent, had insisted he made a commitment. She wondered what Mama and Dad would make of that.

Chapter Two

Coming home from work one afternoon, after a rare early finish, Justin decided to get off the Underground at Embankment, and go on to have a turn around the park. He paused to watch the ducks on the lake. There was an argument between a reluctant duck and a determined drake. He felt sympathy for both parties, and reassured himself that in a week or so they might be in sync. He didn't feel the same about his own situation. Clara, with whom he had found it an ongoing problem to get to commit to their next move, really needed to come down at half-term week and house-hunt with him. As a bank employee, he had been instructed to get their house on the market. Decide where to live. Get on with it.

When he'd first started at Canary Wharf, and was struggling to fit in, he was haunted by Clara's image. He couldn't stop thinking of her beauty, her goldenness, and how she could arouse him just by her proximity. He recalled with affection, and newly acquired sadness, her husky laugh and the way she'd knot her amazing hair up into a topknot absentmindedly, when trying to explain something that engrossed her.

Now he was just as preoccupied with questioning how much she was committed to their marriage. He had a half-formed fear, which he failed to thrust from his consciousness, that she might retreat to Denmark, take Zoe and Carl, go back to Odense near her parents; even worse, even farther away, to bloody Finland, to her grandparents near Kuopio.

Back at the flat, staring out through dusty windows, Justin tried to concentrate on a possible joint future, in which case he still thought Greenwich would be best. There were several schools in the area, admittedly totally unlike their rural church school, but everything could be an adventure for them, if they were positive about their new life. There were the massive parks, access to the river and excellent transport connections. He checked his watch. It was time to Skype home.

Suddenly his phone vibrated. It was Linda, Ling's cousin. She wanted to know if he'd like to join them for the lantern street party in Chinatown. Justin smiled to himself at the thought. He assumed she'd got his number off Ling's phone. She probably felt sorry for him. He couldn't imagine how he might fit in amongst her young, single crowd. Still, it might be fun. He checked his watch again. Now he was late to Skype home. He threw his jacket over a chair, sat at the table near the window and set up the screen.

Clara was annoyed. She'd got the twins ready for bed so they could kiss goodnight and Justin had kept them waiting. The children soon forgot in their excitement to tell him the news. Nana and Grandpa were coming! Clara's parents were about to make an unexpected visit.

'Dad said they will try to catch you whilst they're on some art jolly, before they come up here.'

'I'd like that. They've got my number. I can meet them or they can pop in here. See what time we've all got.' Privately, he hoped they might have some, any, success in encouraging Clara to move to London. He mentioned that he was going to watch the lantern street party and promised the children lanterns. Clara requested a box of Chinese tea. Making an effort not to rush, he eventually blew kisses and said goodnight, closing the laptop. He grabbed his jacket, pausing to remove the mysterious pearl earring. Justin hesitated, fingering its silky smoothness before placing it carefully on the coffee table, then left the flat.

With a few minutes to spare one morning, Justin had gone over to the coffee machine, having left his position, to stretch his legs during a lull. He'd phoned home to see how Clara's parents were enjoying their visit, and having been reassured all was well, he'd given her the news that he was being sent to Shanghai later in the spring with several other members of staff. She had sounded, well, almost irritated, rather than impressed. Deflated, he finished the call with, 'Well, I'd better go. I managed to see Hans and Anna after all. It was good to catch up with them. They do look well.' He paused, 'Give them my love, won't you?' It was an automatic offering to convey such a greeting to a couple he was partly mystified by. They were so different from his own, easy-going parents. Clara had then finished the call, adding lamely, 'Oh well, you'll enjoy the course you're going on now. Shanghai too, when that comes up. Love you.' Before Justin could affirm his feelings too, she let the phone drop into its slot.

Wondering if Jussy, by the tone of his voice, was beginning to give up trying to persuade her to move, was heartening. That telephone call hardly mattered anyway, not now. Her parents were going to help her to stay here at Keeper's. They had rather tentatively, she noticed, brought up the subject of Justin turning down their offer to help buy a flat in London when they'd met up with him. She had been angered by their offer, when all she'd wanted was to force him back to Suffolk. Their thinking had been that it would have been a good investment as there was some cash they wanted to find a home for. Also, they'd hoped to make use of it themselves occasionally. In the event, they had found a better use for this money, from Clara's point of view.

Jane and Rich, neighbours from the other end of the lane, had popped in to catch up with her parents. There were hugs all round, anecdotes of summer barbecues past, even mad winter ones blamed on Danish hardiness. Anna asked them how their online children's clothes business was doing. Jane had made a face. Anna immediately glared at Clara. 'I am sorry, Jane, I didn't mean to pry.' Jane smiled, 'No, please, everything's fine.' She went on to break the news that they'd decided to sell up. They wanted to travel to see their grandchildren in Australia in their winter, when bush fires should be less of an issue. Then they'd like to revisit some youthful far-flung haunts. Spend some ill-gotten gains. Jane grinned, hesitantly.

Rich turned to them, 'It's okay, folks. I want to be open about this. I've been diagnosed with Parkinson's.' It was impossible not to look shocked. Rich continued, 'We don't know how long I'll be well-ish, so we're getting going ASAP.'

Once they'd recovered from the shock, they turned to chatting about Clara and Justin's situation, Danish pastries, Carl and Zoe, dogs, and the current promise of spring, and what Brexit might mean for all of them.

Over lunch, Anna looked at her daughter closely. 'Are you losing weight? You're not dieting are you?' Clara waited for "chicken" which, thankfully, never came. She never weighed herself, but was pretty certain her weight was stable. 'Oh, of course not. It's just so difficult running the house with Justin never here. He doesn't seem to understand I need his presence.' It sounded pathetic and she didn't care. Both parents stared at her, their worried expressions evident.

Anna coughed. 'Well, from what you've just said, I don't know how this could help, but your father and I wondered if you would be interested in Jane's business if your father feels it's a good purchase? The thing against it is, you'd have even more to do, but you may be able to keep on Jane's workers and perhaps find someone to do some cleaning too.' She looked around the untidy kitchen.

Speechless, Clara gazed at each of them in turn. Could they even mean it? What was the catch? Then, a little calmer, she silently thanked Jane and Rich.

'Then, if you go to London, you could move the business with you. You'll always be able to find staff, perhaps outworkers. You worked in admin for that Scandi Design company in Copenhagen all those years,' Anna sighed, giving just a moment's pause to indicate her historic disapproval of her daughter's apprenticeship in a commercial enterprise. There was another small sigh, as she rather grudgingly conceded, 'That experience should give you some idea of how to run this, I would imagine.'

'Oh yes. I'm sure.' Clara ignored the implied disapproval from her mother and was quick to be positive, pushing aside the almost forgotten memories of tight schedules, delivery dates looming, long working hours and online computer problems. She would make this little business work. Clara continued, 'At Scandi Design, they used embroidery on their small clothing items too, mainly traditional. Of course we could do something similar. You know them already, Mama, don't you?' Now she could hear herself gabbling, not allowing space for any doubts to creep in, then forcing herself to slow down, finishing with, 'Are you sure?' Then immediately regretting giving them the opportunity to retract their offer, she followed up immediately with, 'Thank you so much. Perhaps we can discuss details before you go back? I'm sure Justin will be thrilled.' Her father raised an eyebrow.

She was oblivious to everything except this unexpected opportunity. She would make a success of it, she promised herself. Most importantly, the business worked from home. She could continue doing the same. She, they, wouldn't need to move. She was ignoring Justin's progress in his new job. Her father brought her swiftly down to earth, admonishing, 'Let's not get ahead of ourselves, Clara.' This needed some consideration, he reminded her. 'We agree to the idea in principle. I need our solicitor to go over the legalities. Also, we need to clarify the best way to move the money and ensure there are no negative tax implications. Once that's done, and it shouldn't take too long, we can sign the finances across to you. In turn, you can sign with Rich and Jane, if that works.'

'Dad, this is brilliant – amazing for us as a family – but don't we need, I mean you, I suppose, to try to secure the business, just in case they decide to put it on the market? Could you do that? Would they require a deposit, do you think?' Hans regarded his daughter through silver-framed spectacles. She'd never seen him wear spectacles before. That had been just one other new thing in her world today: her handsome father needed specs.

'I'll take a stroll along the lane this afternoon. Have a chat with them both. Leave it an hour or two, give them time to put their feet up after lunch.'

Clara was buzzing. 'Mama, if I got snowed under, until I find my feet that is, would you help embroider dungarees or jackets? I've often helped Jane with folksy embroidery. You know how Grandma used to decorate with daisies and stuff in the Finnish style.' Her mother had not thought she might be called upon to help – how impractical – but found herself nodding reluctantly, not entirely pleased with her daughter's sudden exuberance. If Justin had accepted the flat idea, she could already see it would have been more to their, her, benefit. Hans should have made more of an effort to convince Justin.

Not many house-hunters had ventured along the lane to view Keeper's during that cold winter. Clara had made no effort to tidy up the children's mess, which spread across the kitchen floor between Justin's visits, or to sweep the path – something her mother had sniffed at in disapproval. Her father had got out the yard broom and scooped up the last of the fallen leaves, but not before she'd skidded into the wall one icy night, when wet leaves had frozen, and just saved herself from going flat on her face. She'd grazed her hand, a result of her wilful neglect.

Now spring was threatening, and there were different issues. Primroses popped up, snowdrops were everywhere. In no time the lane would be full of wild violets. Of course not everyone was as transfixed by nature and the simple joys of the seasons, and she did not feel the need to be too tidy or smart around the house. There had, as yet, been no offers, for which she was very glad. If this business went ahead, somehow she and Justin would just have to make it work and stay here. Perhaps he could afford to leave that job after all and get local work. She still believed he could find a job locally. Otherwise, how many compromises could their marriage take? Then there were Carl and Zoe. Carl had taken to pinching other children in class. Zoe, who had been dry since a toddler, had occasionally wet the bed. The only member of the family seemingly unaffected was Arthur.

Chapter Three

Spring was now a real prospect. Time was moving on and Clara had still proved evasive. Justin had started looking for somewhere permanent to live near work. If Clara wouldn't join him, he would have to look as far out on one of the Underground lines as possible. There had to be two bedrooms, so that they could have some weekends and holidays in town. Or it would mean a sofa bed in a one-bed flat, but at least nearer the city. Clara's parents had muddied the waters with their offers of financial help. They were puzzled why he wouldn't purchase a flat with their assistance. They'd reasoned that they could use it from time to time when visiting the UK; he could continue to commute – leave work Friday for Suffolk, and return either very early Monday or late Sunday, though of course they were already aware, it didn't always work like that. He didn't even get home every weekend. He was also reluctant to accept their offer because, although they had expressed every consideration towards his work commitments, he wasn't convinced that they would remember, once they had part ownership. He recalled instances from over the years when they would assume cool, wordless disapproval over some perceived slight, which would create a tense atmosphere, and leave Clara miserable. Somehow he would manage to remain independent. So he turned down their generous offer.

When he did get back to Keeper's, Clara wanted to treat their weekend like a holiday, which in theory was commendable, but he'd noticed that she wasn't actually keeping things up on his behalf. There was a leak in the guttering, causing a stain to form on the wall, which he had now fixed. The gardener had left to travel, and she hadn't focused on a replacement. Neither had she cut the grass over several weeks when he had been in China, although he often mowed right through the winter. She found the ride-on mower easy to use, but thought it was his job, part of his responsibilities. Clara was now talking of embarking on a children's clothing online business, funded by her parents. With some regret he felt he should have accepted their help with the flat in the first place.

Justin was aware her beauty no longer hit him as soon as he set eyes on her. This shock, this sense of loss, partly undid him. He further resolved to get things sorted. He had thought several times of resigning; there would certainly be jostling to take his place if he opened that particular door. He let out a sigh. He was also certain he would be unable to make enough translating documents from home, or from private tuition or anything vaguely connected to languages: enough to keep the home going. He supposed, without enthusiasm, that he could advertise himself for accountancy work. The sudden shudder he felt was not related to his thoughts of reduced circumstances in Suffolk, but did reveal something else. Something else was beneath all this churning away at him.

He was beginning to fit in, starting to enjoy working in Canary Wharf. His degree in Mandarin may have been the clincher, and his overall interest in languages, but he was certain that his grounding in accountancy, and later an MBA, hadn't done any harm. The tensions, the speed of decisions ensuring any new trade was sound, to his surprise, seemed to suit his temperament. His confidence was growing. He was relishing life in a big city. There were also the classy spaces around that part of the city. Greenwich Park was far more extensive than he'd originally thought. Museums, markets, the vibrancy of the West End – it was all very much what he had discovered, to his considerable surprise, that he enjoyed. Though he was reluctant to admit it, the team were right when they called him the country boy. He was a country boy mesmerised by the size, the pace, the variety of London. In that regard, his thoughts sped across to that part of Soho where the arches were painted red. These thoughts he shook off, admonishing himself, pushing away wayward ideas.

One night he'd been out late. Reaching the door of his building, he was grateful the foyer light stayed on all night. He'd been to Chinatown. Feeling the cold penetrating his coat, he had shivered, shrugging off the thought of snow. Too late for that, he'd thought. It was already spring, though it didn't feel much like spring. There was a man in an overcoat leaning against a pillar a little off to the left of the door. There was often some layabout hanging around, hoping for some soft touch, waiting for a passer-by to take pity. The overcoat moved and Justin tensed. He didn't have any cash; he resigned himself to the embarrassment of a vitriolic outpouring and the ensuing disturbance. A comforting thought skipped across his conscience. At least the building he was about to enter had triple glazing.

'Hello, son,' the overcoat said. Oh God, Justin sighed. He couldn't process why his father might be there in the early hours of the morning, though he didn't need to think about one thing. He'd want money; no doubt a bed too. He'd certainly want money. If only Mum had survived, perhaps things might have been different.

'You're burning the candle, son. Had a good night then?' He prodded Justin playfully and hiccupped. Justin shook his head. There were things he wasn't ready to talk about, even think about, certainly not to this man in front of him. No, it was more in despair at the state of his father. He was not the father he wanted, needed or remembered from childhood, though in all honesty, Mum had held everything together. He could really do with some support right now. However it seemed he was to be the grown-up. He sighed again. 'You'd better come up, Dad. Don't puke.'

'You know I'm never sick. I'm quite hurt at the thought.' He was impossible, irrepressible, and to his annoyance, Justin found himself almost grinning as his father shambled before him into the lift. They alighted outside the flat door.

'Like the pad, son. How long for, then? Bet Clara loves coming up for weekends. Kids love it too? Daft question – so much to see. Must be exciting, house-hunting.'

'Dad, what are you doing, stranded at this time of night? You could have phoned.'

'Strangely enough, I did. Left a message. You weren't answering.' Justin cursed under his breath. He'd turned his phone off before they'd gone into the restaurant; he still wasn't sure why. It had been a strange day all round. It had started with a surprise phone call, taking a moment for him to recognise the voice. Josie had forged ahead in her usual breezy manner. He hadn't seen her since New Year at the party. He still felt uncomfortable when he thought of her determined kiss on the lips, when everybody had turned to the person next to them for a celebratory New Year kiss.

'I'm in town meeting an old school friend. You remember Davina?'

'Um, well, not immediately.'

'Doesn't matter. Anyway I'm staying overnight.' They might meet up for a meal, she continued. It would be fun and save her from dying of boredom. Clara, apparently, had encouraged her. Justin's heart sank. What was Clara thinking? Then he recovered, as he thought she would have suggested that Josie should share an evening with her lonely husband. After their meal, as they sat sipping coffee, she pushed her hair behind her ears. One ear had a pearl-drop earring. She smiled at him innocently as his eyes swept from one ear to the other. 'You knew, didn't you?'

'What exactly were you thinking, Josie?' He cringed afterwards at the memory of his prim tone. Her smile stayed fixed, but her eyes lost some of their laughter. 'Oh, don't be a bore, Jus. You've always liked me. It's not as if you and Clara are love's young dream. You know Jeff and I have an understanding.' As it happened, he didn't know to what extent they had an understanding, if at all. He didn't want to be put in the same category, whatever that might be. The evening hadn't ended well. He'd made the excuse of an early start and not long after had put her in a taxi. At the last moment, in some defiance, she'd grabbed him and, gripping his head, had planted him with a firm, slow kiss, laughing as she waved goodbye. In retrospect he admitted to himself it hadn't been at all unpleasant and could have been fun if he'd known what on earth was going on. And he still had the other earring. He'd taken her to Chinatown too, then, unsettled, had strolled back, stopping for a drink on the way. That he regretted too.

'Dad, come and sit over here. Here's a coffee to sober you up a bit.' He perched opposite his father at the kitchen bar. 'What are you doing here, anyway?'

'Coffee's good, Jus. Been to the casino off Wardour Street with some lads from the old days.' Justin groaned. 'No, it was good. Well, it started very well – just didn't end so well and I forgot to get a return ticket. Thought you'd be back at some point. You took a long time. Had a good evening?' Justin gestured for his father to go into the sitting room. He beckoned him to sit on the sofa. His father was looking exhausted, his eyelids drooping.

'Dad, I'm working tomorrow. There's a bedroom through there. We can talk tomorrow.' But he was too late. The old boy was asleep. He left him on the sofa, placing a rug over him and went to bed, feeling guilty he'd taken the only bed. In the morning, his father was still snoring gently when Justin was ready to leave. After standing over him for a few minutes, undecided, Justin left him with a note on the table, some cash, giving instructions on how to fill the coffee machine and to help himself to shaving gear and, reluctantly, the spare key card. Then he thought again and left out more money for him and took back the key card, nervous. His father would want to get back to Wimbledon Village, he reassured himself. Then he realised he'd need a key card anyway, so reluctantly put the spare key card back and left instructions to put it through the door when he left. He hoped Dad would remember.

Over coffee, there was talk in the office of family. Ling listened to Justin's comment that his father had turned up, late at night and unplanned. Uninvited, truth be told.

'You know how privileged you are. Your father sought you out. It is an honour.'

'Ling, it's different in the UK. I think you're being a bit Chinese here.' Ling dug him in the ribs. 'Just be grateful the father, I mean, your father, is still around, accessible. I would be pleased if my poor father was still with us and could visit. I should very much like to meet your father whilst he is in London.'

'Well, I hope he's gone home. It's easy for you. Grandma deals with all your domestic issues. I've got to keep Frederico's flat pristine, ready for when he gets back, and, well, Dad isn't very, well, house-trained when it comes to other people's properties.' Justin regretted saying the last bit; in fact, he regretted most of the conversation. He'd let his anxiety and frustration with his father's downhill journey get to him. When Justin did ring him, he was already making for Waterloo and promised he'd locked the flat carefully. Later, Justin thought of Ling's comments regarding his own father and wondered what his history might be, but the moment passed. Perhaps he might offer information about his father another time. He'd sensed sadness in Ling's voice, but no inclination to elaborate.

Chapter Four

The transformation of the garage had gone well. Clara stood back to admire her handiwork. Chalk white was everywhere, including on the old worktables and chairs which were now topped with clear varnish, on the beams above her, and a little in her hair. The electrician had been in and fixed work points for the machines and had improved the lighting. She'd indulged herself with a string of fairy lights, but stopped short of having them twinkle intermittently. Heating was to be from an abandoned old dual-burner cleaned up with a new shelf and seals, installed in the corner. The cost had been in fitting the chimney and liner from the money her parents had given for the overall project. Now time was of the essence. Jane and Rich had set a date to go off on their travels and were keen to offload fabrics, computers and machinery, and Clara needed to keep orders flowing.

Justin had agreed, somewhat reluctantly, she thought, to help shift the machinery and stock over the long weekend coming up. Thinking about

Justin and how she missed him, but couldn't see where they were going, she'd had feedback from Josie, who'd reported after her evening with him, that he was newly townified, citified even, and a bit cool. She wondered fleetingly how cool and had even thought he might be tempted by Josie's flirtatious manner. By the tone of Josie's voice, it seemed not, and she allowed herself to feel pleased.

Hearing the sound of a vehicle outside, she opened the side door to direct Pete the coalman to the designated corner of the shed, where the For Sale signs had now been shunted. Her reverie was short-lived – it was a taxi. Out climbed a rickety figure of a man wearing a battered fedora and long coat.

'Just came along to see how it's all going, darling. It suits you – you look blooming.' She was annoyed to find herself smoothing the old smock she'd covered her dungarees with. 'Oh, Den,' she attempted to stop desperation from creeping in to her voice, 'how lovely. I didn't know you were in the area. You should have let me know. You will stay for supper?' She knew, absolutely knew, he'd stay for more than supper. He had history. The worst had been an extended weekend, which had lasted for a month. Justin handled his father better, probably because they were related. She was out of her depth. Her own parents were not like this. It had been considerably easier when she had first known Justin, and Lola was still alive. She had been the stronger of the pair and Den had adored her.

'Thought I could give you a hand. Point you in the right direction.' She tried to hold her ground, not knowing what it was. Justin had a lot to answer for, letting the old boy in on her project, knowing how off the wall he could be. She ducked and changed the subject. 'I've finished for now. You must need a cuppa after your journey. Did you come from Wimbledon? Let's go inside and warm up.' 'Yes, train. Left old banger in Wimbledon. Have to get something newer. Where are my favourite twins, then? It's far too quiet. Cuppa? Yes, great.' He turned away from the garage and made for the kitchen, where Arthur, perhaps remembering him from long walks, placed two forelegs on his shoulders and licked the jowly face with enthusiasm.

'At a sleepover in the village. Coming back tomorrow.' Clara sighed. 'Don't encourage him.' Den was twiddling Arthur's ears affectionately.

Den was on a roll, desperate to let Clara know the latest. She found herself unable to stop him. He'd enjoyed a short visit to Justin's Soho flat. Yes, of course it was only rented, still. Pity he couldn't afford to buy a commute flat in Soho – lovely spot these days. No, a house Greenwich way was probably best. Then, if things changed, they could all live there. Grabbing the opportunity of a pause, Clara ushered Den through the porch into the kitchen. 'Go on through by the fire. I'll be in with the tea in a minute.' Now free of Arthur, Den took a deep breath and swung an arm in a wide arc to emphasise how much he'd like to help Clara's enterprise. After all, he was free for a few days and could help where needed. Standing over the kettle, Clara thought positively that at least he hadn't pretended he was in the area by accident, and then still hung about for days. If he was staying, and she was resigned to the fact, then she'd get him up and working. She must lock the booze away, or at least only leave out what she wanted him to drink. Den had wandered off into the sitting room. Before she could walk through with the mugs of tea, she heard glasses clinking.

'Thought I'd have a whisky chaser with the cuppa. One for you – cheers, darling!' He pointed to the tumbler on the coffee table. Clara managed to contain her outrage at his assumption that it was okay to help himself. The contents of the sideboard would be removed after he'd gone up to bed. Den was certainly not what she was accustomed to. Certainly not like her parents. He was charming, clever and impossible.

Two weeks into her new venture and Clara found herself struggling. There was a glitch with the computer programme. Den had professed a working knowledge of such things. She should have been wary of his cavalier manner, but in a situation where she had no expert to hand, she had blindly jumped at his offer of help. Then Arthur had eaten something, which the vet assured her he had been lucky to survive, but that fact hadn't really cheered her. The bill to save him had been eye-watering. There was a suspicion that he'd tasted something with rat poison included. The nearby farm was under suspicion, but Clara knew the farmer would blame her for letting her animal wander. There was no doubt that the general confusion of orders still unfulfilled, then a helper from the village objecting to the chill of the workroom – as the old burner had refused to work with coal, so now she was burning wood too quickly – and then the twins suffering from colds, had all contributed to her next expensive decision.

She was now waiting for someone who advertised in the local paper to come and reset the programmes on the computers. The other thing, she considered, as she sat by the window watching the wind pushing rain across her vision, was that Justin just didn't seem very interested in what was happening at home. It wasn't just the business, or the fact his father wouldn't budge and he'd cleared the remaining Christmas booze, which she thought she'd stashed safely in the shed next to the coal. No, that apart, Justin hadn't been home for three weekends, after the setting up when he and Den seemed not to take things very seriously, even though the twins had been poorly too. Sighing deeply, she couldn't help thinking that it appeared her husband was having a better time than she was and was staying away on purpose. Was he trying to make a point? An old red van stopped in the lane. A figure with its hood up made a dash in the rain to the kitchen door.

'Afternoon, I'm the computer chap, Tom. You rang yesterday evening.' In the porch Tom pushed back his hood. His red hair was caught up in short braids. She was stunned by his eyes. They were an unusual golden colour. He smiled down at her. He stood considerably taller than Clara, though she was tall. Justin teased her she was Viking height, which seemed to please him, or used to please him, she corrected silently. 'Yes, thanks for fitting me in so

42

soon.' Hell, she found herself blushing at the unintended double entendre. She attempted a calm smile in return. 'Come over to the workroom. It was the garage. Well, you can see, can't you?' She was conscious of sounding nervous, talking too quickly, so grabbed her coat from its peg as he pushed his hood up again and they made a dash for the workroom.

Den stretched out. He liked being here. He'd always liked being around beautiful women. Lola had been so lovely. He was grateful his son had chosen a Danish beauty; well, actually Danish–Finnish beauty, he corrected. No requirement to touch, he reassured himself. Seeing that slender figure, unconsciously graceful in dungarees, baggy legs rolled up, displaying an overwintered light tan – beauty just gave him a sense of optimism. There was also the issue of the blonde hair, so unusually pale, long and bundled out of the way. He'd long retired from fashion photography – too long, he now considered – but Den had the beginnings of a plan. He had recently fallen out with his neighbours in Wimbledon Village, due to a small fire caused by him falling asleep and leaving a lit cigarette in an ashtray. It hadn't spread beyond the sitting room, but the fire did lick up the curtains, which caused the windows to overheat and the glass exploded.

After the clear up, he considered putting the house on the market. He'd offered it to Justin, who protested he couldn't possibly afford it. Den understood, of course, with Clara determined to stay put, almost any purchase was out of the question. He could see there was a time limit, as well, for this standoff situation between his ambitious son and stubborn daughter-in-law. Sooner or later, someone, something, would have to give. Still, in the meantime he thought he might have found a new purpose.

Clara had wanted Justin to commute midweek as well as at the week-ends. It just wasn't practical for Justin – even Den could see that. But according to Clara, he didn't come home every weekend any more. Although he was dubious about her venture in making and selling children's clothes, Den admired her for having a go. The sticking point, as far as he could see, was that she loved the idea, but hadn't actually thought through the commitment required and now was slightly overwhelmed. But it was still early days. She wasn't reliable at cooking either, which was where he had become useful, happy to help. He remembered she had made tasty meatballs once. Nice sauce too. But she wasn't very interested, he'd concluded, whereas he got Zoe and Carl helping and having a laugh. This particular morning, he had been to the village on an old bike he'd found in one of the sheds. He'd pumped up the tyres and set off to buy fish for supper. Sadly, there was a slow puncture, which meant he'd pushed the bike back through the woods afterwards. There was some booze in his camera bag. He needed better funds. Still, content for now, he put what he had in the wardrobe, the bag and all, grinning to himself in the mirror as he closed the door. He was almost ready to make his suggestion to Clara and Justin. Either way, he'd need a drink afterwards. He wouldn't risk it before. She'd know in a heartbeat and think it was the drink talking, though he considered his best decisions had usually been made over a drink. Still, show respect and caution and wait until the right time when they were together.

When Den had spilled out of the taxi on his arrival, Clara had seen he had his case of photography gear. Though clumsily attempting to hold onto his fedora, he'd managed to protect the heavy camera slung around his neck. She had wondered, fleetingly, if he was here to go out on the fens, or travel along to the Broads. At least half their visitors went off to look out for some rare bird or other. This use of time bemused her. She'd gone out with Justin in their early days, but standing still until her feet went numb, then returning half frozen, with disappointment in the air, was weird. But that wasn't at all what Den had in mind. Today, he was having a lie-in. There was a suspicion alcohol might be involved. If he ever got up, she'd get him to walk Arthur.

She'd managed to keep him away from the computers since his unsuccessful attempts to sort them out. Even so, they were still blanking or pixilating. When Tom had last called, the third time in a week, they were still in a wet spell. The cobbled path to the workroom remained slippery. As Clara began to slide, Tom grabbed her. For a second she was flustered, as she thought he had held on a fraction longer than necessary, but dismissed it in the presence of his light-hearted grin and the effect of his hands waving, palms out, as if to indicate that nothing other than a save from a fall was intended. She was ashamed to admit to herself that she found him attractive. Bit hippy perhaps, after her very groomed husband; even so, she grinned to herself.

Today it was bright and she'd gone out cheerfully to the workroom at eight fifteen, after the minibus had collected the twins, ready to get the two helpers onto finishing the little jackets that were selling well. To her dismay, she found, on the still-wet ground, her precious notebook, a birthday present from one of Justin's ventures along Regent Street into a classy stationer's. It was now lying skewed open, with several pages sodden and the drawings and notes there indecipherable. On some pages there was an edge of pulp. The wet leather cover leached dye onto her fingers, when she raised it to stroke its silk-like smoothness, now a little wrinkled. A bit of leaf was stuck to it.

She sat down at a computer, tears welling, peeling the leaf away, and feeling miserable. One of her two workers, Mary, or Liz, coughed, not knowing how to approach her. She was oblivious of her surroundings, sunk in the uncertainty of her life and her annoying father-in-law – and, as if there wasn't anything else, Arthur. But there always was, because he got dirty every day, and needed hosing down, and would show gratitude in licks, between shaking water droplets across the utility wall. Clara tried hard not to think too much about her marriage. For now she was relying on memories.

They had been to Morocco a year after they were married and seen the dye pits and the ochre, crimson and viridian of the dyers' arms. Now the deep blue dye of the notebook's cover was on her hands. She put the notebook down carefully on a piece of kitchen roll near the sink and joined Liz and Mary, who were making coffee whilst waiting for further instructions. They were gossiping about the village hall and the local council. Someone had stepped down because of ill health and there was now a vacancy. Alice, their mutual friend, had expressed mild interest at the last election. Liz turned to Clara. 'I wondered if you'd be interested? Alice is a bit out of the village, really.' From that Clara read, too posh – doesn't understand ordinary people, but privately accepted she might be wrong and looking for subtexts.

'Oh, I don't know. Alice has the time to take things up properly. I'm afraid I've got too much on just now.' She turned to point out the patterns, not touching them. 'Here are the designs. If you'd use daisy stitch for the flowers, just denim blue, and the leaves in backstitch. Same colour. Thanks, ladies.' She left them to it and went back to the notebook. The two exchanged glances, which was not lost on Clara who was unsure what it meant and too preoccupied to work it out.

Clara could see she would have to redraw some designs, once the pages were dried out. The cover still held most of its colour, but was sodden. She washed her hands carefully, before exploring the rest of the damage and placed kitchen roll over the cover to avoid more leaching onto her fingers. The paper looked like ragged cloth, the papers creaking as she carefully turned them over. It was difficult not to compare the notebook with her state of mind: rather ragged around the edges, the odd bit ruined, but some things still intact. Oh well, better make the most of it, she sighed.

Chapter Five

The kerb was reinforced with a metal ridge. Destined to be late, Justin half-ran half-strode towards the tube, scrolling down his latest texts. Stepping back to avoid a taxi, he missed his footing, skidding on the metal. He came round, woozy, and with a terrible shooting pain in his right leg. His back also hurt. When he tried to swing off the bed, everything he knew about himself – agile, fit, athletic – counted for nothing. His top half was vaguely familiar, though without any strength. The rest of him seemed a lost cause. He could just bend his neck sufficiently to view the disaster below. There was a strange frame screwed to his right leg, which was also attached to his other leg in two places, above the knee and at the ankle. His chest seemed to be strapped. He was on his own. Curtains were drawn around his bed. Outside someone was screaming. There was also considerable general hubbub and swearing. He guessed he was in A&E, somewhere in London. Initially, he couldn't remember what had happened, but slowly the memory of the lengthy text he was trying to get through, when everything went blank, came back to him.

No doubt Dad meant well, but these frequent texts had got to him. Dad had insisted on texting him almost daily now so that, although Justin wasn't with the family, he certainly knew how they were all doing. Clara had no idea of this development and just Skyped weekly, unless something triggered a phone call. Justin considered his father mistakenly hoped that by explaining all the latest setbacks it might also trigger a desire for his son to come home more frequently. When their neighbours, Jane and Rich, had sold their online business to Clara, courtesy of her parents, which still rankled, they had omitted to mention that the computers were temperamental. Some guy called Tom seemed to be keeping them going for Clara. His name was cropping up more and more frequently. To Justin, it seemed they were all managing quite nicely. This thought, no doubt foolhardy, had even delayed him from going home on Sunday. After working on Saturday, he'd gone to Ronnie Scott's on Sunday with Ling, his mate from work, and now here he was in this god awful place, in this god awful state.

A petite doctor, wearing a headscarf, a reassuring smile and large, dark-framed spectacles, pushed the curtain aside carrying a small tray with a syringe and some ampoules. She placed the tray on the bedside table.

'Where am I? What's going on?'

'Tommy's, Mr Kerr. We've contacted your family, although when we get a second opinion, we may move you to a specialist hospital. Your ankle is badly damaged. Do you know what happened?' Unable to grasp the grave turn of events, he was too tired to answer. He wanted to go back to sleep.

'Your wife is on her way. You were hit by a taxi. You have been X-rayed. As you will have ascertained,' she waved, he thought, rather too nonchalantly for his taste, almost just in passing, at the frame, 'Your right leg is also broken.' She added, as if an afterthought, 'There is a problem with your ribs.' He wanted to yell at this woman, mapping his current state with a detachment no doubt adopted by trauma doctors everywhere, but he didn't have the energy. Also, he wanted to be sure they'd put him out for the essential work. He needn't have worried.

Sometime later, Justin surfaced to new surroundings. He drifted off again, after someone insisted he open his eyes. He was nauseous and heaved into a dish next to him. Then there was Clara, looking worried, obviously, but he detected through his misery a shadow of something else. Surely, it couldn't be exasperation?

Waiting for him to recover consciousness, Clara wriggled around in her seat, bored and worried in equal measure. She'd just checked with home. Den was coping for now. There was a sign in the corridor, outdated, she thought, instructing mobiles to be turned off. Justin's phone was on the bedside table, so he must have used it when he'd been conscious at some point earlier. She picked it up, paused for a millisecond, then started to scan his texts. Guilt had no place here, she told herself, checking there was no sign of Justin waking up. She needed to know about him – who and what he was these days. Once started, she couldn't stop. She flicked down the messages. In between texts to and from Chinese work colleagues, now friends, Justin had been kept more up to date with events at home than Clara had realised. Fascinated, she continued. His father, Den, spy, bloody irritating father-in-law Den, had taken it upon himself to text Justin very frequently, relaying the current lack of progress of the business and that Carl and Zoe were missing their daddy. She resisted snorting out loud, well, what a surprise that is, and briefly checked that Justin still hadn't come to. Lastly, and in some detail, which really angered her, Den had conveyed the help she'd received from Tom. Even her attitude was reported on – according to Den it was defiant. What else could she be, when her husband refused to accept she couldn't live in London, and he refused to commute as much as he obviously was able to?

She closed Messages, put the phone down, stunned. She was right, as she had thought for some time – he had been having a much better time than she was, at least until now. Perhaps she should invite his Chinese friends down for a weekend. She'd quite like to get a grip on where they stood, in terms of how much they were a part of Justin's life. For now, she decided to keep this new information to herself. It was cheating in a way, but then knowledge might prove to be power. Whether it would do any of them any good was debatable. She sighed, depressed.

Several days later, Justin was up in the same hospital he'd been taken to originally. A replacement ankle was deemed not necessary, to his relief, but practising in physio how to cope with crutches, keeping the plastered foot off the floor, was essential. In spite of sore ribs and the difficulty in balancing, he convinced himself he could cope, and with the aid of painkillers, he was intending to get back to work, now he was being discharged.

'Jussy, how?' Now Clara was really worried.

'There's a lift at the flat. Get a taxi each way. Lift at work. Someone might even drive me in. I can do it.'

Without thinking, she blurted out, 'Den said something about Frederico's coming back soon.' Justin turned carefully from concentrating on this new balancing act with crutches. 'Funny, I didn't think I'd mentioned it yet.' Clara found herself flushing. Now she remembered. Frederico had texted Justin with details of his changed plans. 'Perhaps you were rambling under sedation, darling.' Her reply seemed to satisfy him.

'Must have, then. Well, I'll have to get a new flat too.' Clara shook her head. 'Can't you come home for a couple of weeks, at least? You can get a certificate. I've already checked, and the twins ask after you every day.' Justin could feel events becoming even more complicated, possibly up to the wire over London living. He needed to be in town.

'Well, sorry to be a bore, but I need somewhere in town. Can't expect to kip on Frederico's sofa. Not his style I should imagine.' Defeated, Clara picked up her bag and, carrying his things, followed him slowly to the exit, where she'd ordered a taxi.

Leaning back against the old leather, Justin closed his eyes, exhausted from the effort. He mourned the loss of the suit he'd had the accident in. He'd managed to buy a Paul Smith in the sales. The hospital had cut the trousers off him. The elbow of one sleeve was torn, but he planned to rescue the jacket. He'd have suede elbows stitched on. It could look okay with jeans, he thought. He wondered why he allowed himself to care about such superficial things, when he couldn't even walk and there was so much to be worried about. Maybe it was a small thing he had some control over. There was precious little else.

After paying the driver, then carefully hobbling across the pavement, Justin leaned for a moment against the marble wall of the vestibule for balance, as Clara summoned the lift to the ground floor. He was grateful she hadn't rushed back home, though he sensed that might have been her original plan. This slow procedure for moving around was driving him mad. He thought he could be okay with the pain, which was bound to ease in a few days, with the assistance of the hefty prescription handed to him on discharge; but the inconvenience, awkwardness, lack of any possible sudden decision that might be acted upon, was impossible. He didn't much like the look of tracksuit bottoms either, or the oversized long boot on his injured leg and ankle.

As the lift pinged its arrival at the fourth floor, he adjusted his crutches and, negotiating the lobby, waited impatiently whilst Clara fiddled with the entry card to open the door for him. As she followed him into the hallway, closing the door behind her, she noticed how spring sunshine cast a low beam across the hall, their movements disturbing minute dust particles into the air. Spring, she thought. We need to talk about Zoe and Carl's birthday. It's only a couple of weeks now. He must come home for that, and then there's Easter.

The only sensible way to eat was takeaway. Lunchtime was no hindrance to choice. There was the Indian, second to none, Justin said, just round the corner, not worth getting a delivery, and he was sure she'd love it. After she'd agreed, it suddenly registered that in this instance she was expected to go out and queue to collect it. She was peeved; it meant it was down to her. Even the Saturday mobile chippie at home dropped orders off to outlying spots. London was not what it was cracked up to be in any way, although she already knew that. Still, she had a chance to have a look around. Although she hadn't believed Justin, wandering around Soho was okay; she found people even stepped off the pavement where it was narrow to allow oncoming pedestrians room to pass. Traffic was snail-like and cautious as she hurried back with the hot parcel. Justin had managed to get chutney out of the cupboard and some cutlery. They ate out of the cartons. Clara, admitting she was starving, rushed her food, spilling sauce on her top. 'Crikey Clara, good job the kids can't see you eating like this.'

'Haven't eaten really for a couple of days.' She paused to go to the sink to splash the spill, stuffing a tea towel up inside her top to soak up the water.

'I'm sorry about all this, Clara.' He waved at the collection of cartons strewn about. 'Still, it does conjure up quite a picture. Don't normally see dribbling.'

'What, me or the kids?' This was unexpected humour from Clara, relaxing him a little. Perhaps things would be okay. Justin grinned, 'Hah! How are they, by the way?'

'Looking forward to you coming home to celebrate their birthday, and Easter, of course!'

Justin felt that he had just walked aimlessly into a trap. He shouldn't feel like it, but he did. He scolded himself as he did love them; he must make the effort, and it would be an effort with crutches on trains. He would have to manage. 'Have they said what they want yet?'

'I told them they could Skype this evening before bedtime, okay?' It wasn't a question, more a manner of speaking, but he thought it would be fun to see their faces; see what they wanted for their seventh birthdays.

Clara made coffee and they sat, Justin newly drugged up, half dozing, occasionally chatting inconsequentially in a pleasant limbo, letting the sun slide from the building. Clara snuggled up to him, carefully avoiding pressing against his ribs. To feel close was precious. She sighed, just as the landline went.

'Put it on loudspeaker, darling.' Justin leaned back.

'Hi guys. Just checking on progress.'

'Hi Dad.'

'Hi Den.'

'Good, you're both there. Glad you've escaped from the hospital safely.'

'Dad, they were brilliant.'

'Yes, well. How are you, Jus? Can you manage the lift? What about food?'

'Dad, yes, fine. I'm just sorting myself out.' Clara harrumphed in the background. Justin continued, 'Well, yes, I am coping. I will cope. By the way, did I mention Frederico's due back soon? I need to get new lodgings.'

'God, son! That's a big order just at the minute. You can't get around to view places very easily. Good job Clara's with you. She can ferry you about.'

'No, I can't! I need to get back. There are the twins and I need to keep tabs on the business. I've already wasted days stuck in London!'

'Thanks for your support, Clara. I didn't intentionally fall just to annoy you.'

'Hey, you two, hang on a minute. I've got an idea.' Den paused. They all paused.

'How about I look after things this end for a bit? Tom is keeping your clapped-out computers working.'

'Clapped-out?' Justin looked horrified. Were they that bad? Clara pursed her lips and Den rushed on. 'Don't worry, Jus, he's very cheap. And the girls are great. They're already finishing the designs I photographed for the new online catalogue for Clara. I keep them topped up with coffee and flattery. Twins fine too. We all go out after school with Arthur. Did you know he can swim? S'pose dogs can. Zoe jumped in with him. I snapped them. It can go in the catalogue. You know, country living type of thing.'

'Oh my God! Is she okay? Has she caught a cold?'

'She's fine. Speak to them both later. We can manage for food too. I've found the freezer cabinet in the village shop. Very good ready meals. We all choose our favourites,' he added, expecting to impress, 'with veg, of course.'

Justin and Clara looked at each other, momentarily speechless.

'Den, you can't possibly run things more than a few days. It's so kind of you, but there are a million things I need to do. There's the dentist for the twins next Tuesday. Then their cake and the invites for their birthday trip.'

'Got it all, old thing. Looked up on your wall-map diary jobby in the utility. Carly showed me. He likes it because he can look up his play dates in advance. It's like major war ops, your planning. Absolutely brilliant. I can plan for weeks ahead. It's all there before me.'

'Dad, it sounds like you've got everything under control, and we really appreciate it. I need to have a chat with Clara and we'll talk again a bit later. Okay?'

'You two take all the time you need. But it's going along famously here. Even have a little tipple once they're tucked up. Snooze with Arthur by the fire. Where's his shampoo by the way? That chickweed didn't fully come off with a hosing. He's a good-natured old chap though.' With that he rang off.

'Oh my God, what do we do? Chickweed, tipples. Is that supposed to make me feel secure?'

'Slow down. What's a bit of chickweed indoors? We've had worse. Let's get the drift with the kids when they get in from school, and he's not had a tipple. Sounds as if he's enjoying his role of grandad.'

Clara sighed, stood up, stretching, and went across to the kitchen. She made mugs of tea, emptying a box of Danish pastries onto a plate.

'You found that shop, didn't you? I told you. You can get really good Danish here. Don't need to import them from home.'

'Oh, shut up and just eat them.' She rolled her eyes. 'When have I ever ordered Danish from home, then?'

'Got you!' He laughed, then immediately gasped in pain, causing Clara to bite her lip and pass him the next dose of painkillers.

It was nearly six. Time to Skype. There they were, grinning into the camera. Suddenly Zoe's dark looks made her seem bigger than Carl, his delicate blonde features pale in artificial light.

'Hi Daddy! Can I see your leg? Have you got cuts anywhere?' Zoe, nervous and yet excited, wanted to know the details.

'Daddy, are you hurting?' Carl, his face anxious, glanced sideways at Zoe.

'Well, just a bit, sweetheart. But I'm going to feel better with Mummy here and helping.'

There was a long sigh from behind Justin. He resisted turning round to check Clara's intent. He didn't comment, only smiled at the screen.

'Daddy, when you come home with Mummy, can I put some stickers on your leg cover? Look, I've got a whole sheet here. Grandad helped me buy them.' Zoe waved them at the screen. Justin thought he might deflect this new threat to his diminishing dignity, until he'd gathered his thoughts. Instead it led the conversation to more important matters.

'I hope you two have been thinking very hard about what you'd like for your birthdays. I bet you can't think of anything at all!' It was a nanosecond before there was a response.

'Daddy, Grandad took us into Bury for a treat and we've seen watches that are walkie-talkie. You can speak to each other for three kilometres.' Carl expressed the distance by opening his arms as far as they'd go, beyond their vision on the screen. Den's voice came from the background. 'I could get them if you like. Other than that they liked remote control helicopters.' He avoided the impulse to comment that it was almost impossible to get in their rooms already. Clara had already stated no technology that involved sitting down.

'Yes, and you can have pink too! I mean watches,' Zoe piped in.

'We shall have to think about it. Don't forget we are taking you and your friends to that soft play centre where they've got a roller-skating rink too, then for a pizza, so it depends how much that all comes to.' Den broke in again. 'I'll ring you tomorrow. We can chat about details. When are you coming home, Jus? You're bound to have appointments before they let you set off. On the other hand, everything's good here. Clara left me money for food and to pay the workers. Mind, they've asked if I'll do them a portfolio for a calendar to fundraise for the church, like Calendar Girls. If I do extra for their own use, they'll forgo their pay for a couple of weeks. Not bad-looking girls, actually.' There was silence, broken by Carl. 'Yes, Daddy, when can you come home? Tom has stopped behind to chop up that tree that came down in the storm. We've got loads of wood and I learnt how to stack it properly in the store.'

'Stopped behind? Oh, good. Yes, Carly, I'll be home soon. Certainly before your birthdays.'

'Aunty Edie said if going out is too much, because of your leg, we can have a bouncy castle at theirs and a treasure hunt, and a feast. And you can come too!' Zoe waited for what she obviously expected to be overwhelming delight. Initially Justin was speechless, and thought he might even be angry, then very soon there were splinters of relief creeping in to defuse his sense of outrage. Reluctantly, he conceded it might be for the best. Clara moved forward to be clearly seen by the children. 'Now, I know it's very exciting, but Daddy and I will have a chat and speak with the aunts. We shall do something lovely.' Justin couldn't quite grasp how everything seemed to be beyond his reach, beyond his control even. Edie and Alice's generosity was appreciated, obviously, but why hadn't they suggested it to them before saying anything? On another subject, there was the small problem of his father and his evident enthusiasms. And Tom was a bloke he needed to meet.

He would go home soon, that much was clear. He still needed to sort out the flat first. He needed somewhere to come back to. He knew now he couldn't cope with work yet. Goodbyes exchanged, Skyping was over for a few days.

'I need a drink. What would you like? There is some elderflower cordial in the fridge.' Clara patted him on the shoulder as she passed him on the way to get a gin and tonic. She hadn't noticed before, but she could see his hair was thinning a little – not much, but thinning all the same. She thought of Den's full head of hair and wondered if Justin was following Lola's family's genes where hair was concerned. Clara passed him his drink and a small dish of nuts, sitting down opposite him with her drink, giving him space to spread his leg.

'Firstly, there's the small matter of Den and his promiscuous camera.' Clara bridled, unable to imagine how the latest news would go down in the village. The personal portfolios were even more worrying.

'Well, that's a first, I must say. Don't think he's done nudes before. I don't know how we can stop him. Think about how much you'll save, anyway. Don't forget there's the naturist beach. People are quite laid back at home. Don't tell me nudity – and it will only be very discreet – is offensive to your Danish psyche?' Justin tried to reach her to tickle her, but the effort fell short. She made a face at him, changing the subject. 'Y'know, Edie did ring the other day, but I had to go out to the workroom to see to the embroiderer. The computer wouldn't print out the designs. I think Zoe took the phone. No doubt she was instructed to speak to me and forgot that part of the conversation. I'll ring Edie in the morning.'

'Pity they couldn't have run it past us first though. I think Edie and Alice's idea is okay – very generous really. It would be more practical. We can't manage all those kids in two vehicles, even though Dad would do his bit if we hired a people carrier. Then there's me. All the space I need.'

Clara noted, but refrained from commenting, that Justin had actually included himself in the birthday proceedings. She should be able to chat to him to say how pleased she was, but he was tired, she could see from his drawn expression; not only that, she shouldn't have to be pleased. Ah, well. One step, one very awkward step, under the circumstances, she thought, amused at her minimal wit. Yes, one step at a time.

They'd spent their first night together for weeks. It had begun tenderly, with Clara helping Justin remove his tracksuit bottoms, the right leg cut off at the knee, and then gently assisting him off with his sweatshirt and T-shirt.

'Reversal of roles – I should be doing this for you. What d'you think? Ouch!' She'd pulled too quickly at his T-shirt. Once in boxers and a clean T-shirt, and after more painkillers, which he thought he'd take before changing next time, he was eventually comfortable, having forgotten the idea of undressing Clara, and was just too exhausted. It was a strange night, both desperately wanting intimacy but finding Justin's injuries too much of an obstacle. In the end they accepted defeat, with Justin's leg supported on a pillow and a pillow between them. He had dreams of Zoe and Carl, pulling him home.

Clara tried not to move her arms over the separating pillow so slept little, nodding off towards morning. Unsurprisingly, they both awoke tired and restless.

'I need to get back. I must get home. There's everything piling up. Can't imagine how Den's really doing.' Clara pushed her hair up and clipped it with a slide. Some fell back down over one shoulder, but she didn't notice. She was standing halfway between the bathroom and bedroom in her underwear, noting how the early light played over adjacent buildings at this height. Justin was freshly aware of how she was apparently unconscious of her allure, thinking, please get more clothes on. Cover up what I can't have. She broke into his thoughts. 'What if Den comes up for a few days, until you can manage, you know, to dress yourself and do food?' Justin was left downcast. He'd hoped their closeness he'd felt since they'd got back to the flat would encourage Clara to stay for a few more days.

He was also very aware that he needed to find a flat to rent. He knew Dad would fit in, but he couldn't rely on him to stay sober and he needed, if not a driver, then help with taxis. His phone went. It was Ling. 'Morning Ling. How you doing? Yes, Clara's here. You off today? Yes, we'd love it.' He made a questioning face at Clara, who made a face back, in defeat.

'Yes, please. Bring us come cookies or something. We haven't eaten.' He put the phone down.

'He's not bringing fortune cookies is he?' Clara was rattled, unprepared. Although she'd considered that she should meet his colleagues, she'd wanted to be the one to initiate it in her own surroundings. Justin burst out laughing. 'Oh, please! Ling passes the best bakery in the West End on his way over. Probably be blueberry muffins. That okay for you?' It would have been difficult to be unaware of the edge to his voice.

'Oh well, have to be, I suppose.'

Ling, when he rang the bell, had his arms full. Clara went to let him in. There was a moment when they just smiled at each other; mutual introductions were then exchanged as Clara invited him in.

'These are for you.' He proffered a bunch of late violets, surrounded by their little leaves, wrapped in waxed tissue.

'Ling, they are so beautiful. Thank you.' She buried her nose into the delicate petals. They grew wild in the hedgerows at home. She had always been enchanted by their perfume and their frailty and each year there they were again. Ling's smile lit up his face, its warmth reaching out to Clara. He took her free hand. 'Clara, it's so nice to meet you at last.' It was as if she had been kept away from him, she thought. Justin raised an eyebrow, before turning his head away, silently signifying to Clara that he agreed with Ling. Her reluctance to visit had been discussed, she was sure. Perhaps Ling was right; she had stayed away for too long. She had to look down at Ling to meet his gaze, but not as far as she had expected. After all, weren't all Chinese short? Then she was aware that he was still holding her right hand, the violet posy in her other hand, the baker's carrier bag slung over his wrist.

'Okay guys, now you've introduced yourselves, might we get to the items in the bag? I'm actually quite hungry, between painkillers, you know. I'm not feeling so queasy.' Justin paused, impatient, then waved towards Clara. 'Get the coffee, would you, darling?' He made a feeble effort to sound light-hearted. Clara, now suddenly self-conscious, stepped back, catching her heel against Justin's crutches, which were resting against a chair. Ling, in an effort to save her, reached out, but it was too late, and they went down together, doughnuts flying, muffins rolling towards Justin, violets crushed and both of them gasping in shock. Ling quickly recovered, scooping up a couple of doughnuts and placing them on the coffee table. But Clara found getting up painful as Ling tried to help her.

'I think – Ow!' Clara carefully tried her right foot on the floor, supporting her weight on her left foot, and leaning against the back of the chair, tried testing it again. Under the pale tan, Ling could see she was ashen. 'I'm okay. I will hobble a bit till it eases off. Still, could you do the coffee, Ling, please?' She sat carefully. Ling nodded, making light of her request as he smiled en route to get the tray with plates and coffee mugs. He picked up the remaining muffins and doughnuts, dusting them off, avoiding the dust balls under the sofa. Then he assisted Clara across the room to the table near Justin, who, still on edge from observing their accident after the introductions at the doorway, grunted in irritation.

Once they were settled, exquisite muffins and jam doughnuts washed down with very strong coffee helped to some degree to restore emotional equilibrium in the room. Clara enquired about Ling's family and his life in Hong Kong before coming to London. He was brief in his answers, partly reluctant to open up about his family history, but even more, sensing his welcome might be on a knife-edge. He enquired how Clara's ankle was feeling.

'Think it'll be fine. I'll just try putting my weight on it again now.' She held her breath, pushing herself up, gradually gaining full height. 'Oh hell!' she cried out, and slipped back into the chair.

'Honestly, Clara, what is it with you?' Justin's frustration from recent months boiled over. The miserable visits home, courses abroad on which she refused to accompany him as an invited guest, her refusal to bring the children to London for weekends and, to cap it all, beginning a business she seemed ill-equipped to cope with. They could, in all honesty, already be together as a family. Even so, he couldn't believe he'd just said it. Now he couldn't unsay it, nor could he apologise. Clara, disbelieving, stared back at him. 'What d'you mean?'

'Well, you must admit none of this would have happened if you'd agreed to move with the children in the first place.' He pointed to his booted leg. Clara stiffened at the accusation. 'It wasn't anything to do with me. You had an accident. I was at home!'

'Exactly. Dad was texting me every day to reassure me you were okay, which was more than you were doing.' There was a stunned silence. Ling and Clara stared at him. Justin continued, 'I slipped against a metal kerb trying to read the latest from him on my way to work.'

'You were spying on me!' She recalled the long texts she'd skipped through on Justin's phone when he was in hospital. 'And you could have come home more often and seen for yourself!' She felt, maybe illogically, betrayed, but was at a loss as to how to defend herself.

It was clear that his feelings were out in the open now and there seemed little to lose, so he continued, 'I'm sorry, but you're still centre stage. It's all about you, isn't it!' He pointed at her accusingly, adding, 'We're basically stuffed if you're crocked too!' He turned to Ling, sighing. 'Ling, pass me my crutches, would you, please?' The crutches were still on the other side of the room. Ling silently passed him the crutches, experiencing a very strong desire to be elsewhere. As soon as he could, he made his excuses and left. Walking back in weak sunlight, he couldn't help but feel sorry for them both. Ling knew Justin only had a week left in the flat and that he wanted to find somewhere more permanent to rent. He had no desire to interfere, but perhaps he could suggest Neal's flat next door to Grandma's. Neal was going abroad for eighteen months, although Ling didn't know if he wanted to let. He'd find out about the flat and ring them early evening if he had any news.

As he wandered along Frith Street, he paused to watch two pigeons squabbling over a piece of pizza someone had discarded. Nearing Grandma's flat he was still considering the squawking pigeons, and how testy Justin was, and how unforthcoming Clara seemed to be. He pondered whether breaking one's ankle and leg, not to mention cracking one's ribs, then Clara's newly swollen ankle, might reasonably cause domestic friction, leaving aside their difficulties with regard to Justin's need to flat-hunt.

After supper, he rang Neal's bell. A shadow passed across the viewing hole. A woman's voice called out in an accent he thought was French perhaps.

'Ling next door,' he called back. A moment or two later he heard a bolt pull. The door opened to reveal a slender woman of about his age, wrapped in a heavy silk housecoat. Ling loved silk; he forced his glance away from its deep blue folds across her breasts. It was Neal's housecoat. He remembered thinking, on an earlier doorstep encounter, he wouldn't mind one of such quality himself. Her hair was wrapped in a red towel.

'I am sorry,' he began, stepping back, seeing it was obviously an inconvenient time.

'Neal said you might pop round. Ling, you said?' She took in his Chinese appearance. Ling nodded.

'I'm Michele, settling in. He went…' She waved her hand, gesturing towards him. 'You know, Neal – he went a week early. You come in?'

After his disconcerting meeting at Neal's front door, Ling had avoided Michele, who kept unsociable hours and banged doors late at night. Justin, he thought, would not have caused Grandma to grumble. But, he sighed to himself, as they say in the UK, we are where we are.

Chapter Six

Having no news to offer after the disappointment of Neal's flat, Ling waited a few days before suggesting he might pop in to see Clara and Justin again, hoping they'd be in a better temper, and having heard Justin had been given the all-clear to go home. Clara answered the phone. 'Oh yes, Ling. Please do come round. We're having coffee.' He was already out, on his way back to Chinatown. In a few minutes he had arrived. Ling came out of the lift and took a deep breath before ringing the bell.

'Come in, Ling.' Clara smiled, turned and walked carefully ahead of him, favouring her right ankle. He couldn't help but be aware, tall though she was and moving awkwardly though she certainly was, that she had an elegance about her which he found disconcerting. They had been sitting at the table near the window in the wavering morning sun, where he joined them, having noticed through the open bedroom door that some bags were already packed. Once settled, Justin explained to

Ling that he'd been online looking for somewhere to live, ready for when he came back to work.

He glanced at Clara who looked away, having placed a coffee in front of Ling. He might need another mortgage, Justin said. Ling, cautious by nature, wondered how things might have changed. 'But I thought you were renting?'

'Can't get a flat near work, but buying, well, even this,' Justin extended an arm to encompass Frederico's small flat, 'would be well in excess of half a million.' Then Justin elaborated on the idea he'd come up with, which to Ling seemed, initially at least, quite bizarre.

'Take a look at this.' Justin swung his laptop round to display a houseboat. Ling shrugged in disbelief. 'Yeah, they must cost millions. Seen them moored at the marina near work en route for the Continent.'

'No, obviously not those and not there. These are old narrowboats. There are companies who do them up to sell. Some advertise individually too. There may be a chance to rent, if the mortgage falls through. You can get some with permanent moorings for a premium. Not cheap but doable. Services included.' Clara looked across at Ling. 'Can you imagine? You come home to find someone's moved it somewhere. Taken it. Gone. How secure can that be?' Justin grimaced in irritation, endeavouring to remain calm. 'Look, I've tried to explain already. I'm thinking a canal or even a boatyard. It's all tidal. You can only move at high tide anyway, for which you've already booked a slot in advance through the Port of London Authority. Then to move you need a licence to prove ownership.' His enthusiasm was hard to ignore. He found some new particulars online. 'No, not this one, Bow Locks. No, look, this one, Limehouse Cut. It's a canal off the river. You've got to agree, it looks ideal. I could cycle from there, or from a boatyard nearby.' They all peered at the pleasant open view. There was even a man fishing on the opposite bank. Clara sniffed. But Ling was beginning to see a version of the narrowboat idea as a possible solution to Justin's predicament.

'I wondered about this one. Still under restoration, so I could have some input.' Ling found himself offering to help. 'Do you want to have a look before you go home tomorrow? Are you going to make an appointment? I could help you in and out of taxis if you like.' There was a pause. Clara pushed the laptop away and stood up, stretching then wincing. Leaning against the table, she stared at the two men. Justin and Ling held their breaths, wondering what was coming: She twisted her hair over one shoulder. 'Well, it's a long shot, but you've got nothing else. Let's do it.'

It all happened very quickly from there. Justin, grasping the nettle, made the call straight away. They were dropped off near Limehouse Cut. There had been a short heavy shower. There were still small puddles along the towpath, reflecting a returning watery sun.

Justin, though struggling, was in a positive frame of mind. His boot was covered in a white plastic bin bag, taped on by a determined Clara. He'd argued he didn't need it. Clara, through clenched teeth, had insisted. Exhausted by arguing, he gave in. His sore ribs were bearable as long as he didn't turn sideways. He would cope, even if he did look ridiculous.

'If we must go and see this *boat*,' Clara had emphasised the word as she'd covered his leg, 'at least protect your foot from wet and mud.' Still, Justin thought, this was the first time she'd acknowledged he had to do something positive, real, about living part-time in London.

Ling liked water and boats, but he looked dubiously at the half-restored narrowboat, which moved very slightly against the side of the canal. There was nothing to see that lifted his spirits. Work had obviously stopped at the point where it had been restored to a watertight condition below, but the tarpaulin slung over the top didn't look encouraging where it had dipped, and a small pool of rainwater had gathered. They noticed a thin young man of about twenty or so, tall and a little hunched, as if to make himself small in the landscape, standing waiting for them. His ripped jeans and black trainers were no doubt on trend. The thick fleece with hood lowered revealed a pale face, his eyes reflecting the now grey sky. He smiled, his demeanour immediately transformed.

'I'm Wesley Granger. Call me Wes. Grandad, Mr Birtwhistle, will be along soon. I've been tasked with showing you over.' The three of them stared for a moment, surprised by his cultured tone.

Justin gathered himself to speak. 'Good to meet you, Wes. This is my wife, Clara, and Ling, our friend. The boat would be for me, but tricky for me to manoeuvre myself on board today. Ling has his phone with him and if it's okay with you, will come on board with you and video the interior, so I shall be able to see where your grandfather has got with the renovations.' Clara showed no interest in taking on this task when Ling questioned her with raised eyebrows and offered her the phone.

'Would your wife like to see the interior?' Wes hadn't grasped Clara's lack of interest, as she smiled, politely declining. Wes pulled the tarpaulin back to reveal what appeared to be a watertight deck – a liveable narrowboat, lacking in paint and having what appeared to be Perspex portholes. There was also a very narrow access running along each side of the boat's length. Wes and Ling clambered down to the deck as Wes explained the reasoning behind the narrow construction. Ling stretched his arms out, trying to reach both sides.

Wes laughed. 'You may have noticed how narrow the canals are, often only two point thirteen metres, so the beam needs to be two point eight metres maximum to allow leeway each side.' He stood back as Ling began to video, moving forward slowly, turning to include each side of the interior. The galley was nearest the exit, set along portside. There were copper pans hanging above the cooker and utensils next to them. Wes showed Ling the drop-down table with fold-up benches. It was surprisingly tidy, Ling thought, and was briefly reminded of his parents' flat in Hong Kong, where every centimetre was accounted for. This interior looked tired and lived-in, but he was beginning to be impressed by the ingenuity of the narrowboat owner. Next was the living room space, with two freestanding easy chairs, one a rocker. The rocking chair had an old tweed seat cushion, flattened by use. He continued to video, taking in the small wood-burner set between the chairs. A brass telescope was in the corner with an old cloth thrown over it. On a small table stood a globe. Wes pointed out occasional roof lights. The next space was separated by varnished wood panelling, with the lavatory portside and the shower room to starboard. Lastly was a tiny bedroom where a double bed took up almost all the width. Above, there were cupboards and to each side narrow wardrobes.

Wes glanced at his watch. 'That's it, Ling. Shall we go back now? Grandad will have got here by now. Your friend can ask him any questions.' They scrambled back and discovered Wes's grandfather just arriving.

An older version of Wes approached. The difference was immediately visible in as much as he stood very erect. The eyes, pale like Wes's, twinkled. He seemed to be a man who carried himself lightly. 'You've been over Bertha, then? I see Wesley has introduced you.' He looked at Ling, who gestured to Justin and they shook hands.

'Haven't wanted to do anything to her since I stopped travelling with the missus.' He paused here to gather himself with a sigh, then, thrusting out his neatly bearded chin, continued, 'Well, now it's giving me something to set my mind to. Now it's just me and Harvey in the boatyard.' He nodded affectionately towards a small dog. Harvey, a white terrier, stood up, wagged his tail at being mentioned, then sat down, close to his owner and just clear of a puddle.

Justin had leant on his crutches to shake hands with Mr Birtwhistle. Clara nodded in greeting then retreated, taking most of her weight on her left leg again. She leaned against the old brick wall at the side of the canal whilst Ling, surveying Bertha from the towpath, thoughtfully put a forefinger to his lips as he stared at the half-finished boat. If he'd been quicker off the mark, they might have been moving Justin's stuff into Neal's flat by now, instead of being stuck here at the side of a canal viewing a somewhat doubtful investment.

Justin, as if sensing Ling's uncertainty and suddenly nervous about his report and the video he was keen to see, suggested they move to the pub a little way along the canal. He needed to sit down and so did Clara. Mr Birtwhistle and Wes declined, saying they were expected at one of Wes's friends. As he shook hands on departing, Mr Birtwhistle mentioned how busy he was with viewings of the boat. However, when Justin expressed concern, he reassured him that he hadn't yet received any offers. Justin promised to contact him, either way his decision went, very soon. Having shaken hands again, he turned to go. Mr Birtwhistle clapped Wes on the back and made off in the opposite direction, with Harvey trotting alongside, giving them just one look back.

Once they'd shunted along the towpath to the Bulkhead Inn, they found a table inside, where Justin was relieved to dispense with his crutches. He slid carefully on to the window seat as Clara joined him, careful not to knock him, or her foot, under the table. They were both tired. The sun had disappeared again and, on scanning the room, Clara was grateful for the lighting. She could imagine that even with its copper and brass paraphernalia the interior could easily be gloomy. She was cheered by the sight of an open fire burning in the grate at the far side of the room, where a group of walkers had gathered. On returning from placing their orders at the bar, Ling noticed that they both looked drawn. Their drinks came, a coffee for Clara, and two beers. Once the waitress left with their orders for sandwiches and an extra of chips, Ling leaned forward as Clara and Justin, now a little restored, huddled together, commenting on the progress of the video showing the boat's interior.

'I think Mr Birtwhistle might want to refurb to get more for it, but I could manage as is for the time being. I like it.' Justin leaned back to take a sip of his drink, as he pushed to the back of his mind how he might manage with the twins and Clara in that narrow space.

Clara took the phone, concentrating on the pictures of the interior, pausing the video frequently. 'Well, I can see it's old-fashioned, obviously, perhaps a bit grubby, but some chalk paint and a few new bits of furniture, or even some spare from home, would change everything.' The two men, for the second time in a few hours, found themselves speechless. 'Well, look at it!' she exclaimed defensively. 'As long as the electrics and plumbing are safe and the wood-burner checks out, it's not bad, is it? Mooring's crucial, of course,' she added, as Ling reminded them that Mr Birtwhistle had a boatyard.

As their food arrived, Clara removed her elbows from the table to allow space for the plates. The waitress, tiny, probably around eighteen or so, with purple hair, half of it shaved off down one side, and a nose ring, peered over at the open phone as she pushed the plates around. 'There you go. Oh, that's Wes's grandad's boat. You the ones looking at it, are you?'

Regarding her in surprise, bordering on irritation, Justin automatically closed the phone. 'Matter of fact, yes. Did you want to tell us something?' He watched her step back, suddenly deciding her apron needed straightening. 'Well, me and Wes,' she gulped defiantly, then lifting her chin, ploughed on, 'Wes and me sort of grew up together at mine when Mr and Mrs Birtwhistle were away and he was home from boarding school, so I'm interested.'

Justin had started on his sandwiches and through a full mouth decided any information could be useful and in a more approachable tone, he said with a smile, 'Well, if you can spare a few minutes, we'd be very grateful.'

'Well, lunch shift is finished. Just got to clear those tables.' She pointed to places vacated by some walkers. Justin suggested that she join them with a drink when she was ready and to put it on their tab. He had the strong impression she'd have spared the time anyway, drink or no drink. They stuffed their chips and sandwiches down, much hungrier than they'd realised. Ling brought back coffees, and they sat toying with their drinks. It was only a few minutes before the waitress came over with a Coke on ice. Justin was impressed that she hadn't gone for a cocktail with an umbrella, but, he supposed, it was still afternoon. 'Please, take a seat.' She hovered, uncertainly. 'Please?' He pointed to the seat next to Ling, suddenly aware of how intimidating he might sound. He softened his tone and pointing again, said, 'This is Clara, my wife, and this is my friend, Ling.'

'I'm Janine.' She wriggled in her seat and touched her nose ring for reassurance. They couldn't take their eyes off her. She looked around at her audience. 'You want to know about the boat and perhaps some of its history?' Justin nodded, wondering what this child–woman might reveal that could be of any use to them. Still, his leg hurt and he was in no hurry, so he smiled in encouragement. 'Yes, please.' She twirled the ice with her straw, concentrating for a moment on her drink, then took a deep breath and began. 'Mr and Mrs Birtwhistle lived on Bertha after he came out of the merchant navy, because Mrs B couldn't settle on account of them losing their daughter and son-in-law in a terrible car crash, who were Wes's parents. Wes was sent to boarding school on account of Mrs B's nerves when Mr B was away at sea. That was before he retired,' she added.

Her audience hadn't expected this. Their coffees were now forgotten. Once under way, Janine forgot any shyness in telling what was in effect the narrowboat's recent history. 'Mrs B was a delicate lady, see. That's what Mum said. Then Wes didn't want to go up and down the canals on his holidays, so he lived with us, because Mum and Dad were friends with them. He's a painter now, Wes. Well, an artist really, and well off. He's got his own place.'

Slightly confused, but not wanting to stop the flow, Justin nodded for her to continue.

'Well, then about eighteen months ago, Mrs B wasn't very well. Mum said it was cancer of the brain. Anyway, she stepped off the boat on the Manchester Canal when Mr B had gone for groceries.' Clara gasped in shock as Justin and Ling looked on, horrified. Janine nodded, 'It was a terrible shock all round, but Mr B said it was what she wanted. She loved the Manchester Canal, see, and there wasn't any hope.'

Ling turned to her, unable to resist expressing his feelings. 'I am sorry Mr Birtwhistle has suffered so much, Janine. I hope he finds some peace now.' Justin agreed, thinking it was typical of Ling to show compassion even for someone he'd only briefly met.

'Mr B? Well, yes, but he doesn't want to live on the boat now, though he loves it. Are you going to buy it?'

'Not Ling, Janine, but I may.' Janine turned to Justin, as if to concentrate her attentions on the possible purchaser of the boat. 'He's going to restore the old chandlery in the boatyard into a flat, Mum and Dad say. He tells them corny jokes and makes them laugh. Sometimes he has a meal with us. He helps people who come to his boatyard. They bring their boats. He says his reward is that no one sinks! He teaches how to steer and navigate through the canals. He goes out on the estuary too.' She stopped, suddenly self-conscious, aware she had revealed much of Phil Birtwhistle's life in her eagerness to express her support and now was uncertain of her reception. Clara leaned forward to reassure this young woman, who suddenly appeared uncomfortable. 'Thank you, Janine. It's been so kind of you to give us your time.' Standing up and straightening her tiny skirt, Janine looked across at Justin, still with an earnest expression on her face. 'It's a good boat, you know. You should know that, at least. Goodbye then.' She walked behind the bar, then disappeared through a side door. For a few minutes after she'd gone, they remained silent, affected by the tragedy which hung around the boat, and still affected by the young woman's obvious fondness and respect for Mr Birtwhistle and his grandson.

Then Ling, pragmatic as ever, asked Justin and Clara how old their house was.

'What has that got to do with anything?' Clara jumped, as ever edgy and sensitive in regard to Keeper's Cottage. Justin shook his head, exasperated. 'Let Ling speak for goodness sake, Clara.' Ling saw the tension on her face and smiled. 'Sorry! I just meant that any house – or home – which isn't new, has seen sad things as well as good things. Someone was born and even died in your house in the past. That's inevitable!' Justin grinned and pushed Clara's arm. 'Hey, you don't think they should've pushed the boat out and set it alight, body on board, you know, Viking style?' Relieved they'd got away from the fragility of house ownership, she chose to ignore his tasteless comment with a snort. They were all quiet on the way back in the taxi, each busy with their own thoughts. Ling left them at the flat and decided to walk from there. He saw how weary they both looked; even Clara looked dulled down. He wondered what they would decide about the boat. They insisted they'd be able to cope the next day. A courier was collecting most of Justin's bags and a taxi to St Pancras was booked. Den was meeting them at Bury station. 'I couldn't have managed without you. Thanks so much, Ling. You are a good mate, no question.' Justin looked for a moment unsure what else to say. Ling brushed it aside, remembering with a wry smile Justin's irritable reaction when he'd first met Clara – those crushed violets in their fall together, the doughnuts flying. He considered that it would have been difficult to have made up that particular episode. He could still recall the smell of Clara's hair as he fell against her; the smell of bergamot, he thought. As she moved past him, he caught that perfume again.

'Come and stay. We'll let you know about the boat. Justin's working part-time from home for the next month or so, maybe longer. I would avoid the twins' birthday if I were you.' She smiled. He smiled back his thanks and nodded, with no intention of taking up the general invitation. If he received a specific weekend invitation, he might venture into the wilds of Suffolk and risk leaving everything he'd become familiar with. He waved goodbye.

Once again settled at the table under the window, more strong coffee to hand, his leg supported on a chair, Justin started to sift through the video of the boat on his computer. 'Think I'd move the bedroom from the bulkhead, if possible. It would mean sliding past the bedroom to get to the sitting area. Bit tricky, perhaps.'

'Still, Jus, look at the stove. It's sort of in the middle, so would help to heat the whole boat. If it's moved to the far end, it might not prove so efficient in keeping the rest warm.'

'Mr Birtwhistle does do boats up. I know they often have central heating – that's more practical for me. He'll have some ideas for us, anyway. Think I'll ring him and tell him, bank allowing, I'll buy it.' He paused, working out how to broach his current thinking. 'You remember Mum left me a nest egg for what she called a rainy day?' He wondered how the next few minutes would go, but took a deep breath and continued, 'I know we said we'd put it by for the kids to help with their education. But this is definitely a rainy day. Maybe I can gradually put the money back, but I need somewhere to live now, Clara.' He regretted there was the slightest sound of pleading in his tone, with all that lay behind his needing to proceed in this way. There would be no family life in London. To his surprise, she didn't bite his head off.

'No, I'd been wondering if we should raid that. It would mean you wouldn't be completely at the mercy of the bank's decision, though I can't imagine why they would refuse. Enough of the staff have extra mortgages.' Neither of them mentioned that the usual requests were for extensions, or larger properties and in fact, they'd had a second mortgage to put in a kitchen and central heating several years previously, but perhaps not so much for boats of diminishing value –something Ling had warned them of when they were discussing the idea earlier.

But, by having minimal improvements and permitted a small mortgage increase and using Lola's money, they just managed to reach Mr Birtwhistle's asking price, which he accepted. They exchanged solicitors' details. There was no estate agent. Justin explained that he was returning to Suffolk to convalesce. As soon as his solicitor had all the details, they agreed a deposit would be forwarded. Then confirmation of the balance date as soon as possible. They chatted briefly about the few alterations to the boat and, although Justin was hesitant, they did need to sort out beds for the twins. That apart, they'd meet up soon, to make definite plans and fix a timescale.

'Meet up? How're you going to manage it, lad? Mrs Kerr bring you back down from Suffolk, then?' Clara shook her head in immediate refusal. She wasn't home yet from this disastrous trip. A pang of irritation shot through him, but Justin held his temper to quickly change tack. 'I'll bring my father. He'd love to see it, I know – the boat. He'll bring me. He's had to hold the fort for a while, so he'll enjoy a trip down for a change of scene. Get away from the kids and stuff. He'll drive me.' So with that agreed, they said their goodbyes and hung up. The decision was made. Justin, in spite of his relief that he was more or less confident he was not going to be homeless in the city, knew now that the die was cast for a very different life.

Chapter Seven

Clara hummed as she finished packing. They'd Skyped home. Tom had been popping in to ensure the computers were working properly. Den had taken to him and together they'd cleared the spare shed ready for more wood from Thetford Forest where Tom's brother worked and where Tom helped out. The twins were in fine fettle and briefly mentioned slight sniffles had cleared. It seemed they were all expected at Alice and Edie's for the birthday party. Justin commented again it would have been more fun for them to have held it at home. Clara snorted derision at the very idea, plainly relieved she didn't have to deal with it. She considered, as she firmly pushed Justin's remaining shirts into a sports bag, that she could hardly be expected to set up a party long distance, whilst she was trying to look after Justin. However, when she sat on the bed to fold his underwear ready to go into the last bag, she found her mind wandering towards another niggle. She knew Den was coping to some degree, but worrying thoughts of the calendar he was happily tackling with considerable enthusiasm, from his lengthy report that afternoon, for the ladies in the village, bothered her. She wondered fearfully if he'd seen the original *Calendar Girls* film and the deceptive nude look they had very successfully achieved with carefully placed objects. Would Den be as careful? She was glad she'd hidden the remainder of the booze in their bedroom but fretted there would be other things to worry about very soon.

Den met them, driving their Land Rover, the twins and Arthur piled in the back. Justin noticed a couple of fresh dents on the nearside wing, but in the effort to climb in and get Den to take his crutches, and with Carl and Zoe vying for attention, not to mention the excited barking from Arthur, he couldn't find space to ask any questions. Clara sank into the spare seat next to the twins, after hugging them across their seat belts. She was put off immediately by Arthur leaning against the divider, dribbling down the mesh. She wondered, fleetingly, if Den had been walking him properly. Arthur seemed even more hyper than usual, and generously slobbery, but that was normal, she concluded, as she tried to wipe it from her collar. She knew only too well that a short dash round the field was only an Arthur taster. The result, in earlier days, had been chewed chair legs. Still, she thought, as they trundled away from urban surroundings towards open countryside, Zoe and Carl looked properly dressed and seemed happy, so perhaps she should be grateful he'd at least seen to priorities. Nevertheless, she would check the kitchen chair legs once they were home.

Home! Sanity! Chattering voices faded. Here, she thought, was where she belonged. She loved the huge skies at Keeper's Cottage and the way the cottage settled down amongst the surrounding landscape. You could smell the vegetation when walking in the woods; you could see the soil; you knew the wind came from the east far beyond the North Sea, whipping around the Baltic, past Denmark and ever westward, somewhat fancifully, she conceded, perhaps from as far east as Finland and Russia.

Here in Suffolk there was space all around where the children scampered about and stained their fingers picking blackberries in late summer. In the woods they played hide-and-seek where, about now, sweet chestnut leaves would be unfurled but still tender, and they would pick the leaves and strip them out until all that was left were the spines. In autumn they collected the prickly cases, screaming and laughing, and pushed out the nuts to roast on the little coal shovel with the oven glove wrapped around. They gathered pine cones to burn on the fire on chilly nights. She wanted them to cherish these memories and to continue to make memories like this. The thought of transferring them to the broiling metropolis was anathema. She feared what it might cost them all in the end. It never occurred to her that these were specifically her needs, her desires, reminiscent of her times in Finland with her grandparents, where as a child she had felt secure.

On arrival at the cottage, Justin was surprised to see how the season had moved on to the extent that the field which had been seeded showed a fuzz of green, most likely barley, he thought. This meant that for a few months Arthur would need a lead until he was into the woods. They'd often discussed raising the fence height, but he could jump like a deer and they'd put it off. The trees in the lane were in full leaf. Even their tender leaves had begun to mature to a mid-green. Time had passed him by in the city, not that seasons didn't show themselves there too, he thought wryly, but work and then the accident had made him preoccupied. Even their plot in front of the cottage had become wild and needed strimming. In the back garden he noticed that the old shed door was propped open and there was a stack of neatly cut logs stacked inside, also some still waiting to be housed. Ah, this Tom had been busy, as the twins were pleased to report; this was not his father's handiwork, he was quite sure. Dad may have helped, but he had never been a tidy man. Tom was obviously part of Clara's new team, making himself useful. He felt resentment and a pang of jealousy. He was going to find out more about this Tom in the following days and weeks, and label him.

He still loved it here in this idyllic corner of the world, then immediately corrected himself. He loved it because this was where Clara and the children were. After all, this was where he and Clara had settled once they'd married, and he'd thought his job was permanent in Bury. Clara's preference was for Keeper's Cottage, although there was a cottage in Swayle village they could just have afforded, but this made sense, Justin could see. It was in need of work, but there was more space around the cottage and a proper third bedroom. They tackled most of the work themselves, Justin carrying out the heavier jobs, as Clara was heavily pregnant. They were putting down roots, she'd said, for which he'd been reminded frequently lately, he was now responsible for disturbing.

It was a constant surprise to him, not that he'd seriously acknowledged it before, but it was a fact: he was enjoying living in London. It had become more than that, though. Experiencing being at the hub of everything was wonderful, exhilarating. Nevertheless he was torn, knowing Suffolk could still beckon, which led his thoughts on to Clara's new venture. He knew he should show a proper interest, in spite of it still rankling that her parents had upset an already wobbly apple cart by funding her. So far, she'd shied away from involving him after the setting-up weekend, although he guessed she would like some input from him. He knew he'd been offhand, disgruntled, at the outset. Now he'd be around for a while, he'd try to be more positive.

Once everyone had unloaded and they variously staggered with crutches, ran, jumped about, and followed quietly inside, there was the fire to make up in the sitting room, the heating to turn up. Although it was spring, it had turned chilly and Clara felt cold, worried Justin might catch a chill.

As the next weekend loomed large for the twins' party, Alice and Edie had promised to call in, bringing a huge casserole with them. They squeezed around the kitchen table, Alice discussing final plans. They'd got the local conjurer booked in. Zoe, eagerness showing on her face, asked, 'Auntie, is he the one who teaches tricks, too?' Alice looked flummoxed but was quickly rescued by Edie, who reassured Zoe by confirming he would be. Carl wriggled in his seat, anxious. 'Will he be wearing a clown's face? Only the last one was scary. He wasn't smiley, Daddy.' Justin patted Carl's leg, comforting him. 'No, we agreed about that. Am sure the aunts will have that covered, darling.' So then they settled down to the satisfying task of tearing up a French stick to dip in the gravy.

Clara enjoyed this first meal back home for mostly the wrong reasons. She was grateful for the casserole. But what was wonderful was that the party food was organised, the cake booked and the entertainment almost sorted. All she had to do was to go online for party bags and remind Justin to pay for everything. Den had even managed to get all their presents whilst she'd been in London. She felt guilty, wondering why everything seemed such an effort these days. So far she hadn't even been out to check on the latest orders for the business, or to ensure the computers were still okay, or to ask Den after Mary and Liz. She comforted herself with the promise that she would get a grip after a night's sleep.

After some discussion, it was decided Justin would sleep on the sofa bed in the sitting room for the time being. They discussed the stairs and the difficulty for Justin. Den didn't help by suggesting a stairlift. They both glared at him as he defended his idea. 'Only saying. Obviously isn't worth struggling. Think they're cool, myself.' With that he shrugged and left them to it, having stirred things up a bit. At least they'd agreed with each other against his suggestion, which made a change. Daft pair, he thought to himself. Of course Justin needed to be downstairs; there wasn't any need to discuss it. Clara could always join him, as he was sure she would.

He was surprised to discover over the next week or so that in fact this didn't happen, as far as he could tell. Then he conceded that he was at the far end of the cottage in the box room. He hadn't been offered one of the twin's rooms when he'd arrived. He considered the box room was his penance for turning up uninvited, then being allowed to stay. His window overlooked the front garden and their small plot just beyond. Good view, he thought; shame about his bed, as he pushed down on the flat mattress. But he had a plan.

Justin's accident had put everything on hold with regard to his big idea. He'd almost broached the subject to Clara before the current uproar, but then there was Justin's accident and now Justin was preoccupying everyone. He considered he would need to choose his moment carefully. Obviously Clara was staying here and wouldn't move, though Justin seemed to think he could entice her into the big smoke. Now that Den had been around her recently, and seen the way she was determined in her particular, quiet way, he didn't think Justin would stand a chance persuading her to move, and he had some sympathy with her there. He would sell Wimbledon. He liked it here. Originally, he'd thought of a grandad annexe, but had reconsidered. There was that small plot at the front of the cottage. If he could buy that from them, he might build.

The twins' party caused Clara serious pangs of guilt mixed with gratitude. Flopped out after Den had volunteered taxi services and taken the second contingent home, using the Land Rover with the back long seats down, strapping each child in, she found herself thanking Alice and Edie to the point when Edie told her to shut up, laughing, which caused more merriment.

Mystified, and evidently a little pleased, Zoe looked up at Clara. 'Mummy, have you said something wrong? Do you need to say sorry?'

Clara shook her head, ruffling Zoe's dark curls and smiling at her own rare inability to hold back. 'I'll be quiet now for a little while,' was all she offered, leaving both children none the wiser. Eventually they left for home, the twins still high and Justin grey with pain, having left medication at home. Clara drove, with Den sat in the back, ready to relax after his noble efforts collecting and delivering excitable children, thinking of a good strong beer. Clara and Justin chatted about how to show their gratitude. Den had noticed that the small copse Alice and Edie were extending had some saplings. Perhaps a tree would be an idea, he suggested.

'Wouldn't that be a bit over the top, Dad?'

'Not if you decide beforehand how much to spend. A sapling birch could be affordable,' he offered. This led them to discuss fruit trees. Clara recalled an apple had been lost in the winter storm. The twins liked this idea and Justin agreed, so it was decided. It was to be a fruit tree.

So on Easter Saturday they went to a local tree nursery together and insisted Alice and Edie choose a fruit tree, Justin swinging in ungainly fashion on his crutches, the cross bars now covered in foam to protect his hands. They'd considered getting a wheelchair on loan, but the terrain where they lived wasn't level. The severity of his break meant the hospital was keeping him in plaster for longer than he'd planned, in spite of his urgent request to be promoted to a footed boot. So he remained frustrated.

Den was continuing to settle in by the day and the fact that his son was at home, albeit a very touchy son, gave him the added certainty that here was where he wanted to be permanently. There was an added interest, which had been preoccupying him. He was drawn to Liz but was cautious as to how to approach her. She was reserved and self-contained, which he suspected increased her appeal to him. He'd established when he was photographing the calendar volunteers that she didn't have a partner. He loved the way she moved in a loose-limbed, relaxed way; the way she smiled was calm. He guessed she was in her late fifties. He warned himself not to rush things.

They'd almost finished photographing for the calendar. Once that was over, perhaps they might have a picnic during the nice weather. There was a wonderful copper beech in the forest where Tom had taken him to collect wood, well away from the cutting, pollarding and thinning. Well, he might try his luck. Snag was, he had no vehicle just now. He did need more finances. Perhaps he could borrow the Land Rover. Lola was still in his thoughts, but she had always believed in living life to the full. He almost felt her prodding him in the back to get a move on and live a little.

They'd had a terraced cottage in Wimbledon Village all their married life, which they'd struggled to buy as a couple starting out, but it was worth a fortune now and would buy him choices and help with his pension pot. Although he'd travelled, and was often away in his profession as a fashion photographer, it had been a happy time; but of course, everything changed when she died. Now he had found this rural idyll.

Chapter Eight

Phil Birtwhistle had emptied his furniture into the back of the workshop storerooms below the old chandlery in his small boatyard off Limehouse Cut. He had his basic needs there for now, half camping out in one corner, in readiness for the next stage. Bertha was moored nearby. He had completed the installation of drop-down bunks for Justin Kerr. There was something going on in that family; they didn't seem completely together with stuff. He wasn't sure where the Chinese chap, Ling, fitted in. Name of a river fish, he thought, smiling. He liked the idea of that and wondered fleetingly what it might mean in Chinese. Ling seemed on the ball though. He pondered again how they all fitted together. With Bertha to be moored nearby in his boatyard, he could keep a bit of an eye out, not that it was any of his business, but still.

As previously arranged with Justin Kerr, the next day he set off on Bertha, manoeuvring his way through the city waterways, his last trip outward, having checked everything carefully. This was a total treat for him.

He had all he needed, an autopilot, as well as the app for navigation. He kept a two-way radio for emergencies tucked under the galley shelf. He would bring back this Justin chap, who had still been in a leg-support boot when they'd last made contact. He'd told Phil he was ready to get back to the city. There had been no revisiting of Bertha.

So there Phil was at three knots, a bit more on open water, with time to put all his thoughts in order and get ready to design his flat for a life that would be lived permanently on dry land. En route, he was calling in on an old mate from the merchant navy, now living in a shack on West Mersea. They used to drop anchor and feast on oysters in the good times. He allowed himself the nostalgic thought that Mrs B had loved it there. But he was going to make new memories.

He watched the waters spread before him to a milky width, reflecting the pale sky as he cut into open waters. With the reassuring slow chug of the engine, he found himself hovering over Mrs B's memory and that of their daughter, Hester. Hester: dying like she did in that horrific crash. He'd tried to thrust the pain he felt from the memory of that time to a safer place. To think they used to tease Roger about his terrible driving. Thank God, at least they didn't have young Wesley with them. One thing about Roger, he'd been a worrier and had every insurance known to man. Wesley got left a tidy sum. Good job, all things considered, given the state of Mrs B ever after and how she couldn't cope with Wesley.

After West Mersea, he planned to hug the coast past Clacton Sands along towards Pennyhole Bay, where the North Sea could still affect the steadiness of a narrowboat, though he'd go as near as safe to the coast. He intended to pass up the estuary at Harwich, pass the redoubt, where there were cross tides which could push him off course but not enough to worry about. He was confident. He'd be able to pass on up into the River Orwell and moor at Ipswich, which was a bit pricey this time of year, but he'd got a deal at the least fashionable end of the marina for a week.

Justin Kerr had invited him to their place in Suffolk to stay and recover from the outward trip, before they set off again back down to London, when he hoped to teach the lad something of narrowboats. Always curious about how other people lived their lives, he considered being at close quarters might clarify a few things. The poor bloke had had a rough go of it with his accident and his leg slow to recover.

The forecast was for fine weather with a light breeze and he'd determined to make the most of each bit of this last solo trip on Bertha.

He arrived at West Mersea on a warm, sunlit late afternoon. Joel welcomed him with a supper of grilled fish, more beers than planned and old shared seafaring memories, which led to more beers and a hangover.

Arriving with Bertha at Ipswich a day late, he had worried a little if his berth might be taken, but his place was still reserved. He was relieved to find her not amongst yachts but to be moored next to Winnie and Queenie, both restored narrowboats.

He had made it without difficulty, barring the small delay, and although out of practice on open water he now felt better than he had for a while. On the strength of this, he had made contact and was now also planning to meet up with Olly Judd, another old merchant navy friend, who lived on the Broads and whom he hadn't seen since they'd both been widowed. New memories, he thought, smiling at no one.

It was quiet at this end of the marina. He'd texted the Kerrs with his expected later arrival, but so far he could see no one hanging about waiting for him. He threw his bag on deck, locked up, shoved the ancient black leather gloves he wore at the tiller under the shelf and went to wait on the jetty. It was another warm sunny day with salt on the breeze. He drew in a deep breath, expanding a lean chest beneath the navy sweater, and closed his eyes in pleasure. A hand nudged him; a cough followed. Pulled back to the moment, he saw a man of similar age and similar build, with a little more around the middle and chin, and – unlike him – clean-shaven, grinning at him. Den's camera was slung over his shoulder. The men shook hands.

'Knew it was you, Mr Birtwhistle. Heard all about your boat. I'm Den, Justin's dad. How was it coming round the coast?' Den strolled the length of Bertha and back along the pontoon, admiring her high-gloss finish, as he removed his camera from its bag.

'Call me Phil. I was very lucky – good weather. Could've been a lot worse. A bit out of practice, I suppose, but nah, it was okay.' He paused, weighing up this amiable chap. 'You were coming down to take a look. That got scuppered then?'

Den shrugged. 'In the end Jus didn't think it necessary. Tell you the truth, he was struggling with pain then. But he's improving by the day now.' He pointed towards the car park where he'd left Arthur in the Land Rover. 'I'm parked there, but I thought I'd take a few quick snaps of the exterior, if you don't mind. The twins are so excited.'

Phil watched as Den moved around the jetty, snapping from various angles, then, turning his camera off, he replaced the lens cover, slinging the camera back over his shoulder.

'Didn't you want to take some of the interior then?' Phil offered, as Den paused for a moment to have a last look at Bertha.

'Well, I think it best if you show them all. Make it a surprise when they come to see it before you go back.'

Phil shrugged and so they made their way to the Land Rover. He saw what looked like a small horse leaping about in the rear of the vehicle. He wasn't a fan of large dogs. To take his mind off the dog, Phil asked if they could stop at a garage.

'Yes, sure. We pass several.'

'Need to get flowers for Mrs Kerr. Roses perhaps.'

'Oh yes, of course.' Den thought Clara would be polite but not thrilled with garage flowers. Still, there were limits when someone had been at sea for a few days.

At the first garage, Den pulled in to the side. Phil disappeared, reappearing a short while later with a carrier bag and flowers of vivid colours.

'Thought it best to get a few bits,' he grinned, lifting the bag. 'Chocolates, some sweets for the kids. No roses!' He made a face at the mixed bunch.

They drove on, gradually leaving the buildings and traffic behind them, and towards what Den considered heaven. Arthur was making strong whining sounds from the back to Phil's considerable discomfort.

Den said, 'Oh, he's fine. Loves people. Very affectionate.' Phil shifted in his seat. 'Yes, he'll definitely put his front paws on your shoulders first chance and lick your face. Does it to everyone.' Phil didn't answer. 'No, really, he's okay.' Den sensed he hadn't been very convincing.

Half an hour or so later they were stopping in the driveway near the woodshed. Den wondered if Phil might enjoy a whisky later. Clara had been working in the garage workshop and came out to welcome them, but Arthur got in first, having been released. Phil stepped back to avoid the inevitable as Den had described, but Arthur was quick and a big tongue was quickly around Phil's cheeks. Once that was accomplished, Arthur stayed next to him.

'Oh, I'm so sorry, Mr Birtwhistle. Arthur, leave him alone.'

Phil smiled weakly. 'No, it's fine. Call me Phil.'

They shook hands, then Clara led them into the kitchen where Justin was set up to work from the table, his injured leg supported on a chair. He struggled in an attempt to get up.

'No, lad, don't.' Phil put his arm out to stop him. Unfortunately, he was still clutching the flowers. Justin leaned forward to take them and thanked him. Den exchanged glances with Phil with no comment.

Phil proceeded to hand the carrier bag to Clara. 'Thought these might come in handy, love.'

Clara peered into the bag. 'Thank you, Phil, that's very kind. Let me show you your room. Bring your things. Hope you don't mind – Carl is doubling up with Zoe and you've got Carl's. There are some toys about.'

They climbed the stairs and turned right. The room was small, but what impressed Phil was the view. The window overlooked the back garden and across to the nearby fields.

'Bathroom is opposite. See you downstairs for lunch in five minutes or so.'

Phil thanked her and looked around. The bed was narrow, but not a bunk, for which he was grateful. He noticed a spare bed tucked underneath. Having made his way downstairs, he saw a laden table. He realised he hadn't eaten since the previous night and found himself fighting his appetite.

Clara, intending lunch to be casual, had laid out ham, cheese, salad and pickles, with homemade bread and a fruit bowl. They sat at the kitchen table where Justin had pushed his paperwork to one side, so he didn't need to move. Justin sensed that Phil wasn't relaxed which, for some reason, saddened him. They sat for a while over coffee, until Den offered to show Phil around, although Phil noted that that seemed to include Arthur, who'd sat on his feet throughout lunch. The three of them set off after Den popped his head around the door of the garage workshop to speak to the two women working at embroidery. Phil was momentarily jolted by the scene, his head filled with the memory of Mrs B sat in their narrowboat on many an evening with her silks in a shallow basket by her side, her work on her lap. He was pulled back to the present by Den who called goodbye to the women, holding the door for him.

The woods near the cottage were ancient and still managed. They were soon in deep shade; birds flew about. It was cool, almost chilly, and mysterious, Phil thought. They made their way along paths which led them beneath huge leafy umbrellas of green, then paused under a giant beech.

'This is some place, Den. Of course I'm more used to water, narrow canal ways and towpath wildlife. That's not to say I'm not impressed.' They looked up. 'This is some tree, too.'

Den, busy stroking Arthur, smiled in agreement, with thoughts of taking Liz to Thetford Forest, where he'd seen the copper beech. He needed to work on that.

Supper went more easily than lunch for Phil, helped by a few beers Den appeared with. He thought Clara looked a little edgy but couldn't fathom why.

Phil was surprised how well he slept. The twins had caused some excitement when there was a minor fight over who was taking which bed in Zoe's room. He did wonder how they'd manage on drop-down beds on the boat. Then, of course, with some regret, he remembered it wasn't his problem.

Next morning, as Clara got the reluctant children ready to go to friends, Phil, now more comfortable, promised with Clara's permission that they'd all have a picnic on the boat before he and Justin left for London. Then he and Den set off again, Arthur with a watchful eye on his new friend, who today made no effort to move away from him.

Justin watched the two men, Dad as usual waving his arms about, Phil nodding occasionally in agreement over something, with Arthur eager to keep near Phil, as they wandered off out of the back gate towards the woods, then the fields and past the river. Absentmindedly fiddling with a pencil on some scrap paper, he wondered how much time Phil had spent with his feet on dry land over the years, and how he would cope in the future. Well, he sighed to himself, he wasn't the only one. Still, Phil wasn't going to live far from the mooring in the same boatyard; perhaps he'd drop in and see how he was looking after his old boat. To his surprise, he admitted to himself he would enjoy that. Justin liked Phil's gruff manner. He knew it was probably foolish, but he sensed something about him, nothing he could quite register. The girl in the pub, Janine, had given them a glimpse of his life and tragedies, but Justin was intrigued to hear of some of his many travels.

On the trip back to London he thought they would have a chance to get to know each other. He wasn't sure how much he knew about himself these days. He looked down at his stomach, which had never been an issue for him until now. He did know he needed to get into the gym as soon as he could stand properly. Running was still a distant dream.

His attention was arrested by the sight of Clara coming out of the workshop with a pile of parcels to be posted. He observed her loading them into the back of the Land Rover, her hair falling over her face, a strap slipping a little from her shoulder. Instead of an urge to go to her and kiss that beautiful naked shoulder, he found himself regretful and irritated – not by his inability to move adequately quickly to catch the moment, but by her unconscious sensuality and their lack of unison with each other. His irritation subsided as the vehicle moved away along the lane, but he was disgruntled, bored. Here he was, stuck at the kitchen table, trying to keep ahead of work long-distance, which to his relief, he'd managed better than he'd feared – not full-time admittedly, but enough to keep head office off his back. But his recurring thought had been, for a while, that he needed to get back soon.

Clara just carried on, seemingly unaffected by his inability to get about. A thought came to him that she seemed to like the fact that he was anchored here. Well, of course she did – anything to try to keep him here; for her it must seem a temporary triumph. Suddenly, he needed a very strong coffee. He pulled himself up, grabbed his stick and hobbled across to the coffee machine. A small mercy was that he was now promoted to a boot, which he was permitted to put to the floor. He hoped he would soon be out of that too. He had also been presented with a booklet on how to do ankle and leg exercises, but he was getting lethargic and needed more outside stimulation. He missed Ling, missed the other guys, missed the buzz of the city. He remembered Clara had invited Ling to visit, when they'd come home. He'd message Ling now and beg him, if he had to, to come up and visit.

Carl and Zoe were busy with their chores. Justin watched them, both in shorts and T-shirts, scampering to collect logs from the woodshed. They were tussling with each other on the way across the yard, but it was Zoe doing most of it, Justin saw. Zoe was the more forceful, getting to the door first and pulling the bolt back with a flourish. It had always been like this, he thought. He and Clara tried not to interfere unless Carl's lip started to quiver. Even so, he couldn't help feeling for his son. He fretted that Zoe might be showing signs of bullying. He had talked with Clara about it since he'd been back home. It seemed all one could do was watch and wait, intervene when things got beyond acceptable behaviour and see if she grew out of it. So far, there hadn't been any negative reports back from school, as Zoe was doing well. Even so, he winced at the prospect of trouble with her. Clara hadn't missed the opportunity to point out that Zoe had wet the bed, not frequently, but it was worrying. That wasn't all, she'd added. Carl had biffed someone at school, which was totally out of character too – and why would that be? Justin, unable to suggest a reason not connected to their current situation, watched as Clara had wandered from the room, her back speaking volumes.

He returned to watching the competition of the logs. Now Zoe was trying to get ahead of Carl back to the cottage, but Carl was like lightning, in through the doorway to get logs through to the sitting room, to store in the inglenook against the chill of evening.

'Careful, you two. It's not a race. In fact, Grandad has a surprise for you both if you do it nicely.' Den didn't know about this yet, neither did Justin, but he'd think of something soon; he knew there were treats in the table drawer. Den had rushed out as soon as he'd heard the children arguing. Now he was hovering at the door to the woodshed. Justin had tried to forestall him and let the children manage. But Den had insisted he'd like to make sure they were okay. He said he thought some of the piles were a little shaky.

'Thought you were going to sort it out and stack some more with Clara's wonderful Tom, Dad. He's been elusive recently. I've yet to clap eyes on him.' Justin shunted his ankle about on the cushioned stool.

'Perhaps he's been helping his brother in the forest.'

91

Justin resettled in his seat, irritated by the nagging pain in his ankle and life in general and his father's reasonable suggestion in particular. He continued, pointing at Den, 'On the other hand, he could be staying away for diplomacy's sake. Huh, wouldn't be surprised.' There was a waspish tone to his voice. He glared at his father.

Den puffed out air. These days you never knew with Justin how things would turn. He narrowed his eyes at his son, then relaxed and grinned. 'Oops, Jus, put your claws away. No need for that. I'm sure there's nothing there. After all, I'm here and I'd notice, wouldn't I?'

Justin shook his head, unconvinced, and went back to his computer.

Den had wondered about Tom and the way Clara seemed to cheer up when he appeared, his red braids bobbing. Then, he was hardly more than a boy, he reasoned, but again, Clara did have a way with her. Perhaps there was more to it than that. Still, rolling his shoulders to discard these thoughts, right now he needed to concentrate and keep an eye on the woodshed piles, keep an eye on the twins, ensuring they didn't take wood from the back, and hope to goodness the bottle of whisky, and the Prosecco he planned to share with Liz, remained out of sight. He sighed; he'd been a bit slow there with Liz. He'd noticed how she seemed to have an interest in boats in common with Phil and how Phil, who had seemed to be very quiet, found things to chat about with her.

Amongst the hubbub of the twins running back and forth and their continual bickering, he lost concentration again and drifted off, thinking of Liz – how she could look as if she was about to smile, or was it laugh, whilst keeping a straight face. Did he really amuse her, or did she think him foolish? Who could tell? Suddenly his face felt hot. After all, being friendly and a tad flirty was one thing, and being in demand because of his camera, but committing to a rug with food and alcohol in a shady spot and what might ensue, made him in urgent need of spirits right now. So engrossed was he in these uncertainties looming in his life, he did not notice Zoe grabbing at a large log. The log dislodged a row and several tumbled out, falling on Carl who then yelled, hopping about on one foot. Den shouted at her to be careful, immediately worrying if this was in his job description, then not caring, as Zoe dropped the offending log, missing more feet, and rushed off sobbing to her father. Den, after sitting Carl down to remove his sandal and sock to check his foot wasn't damaged, helped him up, endeavouring to soothe him. With one backward glance, he shoved the door shut with his shoe. In that one movement, as the door swung shut, he was horrified to glimpse several cans of beer neatly lined up, plain for all to see. He'd forgotten them. That was a first for him. He was sure he'd finished that particular supply. He was slipping, obviously.

Once the twins had been calmed and the treat he'd apparently promised them was revealed in the form of a fruit bar each, he made an excuse to bring in the last of the wood and left them to enjoy their snack, their voices resounding in his ears as Zoe tried to blame Carl and Carl tried to defend himself. Neither of them mentioned exposing Den's cache. He decided they weren't old enough to consider blackmail, and because they hadn't said anything, he concluded they hadn't seen anything. He moved the beers to the back with the whisky and Prosecco.

That evening, sitting outside, wearing a sweater against the chill, watching the evening sky flaunting greens and pinks, which faded to palest blue as early stars appeared, he pondered further. Phil had come back from exploring the village and had gone to phone his grandson Wesley to check on Harvey, his terrier. The twins were in bed and Clara and Justin were arguing over whether to light a fire in the sitting room. Den remembered mentioning at supper Justin's check-up – day after tomorrow, that was it. Clara was taking him – the twins would be at some school event and Phil was having a few days away on the Broads with an old mate from his merchant navy days. So that would be his opportunity to get organised. He'd move his remaining small stash indoors into his wardrobe drawer – problem solved and there would be no fear of Phil offering to help! Once he had more cash available, he'd get more supplies.

He'd noticed his booze seemed to go down well at the table. Interestingly, no one had refused so far, with the occasional exception of Clara, but he was sure it was only to make a point. Everyone seemed to enjoy his offerings and it did lighten the sometimes sombre atmosphere. It had been a bit tricky getting it from outside to his room so far, but that had been part of the fun – uncertainty. Ah, uncertainty; his thoughts went reluctantly to the unknown contents within the handwritten envelope, forwarded from Wimbledon, and as yet unopened in a drawer in his room. He knew he would soon have to read the contents.

As he was considering this, he noticed a light on in the workroom. Clara must have forgotten to check it at teatime. Rather than bother her, he thought he'd go in, turn it off and lock up. As he opened the door, Liz shot out of her seat.

'Dear God, don't you warn someone when you come into a room?'

Den, just as startled, stood there, unsure what to say.

'Well, what did you want?'

She wasn't quite the relaxed, biddable person he'd imagined her to be, on this occasion. Even so, standing there, the light playing on her bare arms as she held the embroidery she was finishing, he'd snapped her in his mind and would relish that memory. She did look good.

'Well, I'm sorry I startled you, but I saw the light and thought Clara had forgotten to lock up.' He paused, adding lamely, 'I was just sitting outside.' Then added hopefully, 'Lovely evening.'

She sighed, putting down her work on the table. 'Well, I expect it is. I promised Clara I'd finish this order for her but, to be honest, I can't do any more. You can lock up now. I'm going home.'

She picked up a cardigan and slung it round her shoulders, knotting the sleeves over her chest. He recalled the calendar shot and how her small breasts were almost hidden by the garden club's spring flower arrangement. With some effort, he put that memory aside. 'Can I walk you back to the village?' He added, 'I'd enjoy the walk.'

She looked at him thoughtfully. 'Den, that is kind, but I've got my bike, thanks. I need to get home and have a soak. Another long day tomorrow.'

'Of course, yes, I see. Still, once the rush is over and before the next one, perhaps we could have a walk and a drink, or something.'

'I'd like that.'

Suddenly she smiled, properly smiled, almost a grin. He liked it very much. Things were not at all bad, back here in Suffolk.

Chapter Nine

Clara took a landline call. Her surprised tone reached Den, Justin and Phil, as they sat at the kitchen table, followed by her obvious pleasure in hearing the voice at the other end. The twins had been picked up by the minibus. Den and Justin were still hovering over their second coffees. Phil's friend was shortly to collect him to take him to the Broads.

'Yes of course. No, that will be lovely. We'll pick you up at Bury. Ring when you're twenty minutes off. Weather's going to be good!' She placed the phone down carefully. 'I can't believe it! That was Ling. He's coming for the long weekend. He's able to finish early to come here tomorrow, Friday, it would seem without any problem.' She sat down and sipped at her cooling coffee, apparently unbothered by her emphasis on his ability to travel when he wanted to, leaving Den to express his pleasure, before finding himself in a hurry to finish his coffee and move away. Justin couldn't, with any agility or grace, so he ignored the comment except to declare his delight at the prospect of Ling's arrival. Phil also moved away, sensing an atmosphere, having remembered that he needed to bring his bag down to put by the front door in readiness for his departure.

Ling stood in the front bedroom in Grandma's flat. He still felt guilty about taking Grandma's bedroom. Linda, his younger cousin, already had the spare. Grandma insisted she liked her bed in what had been the study, poking at him with a pointed finger. 'I need to be near bathroom, fool!' Linda had taken the trouble to try to convince him too. 'Oh, don't be an idiot, Ling. Can't you see that Grandma loves having us both and bedrooms aren't an issue for her!' He guessed she was probably right and decided to stop worrying. He sat down on the bed, looking idly at his two choices of bag. The one he preferred was a metallic pod. The one he thought was probably more suited to visiting the country for a few days was the soft bag he used for the gym. He patted the metallic pod, which had come with him from Hong Kong three years previously to accompany him to this new life, this Western life.

Working for the bank had given him wings, a reason to leave. Being a native speaker of Cantonese, and of Mandarin, as well as English, had been the deciding factor. He got up, delaying the decision on which bag to use, and looked out of the window. Chinatown Market lay two floors below. Some red pantiles on the permanent stalls were catching the sun, whilst coloured awnings rippled in the afternoon breeze. The double glazing kept much of the racket out, but it was never really quiet. Ling was accustomed to city life and although London and Hong Kong offered very different diversions, they were held safely within the urban sprawl he hadn't ever really ventured much beyond.

He rang Justin on his mobile. 'Hi Jus, do I need a suit? Am just packing, but what about Phil Birtwhistle? Have you got room for both of us?'

'Yes, Phil's gone off to the Broads for the weekend, so you're okay. Room to yourself. Gear? Lord, no! Just casual. Oh, and your swimmer if you fancy wild swimming. I'm walking a bit now. If it's hot we'll have a dunk in the river. Looking forward to seeing you. I can't wait for a laugh.'

'Yes, fine. Okay. Looking forward to seeing you all too. See you this evening.'

Finishing the call, he turned away from the window. Justin couldn't wait for a laugh. He would try not to be the cause of it, obviously. He should take the soft bag then. Hmm, he thought, wild swimming too. Well, he'd seen them in the Albert Dock doing it for charity. Apart from the over-enthusiasm of some of the competitors, he thought wild swimming might not be quite his thing; it would depend on the look of the water. He packed quickly now, deciding to carry a jacket, although the forecast was for dry, hot weather. Then he went into the kitchen to see Grandma. She handed him a plastic box. Cantonese filled the air as Ling tried to make sense of the contents.

'Grandma, what is it?' But she shooed him from the flat, with instructions to open it at the table.

Standing in the corridor of the train, his bag between his feet, jacket around his shoulders, the rhythm of the train rocking him slightly, Ling began to wonder about the visit ahead. Already he could see there were fewer buildings flashing by; fields were opening up, some inhabited by cattle. As the train pushed on, he was conscious every mile took him nearer to Suffolk County and Justin's family, the twins, Justin's father, Den and, of course, Clara, whom he often thought of without quite knowing why.

Apparently Phil Birtwhistle, in whose borrowed room he was to sleep, was away visiting a friend. Ling let out an exaggerated breath, then drew in another. He had to smile at himself – this was the cool guy who liked to think he never lost his equilibrium. Well, this could easily be one of those rare times.

Clara met him. Justin had declined, saying it was pointless as he would merely sit in the front of the Land Rover and wait, whilst Clara did the honours of going to the exit of the train station. He would, instead, be ready at home with the offer of an immediate cold beer and warm greetings.

Ling found himself walking towards Clara amongst the other travellers, not knowing what to expect of the encounter. He reminded himself he knew what to expect visually: her height of course. He saw that she walked easily now, the ankle recovered. She was wearing a loose, flimsy dress almost to the floor above flip-flops, a thin cardigan over all. She waved and smiled. He lifted his jacket and waved back awkwardly. As she approached, for a moment her perfume, bergamot, assailed his nostrils.

'Did you get a seat? I expect you're exhausted,' she rushed on.

Ling hesitated, shaking his head. 'No, I'm fine. It was crowded. Standing room only until near this end, but it was okay.' He thought she wasn't listening.

'The car's this way. Do you mind dogs? You've heard Justin go on about Arthur, I expect. He's in the back. He likes car rides. Only thing is he doesn't always sit down.'

'Dogs? Well, yes, you see all sorts in the park. If I had my own place I might consider a pug. They make me laugh, though of course one would be good company too.'

'Well, Arthur is very gentle but, er, quite a big dog. He's very friendly, actually,' Clara added lamely.

Ling, startled by Arthur's barking when the doors were opened, was embarrassed that his voice carried a querulous tone when he tried to ask jokingly, 'Arthur doesn't eat people, does he?'

'Only if we forget to feed him!'

Ling gave a hesitant laugh. 'I asked for that.'

To Clara it was obvious that the dogs in the city park, to which Ling had referred, must be mainly small breeds. She should have insisted on leaving Arthur at home. It was Justin who had suggested Arthur could be his surrogate, which at the time she'd said was ridiculous. These days it was tricky crossing Justin and it hadn't seemed worth the aggro. She found herself feeling strangely protective of Arthur now, which was a developing attitude she was surprised about. She guessed Justin hadn't stopped to share with Ling any pictures of Arthur from his phone in an idle moment at work.

Clara offered a back seat for Ling's bag and jacket, but Ling chose to keep his bush-style jacket with him on his lap. She didn't comment. It was a warm evening with no sign of rain. She noticed he stroked it once or twice, smoothing it across his knees, and even slipped his hand into one of the numerous pockets on one occasion to check for a tissue. They quickly left the town behind, passing along roads with hedges and open country beyond, bathed in late golden light, which Clara suggested made magic of their surroundings. Ling nodded in agreement, but she had a further sense that Ling wasn't entirely at ease. She thought of the violets he'd brought to the flat in Soho on that fateful day when they'd fallen and she'd hurt her ankle.

'Ling, in spring along here is where wild violets grow. Possibly a bit smaller than those you bought me, but I think of them each time I drive along here. I'm afraid my falling on them rather spoiled them.' She tried a giggle. Ling remained silent, gripping his jacket, then letting go. It hadn't been the right thing to say, she thought.

Ling looked more keenly at the hedge banks. 'Oh, I didn't know they grew around here. Those I bought came from a farm in Cornwall, the woman in the shop said. I saw them and thought, how delicate – and their perfume was so light, you needed to put your nose up close to get it.'

This was getting more awkward by the minute. With relief she could see their turning up ahead. 'Nearly there. It was very kind of you to think of me when it was Jus who was the invalid. Thank you.'

'I guessed you might like something too.' He omitted to say Grandma had instructed him and now he was a fraud, although at least he had liked the idea. He found himself gripping his jacket again and made an effort to relax. If he went on like this it would need an iron over it before he could wear it, then he remembered he'd bought it because of its crease resistance, as well as its showerproof qualities. Perhaps he should try harder to relax. He found himself smiling at the contradiction.

The first sight of the cottage set at the end of a lane, a gravel drive sweeping past the front door to a parking area at the side, the last of the sun catching the bricks, was – for some reason he couldn't quite put his finger on – very pleasing. A man who looked like Justin, but who was older and slightly portly, was outside, a sweater around his shoulders, talking to a slender woman of a similar age, who was smiling at something. He remembered Den and some of his history from Justin. Den waved and said something to the woman, who also waved, then collected a bicycle from a nearby wall and wandered off towards some woods beyond the garden, turning to wave again as she opened a gate to the path, where the setting sun streaked through, now red. Ling resisted the urge to ask how safe the woods might be.

As Clara turned the engine off, Arthur leapt to his feet stirring up the smell of sweat and dog hair, joyful at their arrival, leaving smears of saliva down the back windows. The twins dashed out from the side door, halting immediately on calls from Justin. Ling could see already that Zoe was the bold one of the two. Carl stepped back, quickly finding Zoe's hand to grip. Ling was amused how they were so unalike, yet so like their parents: Zoe as dark as Clara was fair, Carl white-blonde. He was glad to see Justin was managing better than he'd expected and had made considerable progress, admittedly with the aid of a stick.

He and Clara slipped down from their seats, jumping to the fine gravel, the warm evening air carrying the smell of cut grass, and he sneezed. He'd forgotten his antihistamine tablets. Suddenly Ling found himself shaking Den's surprisingly firm hand, being greeted warmly and patted on the back in welcome.

Justin came towards him, grinning broadly. Zoe and Carl stood to attention below him, staring intently at this new visitor. Ling leaned down to speak to them.

'Zoe and Carl, it is so nice to meet you.' They stepped back. He returned to an upright pose, momentarily flummoxed.

'Children, go on in and wash your hands.' She shook her head in embarrassment. 'I'm so sorry, Ling, about that.' The children were still rooted to the spot.

'It's okay, really.'

Arthur was now pulling. Clara found herself apologising again. 'I'll have to let him go, sorry. After he's had a lick, he'll be off round the garden to let off steam.'

Ling struggled not to wince, bracing himself. Having endured hot breath against his face, he determined afresh that a small dog, whatever the circumstances, was preferable. Gathering himself, Ling rummaged in the top of his bag. 'Zoe, Carl, these are Chinese dragon kites for when it's windy. They have long tails, see? Mummy and Daddy will help you assemble them. Zoe, yours is bright red. Carl, yours is bright blue.'

'Can we try them out now, Daddy?' Carl was hopping up and down in anticipation. 'Yes Daddy, we should – straight away!'

'Have you said thank you?'

'Thank you, thank you!' they both piped up.

'Ling, you brought kites to the right place. Suffolk's known for wind. Kids, we'll try them as soon as there's enough lift for them.'

Disappointed, they examined each kite for comparison, delaying even longer the handwashing instructed by Clara. Ling was gratified he'd had the sense to buy duplicates.

'Well, these are for you two, Justin and Clara, for the garden. I hope you can use them. They're Chinese lanterns. I chose nylon rather than paper to withstand some of the elements. There are LED lights to hang in them. Not traditional, exactly.'

Justin and Clara opened the package. 'Well, we can hang these this evening after supper. They will look wonderful in the apple tree. Thank you,

Ling.' Clara leaned forward to kiss his cheek, then, unsure, patted his arm instead.

'Yes, Ling, thanks so much. We need something to brighten the garden up in the evenings. Perfect. Now you must be starving, come on in. Everything's ready. Dad did it. Zoe and Carl laid the table,' Justin commented, hobbling into the kitchen, leaving Clara endeavouring to smile at his receding back.

The kitchen was lit by small candles in the windows, against the approaching dusk. Ling noticed that in the centre of the table someone had picked what he thought looked like wild flowers, thrust in a casual manner into a large jam jar. There was a pervasive strong aroma of spices. They sat at places written by the twins.

'I did yours, Mr Ling,' Zoe declared, looking up at him uncertainly, pointing at the card in front of him.

'Thank you, Zoe. You printed it beautifully. You can just call me Ling, like you are Zoe,' he smiled. Carl nudged Justin.

'Daddy, mine's good too, isn't it?'

Justin looked very carefully at his place card. 'You know Carl, it's perfect. In fact you both did them all very well indeed.' Then Justin turned to get Den's attention. 'Dad, would you like any help with the food?'

Den hesitated; after all, his son wasn't offering on his own account. 'Well, yes please. Clara, would you check the dal on top and the rice?' Den moved over to the oven to pull out the dishes and stepped back smartly to avoid the escaping steam, as Clara moved to help. He turned to Ling. 'Ling, I'm not brilliant at Chinese, but am pie-hot with Indian, mainly Kerala. Lots of veggies and spice – some not too hot for the kids. If you're not keen, then there's salad, but I can see you are a man of mettle!'

Ling, uncertain of Den's meaning, just smiled agreement. He liked Indian food. At the mention of Chinese food, it occurred to him that the box Grandma had given him was still in his bag. He guessed she had made some sticky coconut balls, which might be good with coffee later.

It turned out not to be such a good idea, as Grandma's sweet tooth had won over moderation and the sticky coconut, heavy with condensed milk, stuck to everyone's teeth, which caused unintended hilarity as the twins struggled, adding to the now light-hearted mood, gained from copious amounts of lager having been downed to slake adult thirst. The twins were eventually led off to a late bed by Clara, escaping bath time. Den had suddenly pulled the lagers from the fridge, with the casual remark that Liz'd brought them for him from the village earlier in her panniers. Ling remembered the woman with the bike, mystified where the panniers might be, as he'd only noticed a wicker basket attached to the handlebars. He wondered if it was a fiction, having heard from Justin that his father was unpredictable and could be fanciful.

Ling's bedroom faced the back garden. It was a starlit night and once he'd undressed he drew back the curtains. Here there was little light pollution though a pale glow bled into the sky somewhere beyond the trees. He guessed that might be the nearest village. He looked at his bed. His, it turned out, was a pull-out, from beneath what was normally Carl's bed, but temporarily Phil's. He wasn't accustomed to sharing a bedroom and hoped fervently Phil might find a reason to delay his return from the Broads and his old merchant navy friend until after the long weekend, when Ling would've got the train back to London. Carl's toys were tidily held in colourful boxes against a wall and presumably in the padded window seat, against which he'd stubbed his toe in the dark.

Once he'd lowered himself onto the mattress, he was surprised to find his temporary bed very comfortable. He slept until dawn. He had tossed the duvet off in the night, then pulled it over himself again to settle back to sleep, before realising that he'd been disturbed earlier by shuffling sounds above his head. Now fully awake, he listened intently, fearful there might be rats in the roof. Then the sounds changed to a clear pattering. Next, a bird started chirruping. He turned over, checking his phone in the early half-light. It was four fifteen. Very soon, other birds joined in until the woods beyond the cottage echoed with calls as if in answer to those nearer and above on the roof. In spite of the birdsong, some of it meltingly sweet and haunting, he must have dozed, for when he came to again, the dawn chorus, which was what he guessed he'd heard, was over.

Unable to lie there any longer, with the sun now pouring through the open window, he threw on jogging shorts, a vest, and tied a sweatshirt around his middle. Sitting on Phil's bed to tie his laces, he pondered over how to get past Arthur. After opening his bedroom door very slowly, he peered along the landing. There, her back towards him, turning to go into her bedroom, he glimpsed Clara, her figure against the light in a delicate nightgown. She hadn't seen him, he was sure, but he had seen her and was, for a moment, stunned by the vision he had beheld. Once he was sure that her door had closed, he crept along the landing, holding his breath, then down the stairs, pausing on each tread, then allowing himself a deep breath, tiptoed to the kitchen, hoping he hadn't disturbed anyone. He inched the kitchen door open slowly, where, inevitably, Arthur awaited.

He managed to squeeze into the kitchen, pulling the door behind him. There, his back against the door, he was greeted joyfully by Arthur, with quiet whimpers of delight, up on his hind legs licking Ling's face. Ling, endeavouring and failing to avert his face, managed to grasp Arthur's paws, letting him down gently. He grabbed some kitchen roll and wiped the slime from his face, resigned now that he'd been foolish to even think of leaving Arthur behind. In spite of Arthur's friendly enthusiasm, Ling still felt some nervousness at his bulk. Together they went out into the garden. Ling hadn't seen a lead hanging in the kitchen or in the porch. He hoped Arthur wouldn't run away, but by the manner in which the dog rubbed his coarse coat up against his bare legs constantly, he guessed he would stay near.

Ling looked around, unsure which way to go, the sun on him as he turned. The grass was still heavy with dew; there was a heady feel in the air of approaching heat, insects already busy in a nearby flowerbed. He decided he would take the path into the woods. He hesitated for a moment, admitting to himself that with Arthur resolutely beside him, he was glad of the company in this alien landscape. Having thrown his unwanted sweatshirt over the gate, he started to jog, then picking up speed, ran, Arthur loping easily beside him into a place of deep shadow laced by pale sunlight. Along the pathway, where the sun played across the woodland floor, there were tall feathery plants, their creamy-white froth of flowers giving off a slightly sharp scent, which caused him to stop and sneeze.

Having passed to deeper shade, the sneezing stopped, and they set off again, Ling's thoughts as tangled as some of the woodland he was running through. He thought how Justin seemed very different from the Justin he had become familiar with at work. There, he'd seemed enthused by everything around him, eager to join in with the team, to pull his weight and go with the group to the occasional kick-about in Greenwich Park on a Sunday morning, when he hadn't come back to Suffolk. But since his accident, it was more difficult to feel so relaxed around him; it was tricky to read him. Understandably, he considered, Justin must feel frustrated at his slow progress, but he was doing well and would soon be free of the boot, although it would be some time before they could run together. He wondered if he wanted to anyway. There had been mention of swimming in the river. Perhaps if this weather continued over the weekend it would be fun to cool down in that green water he'd already had a look at. He did ponder over Justin's purchase of a narrowboat. Hopefully, because it would be moored off the canal, it would be secure. It would certainly be more fun to visit than the flat. If Justin could cycle, he could even have his bike strapped to the roof, as he'd already suggested, to Clara's dismay.

Ling allowed himself the luxury of letting his thoughts run to Clara: golden, beautiful, delicate Clara. Older Clara, he reminded himself, although she seemed young to him. Clara, he realised, now that he could see her in her own environment, would struggle to embrace the cut and thrust of city life. Here, amongst the fields and woods, the small villages nearby, with her online designer business for children's clothes – for goodness sake, he thought, even that on her doorstep, in their garden! – here she appeared to flourish in her own way, which was difficult to define. After seeing them in the flat, when Justin had blamed her for his accident, and seeing how they seemed somewhat distant now, it was a stretch to imagine how those two were going to make out.

He mused, if things were different, if she were alone, if the slight frisson he'd felt from her once or twice, if he wasn't imagining it, he could almost see himself with her. That would be, of course, a ridiculous outcome. One city-bred Chinese man with a tall, beautiful, older, he reminded himself again, countryside-rooted Dane! He dismissed his idle thoughts, thinking he should get out more at home, just as they reached the village and Arthur obligingly stopped to await their next direction.

They made short work of the return run. Birdsong in the high canopy followed them through to open, sunny patches of grass. Ling had the outlandish idea that they might even have a picnic there later. He could picture the twins playing ball and romping about. It wasn't far from the garden; he thought Justin might manage. But when they reached the gate, he could see by the slow progress Justin made towards them, it would be best to stay in the garden. He picked up his sweatshirt and followed Arthur.

'Morning Ling.' Justin waved with his free hand as Arthur leapt eagerly towards him, coming to an impressive halt as Justin ordered, 'Sit!' He grinned at this success. 'Doesn't always work. Warm, isn't it? I couldn't sleep either. Our duvets are too thick. Need to get some sheets out. Clara's rummaging now in the airing cupboard. Come on in and have a coffee.'

Ling, too polite to express his preference for a shower, followed into the kitchen. A little later, he excused himself. Upstairs he could hear riotous laughter and screams from Den's room at the end of the corridor, with calls of 'Man overboard!' Den was playing boats on his bed and sending them over the side. There was no sign of Clara as he made his way to the bathroom.

Once Ling had showered and put on clean shorts and T-shirt, he looked at his bed, considering whether he should make it or strip the duvet cover. He was saved by a knock on the door and a call from Clara. He opened the door and helped her pick up the bedding she'd dropped outside his door.

'Morning, Ling. This is for you. It was so hot last night.' She found herself rushing on as she had the previous evening, when she'd met him at the station. There was humour in his eyes, but he thanked her gravely, asking what he should do with the duvet.

'Oh, oh well, best pop it on the window seat in case it turns chilly and we've all been fooled into thinking this could be a heatwave.'

'Oh, yes, right.' With that, he followed her and they went downstairs together. The noise had now subsided from Den's room and the twins appeared, dishevelled and excited as Clara shooed them towards their shared room.

'I'm coming straight back, you two. Shower time! I've got your things out ready. Fetch your towels. I won't be a minute!'

They tumbled over each other, giggling and laughing along the landing.

Clara eventually ushered the twins in for breakfast, as Den followed. Ling sat in a corner with a view of the garden and the gate into the woods. Arthur was sitting on his feet. Justin pushed the dog off.

'He's a pain, Ling. Don't let him smother you.'

Ling immediately defended the dog by patting him, now grateful for his support through the woods, and thought of him as an ally. Justin rolled his eyes in amused defeat. Ling was then distracted by the sight of Liz approaching from the woods. He pointed out her arrival to Den, who moved swiftly to invite her in.

'Oh, come on in, Liz. Quick coffee?'

Liz hesitated, then, smiling, slid onto a seat Den had pulled forward. Ling observed Liz sitting a little awkwardly on the edge of her seat. Today he could get a better look at her. He thought she was in her late fifties – very attractive in a slightly hippy way, with plaits taking up part of her hair into a sort of ponytail. Den tried to ply her with toast and the croissant basket and even one of the hard-boiled eggs still available. She waved it all away politely.

'Thanks no, I can't stay, but I was hoping you could all come tonight. I know Den is involved as an honoured guest, obviously. But once the rest of us have got the months sorted, and there has been a bit of a dispute about that, as you'd expect with the opinionated lot we've got, then we're cooling off with a buffet on the green if it stays dry and the forecast is good. The children are invited. Den will confirm all the pictures are suitable for family viewing.' She turned to smile at Den.

'Grandad, will you make a calendar of us too? I want our own calendar!'

'Zoe, sweetheart, perhaps we can talk about that later.' Den shook his head towards Liz, momentarily rattled at the thought.

'Actually, Den, that's a great idea of Zoe's. Take snaps through the summer of the children for Nana and Grandpa in Denmark for Christmas. They'd love it, as we don't see them very often.'

Justin looked sharply at her, but Clara had changed the subject swiftly, by thanking Liz for the invitation and promising to text her as soon as she'd checked with everyone.

'I want to go, I want to, Mummy!' In her agitation to make her point, Zoe knocked her glass of juice over. It flooded unintended, but neatly, into Carl's lap across his shorts. He leapt up, knocking his chair over.

'Look what she's done, Daddy. She spoils everything and these are my favourites. She knows that!'

Justin – swiftly, considering his physical limitations – stood to pull the chair up, grabbing a tea towel from the nearby rack, and mopped as much of the juice as he could. Clara disappeared to return with a flannel, towel and fresh shorts, taking Carl's hand and leading him into the utility room, making reassuring comments on the superior replacements. Justin attempted to regain attention for Liz's invitation, as she stood up to leave.

'What d'you think, Ling? Give you a chance to have an insight into village life. Food'll be good.'

Ling, caught on the spot and totally out of his depth, managed a smile, then feeling he was expected to show more enthusiasm, nodded in confirmation. As Clara and Carl returned to the kitchen, Justin reported that he thought it would be fun for them all, and they should go to support Den and his photographic efforts.

'I was only thinking it might not be Ling's thing, but are you okay with it, Ling?'

'Of course. I'm happy to go along with what you decide.'

Clara thought his demeanour less certain, as Liz smiled happily at her success to Den, pausing on her way out as he followed closely behind.

'We'll bring some salads and some meats. There's some chicken too. I'll slice some of that from yesterday's supper.'

'Thanks Clara.'

Justin offered beers and lemonade for the children. 'Dad can run us past the off-licence on the way round. We can all go in the Land Rover.'

'See you at seven, then.' Liz waved goodbye and left.

Through the window, Ling absentmindedly watched as Den went out with her. He saw them chatting for a few minutes, then she walked her bike to the gate into the woods and disappeared. He thought she must ride her bike on the route he'd run earlier. He wondered how her tyres coped. Den continued to watch where she had so recently been. Was Den thinking about her tyres too? But he thought not, as he caught him smiling to himself as he turned and came back to the kitchen.

'Well, who's for lunch in the garden later, then perhaps a swim? It's going to be hot enough. What d'you think, Jus?'

They all murmured agreement with Den, later pulling the table and benches under the apple tree for shade. The twins helped to bring out dishes, having bought pies and quiche earlier at the country market in Swayle.

To Ling, the stalls and the stallholders seemed very sedate compared to Chinatown. The pace was much slower in every respect. He enjoyed the novelty. Here, he found he also appeared to be a novelty, as much as, if not more, than Justin's now famous injuries, and was introduced to more people than in the three years since he'd lived in Chinatown. He'd become resigned to shaking proffered hands at work, and had now found himself doing the same here. As his cousin Linda would say, "when in Rome", and privately chided himself for his Chinese reticence.

Mid-afternoon they made their way down to the water's edge, towels slung over shoulders. There were deep spots; a swing rope with a tyre spanned the river under a willow. Initially, Clara paddled with the twins as they yelled that the water was freezing. Den and Ling helped Justin down the bank, carefully hopping as he left his boot on the grass. Once in the gentle flow, the three men swam. Once Zoe and Carl were eventually immersed, they swam like fish, Ling noticed. Clara remained close to the children, swimming with them. Ling found himself trying not to look at her, but it wasn't easy; those golden limbs were mesmerising.

Hauling Justin back up the bank was a precarious operation. The bank seemed more steep than on the way down and they were all of them dripping. Ling worried for his friend, but after almost slipping back, he and Den got a good grip and hauled him up to safety.

'Thanks guys,' Justin grinned. 'That's the most excitement I've had for months!'

'We can do without that sort, son. Nearly had a heart attack myself!'

That evening, after a welcome enforced withdrawal to various bedrooms for a rest, suggested by Clara, plus copious amounts of aftersun cream, then tea and biscuits, they loaded up the Land Rover, leaving Arthur in the kitchen. With Ling's arrival and Justin's progress to a walking boot and stick, they had travelled ahead of them. The stars of the show were, of course, the twelve volunteers who had been photographed for the charity calendar. There was a stall with the photographs laid out at the side of the pub lounge. The women, sashes announcing the month they represented, mixed with the crowd. Ling was astonished to discover that Clara, the outstanding beauty in the room, was not one. Liz was; she wore March. A woman called Mary, whom Liz introduced as a friend and workmate, was November. The months had been decided, after all.

The evening was still, humid and hot. Everyone swiftly vacated the pub for the green, where the pub had set up a bar in readiness for the celebrations.

'Who's going to assemble the calendar, Dad?' Justin was relaxing on a bench, as Den and Ling were on a rug with the twins. Clara was chatting to some villagers Ling hadn't met.

'I've still got contacts, Jus, but it can be put together online. The ladies are dealing with it now – should be ready by September for sale for the Christmas market. Glad my part is done, if I'm honest!'

'I wondered how easy it might have been for you, Den? The ladies all seem very pleased with your efforts. Husbands relaxed too, which says a lot.'

'Well, Ling, we did have a few moments. Clara wasn't included, because we aren't in the village, and was relieved, actually. Then there were some others who wanted to be, but didn't qualify, either, outside the village. Not all have husbands to please, you know. The other stuff I've done, off-piste you might say, hasn't been nearly so tricky.' Den smiled to himself in recollection of some pleasant memories.

Ling, watching, thought Justin's assessment of his father wasn't too far out, and found himself warming to this light-hearted man.

Chapter Ten

Phil was back in contact the next morning. He suggested they all meet at Bertha at the marina in Ipswich at lunchtime, where he was being dropped off by his friend, who was stopping off en route at a supermarket, so that Phil could buy supplies for the picnic. Clara took the call and between them they sorted out details. The heatwave had settled in. It was an uncomfortable drive with no air conditioning, all windows open.

'Daddy, can we get a car like my friend Peter next time? Peter's daddy bought a new SUV and it's got everything!'

'Sounds ideal to me. What d'you think, Jus?' Clara gave Justin a sideways glance as she changed gear.

'Think a narrowboat gets best marks, myself. Wait till you see it, kids. And it's ours, which means it's yours to come and stay!'

Conversation ended as they approached the parking area and could see Phil was waiting, paper carrier bags around his feet, his bag slung over one shoulder. Justin, determined to manage on his own, refused help as he climbed down carefully. Ling was ready with Justin's stick. Clara stood back, biting her lip. Den undid the children's belts and helped them jump down. Phil came forward grinning widely.

'Good morning. It's good to see you all. Hi, Ling. Surprised to see you here!'

'I think Ling is too,' Justin grinned. 'Still, perhaps you'd give me a hand on? I can't wait. Can you others manage? Zoe, Carl, hold Mummy's hands please.'

'Well, the boat's ready. Shall we squeeze in then?'

With that, Phil gathered up his bags, stepped across the narrow gap and dropped the bags, ready to assist the company aboard. Den and Ling, last on board, found themselves huddled in the galley. It was going to be a cosy picnic, though surprisingly cool, they agreed, staring around. The twins loved the drop-down beds, made specifically for their visits, and insisted on testing them, to Phil's satisfaction. The new portholes and roof lights were tested and opened with ease. These had been the last alterations. Phil privately thought the change unnecessary, but they were an indulgence Justin had allowed himself.

Clara was very quiet. She explored the boat's length, looking in the shower facility – it was hardly a room – the toilet opposite and the bedroom at the end. The little stove was also in place in the centre of the boat as before, with an armchair either side, one a rocking chair. Justin sat at the table with the children for the indoor picnic. Phil and Clara settled in the easy chairs and Ling insisted he'd like the floor cushion. Clara slipped a wedge under one of the rockers of her chair to gain some stability.

For the return journey in the Land Rover, Den pulled the side seats down in the back to create more seating, grateful they had a Defender with a long wheelbase. There was non-stop talk of visits to Bertha when Justin was back in the city. Ling had worked out his route to Bank, then the DLR to Limehouse, then a walk to Limehouse Cut. Phil found himself heartened.

These people were going to be around, nearby. He would enjoy the compar.. He looked at the back of Clara's head, determinedly driving them back to her sanctuary, as he saw it. He wondered already, how often he might see her visit his corner of London.

They stopped off for a pub supper. It was too late to start food at home, Clara and Den agreed. They drank to Bertha and Phil's modifications, particularly the drop-down beds, and to Ling and his foray into unknown territory, which he had insisted was a delight, and to Justin's recovery and his return to city life. Lastly, and to Clara's astonishment, Justin raised his glass to toast the success of her new business. As the party seconded the toast, Clara, shaken by Justin's unexpected thoughtfulness, found herself welling up through her smiles of acknowledgement.

Once they were back at the cottage, bedtime loomed, not only for the twins, but for Phil and Ling in that small room. Phil was accustomed to small spaces – he had spent years in bunks with crew and wasn't giving it a thought. Although accustomed to small living spaces, Ling's natural reserve caused him to wonder how sharing with Phil would work, and was glad they were extending the day for as long as possible. They sat in the garden, watching the light fade, savouring the last of the day with a beer and the romance of the newly installed lanterns above them in the apple tree. Justin talked of their plans to sail back down the coast to Limehouse. He'd looked it all up and was obviously impatient to get going.

'You've got one more hospital appointment on Wednesday, that right, Jus?'

'Yeah, Wednesday. Can you take me, Dad? We could take Phil in with us, drop me off and take Phil round the market and whatever else of interest. I can phone when I'm done.'

So it was decided that they'd set off for London on Bertha on Friday, once Justin was given the all-clear to have his records transferred back to St Thomas's.

Ling was getting the midday train back the next day. In the name of their new friendships, and after several more beers, they decided they'd see him off. Clara offered to see to the twins. Eventually, Ling had to bite the bullet and go to bed. Den and Phil were happy to stay out in the moonlight, recounting their various past adventures. Justin admitted defeat and joined Ling as he ambled indoors. He was exhausted by his efforts to manage with his weight on his foot for some of the day, which had caused it to swell; it was now throbbing. They went to their rooms. Justin was sleeping upstairs again. Tonight he would have been happy to crash out on the sofa, but with determination, he plodded upwards.

Ling climbed into his bed, wondering how Phil would squeeze through the narrow space between them. However, he fell asleep and didn't hear him, but was awoken in the early hours by hearty snoring. As soon as it was light, he crept out and went for a run. This time he had no intention of leaving Arthur. He'd wondered who had been in to see to him on their long day out. Someone mentioned Tom, but he didn't meet him and Arthur was indoors when they'd got back.

After breakfast, he stripped his bed and took his towel and bedding down to the utility room, then went to find Phil, who was with Den outside the front wall, on the plot at the front. He'd left Clara and Justin in the kitchen, discussing something about the twins, as they played in the back garden.

'I haven't said anything yet, but what d'you think, Phil?'

Phil shrugged. 'No good talking to me, Den. It sounds okay, but what about Clara and Justin?'

'Yes, well, that's my next step. Oh hello, Ling. We're just looking at the boundary here. How are you?'

'Everything's great, Den,' said Ling. 'I've had such a good time.'

They all wandered back to the garden.

As promised, they went into Bury and waved Ling off. Clara and the twins had smiled their farewells, waving them out of sight. At the station, the men shook hands, Justin adding, 'You do know you saved my life this weekend!' They laughed together, then, drawing away, Ling called back, 'Bye then. See you in London next week!'

That night, Den dropped his bombshell after supper. Phil had gone to the village and the twins were in bed. Once they were seated comfortably in the still-warm, fading evening light, with Ling's lanterns lit in the apple tree, he decided now was the time. Jump in!

'Well, you two, I've made a huge decision! I'd like to settle nearby, outside the front garden, in fact, on that fairly neglected small plot.' Clara's mouth fell open. 'You'd like me nearby, Clara – you know you would. I do the cooking more often than not. Entertain the twins. Walk Arthur. Lots more.'

'But Dad, what about Wimbledon?' That was all Justin could think of to say.

'Selling it, Jus. You may not know it, but anything with an SW19 postcode makes a fortune. Had one offer already. Can't be bothered with the gazumping malarkey myself, so have accepted. Don't want to live in the suburbs. Like it here. Love it, actually. See the grandchildren grow up. Help Clara when you are away. What d'you think?'

'Well, a bit of a shock, to be honest, but, well, okay by me I suppose, although you haven't said what you'd live in. I'm not keen on a caravan parked outside, to be honest.' Justin turned to gauge Clara's reaction, which followed swiftly.

'I hadn't thought you'd want to live here permanently, Den.' Clara's tone was not encouraging.

'Clara, I'm thinking of the money I'm going to make, you know the leap in property values. Help you both out a bit. I can keep myself to myself most of the time, but around when needed. I'd like something like a single-storey lodge, hopefully to be imported and erected by the same company who make them. Once planning is passed, it can happen very quickly.'

'Dad, it sounds as if you've already done your homework, but why haven't you talked about it before?'

'Well, I wanted to get you both together. Phil's gone off to the village for a drink with Liz and Mary before he goes back, and I've only just got a proper offer for Wimbledon, so now was the first definite moment. So what d'you both think? Now's the time to say.'

Justin turned to Clara. 'You know, darling, it could work for us all. The kids'd love to go next door to Grandad's. Babysitter for you when you want to go to the village for a meeting, or to see friends. Last but not least, it would help with the rainy day pot. Sorry, Dad, to mention money, but there it is.'

Den got up to stretch. 'Well, that's fine by me, Jus. Makes the world go round. You two have a think. Personally, I think it's a brainwave. Could be a lot of fun!' With that he picked up his sweater, leaving the two behind in a kind of shock, chuckling to himself as he strolled indoors.

'Jus, you know what he can be like. If he's suddenly got money, he could be, well, a bit unstable.'

It was Clara's polite way of saying, too much into the booze, as Justin well knew. Justin sat for a while, trying to think clearly. His gut feeling was that it was a good idea in every way except one, and it didn't involve alcohol. He wasn't confident that Clara and Dad were temperamentally suited to live cheek by jowl permanently. Still, nothing in life was perfect, as he'd discovered himself, so with some reservation he spent the remainder of the evening convincing Clara that on balance this would be a good move for them all. Eventually, Clara conceded that, in fact, Den did help considerably around the cottage, in particular with cooking. Rather slyly, Justin gently reminded her that she disliked that particular chore.

So, as Clara drove Phil and Justin to Bertha at Ipswich, Den stayed behind at Keeper's and got on to his solicitors to speed up the sale and set the purchase in motion. The day was hot and humid. Carl's comments on his friend's parents' vehicle with air con came back to remind Justin of the age of their Land Rover. Once he was settled back in the city, perhaps they could look at a small runaround for Clara and the kids, with some of Dad's money, and keep the Land Rover for when they needed more seating. He wondered if Dad would purchase a vehicle for himself now he planned to settle in the back of beyond with them. The old bike he used was okay for good weather, but not much use in the winter gales that flew across the fens.

The twins were now allowed to walk to the top of the lane to pick up the bus and they waved Justin off as Clara drove past, tooting at them. She had been tempted to ask Den to drive Justin and Phil to Bertha in order to further make the point that she was detached from this boat purchase. But recent nights with Justin had softened her resolve – their bed had become again a place of mutual pleasure. Sore ribs and gammy ankle and leg were temporarily ignored as they relaxed into enjoying each other and found the space to be kind, forgiving. In retrospect, she wondered if Jussy was so relieved to be finally getting back to the city and his job that he risked certain pain in celebration and was rejoicing in a manner he understood. Who knew? After all, she thought to herself, smiling at recent memories, since he'd managed to navigate the stairs to their bedroom, life – no, correction, bed – had become an interesting, even exciting place again, which eased their daytime relationship into normality. So now she was seeing him off – see him off properly, she thought – and would promise to visit soon.

Justin looked sideways at his wife. Today she looked wonderful, her hair piled up with a small scarf keeping it in place. She wore shorts, which showed off her long legs. A baggy T-shirt fell to her hips. He gave a great sigh which, because of engine noise, no one seemed to notice. The memory that was last night stayed with him today, so what did he think he was doing now, leaving perfection behind? He felt sick with regret. Here he was, about to embark on a journey, which would be the start of a new life, in effect. He was in turmoil, but the die was cast. He'd made this decision not thinking he had a choice, but was now, in retrospect, weighed down with uncertainty.

He cheered himself by recalling how he'd managed to return Josie's earring eventually, without any need for subterfuge. He'd been uncomfortable having to hang on to it. He'd tried at the calendar evening, but there was no real opportunity without giving Josie a chance to make a fuss. Two evenings previously, Josie and Jeff had popped in to check on his progress, knowing he was going back to work full-time. Jeff admired the lanterns Ling had given them. They wanted to buy new lights for their garden, Jeff said. Clara offered to show him how they worked. So Justin and Josie carried on chatting, sat round the kitchen table, drinking and nibbling at snacks. Josie, ever mischievous, exposed one earringless ear to him, grinning. Without hesitating, he'd slid the errant earring across to her from where he sat at the table. He noted her surprised expression, shock even, which gave him some satisfaction. It had been in his pocket just by chance, when he'd taken it to the calendar evening, hoping for an opportunity to return it. He hadn't worn those trousers since that evening. She paused, her hand over the earring as if to slide it back to him.

'Pick it up, Josie.' He'd softened his stern tone with a smile.

'Spoilsport! You're no fun at all,' she'd pouted, reluctantly picking up the earring and sliding its hook through her ear.

There were voices approaching, discussing the merits of nylon lanterns against paper. To Justin's relief, nothing more was said regarding pearl earrings.

Sitting behind Clara and Justin in the Land Rover, Phil was silent, immersed in thoughts of what he was returning to. Once he was back and had got Bertha moored, wired up and the connection details explained to Justin, he would walk across the boatyard to his future and a whole load of work. He'd cleared with Planning to convert the chandlery into a first-floor flat.

Wesley was full of ideas. What Wesley didn't know yet – and Phil grinned to himself at the thought – was that he was going to hand his grandson a paintbrush, a large paintbrush. After all, what use was an artist in the family who couldn't apply gloss? Whilst away, he'd also been keeping tabs on how Harvey, that little scruff of a dog of his, had settled in with Wesley and was going with him to his studio. Clara and Justin had expressed concern too, when he'd mentioned a couple of times that as Harvey was a rescue, he was a little worried for him; after all, Arthur was a rescue and had taken time to settle. However, it seemed all had gone well, with the exception of Harvey's first night, when he'd had an accident by the entrance door. Wesley had insisted it wasn't a problem and thereafter he had made sure they had a stroll as late as possible.

Suddenly they'd arrived at the port and Clara was able to drive most of the way towards their mooring, where they climbed down from the vehicle. With Phil having had the presence of mind to borrow the sack truck from the woodshed, they piled up their bags and set off to Bertha. This was his final trip on her. He'd had second, and many other, thoughts with regard to Justin's purchasing of Bertha. Still, the deed was done, and he was about to have the dubious pleasure of steering himself and Bertha back to Limehouse Cut. Justin and Clara followed him along the jetty at Justin's pace. Justin, legs now exposed by shorts, was relieved of his boot but still walking with a stick, or pole as he liked to correct everyone. It was one of a pair borrowed from Jeff at the last minute. Clara noted that he was still limping. She was worried for him but refrained from commenting. Once they reached the mooring, Phil began unloading the sack truck and was ready to assist Justin on board. He put a hand out to help Clara across to join them. Clara found herself sliding an appreciative hand along the varnished exterior, contemplating the hours Phil had spent working on the boat for them. Okay, he was selling to them and needed to make an effort, but even so she was conscious of the expertise demonstrated by Phil, which made her smile with pleasure. This was their second property after all, she thought, modest though it was. On this occasion she concentrated and took seriously Phil's demonstrations of how everything worked: how the chairs folded and could hang on hooks; how the table folded back up to the side of the cabin, as did full-length single beds for the twins, one of which Phil would sleep in on their journey south.

Although it was far too late to step back from this purchase, Clara still found she had misgivings; she hoped that Jussy knew what he was doing. Was it truly right for them, and what would Lola have made of her son's use of his inheritance? Den was relaxed about it, encouraging even over this latest venture, but then Den was full of unwarranted optimism, which unnerved her.

Her anxiety transferred itself to his plans for this imported lodge outside their garden. Another niggle, but not her business, she knew, was the uncharacteristic reluctance he was demonstrating with regard to opening the letter on his chest of drawers, which she'd noticed again that morning when she'd dropped his laundry on his bed; sometimes the letter disappeared, then returned to its former position. She'd mentioned it to Jussy, but he'd waved her concern aside with the comment, 'That age group, you know. Dad has letters from old contacts from when he was working. He'll get round to it. Anything to share, he'll soon tell us.' Clara decided to agree, dismissing her concerns as misplaced; perhaps she was becoming a tad nosy.

It was time to get going. Phil and Clara exchanged a hug, then Phil turned away discreetly as Justin held Clara and they clung together for a few moments. Justin gently held her head, her hair tumbling down over his hand, as they exchanged a lingering kiss. Pink and reeling slightly, Clara gathered herself to step carefully back to wait near the sack truck. This was a strange moment, when they made their final farewells. Clara waited on the jetty, the sack truck next to her as Phil started the engine. Then, when instructed, she tossed the ropes to him. Justin sat near the tiller and she waved until she couldn't see them for the other moored vessels. She swept a tear away and turned back to drive home, dragging the sack truck along the jetty, forcing herself to concentrate on the journey they had before them, cheered by Phil's confidence. He had the route mapped out carefully over the next few days – stops for fuel and to eat with his friend at West Mersea. Then it would be a chug towards Southend and the mouth of the Thames and gradually away from salt spray, with the lingering smell of seaweed, towards steadier waters, except for cross-currents and tides. She was grateful the weather was forecast to hold.

Phil gestured to the tiller and made space for Justin to pilot the boat. Justin would have preferred to sit back and watch, absorbing the atmosphere, whilst he enjoyed the glittering water, listening to the tinkling on nearby masts and relaxing into the day, feeling free. But knowing he really did need to get a grip, he resisted making the excuse of a weak ankle.

'Okay, sure, yes.'

Phil noticed him adjust his sunglasses. They were those daft things like Wesley's. They reflected a metallic blue. Wesley said they were cool. He shook his head. There was no accounting for some things.

'You'll be fine, lad. Just keep your eyes on what you're doing.'

Justin nodded, sure there couldn't be much to it, and endeavoured to concentrate whilst in his mind's eye he could still see Clara on the jetty as they chugged away from her, still unconnected so far to the physical movement of the boat but sensing a finality, a leaving, a turning point, as they slipped away. He shook his head to clear negative thoughts and comforted himself that it was really a new start for them all. Clara had just surprised him with the reassurance that she'd come down soon with the twins to stay.

Then, forcing himself to concentrate on the present, he gradually got the hang of the steering. Once they were clear of the marina and out into the estuary, he relaxed. In spite of an aching ankle, he was enjoying himself and, grinning at Phil, suggested Phil go below and unpack their supplies whilst he skippered the boat to get more practice in. Initially irritated, not to say doubtful of Justin's capability, Phil looked around, scanning the horizon. He hadn't been blind to Justin's occasional gung-ho tendencies when it suited him. However, he could see there were no obvious obstacles within his vision and there was the navigator's screen on his phone, which he'd take with him down to the galley.

'Okay, lad,' he nodded, noting Justin's pleased expression. All being well, he'd make them a coffee whilst he was at it, so stepped below. He reassured himself the lad did need to become adept at handling the craft. Although he'd given Justin a leaflet on narrowboats and their care, they hadn't discussed tidal flow, wind and forecasts, not to say coping with locks farther along. Justin had already indicated, Phil thought very prematurely, optimistically even, that he wanted to bring Bertha back from time to time and take the family for a holiday around the coast. Still, he had to start somewhere, so he agreed to let him be skipper for a few minutes. There were plenty of more tricky manoeuvres to come when he'd need to be with him.

If Justin perched on the side of the craft, he could still have a good view ahead and give his leg a rest. The rhythm of the engine and their sedate pace gave him a chance to ruminate on the intricacies of the boat. When Phil had arrived at the cottage, he remembered he'd been passed a booklet for new narrowboat owners. He'd glanced at it, of course, but was constantly distracted by surrounding minor events. He had planned to go online later and check everything out. His restless state of mind found the prospect of reading the handbook too tedious.

Now here he was, seeing how much work Phil had put in to smarten up the exterior as well as below decks. Actually handling the craft, feeling the low but reassuring thrum beneath his body, confirmed the reality of this new responsibility. It was also dawning on him that he was going to have to learn how to look after Bertha. Obviously he'd have the booklet, which thankfully he'd packed with his things. The internet would be invaluable, no doubt, and Phil would be nearby across the boatyard. Phil had covered most things, he was sure; it was just that he couldn't really remember much.

The drive belt was new, which apparently meant that the fridge would run and they would have lights too. He'd thought, already somewhat thirsty, stuck as he was in increasingly hot sun, that the fridge was more critical; as the heatwave continued, the cold beers were a serious attraction. They could almost manage without artificial light, as daylight hours were long. He'd enquired about hot water and the shower, as most of his stuff was still at home and being sent by carrier once he was at Limehouse Cut. He pulled his shirt away from his armpits; not too bad, he thought, but it was the first day. The calorifier apparently would do the hot water trick whilst the engine was running.

Bemused by now, he'd stopped short of asking what happened when the engine was off. Perhaps a small generator, he thought, but he gave up asking questions he should have known the answers to. It was after seeing Phil's bushy eyebrows raised more than once, before giving him the requested information, with the added disapproval of a frown, which stopped him. He decided to concentrate on the way ahead. Now Justin regretted his lack of earlier interest and sensed Phil's low opinion of him. He was ashamed that he'd hardly given it a thought, realising rather late in the day how critical knowing operating details were. For some reason that he hadn't yet fathomed, he wanted to please Phil and prove that he wasn't a useless landlubber, or useless overall.

A large mug of coffee came as a welcome surprise. They clinked mugs, raising them in celebration of the real start of their journey. Justin was now grateful for any drink. Maybe beers would be reserved for when they were moored. Phil took over as Justin stood carefully, taking in deep breaths of the salty air. Once their coffees were finished, he gathered up the mugs, their handles looped over a finger, taking them below, carefully stepping down into the galley to the sink; then progressed along the cabin using the wall, chairs, bunks, and anything to hand, to support him to help take the weight off his ankle. There was no room here for his walking pole. He used the loo, then cautiously flushed. It worked. Initially impressed, he couldn't help but wonder how much effluent the tank would take and how he would empty it. He sniffed; at least nothing smelled yet. All this extra stuff to think about; this new home was going to require some input, unlike renting the serviced Soho flat. Rinsing his hands in the small basin, viewing his face, he also decided it was time to lose some weight. Yes, he thought, pushing his head back to minimise an incipient double chin, he would start by cutting down on carbs. At least he would once they were back and moored. Then he would get his bike sent up and start strengthening his ankle. He looked around for a towel, but ended up rubbing his hands on his shorts.

Moving back through the immaculate cabin, and pausing to look around, he sat on the easy chair where the telescope had been. He could see he'd need to find a cleaner to help for the time being, at least until he was totally mobile. He would speak to Phil about it. He remembered the friend of Phil's grandson Wesley, the waitress who'd spoken to them in the pub the day he, Clara and Ling had gone to look at the narrowboat for the first time. Perhaps she might need some extra cash. He remembered she was an art student.

Although they'd only just got going out along the coastline, he was already feeling better, beginning to think ahead about how he was going to live. It would take several days to get into the final mooring where he would settle; it might be a bit longer if they lingered at West Mersea at Phil's mate's, Joel. Fortunately, he wasn't due back at Canary Wharf for a week. He needed to get a grip on timing the tides and how it would affect their progress. But this was the nearest thing to an adventure he'd experienced for a long while, and he was going to relish it, pushing aside the uncharitable thought that he wouldn't have been forced into this except for Clara's bloody-mindedness. Still, maybe she'd bring the twins down now they had a fun place to stay.

He did feel guilty about his increasingly fewer visits home before the accident. He consoled himself that he was doing his best to provide for the family. Commitment to his job was essential to support the family and, as he'd reminded Clara, he was paid well for it. Of course, he mused, there was now her children's clothing business, but from what he could tell, it was more of an indulgence so far than a money-spinner. Ah well, he sighed, it gave her pleasure and she worked hard at it, and he was resigned for now to the fact that he was incapable of changing her attitude.

Justin's lasting memories of that journey from Ipswich to Limehouse Cut filled him with a sense of quiet pleasure. The weather had held and he felt nostalgia for the heat of those days eased with light breezes; for the warm nights moored up whilst enjoying cold beers; for the magic of reflected light on water as they disturbed the waves in passing, and for the slip-slapping sound against the hull. Oh, and those fiery, wild sunsets. He'd relished the many anecdotes Phil recounted with obvious pleasure as a captain of seagoing vessels, further enriched by Joel's company as he welcomed them when they moored at West Mersea. They'd spent time feasting on seafood sitting on Joel's sun-washed veranda, paint peeling all around, completely disregarded by Joel. Justin was grateful for his time with Phil, who'd literally shown him the ropes, and he liked to think they'd become friends along the way.

Some weeks later, after he'd swept the tiny deck when he'd got in from work, Ling texted. Shortly after, he arrived with a curry for three and went across to bring Phil back, who was camping out in a corner of his building, to enjoy supper together. Sitting at the galley table, reminiscing over their recent trip, Ling was puzzled by Phil referring to Justin as "the lad". He remembered Phil from Suffolk, when he'd called Justin "lad" then, and proceeded to pull Justin's leg once they were alone, saying Justin was far too old to be referred to as a lad, bordering as he was on forty. Ling at twenty-six dared to comment that he had felt older than Justin from their first meeting, so perhaps this title was appropriate after all. Justin retaliated by shoving him and as Ling grabbed at the wall-mounted bed opposite, commented, 'See what I mean?' and laughed.

Phil was quite a father figure, Justin felt, untroubled by Ling's teasing. Phil's history – of losing his daughter and son-in-law, then ensuring Wesley had as good a start as he could, then coping with his wife's suicide – had not diminished him. Extraordinary, Justin thought, humbled, which led him to thinking about his circumstances and his own mostly absent father role. He promised himself he must try harder. Justin mused that Dad had never been much of a guiding figure when he'd needed him as a boy. Dad, always clever, full of ideas, slightly wayward, was a fun person, which had been, well, fun. He was doubtless far too old to need a father figure himself now, but he enjoyed the certainty that Phil brought and his proximity across at the boatyard. He was reminded how Dad seemed to have come into his own with Zoe and Carl, which was comforting. He wondered what Dad was up to now and concluded he was almost certainly preoccupied by the process of getting planning permission to put in the lodge, as he called it, on their land next to the cottage.

Chapter Eleven

Some nights Clara would watch Den from her bedroom window. Justin was now gone, and her capacity to sleep seemed to have gone with him. The overwhelming sense she'd felt when she saw him off, that they were going to be fine, was waning. Her hand ran down the edge of the linen curtain. She remembered making these curtains several summers ago, stitching in the shade of the apple tree. Then she'd thought how lucky they were, how this quiet, beautiful place had pulled them in and enfolded them. Now Justin was back in London and Den was on the prowl. She'd left the curtains almost closed so as not to be obvious.

Den had started to slope off some nights after saying goodnight, obviously assuming she thought he'd settled for the night too. She wondered if he was going to see Liz. He'd been going down through the woods often recently, returning sometimes after she'd given up waiting to see him return. Even so, Clara hadn't noticed any significant change in Liz's manner towards him when he put his head around the workroom door most days to exchange pleasantries with Liz and Mary at their benches. The two women had always been good friends. She couldn't ask, but sensed the dynamic had changed between them and wondered if Den was the cause.

On these nights, restless in this solitary existence, Clara wandered about the bedroom, carrying her worries with her, fretting pointlessly, she knew, about them all, but mostly about Den – who now was to be a permanent fixture – and his unorthodox behaviour. Then, of course, there was Justin and the narrowboat – their narrowboat – though in fact in Justin's name. Still, she supposed it came under the umbrella of their property, their marriage. Then her thoughts of a particular umbrella made her smile. When she'd left the beach towel on the bed for Ling on his visit ready for their swim, she'd noticed he'd not only brought a waterproof jacket, but a fold-up umbrella during that settled spell of hot weather. She hadn't commented but had thought it odd, putting it down to a Chinese thing. She was aware how much better-humoured Justin had been during his visit. When she'd expressed her gratitude to him, Ling had just smiled, and made some excuse for Justin. She was still standing there, her hair silvered in the moonlight, when she saw the gate open. It was Den returning, unaware he was being observed. She wondered about confronting him. Perhaps she should come out with it. After all, he was in reality still a guest. She felt entitled to know what was going on.

Walking towards the woods one warm evening, Den could have been heard announcing to the nearby trees, to Lola, 'Wimbledon's had it, old thing!' A lodge outside the garden, one of those things that came kitted out, Dad's Pad, that's what he'd call it. They needed him here at home. He stopped in his tracks on the path to the gate and grinned to himself. See! See! He was already calling this Suffolk base "home". Yes, it would ease everyone's problems, give him extra spending money, help his pension, help Jus and Clara and perhaps calm things down a bit – so long as he had access to his booze, his safety net, when things got a bit tense. What with Clara being stubborn about moving, and her online business beginning to pick up, then, to cap it all, Jus buying the narrowboat, it was difficult to see how things would pan out. He certainly hadn't seen that coming.

He'd looked back at the cottage from the gate. Clara was doing her thing. He'd seen her. She was at her window, probably having a restless time of it. Den reminded himself there were treats in his pocket for Arthur on his return. Didn't want to get Clara annoyed, waking her up. The sun was gone now and there was this magical moment between sunset and dusk, a pause, when the afterglow lit where it fell. High in the cathedral canopy, birdsong echoed through the woods. Not for the first time he wished he'd brought his camera, come to that a sound recorder, but then he smiled to himself. Hmm, might give the wrong impression where he was headed. Out of the woods, he strolled to a cottage on the far side of the green, knocking with the heavy lion knocker, was greeted and entered. Much later, the air now cool, the sky inky, lit by a sliver of a moon, he exited, the door closing quietly behind him as he made his way back towards the wood. He found his torch to help him to keep to the path. There were night noises. He heard a vixen's cry some distance away, as he passed along this now familiar route. Since he had been involved personally with some of the female inhabitants of the village through the calendar photography sessions, it turned out there were women who were looking for male company without any strings. He treated invitations of various kinds with equal enthusiasm and promptly forgot most encounters. In that regard, there seemed to be a temporary misunderstanding between Liz and Mary. He'd fancied Liz from the off, in fact. They'd met up at the pub for a drink a few times. She was a little reserved and he liked her for it. He'd invited her out for a meal once or twice too, which, he had to admit, was after he'd taken Mary for drinks with her son, who wanted to pursue photography at college. Then he'd suggested they meet up again for a more in-depth chat as he'd thought the

131

boy could do with some more guidance. After that Liz was cool with him. Still, other women who'd volunteered to be in the calendar seemed happy to still contact him on his mobile. He'd thought on arrival at the cottage, Keeper's Cottage he reminded himself, liking the play on words, that there would be poor internet availability and was dubious regarding Clara's new online business; but he had been wrong and was now almost prepared to offer obeisance to the tower jutting above a nearby wood, offering everyone around surprisingly good reception. He'd originally used his mobile, rather than Clara's landline, when he was photographing so any cancellations could be rearranged quickly. Recently, Mary had confided in him that Liz no longer wanted her company outside of work and she missed her, wondering if Liz was offended by Den's relaxed behaviour towards her and some other inhabitants. But still, she'd added, somewhat obliquely, he'd thought, Liz wasn't his partner. Den found it difficult to believe that their estrangement could be about him and was bemused by the way women's minds worked.

Then there was Jus who had accused him of using drink as a Lola substitute, when he'd turned up worse for wear at the flat in Soho Square a few months previously. He couldn't remember much about that evening, but hadn't tried to defend himself, though had thought then that he'd never needed an excuse for a drink, and dismissed the idea as vague wanderings on his son's part. Jus had seemed a tad tetchy that night and Den wondered what had got to him.

The thing to keep in mind now, he reminded himself, was moderation. He didn't want to be banished back to Wimbledon at this late stage, particularly since he'd accepted an offer on the house, which was far in excess of what he'd expected, and it looked as if he'd get planning permission as well for the lodge. He certainly didn't fancy sharing the narrowboat with Jus, even temporarily – not that he thought there'd be any offer forthcoming. That was another thing: since the accident, Jus had lost his sense of humour and always seemed on the edge of being testy. He'd improved before he'd returned to London but had been back briefly only once, saying he needed to make up for the lost time taken from work during his injury recovery. He took himself far too seriously, in Den's opinion.

With all that in mind, he considered yet again, with some modesty he thought, he was needed here in his son's absence to help out on several fronts; there were the twins for a start, who were missing their Dad. Not less important, from his point of view, was that his cooking was considerably better than Clara's and it meant they all ate at mealtimes and not when she thought to stop work, not that he'd risk telling her. If he wanted a drink, his rule was generally only one before supper. Even so, he needed to tread carefully.

He'd already risked sharing his beer-shed secret with Tom the computer whizz, who'd helped him stack logs to hide his new consignment, which he'd brought back when he'd gone grocery shopping for Clara in the Land Rover. He was regretting that decision a bit. Tom turned up more than Den had expected. Sometimes Clara joined them on the long seat outside the shed, where he'd offer her a beer from the bowl with ice cubes from the freezer. They'd sip their drinks, going over anything that came to mind, and watch the evening advance with the whirling, tiny bats out for insects, as dusk fell. He'd soon have to start asking Tom for a sub. Still, they were having fun of sorts, and a beer on summer evenings in the garden, with Ling's elegant lamps hanging above them and perfume from Clara's nicotiana border adding to the atmosphere. Yes, a permanent move was obvious. It was going to be such an adventure.

With regard to adventures, his thoughts went to the letter he'd received some weeks previously. He'd recognised the writing immediately. Constanza hadn't written for years. If he hadn't organised redirections for mail, he still wouldn't have heard. Now he'd read the contents, he found himself considering what to do next. He wouldn't rush into anything, having put the letter beneath his socks for the time being. There was plenty to think about with the planning for his new home. For now he would concentrate on that.

Chapter Twelve

As the children broke up for the holidays, there was a flurry of postcards from Alice and Edie. They had gone off across the world on their travels and were still using snail mail in preference to emails to notify all and sundry of where they'd got to. Clara sat at the kitchen table, glancing at the front of the fridge where they'd been displayed. She felt no envy at the energy it must require, she thought, to flit around the world like migrating birds. Their family flit would only involve a trip to Bertha. However, she had no intention of staying there for the whole of the two weeks suggested. She might even get Justin to come back with them. So she closed the business for two weeks. Mary and Liz offered to take some work home. They were in agreement that they could finish off during the break, as neither was going away. Clara, expressing her gratitude, handed them each a bundle of dungarees for embroidering. Privately, she doubted they would get around to finishing much, but she was glad of their offer.

Once she'd locked up, she wandered across to the cottage, pausing to sit with Den for a few minutes, watching with the twins as he was busy fixing the boats Phil had made for them. They had sailed them on the river. String had become entangled and the metal loops holding the string had come adrift, tearing at the soft wood. He had glued them and repainted the damaged pieces. After a while she went into the kitchen, returning with cold drinks. She saw the little boats, now good as new, waiting on the grass for their trip to Limehouse. Carl and Zoe had drifted down to the bottom of the garden and were playing ball with Arthur around the swing. When called, they collected their drinks and sat on the grass near the repaired boats, now arguing over which one belonged to them.

'Stop it, you two. They're identical, unlike you two!' Den was correct in thinking this would bring them up short.

'What d'you mean, Grandad? Why should we be?'

Den leaned back with his drink, giving a contented sigh, unperturbed by their querulous questioning. 'If you were, there wouldn't be arguments. Now go away and check you've packed everything for London!'

Shade was still in this corner, but the heatwave was back and Den could feel the sun coming across the garden towards them in scented waves. It really was bliss. He was staying behind because of commitments, he'd said, but really, he wasn't ready to stay at Phil's building site. He'd pointed out that he could look after Arthur, which was a relief to Clara. The Land Rover was in for serious servicing, so they were travelling by train. Justin had suggested they take Arthur on the train with them. The very thought nearly sank Clara. Apart from the journey, there would be so many new hazards, and all of them squashed in that small space would be challenging enough, without a giant dog to look after.

Clara hadn't asked Den about his social life after all. When she'd considered it calmly, she had decided, for now at least, it really wasn't any of her business. If she were honest, she found herself relying on him more and more to help with the twins, Arthur and around the house. Her only real concern, which Justin had dismissed as nothing to worry about, was that he drank daily. She'd always been aware he was a drinker, unlike her own father, who showed no real interest in alcohol. Still, it never seemed to affect his good nature.

She'd worked out that he stashed booze in his room, or rather in the loft above his bed, well away from the children. Reflecting on this, she realised she'd only actually seen him drunk twice. It was several years ago, when he was living in Wimbledon, just after Lola died. So she shelved her desire to confront him about his habits, thinking he would move to his lodge soon, if his plans came to fruition. There was also the fact that the children loved him being around. She stopped folding and rolling T-shirts, gazing out at the cloudless sky, inevitably comparing him to Justin who, in spite of promises, had only been back briefly since he and Phil had taken the narrowboat back to the city. Even then, it had been specifically to go over his father's plans for the lodge on land next to the cottage, Den's argument being that the lodge was a family investment, and should he move away, for now, he, Den, would have it as an extra income to let out in the summer – a thought which didn't thrill Clara. The sale of the Wimbledon property was going through and it did seem likely that Planning would accept something suitable for the edge of the woods. The only restriction was that it couldn't be used full-time. There would be a clause that it should remain empty for January and February each year. However, Den was working on getting that particular requirement adjusted. Clara had no idea how and hadn't asked. She assumed Justin would have looked into it with his father.

The twins were excited at the prospect of Grandad having his very own lodge, where they could go and stay next door, and pleaded for it to be named after him – Denholme's Lodge – which caused some amusement judging by Den's raised eyebrows. To their cries of support for his name, 'Denholme, Denholme!', he'd added that if he popped his clogs it would be theirs in any case and they'd find a better name.

Indoors, the windows fully open, sounds slipping in from the garden, Clara continued the task of sorting packing for their visit to Limehouse, keeping it to a minimum. Although she hoped to avoid the need for washing, Justin had a washer-dryer and there was a small line on deck. Carl and Zoe had rucksacks. Clara's was larger with wheels and bordering on being overstuffed. She'd decided against taking any provisions. If they used the marina shop, which was a good walk away, she could wheel anything they needed back to the boat.

Justin had taken his bike back with him on his last trip from Suffolk, since his boot had been removed. He relied on using his bike panniers, now that he could manage to cycle, but was careful not to add too much weight since he'd had the last version of the boot removed. Although he still complained he had pain, his ankle was becoming stronger. The idea of deliveries to the mooring point did not seem viable. Still, Janine from the pub, Janine of the purple hair, green nails and nose ring, was helping with the cleaning when she could and also bringing vegetables from her parent's allotment. That was a sort of delivery service, Clara thought. She'd have to make sure Justin paid her properly. She wondered where the allotment might be, now that the Olympic development had swallowed up a huge chunk of land.

Den took them to Bury, where he waved them off and promised to come next time, though Clara wasn't convinced he meant it. If he did, Tom, their computer whizz, had volunteered to look after Arthur.

Ling and his cousin Linda met them at Limehouse, after taking the train from St Pancras. Justin had gone straight to the boat from work in readiness for their arrival. Clara was surprised at the rush of pleasure she felt on greeting Ling. She turned to be introduced to Linda, whose watchful almond eyes observed her. To her relief, the twins behaved naturally towards Ling, whom they had got to know at the cottage, shaking hands with Ling and Linda on Clara's earlier instruction. She was, just for a moment, very proud, then the moment was dispelled when Zoe insisted she didn't want to carry her rucksack, as Ling took Clara's bag. Carl, at this point, saved the day, insisting they were big now and Daddy would be pleased they'd carried their own things. So Zoe continued, grumbling, as Linda applauded them for being grown up enough to have their own rucksacks and to be able to help their mummy with the luggage.

Now Clara was able to observe Linda more closely as they walked towards the taxi, exchanging small talk: she was quite exquisite. Justin had merely mentioned that Ling's cousin was young. She couldn't help but wonder why Justin had only mentioned her in passing, with no real description of this stunning, tiny young woman. Disconcerted, Clara found herself feeling clumsy.

The taxi dropped them off at the end of the lane, where the footpath led straight to the siding where Bertha was moored. Ling had already texted Justin and he walked quite steadily up the ramp to greet them, smiling, and arms open, as Clara beamed, delighted to see Justin looking so much better; altogether better in fact. She couldn't see any sign of a limp – that alone raised her spirits. Perhaps he wouldn't constantly refer to it all being her fault now.

Phil had heard the excited shouts from Zoe and Carl across the boatyard. So Justin's family had arrived. It was good to hear young voices nearby. He was glad the first steps to renovate the chandlery had already been completed. Planning had stipulated that the dry dock and the crane's working area must be totally separated by sturdy fencing as part of improvements and health and safety measures. A new metal exterior staircase was also in place. He'd already got Wesley to draw up plans for the interior. Building Regs had been and sniffed a bit without offering any advice. Planning seemed relaxed, as he had no intention of extending the footprint.

Phil decided to pop over to Bertha later to say hello. In the meantime, he was reviewing for the umpteenth time the atmosphere of the first floor of his almost derelict building. He'd climbed up the new staircase and entered from the side of the building. Dust motes were moving slowly across the beams of sunlight. The air smelt musty. He sniffed again and smiled. Yes, there it was, that familiar, faint aroma of paraffin. There was the question of how much he wanted to upgrade to a modern flat. He liked the nautical feel of the place in its rough state. He chuckled to himself – the eau de paraffin would have to go if he was going to encourage visitors. His thoughts lingered for a moment on Liz and Mary, whom he'd met in Suffolk when he had taken Bertha up to Ipswich to collect Justin. Concentrating on this matter, it was clear he'd need at least two bedrooms. Then, as he was now a landlubber, he'd get himself a proper bathroom, an en suite at that, he thought, and another facility for visitors – a shower room, Wesley had suggested.

Stepping farther into the almost empty space and turning to view large coils of heavy rope, he stopped. It would be so easy to trip over that pile in the gloom. He would have to be wary about showing Clara and the kids around, if they wanted to have a quick look before the interior was sorted. Perhaps they could just look in from the doorway. In the meantime, he'd finished looking around, so locking up, he took himself down to his temporary quarters beneath the chandlery.

The twins and Clara scrambled along the short ramp to the small deck, everyone talking, down into the galley where they stopped short at the little table in astonishment. Ling and Linda stood back, smiling at this moment.

'Daddy, how did you do it? It's Bertha, isn't it?' Zoe shook her head, her mouth open in amazement, as Carl craned forward, 'Daddy, that's so clever. Is it really to eat?'

Justin laughed in delight at their response to his surprise. This cake was a feat of some skill by a chap in a patisserie he'd taken a couple of photos to and just asked the question. It wasn't a problem, the guy had said. Okay to make, just rather expensive. So it was time to cut into Bertha. It was decided

Zoe and Carl would share holding the knife for the initial cut. Clara held her breath, but they managed not to squabble or wreck the cake. Justin then took command and passed the iced sponge round. After celebrating their arrival with delicate slices of cake, washed down with champagne and lemonade, Ling and Linda left them to settle in.

Clara, already feeling crowded, suggested they take some cake over to Phil, whom Justin had joked about, saying he was up to his neck in debris. So here they all were, peering in through the decrepit doorway. Phil, restless, had come back upstairs to put music on. He'd heard them clattering up the stairs, dimmed somewhat by his radio filling this space with resounding Meat Loaf favourites, which he swiftly turned off. It was ridiculously good to see them peering into his personal current mess.

'Well, fancy that! Hello, everyone. Perhaps just come in a couple of steps.'

Carl was enthralled. He could see things, smell things. There were great coils of rope to one side. There were old lanterns lying on their sides and up against them he noted what must be by now dried-out pots of something.

'Can I go and see that desk please, Uncle Phil?'

Phil was still touched that the children addressed him as Uncle, permission for which had earlier been sought and given when he was visiting them in Suffolk. Phil cautioned him to be careful of the rubbish, but nodded. Having tiptoed across the space, Carl stood behind the desk, almost out of sight, joined by Zoe. Two small heads peering across the past, Phil thought.

'What was it for, Uncle Phil? It's very, very big.'

Clara was still poised to hand Phil the cake. Justin stood watching this scene, surprised at the children's interest in the old building and pleased too to see Phil engaged with them. Phil wandered across to the twins.

'Well, guys, this has history. I have to decide whether to keep it.'

As he was talking, Clara came forward and set the cake down on the small horizontal surface of an old desk, above the steep slope of its lid. Justin joined them, curious to see what it was about this old desk that intrigued the twins. He ran a hand over its mahogany slope, feeling its worn surface.

'Yes, Phil. It looks important somehow.'

Clara stood back to examine the cupboard beneath the slope and noticed a wooden bar worn down by years of supporting someone's feet. 'Phil, this needed a stool, I should think, because of this bar where feet went. It's quite high off the floor.'

Phil explained that the chandler sat there, the man who sold all nautical requirements to the people, the bargees.

After a while, the twins tired and Clara took them back to the boat, their drop-down beds now the new excitement to be explored. For a while Justin lingered, suggesting Phil join them for supper, saying he'd prepared for a hungry horde and wanting Phil to feel welcome. Having convinced him, he left Phil to see how Clara was adjusting. He had no worries about the twins. They were fine here, he could see. Clara was more of a challenge.

Chapter Thirteen

Left to himself, memories flooded back to Phil from the days when the chandlery was a bustling centre for canal gossip: Jim Froggitt holding court amongst the disarray of spiked receipts, orders and promises to pay. There were people coming and going all day, up and down the outside rickety staircase. Half the bargees struggled to keep going, as movement of trade by canal dwindled to almost nothing, long before there were water taxis, which now plied their trade, let alone tourist boats exploring the farther reaches of London by water.

Still, somehow Jim had made a profit, retired to the Essex marshes and died aged ninety-six, having lived on his old boat for years. Phil had bought the boatyard freehold, with foresight he was unaware of then, before all the development around sent prices into the realms of major developers. Jim wanted out when the boatyard was more or less a dump, long before there were marinas in the East End docks. Phil had already been renting the workshop on the ground floor for some years. Jim never spent on upkeep, other than replacing the rotten roof with corrugated iron sheeting. That had been a mistake. The ensuing racket every time it rained made his ears hurt, he'd said. Phil chuckled, wondering if that was the final straw and Jim's real reason for clearing out. The roof would be another part of the completed refurbishment: grey slate, an expense he'd decided to afford.

Whilst Mrs B was alive, they'd kept travelling the waterways and, until her death, Phil had let the place sink further into disrepair, just using the workshop intermittently. He was made perfectly aware that he now sat on a fortune. He'd had offers. Thing was, he liked the spot. He could continue repairs and help convert and update the various canal boats, which he was often requested to do by the growing number of houseboat owners.

Now the whole surrounding area was transformed, or in the process of change. Not all for the better, his critical eye considered. Phil was content here, however. He was in demand, and a sense of purpose was energising to him, so he ignored the regular increasing offers for the site, refusing to be persuaded. He wandered across to the filthy windows, and grabbing an old rag, pushed it across the dirt, giving him a glimpse of what would be the view from the living room-cum-kitchen of his first floor flat, overlooking the siding and Bertha moored alongside. Phil couldn't help but feel for Justin, who'd taken trouble to ensure there were some games for the twins and a tablet each to leave on the boat for future visits. He'd mentioned plans to take them to Canary Wharf to one of the restaurants on the ground floor at some point, to show the children the kind of environment where he worked.

Phil gave the window another wipe with the old cloth and saw farther on a glimpse of the canal. A better view would soon be possible when the windows were replaced. He thought a pair of French doors, although Wesley had suggested sliding doors, because of the lack of space. These would give access to the narrow balcony running along the front, making for a nice touch, once he'd made the walkway safe. How to keep the property looking similar, but updated, had its limitations. The site wasn't straightforward, but this didn't bother him. There was no access for a vehicle. There was a path through from the nearby road and, if brave, you might leave a car there. Phil had resisted so far and discouraged Justin from doing the same, which was why he was relieved when he'd learnt Clara had come by train. He gave a last glance around and went back to the entrance, where he locked up and made his way over to Bertha.

Clara was thankful the weather remained fine and they had some meals outside on the small plot next to Bertha's mooring. Justin had thought to buy a small bistro set, which was just big enough to squeeze around. They had trips on the DLR to the city and on the Underground to the West End, firstly to the flat where they had visited Justin in Soho, this time to meet Frederico, the owner who had seen Justin at work and insisted they drop in for coffee en route to meet up with Ling, who wanted them to meet Grandma. But when they arrived to see Ling, Grandma was nowhere to be seen. Embarrassed, Ling took them to a Chinese tea house by way of apology. By now the twins' good behaviour time was running short. London Zoo beckoned, which had been a hit on their previous visit, where Zoe hadn't wanted to leave the gorillas.

Ling went along with them and they stayed for lunch. Clara struggled with the concept of zoos in general. Justin and Ling disagreed, pointing out that endangered species, not unlike Zoe's gorillas, could be protected at zoos. Clara, unconvinced, went off to buy ice creams. This was not her world. The views on the DLR ride amazed her and horrified her in equal measure. So much building! So many weird developments, some looking in danger of not being safe, hanging dangerously in a lopsided fashion. Justin found her reactions bewildering. She had grown up in a city herself.

Night-time presented fresh difficulties for her. At least the twins were exhausted and settled happily in their unconventional beds, but she was edgy at bedtime, convincing herself there was no real privacy for intimacy. Justin, mistakenly, assumed she was making a point regarding his purchase of a city base, disapproving now the deed was done, withdrawing her approval, but she wouldn't talk about it. She was glad when it was time to pack up to go back to Suffolk.

Tidying his old workshop on the ground floor, Phil was distracted by thoughts of Clara. He was puzzled by her. Having been around during her visit, he'd become more aware of how she seemed uncomfortable, sometimes standing, frozen, like a startled deer at any sudden noise from the nearby canal, pushing that long mass of almost white hair into a coil, then letting it go. She seemed in a world of her own half the time. Den, he knew, felt protective of his daughter-in-law, and had mentioned, as if by way of explanation, that she was part Danish, part Finnish. Phil hadn't met many Danes, but she did remind him of the Finnish girls he'd met in his youth, when he'd travelled by motorbike, packed with basic supplies and a very small tent, with a mate. They had gone by ferry to Gothenburg, then up through Sweden. They'd ended up exploring the western side of Finland, before they ran out of money. Friendly young Finns, curious about the outside world, spent time with them. They learnt to forage for food and made fires by silent lakes in the glowing evening light. He remembered how the girls struck him as beautiful and reserved. It was an innocent time. Phil thought the proximity of the city unnerved Clara. She did seem suddenly cheery and more outgoing on the last night, when they'd had a barbecue. Ling came, Wesley brought beers and Janine brought crisps. He thought the visit was a success, for the twins at least.

Phil had always kept a small motorboat tethered next to Bertha for access to a local grocer's on the marina, and the modern chandlery, for small items. He'd taken the twins with him a couple of times. If he needed to he could navigate out to the Thames, the same way that he'd brought in Bertha, but it was slow going because of permissions, tides and locks. So he'd bought himself a second-hand motorbike and kept it in the workshop. He resisted taking them out on that, although Zoe had pleaded with him. It was touching to see how reluctant those two were to go back to the taxi. They'd stroked Bertha and kissed her before they left.

He took another look at how things could be better organised and decided the desk would be useful on the ground floor, here, in the workshop where he'd use it for paperwork when he got back to repairing boats. He reconsidered his finances, stroking Harvey absentmindedly, tucked under his arm. Phil wasn't confident that this area was safe yet for his inquisitive terrier. These days he only had himself to think of and Harvey. He had his merchant navy pension and Mrs B's legacy. Wesley had received an insurance payout when his parents had died in that terrible crash. To begin with, Phil and Mrs B had looked after the poor lad, but he'd wanted to board at art school and, unsure what else to suggest, they encouraged him. He was a good lad. But who knew what he carried inside? Unusually, Phil welled up. But he wasn't inclined to spend time ruminating on the past. He was going to make the most of what he had, keep close to his grandson and take an observer's interest in Justin moored just across the yard. As Justin settled in to life on Bertha, he was gradually becoming better-tempered and more mobile.

Ling was good company, often popping in with his cousin Linda during these light evenings. He'd seen them lolling about on the sloping roof, drinking from cans, laughing. They even came around the back of the workshop to invite him to join them, which sometimes he did. Phil had set up a base for himself in readiness for the big push to get everything done before winter. Ling was fascinated with his hammock. On being offered a try, Ling found himself very quickly tipped out. Amidst laughter, Justin and

Linda resisted, Justin reasoning that he was too clumsy and Linda pleading she couldn't get a good enough grip to haul herself up. The second hammock, set up across the beam for Den, had not been used, so it was full of Phil's clothes. Den had resisted the urge to discover Phil's temporary home, the excuse being the planning permission for the lodge was reaching a critical stage and he needed to be available.

Chapter Fourteen

Clara could have kissed the soil like the Pope, a somewhat dramatic thought, she knew, so relieved was she to be back home. Den had collected them from the station, filling their heads with his news about planning permission for his lodge. It was to go ahead. He asked briefly after Justin and the boat, commenting that he'd go with them next time. The twins were full of excitement, talking over each other in their haste to tell Grandad all their news. Listening to their enthusiasm, Clara conceded that there had been some positive things about their trip to London. The twins had loved being on the water when Phil had taken them out. Harvey, his little dog, was practically adopted by them. It was less clear how she and Justin were placed. They hadn't argued, it was true, but neither was there the old closeness she had treasured and their bed hadn't offered any joy. Her fault, she thought. Arthur leapt to greet them: great big, daft, joyful Arthur. Carl looked up at Clara, grinning. He didn't say anything, but she could see how happy he was. Clara felt a pang of sadness. There was little chance of Justin coming back to Suffolk to live, she could see that now. It wasn't so long ago when she believed she could convince him that he could still commute; that they could work it out. Perhaps they still could, but it would mean that she and the children would have to go to and fro as well. It wasn't the life she wanted for them or for herself.

Gradually, the weather changed. The sun took on a new, softer light. Shadows began creeping nearer the seat in the garden. Not so long now and she would take Zoe and Carl shopping for their new school things for the next term. Looking at Zoe's feet, Clara wondered if her own feet had grown so quickly at her age. She had shot up during the holidays, leaving Carl behind. Carl was sensitive, but pretended he didn't care. Den had a word with him, confiding he had been small until he was sixteen, then, wow!

Carl looked up at him. 'Is that really true, Grandad?' Carl secretly thought Grandad was trying to make him feel better and, after all, sixteen was a very long way off and in the meantime Zoe was very annoying. Still, he took Den's hand anyway, as they went to dig up beetroot for supper.

There were new people moving into the house at the top of the lane. Zoe reported back that there were three children, and that they came from Surrey originally, but had come now from Bury. Later Carl said he'd given Sybil, who was near his age, one of his favourite yellow marbles, which he'd happened to have in his pocket and which she'd admired.

'That was a bit rash, wasn't it? You don't know her yet.' Eyebrows raised, Clara decided she'd better take a bottle of wine along to say hello. She did wonder what Den would say when he discovered his collectable marbles, given as a treasure to Carl for his treasure box, were now being distributed willy-nilly.

'Yes, but she doesn't know anyone yet and she's very nice. I like her already. She's pretty too. I'd like her to be a friend! We can wait for the bus together. Zoe can still wait with us, after all.'

Clara, pretty sure Zoe wouldn't find this arrangement much to her liking, began to fathom out a way to avoid possible ructions, but couldn't find an answer. Really, she thought, it was time they each had more friends of their own, but she'd always assumed Zoe would be the first one to strike out, leaving a sad Carl behind. It appeared that the two older children were at different schools, so there was no chance there for Zoe.

The house at the top of the lane had been empty since Jane and Rich had put the house up for sale and gone travelling. They emailed occasionally to check on how "their" business was doing, regarding the computers, sales, and Liz and Mary. Clara always returned a positive email. Because she felt for them and Rich's medical condition, which would curtail their pleasure at some point, she refrained from any negative comments, aware Parkinson's was enough for anyone to have to think about.

Clara took a bottle of wine from the dresser, which Den had put out for supper, fortunately still unopened, and made her way to her new neighbours. They'd need warning that Den's lodge would be arriving at some point on a huge articulated lorry and to make sure they got their vehicles off the lane. She had neighbours again, which she looked forward to. They were a little older, she discovered: Isla and James Hodges. James was a teacher in Bury; Isla was a shop assistant. Frank was a sixth-former in Bury, Mark at middle school and Sybil, at eight, was at the village school.

Justin came home for half-term, having passed his fortieth birthday whilst in London, unable to come home sooner. He was glad he'd missed any fuss and by the time he stepped on the train, he was confident there would be far too much going on at home for any need to celebrate. He wasn't miserable – he just couldn't understand the importance of birthdays, except for children and as an excuse for presents.

He savoured the views from the train window. It was a beautiful golden autumn, still warm in the sun. Bracken was turning on open ground. Beech trees were beginning to shed yellow leaves. He guessed much of their bounty of nuts had already been harvested by squirrels. As the train slowed to a halt at Bury, he pulled his bag from the rack and joined the short queue to exit.

Clara met him. She had to pick up some kit for Carl, so they stopped for a coffee, looking out over the square, their old familiarity elusive as they sat sipping their drinks.

However, over half-term they had time to relax. Den watched them, the atmosphere between them gradually thawing. Justin was recovered to the extent that he could forget his recent injuries, which improved his temper. They went out together, whilst Den took the twins with Liz for several trips. Clara had no idea how Liz and Den were faring and didn't want to enquire. Suffice to say that Liz was looking much happier recently and Den looked rather smug, an expression that she hoped wouldn't prove to be premature. Den had mentioned in passing that he'd received a letter from an old friend who might visit, once he was under his own roof. She'd been an old flame from when he'd lived in Naples for a spell in his youth. When Clara had related this news to Justin, he was unconcerned.

'Ah, that was the letter you pondered over, I bet. I remember Dad mentioning those days before he met Mum.' He thought for a moment, racking his brains for a name – then it came to him. 'Constanza!'

'Pardon?'

'Just remembered her name. Might stir things up a bit romantically for him.'

'Seems to be getting on well with Liz just now.'

'Well, the lodge hasn't happened yet.'

'No, going to though,' Clara sighed, resigned to the impending upheaval.

As Liz was taking time off, Mary offered to bring in her niece to help in the business as a temporary measure. Elaine was still at school but had plans to do a degree in design. After Clara had met her, she felt that

Elaine was serious. She even made some of her own clothes, so she was given the job of finishing to see how she got on. So Justin and Clara sat out in the garden, went for walks and made love in the peace of the cottage, reigniting their feelings for each other. They took the twins out for the day to Shingle Street where, with the easterlies promising, the kites Ling gave them proved a major attraction.

Then suddenly the week was over. The weather was getting colder. As Clara kissed him goodbye, Justin remarked that she must visit him soon with the twins. There was to be some festival in Chinatown and they were all invited. Clara couldn't help but draw in a breath, as if winded, but managed a half-smile. She guessed it was obvious that she didn't relish a trip to London so soon. But the twins were immediately excited by the thought of another visit to Bertha and everything that was new and exciting.

There was a severe gale, unnamed for a change. A wall fell down in the school playground after being hit by a tree. The council closed the school whilst the debris was cleared. When they all Skyped Justin on that Friday evening, the twins immediately declared they could come to the festival. Clara sat in view behind them, attempting to look pleased. She thought of the journey, the constraints of the narrowboat, how they were crowded into such a small space and this time there would be thick clothes stuffing the hooks near the galley, restricting access.

Den wandered in and declared he'd like to go as well, and he'd prepare Phil for his arrival. After all, he said, Phil had been texting him non-stop, partly about his own chandlery renovations and also querying Den on the lodge situation. Den's building work wouldn't start for at least another fortnight, so he had time to fit a short visit in as well. Justin suggested that they should chance the tricky parking and take the Land Rover to ease the journey.

'Bring Arthur, he can stay with Phil and Dad. Phil's place is looking great. Proper beds now – all mod cons. He's got loads of room.'

'Well, I'll think about Arthur. It might be best if someone this end has him, Jussy. Don't forget Phil's dog and Arthur haven't met.'

Clara shook her head in exasperation and disbelief. Cope with Arthur as well as Den? Then she grinned to herself. Grouping Den with Arthur was a bit unkind. Den was invited, after all, and actually, to be fair, was far more helpful.

Suddenly, in the middle of their discussion for arrangements, the computer died. After a few attempts to get it going again, she gave up. Not as upset as they might have been, the twins scampered off for a bedtime hot chocolate with Den. The computer didn't recover. Clara, frustrated, called Tom the IT man. He was working part-time for his brother in Thetford Forest and promised to call in on his way home. He was late. It was dusk and the air felt cold around him when he knocked on the kitchen door, bringing the cold air in with him.

'Sorry I'm late. We had a puncture with the truck and it took ages to change the wheel.'

Something about the cold air, the smell of pines and his sudden proximity, his red-braided hair strewn with some sawdust from dispatching trees, rendered Clara breathless. She stammered that it was fine and she was very grateful he could spare the time. He looked at her searchingly, his golden eyes quizzical. She sounded different. Usually she seemed quite detached, if he were honest, and not really engaged, yet he found her deeply intriguing – an older woman, no question, but a rare beauty, certainly. He swiftly curtailed any wayward thoughts and set to, accepting a coffee as he worked on the old computer.

The morning was bright and clear. It was time to get going. Clara and the twins were assembled outside the cottage around the Land Rover. Phil had phoned, advising them not to arrive with a pristine vehicle, so to fall in line, the vehicle looked suitably neglected, covered in dust and some dried mud around the wheel hubs. To Clara's irritation, Den was nowhere to be seen, although he'd volunteered to drive and promised to be ready on time. Clara, impatiently huffing, took the twins' bags and stuffed them in the rear of the vehicle after her own. Then Zoe and Carl clambered into the rear seats, arguing over who should sit behind Grandad. Clara ignored them and went across to the workshop to say goodbye to Liz and Mary. Elaine, Mary's niece, was still helping. There were a few final instructions. With sideways glances and a rolling of eyes, unnoticed by Clara in her anxiety to get going and simultaneous reluctance to leave, Liz and Mary promised again to hold the fort and had everyone's number if needed.

Arthur had already been taken over to Tom's by Den, en route to see Liz the previous evening. Tom, when he'd stopped off on his way home on that cold night to sort out the laptop for Clara, had offered to have Arthur, in what she thought was an unexpectedly friendly manner, and she was grateful. At the same time, he'd declined Clara's invitation for soup and rolls, saying that Ed, his brother, had put a casserole in the slow cooker that morning. She wondered briefly, then dismissed the idea, if he might have misconstrued her intentions. She sensed there had been a connection between them for a moment, but he must have been aware of the aroma of soup and seen the big pan on the cooker. And she was innocent in intent! Ah, well. He had looked around as if seeking something. She wondered if he was expecting to see the twins and Den, who had gone off to the village hall teatime cinema and would be back shortly. He took the laptop with him, saying he'd need more time to look at it. Clara confirmed she had a smartphone she could use for the time being. So Tom and laptop had left, Tom saying again he was happy to have Arthur.

Halfway across the yard, Den appeared from the site of his "development", as he called it, and at last they were off. By the time they reached their journey's end, Clara wished they'd travelled down by train. The traffic had been heavy, the children fractious and Den exhausted from attempting to be jolly and play car games and cope with Clara's long silences. He'd have preferred to be somewhere adult with a nice drink. There was relief when they finally found a space near the lane to the boatyard, where Phil waved them into a tight parking spot, having been texted by Den. There he was, sporting a welcoming grin, a red kerchief at his neck and a navy striped jumper snugly covering his neat frame.

As soon as they climbed down, greeted Phil and stretched stiff limbs, Zoe and Carl – jumping up and down with pent-up energy – begged to run on along the lane to Bertha, and before Clara could stop them they were off, laughing and shouting, 'Daddy we're here! We're here!' Justin, waiting on the bank near the gangway, scooped them to him, laughing, breathless at the impact. He realised, even though all parts were now healed, that the time when he could pick them both up together had passed. The others wrestled the various bags out of the Land Rover, including a box of drinks which Clara hadn't noticed when they were loading up. That was hardly surprising as Den had obligingly packed their anoraks the previous evening, covering the offending items. But Phil greeted the box with surprised pleasure as a gift for his hospitality. There was enough, going by weight, for a considerable celebration.

After dropping off Den's things and Phil's gift of booze, they all met up near Bertha with the rest of the bags. Clara, tense from the journey, smiled thinly at Justin, as he slipped the children down and came across to hug her, kissing her on the cheek.

At that moment, Linda, Ling's cousin, appeared at the doorway of the boat, closely followed by Ling, smiling his greeting, 'Clara, Zoe, Carl! And Den! It is so good to see you all again. Oh hello, Phil!'

As Linda, exquisite as before, nodded towards Clara and the twins, Den moved forward swiftly and kissed her on both cheeks. 'Just in case this lot forget I'm here, I'm very pleased to meet you. Linda, isn't it? As beautiful as I'd heard. I'm Justin's dad. Please call me Den.'

There was a perceptible pause, then Justin, obviously mortified, offered an apology. 'I'm sorry about my dad, Linda.' He followed up with an awkward shake of the head – 'He is harmless' – which caused embarrassed laughter. 'Dad's got a trained eye for the camera. He thinks he's still working, Linda. You'll have to forgive him.'

Bemused, Linda nodded.

Clara, watchful, found she was surprised to see how Linda appeared to remain unaffected by the attention and, irrationally, felt annoyed that she had already been on Bertha, wondering why she was there, looking so at home. But then Ling was there too and though she was glad to see him again, this seemed very much their territory, not hers, leaving her feeling like an outsider. But there was no time to ruminate on such things as, after leaving their bags on Bertha, Phil, eager to show off the considerable restoration, hustled them across to the old chandlery to explore the conversion.

It was immediately obvious an impressive change had taken place. Once upstairs, and having walked into the entrance hall at the side of the building, Phil showed them the back of the building, where there were two bedrooms, one en suite with a bath.

'Please note, guys, a bath, full-size. Haven't owned one for years.' He waved towards another bedroom – a box room – and shower room, obviously impatient to usher them into the living area, which ran across the width of the front of the building.

'Uncle Phil, how did you do it so soon?' Zoe twirled around, arms out, and without pausing ran to the French doors, planning to explore the veranda.

'I'll fetch the key in a second, Zoe. We'll all have a look.'

For a moment no one said anything, as Phil enjoyed everyone's obvious surprise. After all, the changes were extraordinary. Justin watched Clara with interest to gauge her reaction. He saw her visible amazement as, mouth slightly agape, she looked around, obviously impressed with the style Phil had achieved. Den, awestruck, immediately booked Phil to help him with his lodge interior once it was ready. Phil grinned with pleasure but shook his head.

'That was Wesley as much if not more than me.'

The floorboards throughout had been cleaned and polished back to a pale gold. The wood on the ceiling and back wall had been painted chalk-white. Old dining chairs were blue, as was a table Phil had rescued from the chandlery and got Wesley to paint. There was a seventies sideboard, with shelves above; this had been left unaltered, except for a good oiling. The shelves were of similar wood. The kitchen area was along one wall, in a deeper blue, with the table nearby. The sitting area had two facing sofas, covered in a textured pale grey fabric, and there were two old armchairs, one the rocker from the boat, which was immediately leapt on by Carl. The old windows along the front had been replaced by narrow French doors, which gave access on to the balcony. Phil's telescope stood nearby, ready for action on clear nights when, wrapped up, he'd wheel it out on the balcony, often with Wesley.

On the wall opposite the kitchen stood a wood burner, already alight. Both Clara and Den were stunned by the stylishness and comfort of Phil's new home, but, as he modestly accepted praise, he referred back to Wesley who would join them for supper later. Carl noticed that the big desk was missing.

'Uncle Phil, you didn't chop it up, did you?' He pointed accusingly at the neat pile of chopped wood near the stove.

Phil, horrified at the thought, exclaimed, 'Of course not, son. I'll show you later – it's downstairs.' Phil explained that the desk was in use in his tidied-up workshop, ready for his paperwork.

What drew Carl next, however, was a small table under a window, to the side of the French doors. It was glass-topped and inside there was a collection of things, which fascinated him. The others, at Phil's suggestion, had gone back to the other rooms to have a closer look. Carl pulled Phil back by the hand.

'What is it, son?'

'Uncle Phil, would you show me those things?'

Phil allowed himself to be led back, straight to his small glass display table.

'Will you tell me about this?' Carl pointed out an old compass, with a string attached.

'That was my father's. He used it when he went climbing.' There was a baby's hairbrush, which had been his daughter's. There was a carved knife made of whalebone, which Phil had come across many years before on Orkney. Carl pointed then to a tiny dull green figure, leaning against a box. That was an onyx Inuit figure from Alaska. Mrs B's wedding ring rested on a tiny velvet cushion, next to her engagement ring. Then there was a medal on a ribbon, which had been presented to Phil by the merchant navy for services rendered. Carl's eyes lit on a tiny model of a ship, which Phil explained one of the men had carved and painted whilst they'd been at sea, which was a copy of his ship. Carl squirmed in pleasure, obviously desperate to touch. Phil looked thoughtful for a moment, then, unclipping the lid, allowed Carl to pick up the various items, before replacing them carefully. He guessed that Carl rarely got to have the first opportunity at anything, so he said quietly, 'This is between us, okay, son? I don't usually open this.' Carl nodded earnestly.

Suddenly, there was uproar from one of the other rooms. Zoe had gone out, disappeared down the stairs and was running to Bertha, when Justin caught sight of her from the box room window.

'What is she doing!' cried Clara, exasperation and fear combined.

'I'll go. It'll be fine,' Justin called as, to everyone's surprise, he leapt into action, running down the staircase and dashing off across the boatyard.

'Well, that's the fastest I've seen Justin move, since, well, for ages,' Clara said lamely. She resisted saying since his accident.

Ling stood next to her watching Justin reach the gangway and catch up with Zoe. Justin turned, then gave a thumbs up and he and Zoe disappeared into Bertha.

'Yes, he is better, trying short runs again,' Ling said. 'We go out at weekends.' As Clara turned to return to the living room, Ling's hand brushed against hers. 'Are you okay, Clara?'

Stunned, Clara looked at him. She didn't know what to say. In that small space she was conscious of his light breathing, the concern in his eyes. She suddenly sat on the bed. 'Erm, mostly,' she found herself saying. It seemed almost as a reflex when he leaned forward and kissed her lightly on the lips. Instead of jumping up, or pushing him away, she remained immobile.

Tears unbidden started to slip down her cheeks.

'Clara, Clara,' he said gently, 'I'm sorry, I didn't mean to upset you. What was I thinking? Come, wipe up those tears. Let's go and see what Carl was on about.'

Clara allowed Ling to take her hand as she struggled to stand. She brushed her tears aside, as he moved away to the door and, looking back at her with a rueful smile, made his way back to the living room. Linda had already gone back to join Phil and Carl to see what Carl had been so excited by. Linda glanced at Ling, giving him a quizzical look, which he ignored. They were gathered around the little display table and turned as Clara entered the room and wandered across to take a closer look. Clara looked flushed, Phil thought. She was sorely tested with little Zoe and her pranks; not to mention her and Justin, living apart most of the time. Perhaps these few days together would bring them closer again. And Ling was a good chap. Phil had seen how he'd acted as peacemaker when he'd visited Suffolk during the summer.

Clara put an arm around Carl's narrow shoulders.

He looked up, beaming. 'Mummy, this is Uncle Phil's memento case. Can we have one?'

Phil ruffled Carl's pale hair. Clara endeavoured to concentrate on what was before her. She noticed Linda watching her, a half-smile on her lips. 'It's a lovely idea, Phil. We could do something at home, I'm sure. It may not be quite as smart, but no, I'm sure we can do something.'

There was a clatter on the stairs, the door opened and Harvey suddenly burst in, tail wagging furiously, followed by Justin and Zoe, holding hands.

'Mummy, I saw Harvey running off to the boat. Daddy and I found him. He may have seen a cat, Daddy said.'

'Oh, good girl. We did wonder what was going on.'

The words, somehow, lacked conviction. Although still recovering from her earlier struggle with events, Clara had to admit that Harvey was an independent dog and seemed to know his own territory. Phil just grinned. Ling and Linda started to make their excuses, waving goodbye as they set off for their walk towards the DLR. Phil followed them out onto the stairs, confirming that they'd all meet up next afternoon at the Chinatown Arch near Leicester Square and come back for a late supper. Back in the living room, Clara was bemused by the finished renovation.

'Phil, how on earth did you get all this work done so quickly? Last time we saw it, it was, well...' She trailed off.

'Some young guys running a building company over at Limehouse Cut in a warehouse got let down over a contract, which was rough for them, but good news for me. I was ready to go and it meant they'd get paid straight off. They've got a small boat I've refurbed for them, so I'd done some work for them already. Have to say they worked like stink and Wesley helped me with finishes. Nice lads, mostly from Warsaw.'

'Well, your new home is really impressive, Phil. I love it. The balcony is a treat.'

'Yes, well, that was original. You probably remember it. We just made it safe.' He chuckled. 'Nearly went through first time I went out there.'

'Phil, we'd better get going to give the kids some tea. Come on over when you're ready for a drink and some supper.'

'See you later, Phil,' Justin said.

With that he and Clara ushered the children out to the stairway and down to Bertha, where Clara paused, drained. After giving the twins some tea, Justin had invited Phil and Den over for supper. They were only having pizza with salad, but it was turning into a long day. She was still unnerved by Ling and his unexpected kiss, then hasty, embarrassed apology.

Chapter Fifteen

Justin and Clara took the twins for a walk along the canal path the
following morning, Zoe and Carl skipping along with Harvey on a lead.
It was cold, but Justin had lit the stove and Bertha was cosy. At lunchtime,
they ate on Bertha, lolling about afterwards until mid-afternoon, when they
prepared for their visit to Chinatown. There was going to be the expected
scramble to get themselves ready in this tiny space. Clara made the decision
not to change. She was still tired from the previous day and they'd be wearing
coats anyway, so, after sending the children to clean their teeth and wash
their faces, she combed her hair, slipping on a band and twisting her hair on
top of her head. Justin watched her, silently. Her hair, he thought, was her
greatest asset, but to be honest, when she did it like that, it made her taller
than him. He looked down to see if she had boots on. Thankfully, they at
least were flat. Interesting, he thought and with some sadness. He couldn't
remember ever feeling negative thoughts regarding her stature until now.

She had always been a golden girl, someone rare and touchingly innocent. He had discovered, with considerable shock, that she was also determined to follow her own star, regardless of cost to them all as a family, and to him in particular.

He knew he'd been pretty difficult after his accident. He couldn't help but blame Clara, remembering how it had come about. Other colleagues had problems he was sure, but not this particular one. There were people from all over working for the company. Most had brought their families and settled around the city, being positive, using it as a time of adventure. What would she do if he got a posting abroad? God, it didn't bear thinking about. He remembered Dad and Mum had had friends who split up when he was small. He'd been frightened by the vitriol which had passed across the dining table during the course of the breakdown of their marriage when the friends had visited. Mum sent him and their two children, who were both somewhere near his age, out to get ice creams from the ice cream van. Not many ice cream vans these days in an emergency, he thought. Then they were instructed to play outside. They'd made a den with an old bedspread and pretended not to hear the raised voices coming from the open windows.

It was a whole year now since he'd been moved to Canary Wharf. He picked at his scarf. It was going to be cold, but inside Bertha the stove was making him too hot. As Clara went to check on the twins in the tiny bathroom, he watched her narrow frame navigate the space, holding on occasionally to the sides, as if they were at sea. He raised his eyebrows at the thought. Clara would never cope with a boat holiday; he could see that now. There was more, as well. It was pretty obvious she didn't even like coming to London, regardless of the twins' enthusiasm. He would avoid the old chestnut regarding his job, not to mention Dad building next door and putting down roots. Well, this weekend anyway, although he was now certain she'd never consider moving.

He looked around at Bertha, beautiful Bertha, so carefully updated and lovingly crafted by Phil. Phil, who was everyone's first call along the canal, who still helped him as a pathetic novice boat owner. Pulling his thoughts back to the present, he shooed his family out, taking up the rear, ushering them like wayward ducks to the doorway and up onto the gravel, which ran alongside the boat. They'd need to get a move on, or they'd miss the Red Dragon parade. Phil came across with Den, who looked refreshed, having crashed out almost as soon as they'd arrived, and having taken it easy since. They made their way along the footpath to get the train.

Once at Chinatown Arch where they'd agreed to meet, Clara was convinced they'd be very lucky to find Ling and Linda in the crowd. She stood huddled close to the others, hands resting on the twins' shoulders. Zoe and Carl, mouths open and heads swivelling around to catch as much of the scene as possible, suddenly started to jump up and down to get Ling and Linda's attention as they made their way towards the group through the throng. They had a stranger with them. She was Chinese, elderly, wearing traditional black trousers and a fine embroidered jacket. Her hair, still black, was in a knot at the back of her head, unlike Linda's short bob. Zoe remembered about China from school where they were covering some aspects of worldwide history. She stared down at the old lady's feet. They were small, she thought, but she wore normal flat black pumps, just like hers, only Zoe's were red.

Justin moved forward, to greet this unknown person. The old woman reciprocated. They exchanged a few words, then Ling and Linda approached to introduce their grandma to the others. Grandma spoke very little English, which hardly mattered, since there was so much going on around them – not only the colours and smells but above all the noise. Whilst Chinese music played, suddenly a huge red dragon appeared from somewhere ahead. Its bulbous eyes appeared to be seeking someone out, as it twisted and turned along the central walkway. As the dragon got nearer, and as they were near the front, Carl saw legs running about beneath the costume and pointing, laughed out loud in excitement. It was already nearly dark now and the huge lanterns bobbed about cheerfully high above them in every colour, carried on tall poles.

They tried street food. Grandma would point and, in sharp tones, say, 'Good! Try!' Ling and Linda nodded, smiling in agreement. They bought a variety of foods sold in little bowls, then sat on benches to taste and compare flavours, until they reached the stalls selling mooncakes, made for the Moon Festival in autumn, when the moon is full. The stallholders pointed upwards, where a low moon hung above, in the cold air. There were various sizes of cake to buy, an intricate design imprinted on each. They were really more of a pie than cake, with a salty crust and a soft filling. Some had savoury fillings, some had a duck-egg yolk in the middle. Zoe and Carl both made faces at the thought. The sweet-filled options were more to their taste, with almond and apricot and many other mixtures. Here their Chinese friends disagreed as to which were best. Justin was ready to try a savoury cake. Den and Phil decided to share two different flavours. Clara protested that she couldn't eat another thing, although, she added quickly, they all looked tempting. The twins chose a sweet mooncake and they all found another bench to sit on whilst they tried these delicacies. The main parade was now in full swing as the dragon made his way back to the start, followed by a Chinese band of cymbals and tambourines and instruments that resembled long horns, followed by drums and dancers in colourful costumes.

Finally, as the evening began to wind down, Grandma invited them, through Ling, to go up to her flat for a drink before they made their way back to Limehouse. Clara, looking at the twins, who had stood up well until now, took the lead and thanked the old lady, politely refusing, explaining that the children had been on the go since early in the day. Grandma looked at them both, then at Clara and nodded with a smile that showed uneven yellow teeth. Clara had the uncomfortable feeling that Grandma could see through her excuses. Truly, the hubbub, the long day and tension had done for her. In fact, the twins were still bouncing, but she insisted, so they all began to say their farewells.

Before they left, as supper at Phil's was now scuppered by all the street food they'd devoured, Phil insisted they all go to his flat for lunch the next day. There were many smiles and Ling, Linda and Grandma turned and disappeared into the now thinning crowd. By the time they reached Limehouse Cut, everyone was flagging. The day had finally caught up with Carl and Zoe, who were being encouraged not to squabble with promises of a ride on Phil's motorboat before they went back to Suffolk. Den had been quiet for some time.

'You okay, Dad?'

Den grinned. 'Course, Jus. Just been thinking about an old friend I heard from recently. Retired now, like me. He's got a boat somewhere around here. Thought I'd pop in in the morning if he's around and give him a quick visit.'

'Do I know him then?'

'Cedric Brown. We worked together for several years. He set up some spectacular shoots for *Vogue*. He's quite a flamboyant character – he used to wear long, red velvet coats, for a start.'

'Oh, him! Yes, he came for dinner once. Didn't he bring a parrot with him?'

Den chuckled. 'Those were the days! I'll give him a ring in the morning.'

'Grandad, a real parrot! Can we come too?' Carl, suddenly wide awake, begged.

'I'm sure you can, if Mummy and Daddy agree. Still he has to be there first, so we'll see tomorrow. I can't promise the parrot, by the way.'

They were back at Bertha. Phil and Den waved goodnight. Harvey was looking out through the French doors of the chandlery, barking at their return, as he had the previous evening on everyone's arrival.

Justin unlocked the door to Bertha, ushering the children down into the cabin, followed by Clara, whose hair had slipped out of its coil, and now fell down over her shoulder. He so wanted to touch it, just for a second, but caution won, as he remembered how cool she seemed.

The next morning Den tried to get hold of Cedric, but his call went to voicemail. The twins, Carl in particular, were disappointed. Justin took the twins to Greenwich to see the Cutty Sark, which was intended to make up for not discovering if Cedric was in and still had his parrot. Phil collared Den to help prepare vegetables for lunch. Ling and Linda were going to join them, but Grandma had declined.

Against her better judgement, Clara offered to take Harvey for a stroll along the canal to get him out from under Phil's feet, as he prepared the chicken. Justin had suggested they both take the children to Greenwich, where Justin had thought they might have had a look at where he'd hoped Clara would consider moving. She didn't want to see Greenwich and declined, suggesting he take the children. He shrugged, rebuffed, and merely replied, 'Okay, if that's what you want.'

Den resisted asking why she hadn't gone with Justin and the children. There was no knowing how her mind worked, or Justin's, for that matter. The morning was bright, so the two men sat on the balcony for a few minutes with their coffee. They watched as Clara disentangled herself from the lead Harvey had wrapped around her legs. She laughed and waved to them as she disappeared along the path. After the men had finished their preparations for lunch, Phil ushered Den back outside with a lager where they relaxed on the balcony, idly watching to see when Clara or Justin and the twins might reappear.

Den could hardly wait for Wesley to arrive. Phil said he was very good at anything to do with design and they could put their heads together, if he wanted. Den hoped Wesley would go through his ideas with him. Now everything was in place with regard to permissions, he needed to crack on with specifics. He grinned to himself. He knew he was inclined to change his mind. Another head would be good, so long as the other head wasn't too outlandish. The footprint and wooden exterior were already decided, but not the interior, or the company from which to purchase.

He allowed himself a cautionary note. Supposing, once the lodge was completed, he found living on the edge of the woods, a mile from the nearest village, too quiet. What then? He could almost see Lola frowning at him. She had been his stabilising force. So far, he'd enjoyed staying with Clara and the children. He did feel a pull to the grandchildren and in all honesty he was concerned for Clara, which turned his thoughts to his son and that narrowboat. She'd revealed to him, with a regretful grimace, after her previous visit, that she'd found it claustrophobic. When he'd shown his concern, she'd admitted, with a somewhat rueful smile, that even so, the children loved it.

He couldn't see how those two were going to survive this current living situation. Justin seemed more adjusted to this city living than Den felt entirely happy about – contrary to the beginning, when Justin had really worried how he'd fit in with the demands of city working life. Jus certainly didn't get to Suffolk as much as he could, Den was sure. Well, if he, Den, couldn't settle into permanent living in Suffolk, he'd move up near Jus and Phil. He liked Phil. Then there'd be Cedric somewhere along the canal. Perhaps he'd get Phil to look out for a boat for him; nothing grand, of course, something like Bertha. It seemed the main issue was permanent mooring. He'd have to pay top dollar to get that, according to everyone's conversations. Good job Wimbledon fetched so much. He could afford two pads!

What if he could get Liz to come with him? Trouble was, he was sure she had a soft spot for Phil, although as far as he knew they hadn't met up since Phil brought the boat back from Ipswich. He hadn't invited her this time after all. He didn't want to muddy the waters against himself at this early stage. His reverie was interrupted by his phone.

'Hello, you old devil. This is your mucker, Cedric!'

Den raised his eyebrows. That sounded a bit hearty for Cedric. He stared at his phone, before returning the greeting. 'Hello, Cedric. Nice of you to get back to me. How are you these days?'

'Never better. Got myself a cosy set-up here. You must come round. You'll love how I've done up my boat.'

Den wasn't so sure about Cedric's taste, but he was keen to see how different his houseboat might be from Jus's. He was about to broach the subject of Cedric's unusual taste in pets on behalf of Carl, when he saw Clara returning with Harvey. There was something wrong. They were both covered in mud and Clara was holding her free arm to her chest.

'Cedric, can I ring you back in half an hour? Bit of a crisis here. Bye.'

He was already down the staircase, when he could see at a glance, Clara's face was bleeding. He ran towards her. 'What's happened? Are you hurt? Let me take Harvey. Better keep him on his lead till he's cleaned off.'

Clara had stopped at the bottom of the staircase, holding on to the rail, as if for support.

'Can you manage the stairs?' He waited for her to respond. Then he saw tears welling. 'Whatever is it? Tell me.'

'Out here. I don't want the others to hear.'

'They're not back yet. Ling and Linda haven't arrived. There's only Phil. He's laying the table.' They sat down on the cold steps. Den wanted to put his arm round her, but refrained. He tied Harvey to the bottom post, where, to Den's surprise he sat quietly.

'I...' She was struggling to speak.

'Take your time.'

A deep groan followed. 'I stopped to chat to a man. He looked pleasant. He was washing the roof of his boat. A sort of equivalent to washing the car on a Sunday morning, I thought.'

'Yes?' Den waited.

'He hopped off his boat to say hello to Harvey. Well, that's what I thought. Then he went to touch me. Frightened the life out of me.'

'Touch you. How?' Den heard anger in his voice.

'I hadn't noticed, but I had a bird dropping on my shoulder.'

Den acknowledged that that was more than likely. The gulls were everywhere along this stretch. Even so, the bloke could have just pointed it out to her. He didn't need to invade her space, which had obviously rattled her. 'But that doesn't explain how you both got so filthy, or the blood trickling down your face. And what about your arm?'

'I feel so stupid. I panicked and jumped back. Harvey went for the guy. I tried to pull him away. It was muddy just there. I yanked hard at Harvey, who tore one of this guy's sleeves. After a few tries, it worked and we fell back into the brambles at the side of the path. Somehow I twisted as I went down, catching my face, and wrenched my arm. The guy I had been talking to, when I stood up again, looked at me with a horrified expression, said he was sorry and disappeared quickly inside his boat.'

'Man's an arse. Should have walked you back at least.'

'Glad he didn't – and I owe him a shirt.' She mopped up the remains of a tear. 'You know, I feel so humiliated, because I overreacted like a hysterical teenager. Please don't tell the others, especially Jussy. He'll just laugh at me.' There was a pause. Den waited again; he felt sorry for her. She said, apologetically, 'I am sorry, Den.'

'No, no, not your fault. But are you okay now to go and get cleaned up? No need to explain. I'll hose Harvey off down here. He won't mind. I've seen Phil do it.'

Den watched as Clara trudged up the stairs. Something was going on with his son and Clara, which was deeper and more complex than them living in separate dwellings. After all, loads of couples managed to cope. Ah well, all would sort itself out in time.

After cleaning up Harvey, Den went to the spare fridge in the workshop to fetch out the fruit juices ready for the children, which Phil had asked him to do about an hour previously. He'd catch Cedric later; perhaps slip along with Carl and Zoe in the afternoon. He wondered how Clara would cover the scratches on her face. He knew from his photography days at work that make-up was a wonderful thing, but Clara didn't appear to wear any normally, so perhaps she would be unable to avoid some attention.

It was after lunch before Den remembered Cedric. Ling and Linda's arrival deflected to some extent Justin's concern over the swollen scratch down the side of Clara's face. Other than brushing aside any concern he might have felt, she remained subdued. Jus was irritatingly hyper, Den thought, full of how he and the kids had had a great time; there had been a sort of country market nearby and they'd bought toffee apples. Clara raised eyebrows at this, but didn't comment. Ling chatted to Phil about Western versus Chinese food and was admiring of his roast lunch.

Den was aware of something unspoken going on. It was difficult to be sure, but Linda seemed to be watching Jus more than absolutely necessary. Occasionally Jus would catch her glance and smile back. Fruit salad and coffees over, Den excused himself and went out on the balcony to ring Cedric. Before he did so, he looked back at the party, now relaxing. He wondered if Phil had noticed anything previously between Linda and Jus, and how he could broach the subject. He knew Ling and Linda often hung out at the boat. Linda was so young though! But it wouldn't have made any difference if they'd been similar ages, he told himself. The thought of his son messing about with a twenty-something, when Den had thought he was still trying to make his marriage work, came as an uncomfortable thought.

Deciding to concentrate on his attempt to reach Cedric, he pressed redial and got an answer immediately, shelving his fears as those of harmless flirting by two attractive people over a lunch table. Cedric was moored in a private marina about half a kilometre away. He was most enthusiastic about Den bringing Zoe and Carl to visit. This time, Den remembered to ask about the parrot.

'Don't tell the sprogs, Denholme, old chap, but I've got something much better. Keep 'em busy while we get a snifter in. Boyfriend's out mowing his bowling green: goes in for competitions, got medals. Can't see it myself, but he's happy, so I'm happy. Big tournament coming up, so Sunday cut. Meet him next time. Teddy's nearer your boy's age. Think I may have seen him at the restaurant with a Chinese couple a few weeks ago. Wasn't sure and didn't know he was working up here, then. Though, if I was right, he looks just like you, still. Teddy and I were celebrating Teddy's fortieth.'

Mentally breathless, Den agreed two thirty and finished the call, deciding he'd have a quiet word regarding Cedric's enthusiasm for referring to him as Denholme, which always put him in mind of a pre-war bungalow.

Clara made Zoe and Carl wash their faces and comb their hair, under supervision. She had to make an effort not to hold her face, which was stinging and burning. Then she went to assist Phil to clear up the lunch things. Justin wanted to show Ling something he was studying in Cantonese history and Linda tagged along over to Bertha.

Clara found Phil easy to be with, and once they'd cleared everything away, they settled down to stretch out on the sofas, after Phil insisted on spraying Clara's scratch with some dry antiseptic, which was bright yellow. She glanced at herself and decided she didn't care. There were Sunday papers and magazines to thumb through. After a while she found herself nodding off. Phil watched her and decided a sleep would relax her. She seemed to carry tension around with her and it concerned him, having known it before in his wife. He didn't really know how she and Justin were getting on, but they didn't seem in any kind of harmony, from what he could make out. He decided he'd have forty winks too and pulled a stool up to rest his legs.

Chapter Sixteen

Cedric's directions were easy to follow as they walked along the towpath in thin sunlight. The boat was a Dutch barge and, by Bertha's standards, large. It was wide too and its rooms seemed light and airy in comparison. There were overhanging trees with late leaves still hanging on. The surprise for the children, after they'd goggled at Cedric's red velvet coat and cap with a long matching tassel, was what roosted and fed in the trees. There was, it seemed to Den, a tree full of green parakeets, all squawking and squabbling. They had escaped or had been let free, Cedric told the children and, because of the mild city climate, they had thrived and multiplied. He liked to photograph them. Now they were free, they didn't need to go anywhere else. The feeders hanging in the tree attested to his commitment. Completely overwhelmed, the twins were given treats to put along the deck, where the birds would come over and feed. They were very tame and if the twins were patient the birds might even feed from an outstretched hand.

Den wasn't happy about the children on the deck on their own, but Cedric had safety arrangements covered. They'd brought their life jackets with them and Cedric had what he called dog leads attached to the deck on one end and harnesses for the children on the other.

'Teddy's nephews come to stay. I devised these so they can't wander or go over the side. Drinks coming up, twins, then your grandpa and I are going below for a catch-up, okay?'

Bemused, they nodded silently. This was unlike anything they had ever known.

In the spacious sitting area, Den wandered around looking out of windows and admiring paintings hanging on the upright sides of the boat, whilst Cedric organised drinks. There were several pictures of Cedric with, he assumed, Teddy. Teddy was a tall, wiry-looking outdoor type, with bright blue eyes, mid-brown hair and what looked like a small tattoo on the back of his right wrist, the hand dangling round Cedric's shoulder. He wondered how long they'd been together. In his youth Cedric had been a partygoer, a frequenter of clubs, but so had he, Den remembered, thinking fondly of fun times. Then, he'd met Lola and they'd got married. Cedric had gone on much longer chasing his dream. Perhaps he'd found his with Teddy. He looked like a nice boy, or man, of course, man.

Den found himself beguiled by a very good whisky, with a dash of water. Then there were the memories brought back over a second glass. He and Cedric recalled how they had risked driving home in the old days, after just such an indulgent hour in the nearest pub, following a trying day on a photo shoot with truculent models dressed in outfits for the forthcoming season – which meant the poor girls were either freezing or boiling. It was all so different now with technology. They reminisced happily until there was a wail and a loud shout from on deck. They both rushed above to see blood gushing from Zoe's hand and Carl shooing a bird away by flapping his arms about and shouting, 'Bad bird! Bad bird!'

Cedric unclipped their harnesses and in some style produced a large blue silk handkerchief, wrapping it tightly around Zoe's hand, then led the children down to the galley to his first aid kit, explaining as they went, 'I just happen to have some emoji plasters for such an occasion, Zoe, so once we've cleaned you up you can choose which face you'd like.'

Zoe, overwhelmed by the silk handkerchief and the bobbing tassel on Cedric's cap, wanted to see the plasters. Carl looked over her shoulder and asked if he could have one too. After all, he had shooed the parakeet away. He chose an emoji with its tongue sticking out. Zoe chose one with a cap and tassel. Den, unaccustomed to being in the background where the twins were concerned, decided Cedric should have warned them that they shouldn't try to feed wild birds from their hands.

'Oh, come on, Denholme.'

The twins looked up at Den. No one called him that. They'd tried once over the possible name of his lodge and got reprimanded. But it seemed Cedric was different.

'Oh, come on, nothing terrible happened, and it was fun overall, wasn't it, kids?'

They nodded in unison. It had been a very exciting afternoon. Even the elderflower ice lollies and baby meringues had been different, in blues and reds and greens. There would be so much to report when they got back to Suffolk. Cedric's outfit was something to remember as well. He was like a magician, Carl said, as they set off on their walk back to Bertha.

It was worth noting, thought Den, that some old friends could turn out to be quite a handful. Still, the whisky was excellent; Cedric had always had good taste in that regard. His earlier thoughts about looking out for a houseboat had diminished slightly. Cedric's mooring was over eight thousand a year. Justin's was much cheaper, but that was thanks to Phil and there wasn't really room for two boats at that mooring. There was the matter of dry-dock maintenance every three years and then there were emptying charges, plus water and electricity. It would be more fun, he decided, to hire a narrowboat and cruise along French waterways in the summer, enjoying the bounty of vineyards and eating lots of fish, and then hand the boat back at the end. If he chose the school holidays, perhaps they could all go.

Once they neared Bertha and the chandlery, Den allowed the children to run on ahead. Everyone had assembled around Phil's barbecue. The smell of sausages permeated the late afternoon air. It was almost dusk, and everyone had fleeces on over sweaters. Clara went to meet them with extra jackets for the twins. They talked over each other in their excitement to be first with all the news of their afternoon. Clara saw the plasters immediately.

'Oh my goodness, what happened?'

'I got bitten by a parakeet. Carl has a plaster as a reward for shooing it away.'

'Den, you know parakeets can carry an infection transferable to humans?'

'Never heard of it myself. I'm sorry, but Cedric's partner's nephews feed them all the time. He never mentioned it.'

'Well, we'll keep an eye on her.'

Den was at a loss. He wondered whether they should take Zoe to the nearest A&E for a tetanus jab, but Jus said that they'd all had them previously. Den was by now overwrought with guilt. He thought that looking after children was more problematic than being a traffic warden, not that he had any personal experience of that, but he'd heard enough. Still, the twins seemed fine, and Zoe was full of beans as usual.

The sausage barbecue was a little subdued. Sunday evening meant that thoughts were turning to the working week. Ling and Linda made their excuses fairly early, saying they needed to get back because Grandma went to bed early on Sundays. She helped at the Immigration Support Centre in Chinatown on Mondays and they didn't want to disturb her when they got in.

Clara, less of a fish out of water now that she had further established a friendly rapport with Phil, relaxed for the remainder of the evening. After all, she would be going back to Suffolk in the morning – but that wasn't without its own problems. She was upset that Justin hadn't made any plans to come to Suffolk, although, almost begging him, she'd found herself subconsciously twisting her gold wedding ring round and round her finger. She tried not to dwell on that aspect for now.

She'd turned away from him the previous night and he had been sullen in the morning. When she'd tried to explain again that she felt they didn't have privacy, he wouldn't listen and over breakfast had almost ignored her, saying, with raised eyebrows and a cold expression, that what was the point in making the effort to make the journey up to Suffolk when she wasn't interested in him, which had prompted her to plead, 'What about the children? Then there's Den too – and I haven't changed. It's just that everything else has. At least try and come home soon.'

'No. You come down with the children. There's so much more to do here. I'll have a word with Phil. He'd love to have them stay over there for a night. Harvey loves them too. You might even consider sleeping with me properly.' As soon as it was out, he hated himself, but left it in the air between them. His blunt refusal to come home and, she felt, cruel comments regarding her feelings and their sleeping arrangements, left her depressed. They had reached a new impasse and she wasn't sure how to get beyond it. It was a falsely jolly departure and a dreary ride home for Clara. Den offered to drive, but she said she'd be fine and Den guessed she wanted something to concentrate on.

That evening Tom dropped by with an exuberant Arthur, who lavished them all with his attention. In his enthusiasm, Clara was almost knocked over, but she didn't care and ruffled his coat as she recovered.

'Have you been in the wars elsewhere, then?' Tom, golden eyes concerned, pointed at the red scratch down Clara's cheek as she put her hand to it.

'Just a tangle with a small dog and some brambles.' She dismissed the livid scratch with a smile.

'Tomtom, guess what? I got bitten by a wild parakeet!' Zoe displayed her fresh plaster. 'There were lots in the tree.'

'Wow, kids! That was an adventure, then. I've seen them wild too, but in Oz, you know.'

'These came a long way then, Tomtom, and I shooed them away!'

Clara, seeing how proud Carl stood, recounting the story, was overwhelmed in that moment with tenderness for him, but was immediately distracted by gruntings from Den, as he dumped their baggage in the hall. Pulling herself together, she thanked Den for unloading, as he wandered in saying he was gasping. Clara turned to offer Tom a drink.

'Love a coffee if you're making one.'

Clara moved to the fridge to fetch milk for the children's hot chocolate as Den set the coffee machine.

'Take a seat, Tom. Biscuits are in the tin. Help yourself. Children, just two each, now. Tom, we owe you for having Arthur.' Clara had meant to bring back something from London, but hadn't got around to it.

'I may have just the thing for you to share with your brother. I'll be back in a minute.' Den reappeared with a bottle of whisky. 'Thought it'd be just the job after a day in the forest, when you've been chilled to the bone, as you thaw out by the fire.' Den placed it in front of Tom, who picked it up, admiring its amber glow.

'That's very decent of you. It'll be a pleasure to look after Arthur next time, if this is the reward!'

Clara brought the coffees over, after giving the children their drinks. They sat around for a while, the twins recounting their various experiences until Clara sent them up to bed, deciding that showers could wait until the morning. Den promised to tuck them in in ten minutes or so. When Den went up as promised, Tom and Clara sat, sipping their coffees. Clara nibbled a biscuit. Tom was unsure how soon he should leave, thinking he should at least wait until Den reappeared. As the state of the workshop computers needed addressing, he decided to bring up the subject. There was, as well, the laptop, which he'd cleaned up and got working.

'They're limping along, Clara. Think you're looking at replacements next year.'

'Can you keep them going until after Christmas, d'you think? Then I think the business will take it.' She grimaced. 'Before, and I'll have to call on our credit card.'

Tom agreed to do his best, as Den came in, saying he needed a real drink now. Tom got up to leave as Clara thanked him again. Once he'd gone, she shared a nightcap with Den, which pleased him, but perturbed him at the same time. When she insisted on paying for Tom's whisky, Den insisted with equal fervour that she didn't owe him a thing and, in truth, she knew this was true and they left it at that.

The next afternoon, when she went to the front door to check for post, there was a note through the letterbox. On opening the door, she found a large box sitting on the tiles, addressed to her. On the kitchen table, she tentatively opened the lid to discover a large spray of mixed flowers, bunched carefully, the stems in a gel pod. She was certain there'd been a mistake; they couldn't be for her. Justin never, but never, gave her flowers. She prodded the gel sack – no need for a vase, then. The card at the bottom of the box was folded. She sat down carefully, opening the card to read the message. It was from Justin. "I want to be better than this. Please forgive me. I'll come home soon. I want to come home soon. Will Skype you all in a day or two with a date. I love you. Justin." Clara lifted the pod and settled it on the dresser. There were freesias amongst the selection, and soon the kitchen was filled with their heady perfume. She shoved the card behind other post leaning on a shelf of the dresser, unconvinced that Justin had initiated this. Negative thoughts sat on her chest like a weight. After his outburst before she'd left, it was hard to imagine he'd had such a swift turnaround. She sat staring at the flowers, eventually concluding that whoever or whatever had prompted him to send them, this was better than how they'd left things.

Clara remained sceptical, but Justin did come home two weeks later, late on a Friday night. He'd spoken with Human Resources, offering himself for some Christmas duties in order to have flexibility during the installation of his father's new property, but didn't mention his manoeuvre with Clara. Neither did he remind her how his department was expanding, during which time, already begun, everyone was doing overtime, often into Saturdays, as it wouldn't have been met with any sympathy.

As it happened, his request for time to go home was sanctioned. He saw the foundations already laid for the installation of Den's lodge. He trod very carefully around these and around Clara's feelings. She had thanked him in a cool manner for the flowers, without referring to the message. He would never know if she'd read it unless he actually asked. He decided to leave it. They both flopped by a resurrected fire, sipping at drinks. Den insisted, with a large glass of wine, on busying himself doing something about Saturday's lunch – they would all go to the market in the morning. The twins were long gone to bed.

Justin, glancing across at Clara, risked stroking across the back of a nearby hand, very lightly, gently, smiling questioningly. She didn't flinch or move her hand, so he chanced leaning forward to kiss her nearest cheek. This went well, as she turned and kissed him. After watching the dying embers and sipping more wine, they wandered out to see Den. Now that preparations were complete, he was sitting with his feet up on a chair, reading.

'You two going up now, then? Think I'll be up soon. Oh, by the way, Jus, I have invited Constanza in the New Year. I might have mentioned it before. Just old mates, you remember? Once I've settled in.'

Justin's mouth worked a second too long before he managed an answer. 'Dad, I only remember what you've told me. Up to you anyway. Night then.'

'Night you two.' He put his book down, stretching a stiff back as he stood up. He'd half expected some reaction, eyebrow raising at the very least, but Jus seemed to have other things on his mind, for which Den was grateful. He hadn't mentioned it to Liz yet, but there was plenty of time to get people used to the idea that he might like to catch up with old friends. Ah, well. He sighed at distant memories. Thing was, she'd been much more than a friend, but he'd never talked about it. After all, they'd both been so young and life had moved on. He turned off the lights, said goodnight to Arthur and made his way to the box room – the box room for now, but not for much longer. He was going to have a good-sized bedroom in his new place.

The weekend passed all too quickly, but Justin, determined not to undo the rapprochement achieved, promised he'd come home again soon. He added, deflating Clara, that Dad would need some help too. It wouldn't be just for her sake, after all.

Chapter Seventeen

Having gone to work one dank, cold morning on his bike, and realising he'd left some paperwork on Bertha, Justin, annoyed with his carelessness, rode back to the boatyard. There were two bikes leaning against each other. He recognised Janine's bike and wondered who was helping her. She was a nice kid, he thought. Opening the main door to the cabin, his greeting died on his lips. There, standing on a plastic sheet, was Janine, Wesley in front of her, a paintbrush in one hand, hairdryer in the other. There were pots of various paints on a stool. If Justin could have thought of anything to say he would have mentioned he was grateful for the proliferation of plastic to protect the boat. Instead he found himself staring at two tigers' eyes with protruding pupils and, below them, splendid orange whiskers above an open mouth with snarling teeth, all this above a neat purple triangle. That's the first time I've seen a purple pubis, he thought, then reconsidered. Janine had been painted with a bikini bottom, with fluff stuck on. Slightly relieved, but still bemused, he waited to learn more as he stared at her painted body.

'Oh hi, Justin, Mr Kerr. Sorry for the inconvenience. We did the cleaning first though.'

'Yes, we've almost finished, in fact,' added a sheepish Wesley, who had put down the paintbrush, but was waving the hairdryer in emphasis.

'What on earth is going on here? And why here, anyway?' Justin, too astonished to be angry, waited for some sort of explanation, adding, 'There's a dressing gown behind the shower room door, Janine.'

'Oh thanks. Can't put anything on just yet. The paint hasn't quite dried and I don't want to smudge.'

Justin, short of time, but lost in this surreal world, begged for a quick explanation. He had to dash back to work. There was an important meeting almost due.

'Would have done it at home, but Mum's got a friend visiting. Then Wes's grandad has gone out and forgot to leave a key for the workshop. We haven't got much time, you see. College is having a human installation competition. Three of us are being jungle animals. It's tonight. Tiger, that's me of course, then an elephant and a hippo. It's going to be in the main hall for all the students in my year, and guests.'

Justin nodded, dumbly. There wasn't time to query the ethics, moral or otherwise, of a teenager being practically naked, and being covered in body paint by an ex-student, who was certainly qualified, by the look of the artistry. He left them to it. He might dine out on this for some while if he dared repeat what he had just seen. No doubt there might be questions regarding his favourite drug of the moment. He hesitated to think how the elephant and hippo might look. He hadn't asked if they were male or female. He also wondered what the judges might think of a tiger with a purple beard and what the guests might make of nude installations overall. Nearing the office, he shook off his mental wanderings. It was all a bit beyond him.

As Clara stood inside the front door, having emptied the mailbox, she saw Den pottering about in the lodge with Arthur following close behind. Arthur's head was all that was visible through the windows, with an occasional glimpse of a wagging tail. Thankfully, she thought, it had been a dry autumn. She smiled to herself. The lodge had arrived at Harwich from Finland via Sweden, then Denmark, virtually flat-pack, but astonishingly, to her at least, complete. After initial reservations about having a building so close, she found she was actually quite excited by the prospect. That it had travelled from her maternal grandparents' country to settle here, drew her to its warm wood. She found herself needing to touch it. Phil's grandson, Wesley, had spent time with them when they'd gone to London for the Chinese Festival. Den showed everyone his research for the lodge, but had only skipped around a few websites. Wesley showed enthusiasm about the possible design of the lodge's interior and became involved. Together they spent what to everyone else seemed a very short time researching and exchanging feverish emails. Den's sense of urgency lent speed to the enterprise to Justin's concern. But Justin was busy with the expansion of the department at work. He heard Den had decided on triple-insulated walls, roof and windows. Doors were to be as standard, which all seemed to make sense.

The structure was ordered, the delivery date agreed and suddenly there it was, an enormous transporter blocking their end of the lane. Justin managed to take a few days off and was there to see three muscular, big-bearded guys jump down from the transporter. They spoke good English. After checking the foundations and ground plans over coffee, they got everything unloaded, working till after dark, using huge arc lights rigged up in nearby trees. The lodge was erected over three long days, all services working, with trades and more muscle contracted in. Just as quickly, the three men departed to cheery farewells, returning to Finland to accompany the next lodge, which was to be erected in Holland.

Clara had savoured their exuberance and even spoke a little laboured Finnish to their resounding cheers, but even so, she was grateful that they retired to their own sleeping arrangements on the transporter. The other trades were local. Justin returned to London. His visit had been good. All the excitement of Den's development had eased their path together – there was so much going on and no time to reflect, for a change. Everything was, for now at least, in the present. She glanced across the lane. All that was left to remind them now of the recent disturbance were the deep furrows the gigantic vehicle had left behind. Now the lodge stood neatly amongst the trees. Den had chosen furniture from his house in Wimbledon, which had been stored and delivered two days after the lodge was ready. Water was in, heating was on, the sewerage pipes were connected to the new sewage treatment plant, where a team had moved in with diggers to install it after clearing the old site. When the team retreated, it was mainly buried by Den, Justin and their new neighbour, James, whose eldest, Frank, also pitched in, just leaving the lid visible for access, before they got an expert in to finish the electrics and for Building Regs to check.

Since the flower bouquet event, Justin seemed more like his old self, Clara was relieved to note, and did not show resentment towards her decision to stay put. Because of everything else going on, she had been happy to make little of her birthday this year and was then surprised and pleased to receive a replacement notebook from Justin, gift-wrapped from the same shop as the one she'd part-ruined in the garden earlier in the year.

The year was moving on now, drawing to its inevitable close. They would soon need to plan for Christmas. Alice and Edie, who normally featured in their Christmas and New Year celebrations, were extending their travelling into the new year. She left the workroom piled up with orders, leaving Liz and Mary busy packing them, to go and let Arthur out and grab a soup for lunch, whilst thinking of how to organise this particular Christmas. Perhaps Justin would like to invite Ling and Linda. She'd since dismissed Ling's brief kiss as a sympathy vote at a difficult time. Justin was certain to come home, as the office closed over the celebratory days, but she was unsure for how long, trying to remember if he'd taken annual leave the previous Christmas. She'd have to check with him, although, because of his accident, she worried if he'd have any extra leave left. She wondered if her parents would come across from Denmark.

Clara remembered that Ling had mentioned he was a nominal Christian. When she'd expressed surprise, as she had assumed him to be a Buddhist or a Daoist, he explained many Hong Kong Chinese were Christian – dating back to the nineteenth century when Christianity had been imposed by the British, and native religions were suppressed – which now led her to ponder whether they should also invite Ling's grandma for Christmas, if they liked the idea. She'd have to speak to Den, assuming he'd join them and Liz would like to be with them. Then she'd need to borrow one lodge bedroom at least. She guessed Phil would have his own arrangements.

Justin sat near Bertha's stove. Suddenly, it had turned very cold. There had been ice on the roof that morning. Looking out, he was surprised to see Phil sitting on his bench, drinking a coffee. Harvey was sitting next to him. It was Sunday. Later, he'd Skype home. Curious about why Phil would choose to sit outside on a frosty day like this, he turned the stove down, picked up a fleece and went up to join his friend.

'Morning, lad. Have a pew.'

Harvey jumped down to greet him.

'What are you doing Phil? It's freezing!'

'I like it. I've been in much colder places, trust me. I like winter – got thick socks, warm boots, thermals.' He chuckled at Justin's discomfort. 'You'll soon get colder if you go about with deck shoes on in this weather.'

Justin looked down and grinned. 'Well, I wasn't coming out. Just curious as to why you were.'

'Finished a book about shipping during the Second World War last night and didn't sleep too well. Then thought how fortunate we are today. Hence a strong coffee and a bit of fresh air. More coffee upstairs. Fancy some?'

'Yeah, okay, thanks. Better than staying out here. I know what you mean though. More distant, but I've been reading about the Opium Wars. Unlike the Second World War, we don't come out of that well. Factual stuff can be disturbing, if you see what I mean.'

Phil looked at him from under bushy eyebrows. The lad wasn't wrong.

Justin, almost out of credit with time off, finished late and Clara picked him up at Bury station. They drove straight home in the inky, early winter night, trees showing their gnarled fingers, leaves now carpeting the lanes. It was, Justin thought, more miserable here than in the city, as, subconsciously, here weather and seasons held one in their grip. Still, Clara was in a good mood, which cheered him. She'd blurted out as soon as they'd met, that she had some good news.

As they pulled into the cottage driveway, he could see lights on in Den's new home. The twins were with him, but as soon as they heard the Land Rover, they leapt out from the front door and ran to him. Justin grabbed them both and hugged them.

'Daddy, Daddy we're all going to Great-Granny's for her birthday. We're going to go with Nana and Grandpa too. They're coming from Odense first to stay with us here too!'

Justin tried to turn to Clara to make sense of what Carl was saying, but Zoe was grabbing him, obviously desperate not to be left out and, for her, looking uncertain about this news.

'We're staying for Christmas too. We can go on snowmobiles. Will I like snowmobiles, d'you think?'

Clara looked shifty, he thought. 'Was this the good news you mentioned?' Mentally, he already wondered how to avoid this visit. He found his good mood slipping away. Apart from everything else, time being the main factor, Finland during the winter was not what he would have described as good news. There was the drinking, the low light levels, which he hated, and the cold. Although bitterly cold, Kuopio didn't always even have snow at Christmas. They'd probably have to travel farther up north for that. Probably visit other elderly relatives. He looked across at Den, who had followed the children out. 'You going too, Dad?'

Den grinned widely. He could read his son like an open book. Didn't have to mention the social life his son would prefer him not to indulge in. 'I've been invited, so yes.' He added unnecessarily, grin deepening, 'It'll be exciting.'

At least Clara had the decency to sound apologetic. 'Well, Granny will be ninety and Grandpop wants to have a big celebration and get all the family together.'

They were still grouped outside. Clara opened the kitchen door. Now Arthur, who had also been at Den's, pushed through to his bowl. The children, excited by their news, and tired – it was long past their bedtime – were still wired. They jumped up and down for their hot chocolate. Den followed Clara, as she called the twins to calm down.

Still outside, Justin halted. In his annoyance he took it out on the decorative copper coal scuttle, until then sitting neatly by the doormat, planted up for the winter. He knocked the contents flying. Blame the dog, he thought. The coal scuttle originated from Clara's Finnish grandparents, Granny and Grandpop. When he and Clara had been there on holiday one summer, the grandparents had converted from coal to oil. The story went that when she was little, even until she left school, Clara stayed with them for most holidays. It had been Clara's job to fill the scuttle and bring it in to the range, whenever needed. Grandpop had presented it to her on that summer holiday, as an amusing memento, all those years later. To Justin's surprise, she'd treasured it and brought it home. Grudgingly, he now felt himself impressed – the old boy had made a good job of his copper work. The scuttle could withstand considerably more abuse than that which he'd just inflicted on it.

There was one consolation, as far as Justin was concerned – they wouldn't have to go foraging at this time of year. He could already see in his mind's eye the rows of bottled and salted goodies which Clara's granny would have put by for their pleasure, not to mention her own brew of Lakka, the cloudberry liqueur that could knock an innocent clean out.

'Darling, don't look so underwhelmed. Grandpop has booked us an internal flight so we don't have that long drive from Helsinki.'

That didn't mean Grandpop was paying, Justin thought. He'd been caught out before. Dad was talking of Liz going too, as he'd been invited plus one, if he could find someone, Grandpop had apparently said jokingly. If only people would stick to being careful with what they offered, Justin thought, but quickly modified his view. Liz was, if anything, a sobering influence on his father, which would be a good thing when they were surrounded by drinks of every variety known to man and a few not heard of before.

They were all to stay in a house near the farm, which the considerate Grandpop had vetted and booked for them. There was a vehicle included. Justin assumed winter tyres, if not studded, would be fitted. Grandpop would see to the legal side of that as well. He'd fancied a few days off in Suffolk over Christmas, perhaps with Ling and Linda, as Clara had previously suggested. Now, irrationally, he was sure they'd get snowed in in Finland and be unable to escape home. This was all before he'd dropped his bags and sat at the kitchen table.

Clara was in the best of humours. They were going where her memories were all good. Unfortunately, it was always an expensive trip. Sometimes in previous years, just she and her mother had gone to Kuopio for a few days, always in summer, when Justin took leave and looked after the twins. They'd taken the twins once for a week, but she hadn't been in winter for years and the children never. The prospect of going to the frozen lakes, seeing the spruce bare and hearing the wind playing through the frosted pines, filled her heart with joy.

The rest of that weekend was littered with everyone's excitement over the forthcoming trip. Clara loved to ski and skate around the archipelago. Grandpop had already informed them the ice was doing well. Should they take their own gear or rent? Should they book the twins in for classes? Would there be time even for an organised snow-walk or a sleigh ride?

They were watching the weather forecasts avidly. If eastern Finland didn't get snow, at least it would be very cold and Christmassy, Liz noted. Den and Liz went out and bought warm boots and inner linings for their coats. Hats with ear covers were next and gloves with mitten covers. Then they disappeared one Saturday to Planet Ice in Norwich for a short course in ice skating with the twins.

Chapter Eighteen

Justin was getting daily reports by Snapchat and all other means anyone chose. He confided in Ling that he hated the almost dark and the bitter cold of winter in Finland. Summer was a different thing entirely, he explained, with the almost constant light, outdoor living and the gentle warmth – that is, if you missed June and plagues of midges.

Ling accused Justin of constant moaning like an old man, which brought Justin up short, pointing out that, after all, he wasn't moving there, only visiting family for a double celebration. It should be fun. Ling quite fancied the idea. It appealed to his newly discovered sense of adventure. He thought he'd been cold when he arrived in the UK, but this sounded arctic and strangely exotic. He'd hired skates each year as they set up rinks around London. He'd taken Linda too, but she couldn't keep upright and dissolved into giggles, as well as bruising herself.

Justin revealed, still set on negativity, 'I've already volunteered for skeleton staff backup. If it doesn't come up, then I'll accept my lot.' He grimaced. 'If it does, I'll take it.'

Ling surveyed him seriously. 'Do you really mean that Jus? Think of it. It's a big family thing, Clara's parents coming over to visit you, and travel on together after a few days here – Den and Liz already half-packed. The twins excited. Can you really justify backing out? They'll never forgive you.'

Justin gave a deep sigh. Of course, Ling was right. He'd have to grin and bear it. Not so different from millions of other poor sods jostling with each other over Christmas, he supposed. He did have second thoughts about the run-up, however. There'd be Grandpop's organised parade around the farm in a celebration of the Festival of Light from days in Sweden in his youth, followed by partying, alcohol and the cold again. He'd escape all that somehow. These days he had aching ribs and an aching ankle in the cold, a reminder of his fateful accident in London. He was tempted to tell Clara of his continued physical aches, but she'd think he was getting at her. It wouldn't help. He'd ski and skate. Perhaps he'd take a leaf out of Dad's book and make sure he had plenty of booze to deaden the pain. He'd certainly get a script for painkillers.

Clara was worried that Tom was popping in more frequently to tweak and check on the computers. When she'd queried if they were failing, he'd reassured her he was only playing safe. In gratitude, Clara invited Tom to stay to eat and, after declining a couple of times on the grounds of intruding and still being in his work clothes, he accepted, after insistence by Den and the twins, texting his brother to go on to eat without him. Zoe and Carl used Tom as entertainment to Clara's discomfort. He laughed off any awkwardness she felt. There was his sleeve tattoo: he'd described the meaning of the sun and moon in blues and reds, referencing a respect for the natural world; then the ring of knots in black entwined around and down his arm, referring to his Celtic ancestry. There was also the small matter of a maze.

This, he explained, leaning forward, his curly braids falling across his face, was a generic similarity to an Indian tattoo, which protected the wearer from bad things, the devils unable to find their way out.

'What's generic, Tomtom?' Zoe asked, as she traced a finger into the maze.

Clara had stood by squirming slightly at the children's innocent boldness and their insistence on continuing to call him Tomtom, which Tom just laughed at.

'Generic? Well, not linked to a certain thing, so as not to offend anyone who may use a special maze as part of their belief.'

Den watching, sipped his beer, thinking that this young man, quite innocently, was filling a gap for the children. He hoped that the same didn't apply to his pink-cheeked daughter-in-law.

'What bad things?' questioned Carl, his eyes giving away his concern.

'All sorts, but it doesn't matter, because I'm protected.'

After explaining meanings of the signs and stories each section represented, they moved on without pause to ask how he did his hair. At this point, Clara laughingly called a halt to their inquisition. Tom's hair actually confused and fascinated her, but she was embarrassed by the twins' open curiosity. Tom just shook his head, making the braids dance, and left it at that. Clara had wanted to touch the short silky braids. She'd seen people on TV with braids. He was intriguing; then there were those golden eyes. She imagined him relaxing with her and Justin and possibly Ling, who was around his age, and Ling's cousin, Linda, but found herself mentally excluding Linda, finding Linda unnecessary to the mix.

Clara had always taken for granted that she had an easy affinity with men, which was missing from her contact with women. With women, she seemed to have to work at the process of making friends. Of course it was vain of her, but the truth was simple as, flushing slightly at the conceit, she acknowledged she didn't need to do anything – men just seemed to like her.

Of course, she didn't lust after them, of course not, she hurriedly told herself, with the exception of Justin. That brought her up short. Oh, how she had wanted him – his lean frame, dark eyes, wavy hair. There was his energy, hardly contained, his quick intelligence and, now rarely, his company. Looking out blankly at the night, it was clear to her that even her desire for him was faltering. For a moment the recent memory of Tom's laughing golden eyes stopped her in her tracks. Then she turned away from the window and, picking up a discarded tea towel, placed it back on the rail, turned off the lights and made her way upstairs.

Clara had just finished handing the last parcels of children's clothes to the carrier for Christmas delivery. There was still plenty of work to do, but the urgency was over. Liz and Mary had stopped with her for a celebratory coffee and shortbread biscuits, before Clara left them to check up on the twins, who were being entertained by Den. The phone went. She saw on the visual it was Justin. He said he was on some rota, brought about because of the time he'd taken off when he was recovering from his accident. Initially, she was dumbstruck and could scarcely believe it.

'Really? Really, you are impossible! How could you? Mama and Dad will be here soon. They can manage to arrive in time for pre-Christmas celebrations with us. You do know that they've put themselves out to spend time with us as a family, before we all fly to Helsinki, then on to Kuopio, where it'll all get more hectic. I can't believe you!'

It would be impossible to miss the emphasis on "as a family" in the tirade. She had omitted to mention that these wonderful people were retired and, Justin considered, turning into meddlers with regard to the "family" as Clara put it. He thought, yes, if he were honest, why bother? He disliked the claustrophobia they inadvertently generated. He immediately modified his thinking. Of course it wasn't their fault, as such; it was partly his dislike of being trapped by any situation. Now he was going to lie even further. 'Clara, I'm sorry. It's part of the job and important to follow the rules. Next year I shall be more settled in and have more say.' He hated himself, but reminded her of his recent visit, which hadn't been easy to organise. 'Well, don't forget, I did manage to see the nativity play. I know it was a quick visit, but I managed it. Give me a little slack, darling. I'll meet you all at Helsinki Airport.'

'Huh, only because you wanted to. I think I hate you!' she shouted, slamming the phone down.

Justin's ears rang. He held the phone, considering it. That was a bit extreme, he thought. Still, it was done. He felt guilty and relieved at the same time. He did feel for Clara, but he was tired and he was busy and really was on standby for work. However, he cheered himself with recalling his recent overnight visit for the nativity play. It was the play itself and the events during it which he would remember, partly from embarrassment, but mainly with some amusement. Zoe was considered to be, by the school at least, sufficiently mature to take the role of Mary, kitted out in a blue costume, run up by Clara. It was a little too long, but Clara hitched it up over its girdle. Carl was one of the wise men, carrying a box covered in gold foil. Den took photos of them before they left.

The play went well until one of the shepherds unwittingly stood on Mary's gown, which had now slipped below the restraining girdle, as she made to put baby Jesus in his crib. Trapped, she hissed at him to move his foot. He looked at her, uncomprehending, so she took the matter into her own hands, yanking the gown hard, really hard. The astonishment on the shepherd's face as he flew backwards was something to behold, followed immediately by horrified gasps from the audience. The shepherd, having quickly recovered himself, swiped Mary with his crook. Mary immediately hit him back with baby Jesus, who had his own voice, and cried 'Mama'. Carl, to everyone's surprise, took Zoe's side, dropped his gold foil box and joined in. Shepherds were now hitting each other with their crooks. Sybil, Carl's friend from the top of the lane, stood guard over his gold foil box for him. Before the curtains were hurriedly closed, some of the first-year animals could be seen escaping to the sides.

The headmaster, Mr Dogherty, came to the front of the stage, and announced a short interval whilst the cast regrouped. There were irate parents, worried parents and, it had to be said, some very amused parents, of whom Justin was one. Clara was mortified. It was all her fault, she decided. She should have made more effort with Zoe's costume. Justin considered it was a riotous success, riot being the best part, and no one was hurt. The second effort concluded without incident, which was thanks in no small part to Mr Dogherty who, backstage, had calmed the cast, apparently suggesting that the second attempt would be called the second house, as in professional theatres. Justin considered the trip worth every penny of his last-minute, pricey rail ticket.

Clara's parents arrived. They hadn't seen Den's new home. Years before, they'd visited his terraced cottage, when he and Lola lived in Wimbledon Village. The lodge was, in fact, considerably bigger, culturally more Scandinavian and very much to their taste.

'Velkommen, Anna, Hans. Do come in to my new establishment.'

'Hej, Denholme, tak. Can't see a sauna anywhere. That in your plans?' Hans enquired innocently, after settling down in an old leather armchair from the seventies, which was definitely not Scandinavian. He smiled, looking around as if expecting a sauna to be fitted into a corner.

Den hadn't given a sauna a thought, as his startled expression indicated. Still, attempting not to be outdone by this smooth Dane, who was already testing his good humour, not quite wrong-footing him, he took a deep breath, attempting to sound blasé. 'I prefer steam rooms to saunas, myself. We go to the spa in Bury. Running one here wouldn't be practical for me. I'd never keep up with the care of it. I assume you have one at home, then?'

'No,' Hans laughed. 'Not exclusively. We share with next door. It's in the copse between us.'

There were things, questions, Den would have liked to have asked about the semantics of such an arrangement, but instead he drifted off into his own thoughts as Hans sipped at his pre-supper drink. Anna came in to report to Hans on the progress made in Clara's workshop and on the charm of Liz and Mary. Taking the glass offered, she proceeded to ask after the twins and, embarrassingly of course for Den, about Justin's continued absence, which obviously concerned her. Den smiled back at her, having decided nothing he could say would help.

Den knew there was a sauna at Clara's grandparents' place in Finland. They'd even joked, he and Liz, about switching each other with birch twigs from the forest and rolling in snow. Hans merely continued to smile. Was it turning into a smile-off? Den wondered. It was going to be a long week. There was something about that couple which irritated him. Smug was an option, although he hadn't quite worked them out. They were pleasant, friendly, very blonde. Maybe it was the blondeness, simple as that. Oh, and the slimness – their glowing fitness, which caused his stomach to tighten temporarily. Still, they did love a drink, but even that never seemed to affect their sobriety, which was annoying as well. And he'd only been to the spa to keep Clara and the children company, when Justin had booked them tickets for a surprise day treat after he'd cancelled a weekend home. But he didn't explain, partly not to put Justin in an even poorer light, and partly because he didn't deem it worth clarification.

Liz and Mary had been busy when Anna had appeared, popping her head around the workroom door to enquire if it was convenient to come in, before walking in and closing the door behind her. She was stunning, they agreed. She was not as tall as Clara. Her hair was styled in a short bob and she had faded blue eyes surrounded by thick fair lashes. Her pale, golden skin – the same Scandinavian gold as her daughter's – was only lightly lined.

She was slender with a neat, stylish appearance, her cashmere dress and dark green tights matching, above silver trainers. She had an off-white stole slung around her shoulders, highlighting small silver drop earrings. Both Liz and Mary had been impressed, watching as Anna said goodbye, before she leant down to fondle and examine a little dungaree set with its own jacket, laid out on the testing bench.

'Really sweet,' she'd commented, turning back to smile at the two women, whose sewing had ceased whilst they watched. After they heard her footsteps fade towards the lodge, they burst out into nervous laughter.

'Well, what did you think? Was she checking up on us? She didn't come across with Clara. Where is Clara, anyway? I want to get off early.'

'I'm staying – taking a change of clothes over to Den's. I wonder if she realises I stay there occasionally.'

'Good luck with that. She seems a bit schoolmarmy to me. Not that it's any of her business. What's Hans like?'

'I'll tell you tomorrow. He'll be at supper.'

Mary got up and stretched. 'It's time. I need to get off. Choir practice tonight.'

'Make my apologies, won't you? I'm going to miss the fun. Still, Finland beckons, or rather, the Danes!'

With that they both packed away their work as Clara came in to shut down the computers and lock up. Liz wondered if there would be an interrogation from Clara's parents as to why Justin wasn't joining them. She felt for Den. She hoped there wouldn't be a disapproving atmosphere over the main course, which, she knew, Den had prepared. Then there were the days ahead before they flew to Helsinki. The latest news was that Justin was meeting them there for their onward domestic flight. The trip wasn't going to be without its moments, she thought.

Liz made her way across to the lodge to be introduced to Hans, prior to going back to the cottage for supper with them all, and to drop her things in Den's bedroom. Now not in the employee role, but as Den's guest, Liz politely enquired how Hans and Anna's journey had gone. The Great Danes, as Den privately referred to them, were eager to regale how tiresome their trip had been. They'd hired a car from Norwich Airport, after flying in from Billund, having endured a train up from Odense and a delayed switch at Schiphol. In the past, they'd driven across the Dover–Calais route, but this time of year, driving down through Germany, efficient and open though the roads were, it could be a very onerous business. Den thought perhaps they had looked a little travel-weary on arrival. But now, after showers and unpacking, they were obviously refreshed. Liz had noted Den's assessment of Clara's parents, but had found Anna pleasant and interested in how the business was developing, when she'd called in at the workshop. But then, of course, she would wouldn't she, Liz thought, a little cynically. She'd heard through Mary that Clara's parents had been involved in the business's purchase. Liz hadn't asked Den how the whole scenario had gone down with Justin, but thought it odd.

Chapter Nineteen

Justin was lounging back in the rocking chair. Ling was lying across a floor cushion and Linda sat cross-legged on the Persian rug, near the stove. There was a bottle of wine open and some pizza left on the low table.

Linda leaned towards Justin, 'Justin, can I ask how you got interested in Mandarin?'

Justin grinned, 'Actually, two Chinese friends started me off. Roy and Ray,' he said. Roy and Ray had lived at the bottom of the hill, above the Peking House Takeaway. They'd played on the common together from when they'd met at the age of eight or so. Later, Mandarin was offered at school, and Mum and Dad had encouraged him. By now he'd been accepted into the takeaway kitchen as a washer-up, and Mandarin was spoken around him.

Linda asked, 'Weren't you teased?'

Justin nodded, 'Of course, but I was stubborn too!' and he'd persevered. He did well at A levels and chose Mandarin at university. He was very lucky, he said, for Dad secured him a six-month placement with a Chinese camera company he'd had dealings with in Shanghai. 'To Dad's disappointment I never learnt much about photography,' he laughed.

Ling was more interested to know about Hans and Anna's visit. 'Did you say your in-laws are coming to the UK from Denmark, before flying on to Finland?'

'I know, Ling,' Justin made a grimace, 'the reasoning behind why Hans and Anna thought it sensible to drag themselves here, before setting off again in a week to Helsinki, is a lesson in Hans–Anna think. I've no idea!' They had professed that their decision made sense and that they enjoyed shopping in the UK, intending to have a trip to Norwich, which would give them time with the UK end of the family, before they all flew to Helsinki and on to Kuopio. Justin shrugged, 'That's families for you. They've brought all our presents to leave here and are going shopping for the Finland lot to wrap and take to Kuopio. They like making a deal out of being organised. It's a bit cruel of me to say so, but they're more about effect than feeling, if you follow me. Clara will be smiling through clenched teeth before they all get to the airport. I suppose I should've made more effort to go home.'

Ling shook his head at his friend, laughing in disbelief. 'Jus, if I didn't know you better, I'd think you meant it.'

Justin rocked forward and kicked Ling, as Ling avoided him by swiftly leaning left.

'Well, I don't mind some of the Finnish experience.' Justin waved a hand in an expansive manner. 'It can be fun when everyone descends on the farm, if I'm honest. They do know how to party.'

'Then you've got the sauna experience to look forward to as well.'

'You keen on saunas, Ling?'

'Oh, come on, I've lived here long enough to try your steam rooms and saunas. We have traditional bath houses and steam baths in Hong Kong too, you know. Here there's the hammam in Camberwell Road, for a start.

Thought you'd use it for your aches and pains you're always going on about,' Ling retorted.

Linda cut in, 'I've been to the spa at the Hong Kong Jockey Club. It's great.'

'Wow, who paid, Linda? No, don't tell me.' Ling laughed, as Linda rolled her eyes.

'You know very well that Uncle Anan did.' She turned to Justin. 'He spoils us when we visit. He didn't have kids, so after our parents died in the Ruichang earthquake, he sort of adopted us.'

Justin stopped his chair mid-rock. He looked from one to the other. 'Ruichang earthquake?'

'Yes, in 2005, we were looked after by family. Our parents worked for a building project as engineers on contract,' Linda said, 'in mainland China.'

'Oh God, I'm so sorry.' Justin was out of his depth, stricken. The light atmosphere of the evening had evaporated with this revelation.

Linda, watching Justin, leant across to pat his hand, which was now gripping the arm of the rocker. 'It's okay, Justin. We can talk about it now. It was a long time ago.'

'We stayed with Uncle Anan a lot. He is, well, he's comfortably off,' Ling offered as a way of explanation.

Ling had never talked about his parents. It was a gap in their friendship which Justin hadn't ever felt he could bridge. He remembered something Ling had mentioned once, when he was disagreeing with Linda over something. He hadn't gone into details, but had muttered that Linda hadn't really dealt with things entirely. Now, for the first time, Justin saw Linda as vulnerable. Her delicate features tensed, then recovered their smoothness with, he thought, considerable composure. He desperately wanted to take her in his arms, stroke that silken head, take in her sweet smell and keep her safe from harm. She and Justin often exchanged flirtatious glances, with the occasional slipping of a hand, casually touched. Taken aback at this sudden force of feeling, he pulled himself upright. He looked across at Ling, who was staring at him.

'Yeah, well, now you know. We've had to get used to it and just get on with it. Linda came here straight away and Grandma brought her up. I stayed in Hong Kong, finished school and university and got a job in the bank. Uncle Anan helped and I stayed with him. Then I got a transfer here. Not going back.' He gave a rueful smile, adding, 'Not as keen on languages as you, Jus. I'm happy to stay here. Mandarin, Cantonese and English will do me. Our parents' death is history, just part of our history now, Jus, but Linda and I do look out for each other.'

Justin nodded, at a loss as to what he could say which might be appropriate, then said nothing. Had Ling read him? He wondered, worried.

Their light-hearted evening over, a solemn atmosphere filled Bertha's confined space.

'We'd better be off, Jus.' Ling stood up and took the remaining pizza along to the galley, then texted for a taxi. Linda pulled herself up from the rug as Justin put out a hand for her to grab.

'Don't be upset, Jus. We are okay. We've learnt how to cope. Really.' Stroking his back as if to comfort him, she moved away towards the door. 'We are Chinese, you know!'

'That's true!' Justin grinned, as Ling returned with their coats.

'See you in the morning, Jus. Thanks for supper.'

'Yes, and the wine,' Linda added, tiny in her winter coat.

After they'd gone, Justin sat with the rest of the wine. What an evening. How contained they both were. And he couldn't get Linda out of his head. There was the paleness of her skin and the darkness of those eyes, which held their own secrets, and the pearl earrings she always wore. He'd wondered, he realised now, why a young woman might wear the same jewellery constantly. Somewhat fancifully, he considered that the earrings may have been her mother's and was almost overcome with tenderness for her.

His train of thought landed on his own circumstances. He still missed his mother, but he'd been an adult, after all, when she had died. There'd been Dad, although he'd sort of closed down for a while and drank more. Clara was always quietly supportive. Ah, Clara. Suddenly the wine was vinegary and he took it across to the galley, where he tossed it down the sink and finished clearing up. He paused, leaning against the worktop, head bowed, feeling forlorn, aware of his own sense of loss, living here on his own. He had become less of a husband, and without doubt less of a father, in the year he'd been apart from his family. Perhaps, he thought, without much optimism, perhaps Christmas would help them to find a way. After all, they would be together, but, emitting a deep sigh, hardly in neutral territory.

Lying in bed later, with the boat occasionally rocking from the ebb and flow out on the canal, he went over the evening again. Something had been triggered in him when Ling had said he was content with the languages he was now familiar with. Justin was very different. He hadn't got far into Danish or Finnish, partly because it seemed pointless as most people he came across spoke some English. His feet cold, he pushed one hot-water bottle down the bed. However, he did love tone-sensitive Cantonese and used it at work, as he did Mandarin. Then there was Italian, guttural German, the elegance of French. He wondered where he would direct his enthusiasm next.

Yet, he considered, so many sounds held their own attractions. He missed the soulful sound of swans flying over the marshes in Suffolk. A very different pleasure was that of the canal ducks, which quacked and waddled onto the deck from the bank and even roosted there, which made him smile. There was the sudden memory of the twins, laughing, screaming and shouting in the garden, splashing through the hose, which had been rigged on a garden fork. The twins: his heart lurched. Oh God, what was he going to do? He rolled over, grabbed the other hot-water bottle to put against his back and attempted to settle. Hot-water bottles were his eternal salve against insomnia.

News from Finland was that the lakes were already frozen and the snow had settled. Skyping Justin with the children the previous evening, Clara swallowed her continued anger and they made decisions. They would hire skis once they were there, after Justin said he was unsure if his ankle could take it. Then he'd thought that to compromise and save his still-sensitive ankle, they might go cross-country skiing. The twins, bored now, disappeared to go across to Den's to say goodnight. Continuing their planning, Clara commented that Grandpop had mentioned to her in one text that he'd take the twins into the forest on snowshoes as well, and they could hire them at the same place.

Over breakfast the following morning, the twins discussed their forthcoming packing.

'I'm taking my rucksack, my new red one. My old one's got a hole from London. We can take our tablets, Grandad said.'

This announcement from Carl was news to Clara, but she wasn't feeling up to entering into disputes and she let it go.

'We're taking our watches, Mummy, the ones we had for our birthday, so we can find each other.'

Clara was surprised Zoe was concerned about such things, that there might even be a need to find Carl in her world, but she couldn't make herself concentrate. She was still preoccupied by the events of the previous evening after she and Justin had finished planning. Almost as soon as Mama and Dad had arrived, Mama had insisted on them having a real tree. She had given Clara's artificial tree a cluck of displeasure.

'But, Mama, we'll be away for most of the time!'

'It is a matter of principle. You'll be back before New Year and it will give the children something much better to decorate.'

As soon as she was introduced to Tom, as he had arrived to deliver some logs, she had requested a tree. Tom, confused, stood nonplussed.

'For here, of course, for the cottage. You sell trees, I believe?' Her tone had been imperious, as if she were questioning his capacity to understand a simple request. Clara, standing behind her mother, had made a helpless gesture. Tom had shrugged, guessing this had more to do with some sort of control and little to do with trees.

'What size would you like?'

This was quickly decided upon, bearing in mind the low-ish ceilings. 'Oh, one metre sixty should be fine, thank you. I'll pay you now.' With that Clara's mother had opened her silver bag, producing several notes. Thus settled, she had left them to seek out Hans to inform him that a proper tree had been ordered.

'Tom, I do apologise. Mama can be unnecessarily, well, crisp, almost rude. Sorry!'

'No worries. I meet all sorts.'

Tom had returned sometime later, having sorted a suitable tree from the forest yard, and left them their Christmas tree in the sitting room, having set it up for them in a bucket, which would be covered by Christmas paper. As he'd stood up, Clara saw his braids were caught with pine needles and, without thinking, leaned forward to pull them out. Tom, turning, looked at her searchingly, as she quickly stepped back, aware she was in his space. Hans then appeared from Den's lodge, to deliver everyone's Christmas presents to go under the tree. Clara saw Tom out, where he swiftly bade her goodnight and left, climbing into the forestry truck and giving a toot as he left.

'Helpful chap, that Tom youngster.' Hans gestured towards the tree. Clara smiled in agreement. Hans insisted their gifts were not to be touched until after Finland, on New Year's Eve. Hans had admonished Zoe as she grabbed a label to read who the recipient might be.

'But I want to take mine with me, Grandpa, if I can't have them now!' she pouted.

Clara shook her head and wished for once she might be in control of just one event, just one thing. She sighed, removing Zoe's small fist from the gift tag, and placed the presents on the shelf opposite, leaving space to decorate the tree. 'No, darling. Nana and Grandpa want you to have something to look forward to when we come back, as they will be staying on for a while. There will be presents from Daddy and me and from everyone else in Finland too while we are there.'

Later that evening, Clara, desperate to share her feelings with someone, took a deep breath and rang Justin. He was reclining in his easy chair, nursing a brandy, boots resting up on the dying stove.

'Hi, darling. How's it going?' Justin looked at his watch. This late, and so soon? They'd already Skyped earlier with the children.

'How d'you think, Jussy? It's no fun with Mama and Dad dropping hints about you not being here. Are you sure you can't finish so we can all travel together?'

Justin sighed. He felt guilty, but the year apart had taken its toll. Though he missed them all, he realised there was nothing that would improve things so far as he could see. He already was facing several days with in-laws en masse and he'd fixed wriggle room to avoid total immersion. He reverted to his old mantra, squirming slightly. 'Y'know, it didn't have to be like this. If you'd come here to live, we'd have been together, anyway. Not on the boat, of course. But there were nice houses in Greenwich, if you remember, and loads of open spaces.'

'I can't believe that's all you can say. You know you are a callous bastard!' She was tempted to throw the phone at the wall, but instead pointed out that nice houses in Greenwich were very small and everything was urban and, well, had sharp edges.

Justin laughed. It wasn't how he saw life in the city, at least, not any more.

She ploughed on. 'You know the children are happy here. I'm happy here. I hated all my childhood, being parked with anyone across the city, so Mama and Dad could do their precious work. I never liked town living. Here

I've got roots and feel safe. Remember why we chose this cottage? Remember how you said it was heaven? Well, it still is. I'm not moving. Period. Full stop. If it means no more us, I'll just buy you out!'

That was a new one. He wondered if her parents were involved now. He knew from the figures that her business was only just breaking even.

'I can't see how we can work things out, Jussy.' Now she was crying into the phone. She sniffed in his ear. Then she went off again. 'The business is working too. It'll be better once we have new computers.' She added as an afterthought, 'Tom says they're on borrowed time.'

'Order two new ones. Get Tom to choose with you. He'll know what you need. It's my Christmas present to make up for all my shortcomings.' He attempted a short laugh, thinking of the state of his credit card. They needed him to be earning a good salary. Life was expensive. Her persistent idea that he could earn enough translating from home, or doing freelance bookkeeping didn't hold any appeal for him. Neither was he confident that he could generate enough steady income. He'd met one or two lecturers from the University of East Anglia when he was on a course. It was different for them, as they translated books, or wrote papers, as well as lecturing. She must have approached her parents, who'd already bought her the business, after he'd refused to accept their help in buying a flat. They were a law unto themselves, those two: too smooth by a long way, unlike Dad.

He wondered briefly how Dad would cope if they split up, properly split. Dad loved being in his new lodge, loved being near the twins. There was Liz as well, now. Hell! he thought. He had drifted, to be brought back to what Clara was now saying.

'Computers won't bring you home! All we need is you here and everything will be fine again.' She stretched out on the double bed, waving her free hand over the empty half of the bed. 'I'm so lonely, Jussy.'

'Listen, we'll be together in a few days. Perhaps we can make some plans. I'll get some time off in the new year, when the leave starts up again. Half-term week? What d'you say?'

Defeated, Clara agreed. Justin sent a smackeroo of a kiss down the line, which made her snort through her blocked-up nose, as he reminded her to talk to Tom about her computers. Justin had met Tom several times now. He was very young, he thought, but okay. More than that, he was proving supportive towards Clara's business and had come up with some new ideas for online promotions. Clara had obviously warmed to him. It wasn't clear if it was personal, or more business self-interest.

It was a frosty morning, and Clara still felt bruised from the phone call the night before. She shouldn't have gone so far. Still, Justin needed to know how unhappy she was. The window was steamed up. Arthur was sitting on her feet as she sipped at a strong coffee, whilst he nibbled at the gift of a corner of her toast. She tried to ignore the twins.

'Mummy, we haven't got any snowshoes. Does Great-Grandpop know? How can we get some?' Zoe asked anxiously, her face creased in concern. 'I'm not sure I want to walk in the snow in the forest anyway. Skating was fun when we went to the ice rink, but we had chocolate straight after and Liz said we should always have hot chocolate after skating.'

Clara wondered if Justin's reticence about going to Finland had transferred to Zoe. Zoe, who was normally the forward one of the twins, now seemed floored by the thought of it. She was like Justin where Finland was concerned, she thought, somewhat wryly: particularly good at pointing out snags when she, Clara, desperately wanted things to go well.

Carl rolled his eyes. 'Don't be daft. You hire them from the ski-hire shop, don't you, Mummy, and skates?'

'Yes you do. We discussed it last night. We'll go into Kuopio. They strap on over walking boots.'

Oh my goodness, she realised, she needed to take them shopping for waterproof walking boots or waterproof trainers. She'd left that a bit late. Good job the children brought the subject up. She'd got carried away with the romance of it all. That was all it took to miss something. Managing alone was infuriating, whilst Justin swanned about like a bachelor and only deigned to join them when it suited him. Well, she'd brought him up short now. He needed to decide what his priorities were pretty quickly. Her business was beginning to show promise. New computers would improve their scope, but independence, which had crossed her mind, was still a distant dream, even if she sought it.

Carl couldn't wait to get to the farm and winter adventures. He knew Great-Grandpop still skied and lake-walked. He wondered if it might be possible to stay at the farm, so he wouldn't miss any adventures. Poppa said, too, they could ice-fish on the lake, when they'd last Skyped.

'Daddy said we're going to use Great-Gran's sauna and roll in the snow with nothing on after. I don't want to!' Zoe continued, expressing her fears.

'Oh, for goodness sake, Daddy was teasing, that's all. I think it'll be fun!' Carl wasn't going to let anything put him off this adventure.

Clara tried to brush aside Zoe's qualms. It was hard for her to see things through Zoe's eyes. She was so excited, she told them. This was where she'd always spent Christmas as a child with her parents and grandparents and their extended family. There was so much to do. At least Carl was suddenly confident, positive and excited. She would hold on to that.

'But isn't it dark all day? And why didn't you visit Grandpa Hans's mummy and daddy at Christmas?' Zoe demanded.

Clara sighed, feeling the weight of Zoe's questions. 'We saw them all year, because they lived in Odense, then they moved to Copenhagen, where I met Daddy. They were very old by then and they died just after Daddy and I married.'

Carl was already in Finland in his head. He didn't want to hear any stuff about other Great-Grandpas and Great-Nanas who were dead. Anyway, Copenhagen and Odense were cities and he didn't think much of them when they'd visited in any case.

Chapter Twenty

Justin missed his flight, and so he missed his family at Helsinki. He couldn't begin to explain how he could do such an unforgiveable thing. He eventually reached Kuopio late on the twenty-third, only making it for the main festive day of Christmas Eve by persistence and expensive tickets, to Clara's fury. She borrowed Poppa's car and drove through the freezing night to pick him up. She was tempted to leave him at the airport. She wouldn't allow Poppa to drive out so late and Den had had a drink, like all the other adults.

As Justin saw Clara at the terminal, he dropped his bag and coat to hug her.

'Cretin! Cretin!' she hissed, turned and marched off, the fur tags on her tall boots following her rhythm.

He scooped up his things and scurried after her.

'Boot!' she pointed as he heard the vehicle unlock.

God, did she want him to get in the boot? Justin tentatively dropped his bags in. She snapped the boot shut, and he pulled his fingers back quickly.

'Back seat!'

'I know I'm in disgrace, but isn't that a bit extreme?' His tone was plaintive, angering her further.

'Think yourself fortunate I bothered to get you at all!' Then, as he accepted his lot and settled in to the warm interior, she barked, 'Front seat overheating. Should have let you burn!'

At this, he made a face, which she caught in the mirror. Clara was determined not to give an inch. He'd gone too far and, although she'd recognised guilt on his face, as she'd expected, she noted a subtle difference about him, which she hadn't quite worked out yet.

They arrived at their lodgings in the early hours, keeping Grandpop's vehicle overnight. He'd insisted she use his car, although the hired one seemed fine to Clara. They were both exhausted and, once they'd crept upstairs, collapsed into bed. They had separate duvets on the huge bed. Justin rolled himself up in his and stayed carefully well away from the centre. Clara looked at him pityingly and slipped beneath hers without speaking.

Exhausted, but tense, Justin still couldn't sleep. He was reliving his experiences of the previous two days, the latter of which should have seen him travelling to Helsinki. Firstly, there'd been a drinks party at work, which Ling convinced him he needed to attend. Afterwards, he'd wobbled back to Bertha on his bike and had managed to remember to strap it to the roof. He was still reeling from his meeting with a senior colleague over drinks and fairly boring nibbles. The colleague had thrown up a few suggestions with regard to Justin's job, involving working abroad in the future. Justin's head had buzzed. He guessed it would mean working in mainland China or possibly elsewhere. He managed to sound calm but positive, although privately he was amazed. Why him? he'd wondered. He'd been in Canary Wharf for a little over a year and was only now finding his feet. Once alone, he went to get another drink. Ling had approached as he turned to mingle with the crowd, grinning.

'You know something I don't, Ling?'

'Well, you do know the bank is expanding. Those who are fluent in European languages as well as Mandarin or Cantonese are of interest apparently, as well as accountancy, naturally. Mr Sharaf had a word just to get a feel of whether you might be worth speaking to.'

'Oh, thanks, Ling,' Justin said dryly. 'Why on earth didn't he just ask me straight out?'

'Well, I trained under him when I got here from Hong Kong. We got to know each other quite well. He's had supper at Grandma's.'

Justin raised an eyebrow. 'Oh well, that explains everything. He had supper at Grandma's then, like me!'

Mildly exasperated, Ling shook his head, 'Don't forget, working for the bank all those years, before it became this international enterprise, counts for something too. Not everyone gets his attention. Don't deny you're ambitious, so be grateful! And be ready for a serious interview in the new year.'

'What, yours or ours? New Year, I mean!' Justin was tetchy, out of his depth.

Ling laughed at him. 'Idiot. My only reservation, concern, was how your family might fit in.'

'Christ, you didn't mention that, did you?'

'Of course not! Not my business, but good luck anyway! Come on, let's go over and chat to some of the others.'

Then, after another half hour or so, they'd left. Justin had been surprised by Ling's sudden hearty pat on the back, encouraging him to make the most of Finland. A little wrong-footed, Justin managed to gather himself sufficiently to send good wishes to Linda and Grandma.

The houseboat was warm, the stove still alight. Justin had packed for the flight in advance and thrown his bags in the wardrobe. There was still a day and night to go, before catching an early flight on the twenty-third. Impressed with his organisational skills, and relieved that he wasn't sharing in the inevitable hubbub in Suffolk, he had treated himself to a brandy and sat back, trying to grasp the full meaning of the events of the evening. How he would broach the subject to Clara was going to be challenging. Best not over Christmas, then.

He had leaned forward to top up his drink. There were plans to have lunch with Phil the next day. A bottle of whisky stood on the shelf along with a spare key for Phil, who had offered to keep the stove alight. Afterwards, he'd planned an early night to follow and a very early start the next morning for the airport to catch his flight to Helsinki and meet up with the family's flight.

Someone was knocking on the door. He must have dozed off. He'd looked at his watch and seen it was twelve thirty. Thinking it must be a drunk off their route home, he'd picked up the poker, before looking through the spy hole. There was a pair of antlers, and he heard a giggle. He'd opened the door to find Linda leaning against the door jamb.

'Just wanted to say Happy Christmas in person!' She'd fallen forward and Justin had caught her in his arms.

'Whoa! What are you doing here, Linda? You are way off course.'

'Didn't text, didn't phone. Wanted to surprise you!'

'Surprise? Well you've done that alright!'

She had moved forward, her antlers slipping sideways, to reach up to him. 'Wanted to kiss you – Happy Christmas. Can't do it sober.' She had giggled again. 'Wanted to, sober, I mean, but not right. Drunk okay though.'

Totally confused, Justin hadn't wanted to dwell on how adorable she appeared. Somehow, he'd have to get her home, get hold of Ling and let him know she was okay. There must still be taxis. He'd ring the people he normally used, take her down to the main road and make sure she was safely on her way. Linda had drawn herself up to her full height, which was considerably shorter than his.

'Not going anywhere. Too late. Have to stay.'

He had looked again at his watch. 'I have to let Ling know you're okay, for Grandma's sake.'

'For fuck's sake, Justin, I'm a grown-up.'

'Even so, you were expected home at some point, weren't you?'

'Now you're boring.' Suddenly she sat down. 'Might be sick.'

He had tripped over the stool, trying to grab a bowl from the sink. It was too late by the time he'd recovered his balance and placed the bowl in front of her. She had puked down her front. The smell was reaching the confines of the narrowboat. Justin had immediately started running hot water and squirted washing-up liquid into the bowl, adding a cloth. He wasn't thinking – he had only responded to the result of puke, as he would for the children. A dash of disinfectant had gone in too.

'Feel much better now – have to wash all this though.'

She had started to undress; the antlers were becoming an obstacle. He hadn't known how to stop her, so he'd guided her to the bathroom and the bathrobe on the back of the door, closing the door behind her. Then he had panicked. Supposing she locked herself in and passed out? He'd opened the door a little. 'Don't shut the door, Linda. Leave it ajar, okay?' All he'd got was another giggle, then the hiss of the shower. He'd unlocked the door, picked up the bowl and threw the contents overboard, leaving the bowl and cloth on deck. He'd unlatched the porthole windows, causing a murky blast of canal air to sweep through. Still with the shower going, he'd built up the stove, closing the portholes. He'd sniffed the air. It was a bit on the watery side, but nothing worse. Then he'd sat down, running his hands through his hair.

It was nearly one, but even so he'd have to try and get hold of Ling to let him know where his cousin was. He'd have to tell him she was a bit tipsy as well, although she was a lot more than that. Now she would be in his bathrobe too. So he couldn't put her in a taxi like that. It all became irrelevant anyway, when Ling's phone went to voicemail. He hadn't left a message immediately;

he'd needed to think what he should do next. Of course! Clara had left some things on Bertha. He'd rummaged through the drawers. There was a sweater. He'd held it up. It would be like a dress on Linda. Her underwear was probably unaffected by her puke, so it might do to get her home. She was standing behind him.

'That yours? Bit narrow. Must have washed it on hot.'

She'd grabbed the sweater. For a moment she'd been standing there naked. Then she'd slipped the sweater on, the bathrobe around her feet. If he could have gathered his thoughts, or her at that moment, he would have done, but at that point he'd still imagined he had an element of control. He had seen how the delicate jade sweater suited her far more than it did Clara, but his new concern was that she wasn't wearing any underwear. It was freezing and he couldn't send her home like that.

His life was turning into a tragi–comedy and there'd be Ling to deal with if he behaved badly with Linda. Re-run that, he thought, groaning: Linda had been somewhere in his head, had been since he first saw her at Grandma's and had endeavoured then to dismiss her from his thoughts.

'Feel fine now!' She'd grinned up at him, gone to her bag and pulled out a small packet of white powder. 'D'you fancy some? Good at party time. You agree?'

Some people at work used it. It seemed to be everywhere. He'd tried it several times and had liked the effect. So far he'd never fancied using when on his own. He certainly wasn't on his own now.

'Yeah, okay then.'

'You mind if I do too?'

'Course not. You won't be sick on it again?'

She had laughed. 'I shouldn't drink and take it at the same time, is all.'

'Fine, then let's!' He had known he was lost to his fate then. 'Sure you feel better now?'

She'd beamed at him. She wanted him. 'Still want a kiss.'

Leaning in, she pursed her lips, soft pink, very near, her breath smelling of toothpaste, his toothpaste, her pupils enlarged, his cologne coming towards him from her warm body. He knew everything was wrong about this. Later he considered perhaps she wasn't quite as drunk as she'd made out.

Lying in his arms the next morning, she had smiled up at him. 'Knew I'd have to be devious to get you this far. Had a couple of lines of coke to make sure. Forgot coke and booze together don't agree with me. Still, it worked!' Relaxed, she'd waved an arm in the air. 'I've wanted to since I first saw you, all new in London and lovely. Now you're quite the townie.'

He was totally out of his depth in every way. She wasn't anything like the image he'd had of her before last night. It was obvious he was no good at reading people. He'd thought her slightly cool towards him, flirtatious yet composed, as if it was just a game to play. Now he had to reassess himself too. He'd crossed to a place where he thought he would never go, not in reality anyway. He'd resorted to watching porn some nights; it hadn't made him feel better. Justin hardly knew what to say. He'd probably lost a good friend in Ling. Then there was Clara – what if she found out? Found out? What had he been thinking? Had Linda thought this was a laugh? Could it even have been a bet? Still, there he'd been in bed with a very biddable, beautiful, not to say eager woman. And it was Christmas, after all.

'Linda, you must phone your Grandma. Tell her something. Not this, of course!'

She'd dismissed the idea with another wave of her hand. 'Now we are here,' she'd grinned up at him, 'and we are where we are, as I think you might say, can we do it again, please? I don't have work.' She'd poked a finger at him. 'Neither do you. I asked Ling.'

Startled, Justin faced her.

'Oh, it's okay, he doesn't have a clue.'

Justin hadn't bothered to explain to her that in his experience Ling was very intuitive and mostly aware of everything around him.

'You fly out first thing tomorrow morning. That means we've got all day!'

She'd pulled him down to her. Oh hell, or actually, heaven, he'd thought. He had thought, unused to such subterfuge, that actually, if it was dark when Linda left, Phil might not see her go, if he was lucky. Lucky! Was he a stranger to himself?

Linda had indeed crept out, when Justin went across to Phil's. They had got away with it, Justin thought. Linda had put her things through the washer-dryer. When she'd left, she looked wonderful: her hair so smooth and glossy, her skin its perfect white, her eyes black and full of mischief. He hadn't been able to think clearly and didn't try. He and Phil had stayed up to celebrate with the whisky Justin had taken him. They'd reminisced about the trip down the coast from Suffolk in the summer and how pleasurable that had been for both of them. They'd sat over the supper Phil had cooked. He hadn't questioned why Justin had changed his arrangements to meet up. Then, after getting back from Phil's and congratulating himself on keeping everything under wraps, he'd forgotten to set his phone alarm and had overslept. He'd missed his flight. It wasn't easy to get another so near to Christmas. He'd almost given up but had managed a flight to Helsinki, where he'd caught an even later domestic flight to Kuopio.

So here he was, still awake, still rolled up in his duvet, with Clara still over the other side of the bed and it was nearly time when the twins would wake up ready for Christmas Eve.

Chapter Twenty-One

Phil had been keeping the stove going on Bertha for Justin. To his surprise, on Boxing Day, as he was entertaining Wesley as well as Janine and several old friends living along the Cut, Ling appeared at his door, smiling apologetically.

'Merry Christmas! I'm sorry to trouble you, Phil.'

'No, come on in and join us. You've met Wesley, my grandson, and Janine, his friend.'

Ling had heard about the occasion when Justin had come across those two, body-painting Janine on Bertha, after they'd finished cleaning the boat. Phil quickly went round the table, and everyone nodded and smiled, raising glasses.

'I do apologise, Phil. No, I won't stay. It's only that I'm going to a party later. Justin borrowed my reindeer antlers before Christmas. I wonder if I could inconvenience you to pop over to Bertha and see if they're lying around?'

Phil looked at him searchingly, but picked a key off the hook near the door, gesturing to the watchful guests. 'Of course, lad, and you lot, leave me some booze and don't touch pudding till I'm back. Okay!' With that he strode to the doorway, and beckoning Ling to follow, ran down the outside stairs and walked briskly across to Bertha, where he quickly unlocked the cabin door. Turning on the light, he stepped down into the interior, with Ling close behind.

Glancing quickly around, it was clear how tidy Justin was. Everything was immaculate. There wasn't anything out of place, as Phil had already observed, in stoking the stove. But Ling walked through to the bedroom, where the door was open. The bed was made up ready for Justin's return. Phil watched him moving through the boat, obviously with an idea of where to look. The antlers weren't lying on a chair or on the table. Phil turned round ready to leave, but stopped when he heard Ling scraping about on the bedroom floor.

'Aha, got them! Thought so,' Ling cried, triumphant, appearing from under the bed, antlers waving in mid-air.

'How did you guess they were there? Never have thought to look. Good for you.'

Phil shook his head in admiration, tinged with some bemusement. Who needed antlers to have a good time at a party? Still, he wasn't young anymore. Who knew what was essential?

'Instinct, I'm afraid. Thanks, Phil. I won't keep you.'

'No worries, lad. I'll feed the stove while I'm here.' Then they left, Phil locking up.

After shaking hands with Ling, Phil returned to the chandlery flat, and Ling got on his bike, now sporting a pair of antlers tied over the handlebars, and rode away along the towpath. Anyone observing would have noted his knees seemed at a wide angle from the handlebars. This was a borrowed bike from a neighbour who was obviously smaller. But Ling's thoughts were firmly on Linda. Her outward appearance was deceptively self-contained, and now he worried about her moral integrity. Even deeper was the worry that she still harboured grief from her childhood loss, manifesting itself in her particular adult behaviour. He wanted to talk to her. Again. Would talk to her again.

What she had overlooked during her recent sortie along the canal was the GPS app they had on their phones. He'd known where she was when she failed to return home that night. He'd even got as far as thinking he should intervene, then mentally stepped back, hoping, somewhat naively he now thought, as he swerved around a puddle, that Justin would send her home in a taxi. Goodness knows what state she'd been in. He adjusted the headlight as he rode; the antlers were pushing against the light. This was not a state-of-the-art bike, but he'd avoided the unknown beneath the puddle and a possible puncture. This bike had worked and it had been available.

It was impossible for Ling not to recognise the difficulties Justin was facing in his domestic life. Instinct told him that Justin's fate was probably sealed after that night with his cousin. Night and best part of a day, he corrected. She hadn't returned until the following evening – immaculate, he had to admit, and glowing and evasive at the same time. He hated himself for thinking the worst of them. He doubted Justin would have admitted his time with Linda to Clara during his Christmas in Finland. As for Linda, well, he had absolutely no idea what her feelings might be or what she was up to. He already knew more than he wanted to, but he did know and would have to try to help her. He needed to protect Grandma, if nothing else. She'd be horrified to learn her granddaughter had made a play for an older man. Correction: older married man – or men even? He sighed. That was by no means the worst of it. Ling knew she was occasionally dabbling in cocaine. It was normal for the fashion crowd she mixed with. She may have been high when she'd ended up at Bertha that fateful night and drunk as well, he guessed.

Back in Chinatown, he got the bike in the lift, undoing the reindeer antlers, and returned it to the store at the end of the corridor. He pressed his neighbour's entryphone to report the return of the bike and went on to the family flat. Linda had gone out. Grandma was playing cards with an old lady from along the corridor, with whom she had been friends since she'd arrived in the UK. Ling declined to join them. He was depressed and tired. Passing Linda's room, he stopped and decided to place the antlers on her bed. He realised he was hungry after all and changed his mind about a snack and drink. Passing Grandma, as he went to the fridge, he noticed she was holding the winning card, having given her friends a cursory glance as he'd walked past on his way in. To his surprise, a moment or two later, Grandma admitted defeat, to the pleasure of her old friend, as she quickly gathered up the cards, and suggested some snacks and a hot drink.

Taking a tray to his room, Ling paused again outside Linda's room, then taking his tray on through, sliding it onto the desk, he went back and picked up the antlers. He'd have to be more careful about confronting Linda. He would wait until Grandma was out for a while. He didn't want Linda bouncing in and making a scene. The cocaine issue was something else he didn't know how to handle. Everyone, it seemed, almost everyone, seemed to treat it as normal to use at a party and more or less everywhere else.

How he was going to cope, working with Justin when they started back in the new year, he still had no idea either. His thoughts had been with Clara too. He worried how honourable his concerns might be. Overall, the scenario offered potential for chaos all round.

Justin was still disconnected by his recent experiences, finding the buzz of the others and their obvious excitement as if they inhabited a different planet. Christmas Eve was here. The big day! Zoe had caught the mood at last, for as Carl went to gather up their snowshoes and other equipment in the lobby, there was a tussle. Zoe insisted she wanted to carry her own things ready for the day ahead. Clara, relieved that her daughter had finally decided to join in the spirit of their Christmas, hardly minded the minor disruption. She looked around to find Justin. He was still at the pine table, absently stirring his coffee, his muffin scarcely touched. His preoccupied features worried her. She knew that somehow he was different. For a moment, her ebullient mood fled and a cold inner fear overtook her. Angered that he could still make her feel anything, she turned away to gather up more coats, earmuffs and gloves.

'Justin, if you've finished, bring the bags of presents out from our room. Please!'

He looked up, grinning, but not really connected.

'Justin, we're off. Now! Presents!'

'Yes, yes! Got it!' He scraped his chair back too quickly. The chair toppled over, the seat pad skidded across the wooden floor, stopping short of Den and Liz, as they came through from the passageway, laughing, arm in arm.

'Oops, here we are, son!' Den scooped up the pad and handed it over. Justin nodded, making a face, grinning as he took it back and set it on the seat.

Finally they piled into the hired vehicle, the air almost solid. The overnight temperature had dropped like a stone, causing everyone to feel the rasp of the cold air. Clara threw her things into Grandpop's vehicle, placing a thick cushion on the overheating passenger seat, and called across to Justin to drive the others. Hans stepped in, insisting that, as Justin had had such a difficult time getting to where they now were, it was only fair that he should take it easy. Justin stepped back, sensing that Hans, though he had spoken innocently enough, was as usual being Hans. Silently, he admitted how grim he felt, but not for the reason Hans had suggested.

As they left the road, the farm appeared, standing proud of the surrounding semi-deciduous forest, set on a slight incline, painted rust-red, the corner uprights dark beige, the steep roof slate-grey and almost clear of snow. Somebody had cleared the small area near the side veranda. Liz, ever cautious, glanced up and was relieved to observe that the veranda roof had been swept too. She thought about it for a second or two, deciding someone had leaned out from upstairs windows. This, she thought, was an unusually smart farm.

They parked near one of the barns and everyone piled out. Underfoot it was icy. There were squeals from the children as their feet skidded about. Inside the house there were thick socks for everyone, hanging on named pegs in the side hall, where in the past workers would have left their things as they came in for meals. Clara's heart was suddenly full. There was so much care given to details. Everyone exclaimed their delight as their hosts came forward to greet them in the side hall.

'Greetings to you all! Everyone, please call me Grandpop!' Grandpop threw his arms wide to encompass the huddle in front of him.

Liz observed how tall and erect he was, and appeared to still be muscular. She thought perhaps the outdoor farm life, which must be challenging here, had kept him strong.

His wife came forward, tall also, slender, slightly bent, although she moved freely. Liz recognised her in Clara immediately, for she had similar hair, now completely white, but tied up carelessly, just as Clara often did. Her eyes were pale blue too, twinkling and welcoming. There was something about her, which, though not obvious immediately, made Liz regard her as someone she would enjoy getting to know. No wonder Clara often waxed lyrical about her grandparents, even though Maya, as she insisted everyone called her, was about to celebrate her ninetieth birthday with them.

Once the Christmas greetings were completed, and hot drinks distributed, and cinnamon buns piled up on dishes on the kitchen table and handed round, there was the serious business of deciding the order for taking advantage of the sauna. Grandpop had built it for the family many years before. It was in traditional style: modest, with room for four at any one time. Clara noticed that the wood of the door was new. Wood slats had been replaced over the years as the original benches aged. The roof was in its third life. There was a concession to modernity, with electric heaters replacing the traditional wood burner. Everyone except Justin and Zoe jostled for their turn in the sauna, which heralded the true beginning of this Finnish Christmas. Zoe, shocked, refused to be part of it. Carl sat in with Grandpop and Den. Maya went in with Clara and Liz, then Hans and Anna. Justin, looking ruefully at his determined daughter, decided they must be brave too.

'Zoe, we can do this. If we do it now, we won't be pestered again. Let's pretend we don't care. We're just doing it to keep everyone happy. We aren't really bothered at all.'

He had no idea if it would work. A little later, when everyone else was being shown the huskies being fed in their pen, Zoe, affecting no interest in howling dogs, but truly quite frightened of them, reappeared wrapped up in her long coat.

'Got my cozzie on, Daddy, after all. This is mad!' she harrumphed.

Justin thought quickly: he'd have to manage with his boxers; better not delay. Zoe could at any minute change her mind. So, as the sauna was now vacant, they slid along the path, in uncoordinated fashion, holding hands.

'I'm still not going to roll in the snow!'

Justin laughed. It was such a relief to have something to laugh at. 'Darling, I'm totally with you on that!'

'Good!' she exclaimed.

On their return, Zoe suddenly stopped in her tracks. She whispered, 'Daddy, deer!' She pointed across to the edge of brush, ahead of the forest. There, totally still, was a small reindeer, its breath creating a haze around its heavy head. Zoe declared that it was just like home after all, just with more snow and funny deer.

Once back indoors, it had become Zoe's day. She described how the deer had stretched its neck, shook its antlers, then casually turned and disappeared amongst the undergrowth and into the forest. Not only that, she insisted, but she had helped Daddy brave the sauna. Everything for Zoe was looking up, and later Father Christmas would call to ask if the children had been good. She was confident her report would put her in line for lots of presents.

Carl wasn't to be outdone. He and Grandpop sneaked out when most people were helping Maya in the kitchen. Grandpop showed him where a fishing hole had been bored through the lake ice. They tried a line, waiting patiently, looking down into the icy depths, breath billowing around them. It was already dusk. They had brought a lantern on a pole, which Grandpop had stuck into the ice. At last, there was a tug. It was a small pike. They had photographed it in Carl's gloved mittens, then gently unhooked it and slipped it back to the depths. They returned, taking off their outer gear in the side hall, picking out thick socks from the hooks. As they stuffed their feet into the socks, Carl's questions of why they couldn't bring the pike in to cook required an explanation that pike must be given a chance to grow.

There were scents of nutmeg, cinnamon and other herbs and spices assailing their nostrils. Once in the kitchen, they were handed spicy, hot, fruit drinks. Grown-ups were busy fitting real candles on the tree in the long dining room ready for dinner time, when they would be lit.

Clara found Justin knelt down, setting out the presents beneath the tree. The tree having been finished, the others were elsewhere. She thought, seeing his back bent over as he placed the wrapped gifts, as instructed by Maya, that Justin looked forlorn, out of place here. Unexpectedly, she was suddenly overcome by sadness.

'Jussy, what is it? What's the matter? Really the matter, I mean.'

Wrong-footed by Clara's soft, concerned tone, he nearly blurted out his guilt, but he took a deep breath and sat back on his heels. 'All good here!' he replied, and managed to half turn to give her what he hoped was a reassuring smile.

Clara, unconvinced, sighed. The day moved quickly into late afternoon and the deepest winter darkness.

Everyone except the children relaxed after dinner, waiting for the door knocker. Almost immediately Zoe and Carl were on their feet, held back for a moment by a smiling Maya whilst the visitor called out to them, 'Are there children here?' They were quick to answer, jumping up and down in excitement. 'Have you been good this year?' Even quicker came the answers, then everyone piled into the front hall to see Father Christmas with his sack spread out as he reached down to find presents for Zoe and Carl.

Den thought that Christmas Eve in Finland was turning out to be quite magical. There was still the matter of the children's stockings to be put on their beds, ready for the morning. He hoped Justin had done his bit in that regard. Personally, he wasn't much bothered by presents, but it was fun to watch the handing out from under the tree and the exclamations, genuine or otherwise, at the surprises unwrapped. The Great Danes had put their gifts under the Suffolk tree for when the Brits got back, which caused an unnecessary imbalance he thought, for they weren't returning, but staying on for New Year, which meant that during the evening they would receive more gifts than the Brits. What nonsense, if you stopped to think, so he didn't – and accepted another unfamiliar liqueur, before the visitors returned to their rented house.

The twins awoke to find that Father Christmas had found time to return and leave them stockings filled with goodies. Father Christmas had taken advice from previous years and had left nothing which would create excessive noise. With instructions to stay in their room until called, they amused themselves until around six, when, throwing all caution to the wind, they landed on their parents' bed, squealing with excitement. Fortunately for them all, Justin had considered what an idiot he was and had unravelled his duvet during the night. Clara had allowed her hand to reach across to him. Smiling in response, he raised his open duvet in invitation to his side of the bed. The strong nightcaps they'd enjoyed once back at their rented house had given Clara the courage to insist he reach across to her. Obligingly, he wriggled over. They were both exhausted by recent events. Clara seemed content to settle into her favourite spoon position. Justin was relieved she settled in behind him, partly for the lack of her wayward hair in his face and his chaste condition remained unnoticed. Eventually, they fell asleep, which was how the twins found them.

Christmas Day they all decided to snow-walk across to the farm. It was a later start than on Christmas Eve morning and the reluctant dawn was approaching on the horizon by the time they set off for the half-kilometre walk. The sky was enormous and still full of stars against a fading navy. They would all breakfast together to celebrate Maya's birthday. She had insisted on no presents. Later there were plans to visit Kristen, Maya's granddaughter, Clara's cousin, for a celebration lunch. Kristen was the daughter of their son Affried, Anna's brother, who had died many years previously. Clara had explained on the walk over to the farm that it was a subject no one discussed. It was to be a joyful day, with no sadness permitted. They were invited for a celebration lunch, travelling by dog sleds and snowmobiles.

Over breakfast, it was decided who would travel the five kilometres with whom. Hans had experience of mushing, so he and Grandpop would take both dog sleds with an adult and one child each. Maya and Grandpop were caring for some neighbours' huskies and had previously arranged to exercise them whilst the neighbours were in Tenerife. They would borrow a snowmobile to match their own, so Justin and Clara, and Den and Liz would drive across with those, after a short practice turn around the farm.

Kristen's American husband, Arnold, worked as an astronomer, based mostly in Helsinki, and sidelined for the tourist industry. Anna talked of how he would be able to suggest when they were most likely to see an aurora, which was something to do with charged particles from the sun reacting with atoms in the upper atmosphere. Hans nodded earnest agreement.

'Big green sweeps across the sky, Carl. Sometimes blue too, as if controlled by an amazing magician.' Maya's faded eyes shone as she explained the lights to the children. She was never less than astonished by this wonder, even after a lifetime.

'But, Maya, isn't it frightening? I'm not sure. Supposing it falls down on us?'

Maya took both of Zoe's hands, explaining that the aurora was only light effects and nothing solid. She handed Zoe a marzipan fruit from the tree to take her mind off it.

'Maya, can I have a chocolate one, please? I don't like those.' Carl, not bothered by the idea of a green swirling sky, was concerned he might miss out on a tree favour. He pointed at Zoe's almost finished treat.

'Of course, darling – here.' After that, Maya shooed them off. It was time to dress up against the cold.

Justin recalled, looking back on that day, that it was the best – the best he could remember for a long time. Kristen met them with garlands for their hair. The men joined in, wearing the strange adornments with considerable aplomb. Den voiced a popular opinion when he said they were much more fun than paper hats, though a bit itchy.

In bed that night, their skins glowing from the extreme cold on their journey back, there seemed space in their hearts to be close. Justin and Clara made love, gently, tenderly, taking their time, as if in fact all the time in the world was theirs, then Justin slept peacefully, with Clara cradled in his arms. Next morning, he reviewed his earlier concerns about his visit. Now, suddenly, there hardly seemed enough time to enjoy their surroundings and their newly rekindled warmth for each other.

Chapter Twenty-Two

Justin had turned his phone off. Whilst in the bathroom, he decided he needed to check for any messages. There was a long list of texts from Linda, urging him to contact her urgently, which immediately filled him with foreboding. He wiped them. There was a voicemail he didn't recognise, and he listened to it. Stunned, he listened again. 'This is Mr Zhu speaking. I am in St Petersburg, visiting my wife's family. Please return my call as soon as you can. Mr Sharaf has been in contact with me from Canary Wharf.' Justin sat on the toilet, thinking back to the drinks do at work, when Mr Sharaf had spoken to him. He couldn't phone from the bathroom. He decided he'd have to talk to Clara about the voicemail. He'd ring from the bedroom, where the reception might be better. He took a deep breath; he knew he couldn't ignore Mr Zhu. The cost was immediately evident.

Suddenly, Christmas was over. Clara was furious with him for allowing their fractured real lives to taint this idyll, pointing at him with an accusing finger, 'This man will want to see you whilst you are both in the vicinity. It'll save a fortune for the company. Do what you like, but you will regret it, I promise!'

Flying back to Helsinki, Clara congratulated herself on how well she had navigated the celebrations, without giving way to her feelings of disappointment and anger with Justin. She hadn't wanted to ruin everything for the old folks, or for the children, but it hadn't been easy. She even made an effort now to smile as Justin touched her arm to attract her attention.

'I'm really sorry about flying on to St Petersburg when we land. Christmas doesn't mean much to some of our international staff, I'm afraid.' He shook his head and placed his hands, palms up. 'What can you do? And knowing I'd be fairly close anyway. Sorry,' he added lamely.

'You really are a prize.' She paused as Carl looked up at her terse tone. 'What about the rest of the children's holidays? I'm supposed to do everything, I suppose.'

'Well, I can only apologise. I doubt you'll believe me, but I did tell you as soon as I got the message. It's about expansion and about promotion too.' He did sound a bit whiney, he thought.

'Oh, you'll love that, then.' She whispered her response to avoid any more worried looks from Carl who had settled into a game. However, there was no mistaking her waspish tone.

'I'll be back ASAP. There'll still be time to go to the panto and perhaps go with Dad and Liz and the kids to the ice rink again. They did so well here.' He gestured towards the scene from the cabin window, where lights were already beginning to puncture the black, showing an imminent descent to Helsinki Airport. 'I've got a two-hour delay for my flight, so I can see you through to your waiting area. Think you've got about forty minutes, so not long to wait, and Dad and Liz will help.'

'Don't patronise me. If you aren't coming with us, then as far as I'm concerned, you can –' Here, she stopped herself. The angry whispering was causing Carl to look up again.

Den and Liz had got the gist of the latest difficulties and had talked briefly. Liz had tried not to give an opinion. Prior to leaving the rented house, she'd sat on their bed, watching Den throwing his stuff into his bag. She had stripped the bed as requested on the list of instructions pinned to the back of the door. She stroked the bed, thoughtfully. She was thinking how brief and wonderful their Christmas was, and how she enjoyed being part of Den's life, but she sensed that her loyalty to Clara was pulling her away from Den's enthusiasm for his son's ambitions.

Now here they all were, standing in Helsinki Airport about to say goodbye to Justin.

'Dad, I have to do this. I'll be back in a couple of days. Would you mind walking Arthur, please? Fetch him from Tom's?'

Den stopped abruptly, nearly causing Liz to trip. Mouth open, he was momentarily not connecting home with the airport. Then, grinning, he gave Justin a friendly shove, 'Son, you never know, this could be your big chance. Bit extraordinary, isn't it?'

'Huh, very,' Clara added dryly, turning to Den. 'Exactly what kind of big chance did you have in mind, Den? Another move perhaps? Even farther away from me, from us?' Her anger at Justin was palpable; this recent change of plans was too much to bear. No one understood. She was supposed to fit in and she had no desire to. Her face was burning now. She scraped her hair away from her face as a solitary tear fell to her further annoyance. Liz observing, not sure how to help, was surprised that no one was giving this small drama even a moment's notice. Perhaps, she thought sadly, this wasn't a rare scene in any airport after the Christmas festivities. There really wasn't time to appease Clara. They needed to make their way to the next departure lounge. Justin kissed the children and hugged Den and Liz. Clara shoved Justin away from her, moving off quickly as she pushed her trolley and called Zoe and Carl to follow.

He watched them hurry away, waving reassuringly, feeling regret that Ling had warned him to be ready when a meeting was called and be sure to be available. He'd suggested the call would be in the new year. He wondered why it had come early? Without the nod from Ling, he'd certainly have apologised and explained that he was unable to attend a meeting over the break. But really, would he? After all, St Petersburg wasn't far away. He'd be there in time for supper.

Justin landed in a light snowfall, with no delays. It was bitterly cold, with wind whipping the flakes sideways across the passengers as they disembarked. He'd spent the flight looking at the latest texts Linda had sent him, before deciding what to do next. If she were to be believed, their time together mattered to her, but if he were honest, he was still confused. He couldn't get the memory of her into any order in his mind and hadn't answered her. There was the fear of discovery, of which he was ashamed. No less was the knowledge that he hadn't wanted to resist her advances, even knowing, at least that night, that she was drunk on arrival. Then he'd wondered if she were having some sort of laugh at his expense, but if so, he'd been a willing fall guy. At last, making a decision, he texted a reply quickly. It wouldn't send, so he left it on draft to send once he was in the hotel.

He checked the address of the hotel on his phone. He'd already started on a Beginner's Russian app. Russian was not a language he'd previously given any thought to. There was to be someone to meet him at the airport. The reality wasn't quite as he'd hoped, however. On looking around, he was surprised at the shabbiness of his new surroundings and the unexpected stuffiness in the air. Striding towards the exit, he scanned the few people listlessly standing there. After he got his eye in and concentrated, he saw his name on a card held up by a burly, fur-hatted, heavily coated and grey-bearded man. Justin approached him to shake hands and introduce himself in an attempt at Russian. The man, unsmiling, looked at his outstretched hand as if uncomprehending.

Without speaking, he gestured for Justin to follow. How could this man be sure Justin was who he said he was? How did he know where this giant of a man straight off the steppes was going to take him? But he followed, not knowing what else to do. Steppes Man was the driver, obviously, he reassured himself, hired to collect a medium-height, dark-haired European who said he was Justin Kerr, if Steppes Man understood tourist Russian. Justin had expected a company man with whom he would perhaps exchange a few pleasantries on the way to their car. He almost laughed at his perceived idea of his own importance. He should have been grateful his name hadn't been in Cyrillic on the board, in which case, he'd still be wandering up and down the airport. He experimented again, hopefully, with his downloaded beginner's Russian, which caused a dismayed grunt from the driver.

The blast of freezing air which hit them as they left the heat of the airport caused the driver to pull his duffel coat tighter and smack his hat down lower on his head over his wiry grey hair, ear flaps hanging. Justin, momentarily breathless, the freezing air hitting his lungs, hurting him, wished he had a scarf to cover his mouth and he regretted deciding to pack his own hat in his bag. Still, once his bag was thrown in the boot and he was directed to the back seat, he was out of the extreme cold, and the anonymous driver set off without any concession to his gears, to the ice beneath them, or his passenger. But they were on their way.

He was already weary. Leaving Pulkovo Airport behind them, he'd checked on his phone the distance between the airport and St Petersburg. There was still a twenty-three-kilometre drive into St Petersburg before they would reach his hotel. It had been a difficult day emotionally. After Justin gave up trying to get the driver to turn his wild music down, he pushed the divider as far across as it would go. His thinking numbed, he dozed for a while, cocooned inside the vehicle as it bumped along, nothing much to be seen through the cab window, except snow sliding and sticking.

He was jostled awake by a sharp swerve and loud expletives from the front of the cab. The vehicle steadied. Now determined to remain awake, Justin's thoughts drifted, hovering around Clara and her life away from him. She'd made it clear over the months that moving wasn't a part of any plans she might have. Correction: he wasn't sure she had any plans at all, other than staying at Keeper's Cottage. She did have that new business her parents had purchased for her. He shook his head. It still smacked of subversion to him. How that would pan out was yet to be seen. Clara said she was part of the community and knew everyone, even though she didn't mix a great deal, and that the children were settled, which was another weapon of hers.

Sitting here in this strange limbo, he allowed himself to wonder if she might look for someone else, or had already met someone. Well, if what she kept on about was what she really wanted, this new wonder would have to be a locally based, unambitious prat: a dickhead in fact. His assessment was not generous but gave him momentary pleasure. He sat upright as the car swerved again, throwing him, within the confines of the seatbelt, towards the divider. Straightening up, he resigned himself to the fact that Clara's partner was unlikely to be him, not in the end, bearing in mind the unambitious part didn't fit him any longer. It wasn't even the recent messes he'd made of his flights over Christmas. No, his thinking was, of course, triggered by the events on the houseboat with Linda. Who knew if he and Linda might have something together? The desperate need to be honest with himself, stemming from that event, made his gut churn.

He hadn't faced anything properly during the year. He had fooled himself, imagining he and Clara would ultimately find a way to live together again, even if he continued to work in London. Recalling again her constant plea that he should work from home, freelance translating, nearly made him snort in frustration. Now the possibility that he might be asked to move again and that he was intrigued by the prospect, would anger – had already angered – her further. Chances were it wouldn't be anywhere rural, or even in the UK.

The old Merc hit another rough bump. He gasped and the driver swore, steadied the car and they drove on. They hit another bump, and his thoughts bumped with him to the twins. It was hardly surprising they loved visiting him at the houseboat, but it was only that, a visit, he was perfectly aware. If he and Clara had found a proper home, say in Greenwich or nearby, he was still convinced they could all have made a go of it. There were good schools, lots of open spaces, and the nearby excitement of the city and the West End. Now he might be moving again, so perhaps his idea hadn't been so good after all. But he might have been happy to stay at Canary Wharf if the family had moved to Greenwich. Perhaps he wouldn't have been so eager to try more new experiences. Who knew? Still, it was academic now. Clara would be swift to point out the shortcomings in his plan to move them to London in the first place, should there be another opportunity of change for him.

It was, after all, he thought, now maudlin from cold and tiredness, normal for the mother to bring the children up, if it came to it. He was shivering. Somehow one of the bumps had stopped the heater. He pulled his coat tighter around him. Now very tired, he was guilty of allowing his fears to run away with him. If the worst happened, what he wanted was to avoid anything which might add to the twins' anguish. He couldn't imagine working in some foreign country and coping with two small children on his own, should that unlikely scenario come about. Money bought many services, he was totally aware, but, looking at himself with a considerable element of dislike, he knew he didn't want to have to embark on such a route. Holidays he would enjoy. Snorting loudly at his own weasel thoughts brought a sharp glare from the driver's mirror.

Back in his interior world, he thought of Dad. Dad was already settled next door to the cottage in his new lodge and busy putting down roots. It was early days, but he seemed happier than he'd been for years, pottering about, helping with the twins and cooking considerably better meals than Clara ever had, or desired to. Then, of course, there was Liz, hovering ever closer.

Clara's past, as she had recounted to him one night when they were still new to each other, lying in his bed in his arms, now weighed heavily on him. He could picture her, a quiet girl, loving the countryside and not happy in the city, at school in Odense. When not booked into after-school clubs during term time, during the holidays she was sent off to Finland, outside Kuopio. Her grandparents, though busy, often included her in their day. Other times she'd had the freedom of the forest and lakes, with other children around. And there was always, in summer at least, foraging for herbs and berries, he thought, wryly. It was a pastime that had never appealed to him.

Watching Clara over Christmas, even though there was tension between them, he could see it was almost as if she was letting a breath out slowly, her limbs relaxing. One day, after they'd congregated at the farm and had coffee and snifters, as the oldies called it, the twins went out on the lake with Den and Liz, whilst he set off for a walk to the forest, having accustomed himself to snowshoes. He'd seen a barn door open and decided to peep inside. He knew that Clara's grandparents were in the process of having some farm buildings restored to let out in summer when the days were very long and the weather mild. He was momentarily startled to see that Clara was inside the barn with a tape measure, pacing out, then stopping and turning. When she saw him, she was obviously flustered. He was unsure whether it was because of his presence or because of what she was doing.

'Can I help?' he had offered, when what he really wanted to say was something along the lines of, what on earth are you doing?

'No! No, thanks. Just trying to work out what Poppa was on about.'

She'd scrabbled the tape measure into a small bundle and shoved it in her pocket, closing a notepad as she brushed past him. She didn't have snowshoes on, so her boots sank awkwardly as she attempted to hurry back to the farmhouse. He remembered he'd stood and watched her for a while, then continued on his walk into the beginnings of a rose-coloured sunset. When he'd mentioned again later, out of curiosity, what she was doing, she'd made some vague comment about helping Poppa. He still wondered what that had been about. A random fear was that she might take the twins to Finland, to her grandparents, which he just as swiftly dismissed as unrealistic ramblings on a difficult day.

He shook his head. The snow had stopped. Justin stared out. They had arrived. Trees all along the city roadside were sparkling with lights. It was very cheering. Light at last. St Petersburg at last. He'd survived the nightmare drive! The car slewed into the kerb. Justin slipped forward on the seat. They had reached the hotel. The driver gestured to him to get out. Stiff as he was, and freezing too, he managed to scrabble himself together, opened the door and stepped out into fresh snow. Expecting the driver to get out too, he waited on the pavement. But the driver hooted his horn and gesticulated for Justin to go to the rear and retrieve his bag. Skidding to the boot, he did so and stuffed his rouble notes, which he'd intended for Steppes Man, back in his pocket and slid awkwardly towards the hotel entrance.

Once inside the heated building, skin burning from the cold, and no longer being jostled about by road conditions exacerbated by Steppes Man's driving, Justin took a deep breath of relief. Here was normality. He began to feel less disorientated and made his way to reception. This was a good international hotel. He saw the many languages offering a welcome. After signing in and having his passport copied by a dark-haired, dark-eyed, middle-aged man, who spoke impeccable English, he became aware of a young woman farther along at the reception counter, observing him closely. He looked up, catching her gaze.

Tired and shaken as he still was by the rough treatment inflicted by his taxi driver, he was tempted to be childish and ask her what she was looking at. Her broad Russian face broke into a beam. She nodded and beckoned him along the console. He saw her name badge. She was Helena. Somewhat sharply, not knowing or caring if English was in her remit, he addressed her.

'Helena, isn't it?' He softened his greeting with a tired smile, as he stated the obvious. All he could think of was a hot shower and a large brandy, the winter staple of St Petersburg, according to the old folks. And food.

'Mr Zhu asked me to hand this to you, sir. Please enjoy your stay with us, sir.' She beamed again. There was no hint of irony.

Somewhat mollified, he managed another smile, his lips sticking to his teeth. He gave her a nod and stuffed the envelope in his pocket. As he made his way towards the lift, he was offered assistance with his bag by a bellhop in a uniform reminiscent of an old American movie. He wore a pillbox cap and a jacket with two rows of brass buttons. The gold stripes down his trousers matched the gold rim of his pillbox. Thinking that the boy was probably one step up from slave labour, Justin accepted and they entered the lift. On the fourth floor they got out and the bellhop trundled his bag along a well-lit, carpeted corridor. Using his card key, Justin entered his room. He had two one-hundred notes ready and passed them to the child-sized hand. The boy slipped the notes into a pocket, nodded acceptance, saluted and departed.

Justin dropped his coat on the chair by the heavily curtained window and collapsed across the vast bed. He couldn't remember when he had last eaten, but didn't have the energy to go down to one of the restaurants. He scanned room service. Pulling himself up, he rang down to reception, ordering caviar on blinis, a steak, some pastries and a pot of coffee. He'd take brandy from the minibar. He got his phone out and texted home to report that he'd arrived and where he was, not that Clara would be interested in her current frame of mind. He copied the information to Dad, who would be. He sent love to the twins, then, at last, sent his message to Linda. Done it, he thought. There was a knock on the door. He dragged himself up, picked up his coat, and remembering Mr Zhu's note, he removed it from his coat pocket, the envelope now crumpled, then opened the door. The bellhop had returned. Justin gestured towards a side table and Justin handed over another tip. Four hundred roubles down, but less than a fiver all told. He'd dropped

Mr Zhu's note onto the bed. As soon as he'd eaten, and gathered himself, he resolved to read it.

'Thank you, sir!' The boy saluted and turned sharply, marching off along the corridor, grinning to himself.

That boy will go far and his English is better than my Russian, Justin smiled to himself. This was a much more positive experience than with the taxi driver. He seriously considered that the drive had almost been like a test. He wondered idly if he had passed.

Chapter Twenty-Three

Clara had her feet up on the coffee table, a glass of red wine in front of her, the bottle already almost empty. Her long hair fell around her shoulders. After she twiddled it back into a topknot, pushing a pin into it, she wriggled back against the cushions and let out a long sigh. She wished she were still in Finland with Maya and Poppa. Her lucky parents had stayed on to visit other relatives too. Oh well. Den wandered in with Arthur at his heels, now calm after having greeted everyone with his usual slobbering delight.

'Tom said Arthur got a rabbit and brought it in.'

'Oh, God, I hope they managed to get it off him.'

'Not in time, sadly. Christmas Day too. Their mum was staying and cleared up. She sounds a character,' Den added, with admiration.

'I'm surprised the boys didn't jump to it. Hope nothing got spoiled, apart from the rabbit, that is.'

She giggled, surprising Den, but then he thought, this was booze speaking and was surprised she'd got stuck in so soon. He would join her, but fancied a spirit. He looked around. Since he'd moved next door, he'd noticed alcohol had reappeared on Clara's dresser. He wouldn't take it personally, he decided, though the cottage had been dry for most of his stay. He now nodded towards the whisky. Seeing him looking hopefully at the bottle, she waved to help himself. What the hell, she thought, everything's fallen apart – let's all get drunk. She took another swig, turning to Den.

'Den, d'you know what Justin's really up to?'

That was unexpected. Den gathered himself, sipped carefully at the delicate flavours of his whisky, looking thoughtfully down into the amber liquid, trying to work out what to say, with least damage all round. 'Um, well, no. Whatever, I'm sure it's meant for the best.' He paused, as Clara snorted very loudly.

'Ha! You can do better than that, Den. Where's your inner man gone all of a sudden? Be tough, honest. It's over for Jussy and me. Right?'

Christ, not for him to say, that was for sure. He shook his head in disbelief at her. She wouldn't move anywhere and Jus was ambitious. What could they do? Knock their heads together perhaps? How could he tell his beloved daughter-in-law that it was obvious she wasn't totally committed to his ambitious son? It was most unlike Den, but he couldn't think of anything light-hearted to offer. So he looked down at Arthur and pulled his ears, gently.

'Urgh! I knew it. You won't face up to what's happening in front of your eyes, Den! You could have made a difference with Justin. He sort of worships you. Sort of.'

Feeling damned with faint praise, Den shook his head. He hadn't expected that. 'No, don't think so, sweetheart. If only! I have – how shall I put it? – too many shortcomings.' He was thinking of his son's many disapproving glances over the years connected to him returning home late often, drunk on occasion, or returning not at all sometimes. There would be more reasons if he could think clearly.

She dismissed his offering. 'Oh, you know what I mean.'

Den thought there was little to lose by being honest with her about his own working life. 'Yes, but my job took me everywhere, Clara. Lola stayed in Wimbledon term time but would come out to where we were doing shoots anywhere in the world. Sometimes we booked a tutor for Justin if the shoot was running over. It was good for him and it meant we all had an adventure. Then, when I'd finished the contract, I'd go back to Wimbledon. But Lola supported what I was doing. She got it, Clara.' He tried to resist showing any frustration he felt. At least she could make more effort to visit the narrowboat. The twins loved to visit. He wondered, but didn't dare ask, how she expected to run the household if they split up. He knew from Liz that the business was only just breaking even and her parents had financed that for her. Ah, Anna and Hans, he thought. He had noticed the three of them with heads together once or twice when they were in Finland. She was talking again.

'Huh! Well, good for Lola.'

Clara took another sip. Her glass was almost empty and Den was beginning to feel she was near an empty glass with regard to his sympathy too. She seemed almost oblivious to her audience now.

'I did like her Den, truly. She was lovely to me, but she was very different from me too. Justin should understand that I need to be rooted. My upbringing sort of disorientated me. He really shouldn't be thinking of going off anywhere.' She stifled a small sob.

Den ground his teeth in impatience. His conclusion was that Clara hadn't quite grown up, poor girl; poor Justin too. There Justin was, poised to do well at work, with his marriage slipping away from him at the same time.

Den was exhausted now and needed to get his head down. They had been travelling all day. He got up, stretched and moved his back carefully. Snow-walking and skating had caused him to become acquainted with muscles he'd forgotten he had. He went over to Clara, who was staring at the empty wine bottle. In spite of their difficult conversation, he felt compassion for her. He gently kissed the top of her head goodnight, and taking his glass to the kitchen, went on across the lane to his lodge.

Arthur seemed to think he was needed with Clara. He shuffled to her and lay across her feet and for once she didn't push him away. Depressed, slightly drunk and tired as she was, she was startled when Zoe suddenly appeared before her, dragging her oversized teddy.

'Carl was shouting in his sleep,' she pouted.

It was typical of Zoe to cover her back by incriminating Carl. Clara wondered if she'd have done the same if she hadn't been an only child. There was another reason for Zoe's appearance, which Zoe immediately made clear.

'Mummy, Maya said to Grandad Den you want to live in Finland. We aren't going to, are we?'

Now fully awake and seeing the fear in Zoe's eyes, Clara hugged her. Den hadn't said anything, but deep in the recesses of her mind, where wishes resided, was the barn at Grandpop's farm. She held Zoe before her, pushing her curls gently from her face. 'The oldies just have fancies of their own, darling. They would like everyone near to them. Silly oldies!'

Zoe looked searchingly at Clara, and perceiving reassurance, snuggled in.

Justin's morning was free. Mr Zhu had requested his presence in the penthouse suite at three o'clock, smart casual dress requested. Justin had smiled to himself. He couldn't help thinking how ridiculous the dress code was. He assumed that Mr Zhu knew he'd diverted straight from a Finnish family Christmas. Was this a clue as to what kind of man he might be confronted with, what generation even? He dismissed any idea of trying to figure out whom he would be meeting from the brief but exact communication. Regardless, he thought, it would be fun to do a bit of shopping. He'd heard prices were higher than at home, but what the hell! That's what he'd thought in very different circumstances only a few days ago: what the hell. He took a deep breath and quickly looked at his phone. No new messages from Linda. The flurry had ceased. He thought he was relieved. He would have to confront what issues had arisen from what he supposed was his deplorable behaviour. He hesitated, turned and looked out at the morning dark. No, he couldn't squirm out of it. Somehow that mess would need resolving but, obviously, not from here. He endeavoured to dismiss his domestic plight from his immediate concerns, dropped the phone on the bed and reviewed his scant wardrobe.

He already had a grey cashmere sweater from Dad and Liz and a Paul Smith white button-down shirt from Clara and the kids. He examined Maya and Poppa's offering of a silk knitted tie. It was in shades of grey and very classy. He was being coordinated from afar. He looked down with a critical eye at the comfy black cords he wore for travelling. They were baggy, definitely an item to improve on then. Unlike most of his friends, with the exception perhaps of Ling, whose name he quickly pushed to one side, he found clothes shopping to be a pleasure. Now he fancied narrow trousers – some moleskins, or wool, in black would be good, with a bit of stretch, perhaps. Then, looking down at his feet, he was reminded he only had boots with him. Clean boots now, since he'd left them for valeting, but boots nevertheless. He should look out shoes too, if there was time. He'd decided against a jacket already. He'd observed from the hotel lounge a preponderance of leather cuffs and elbows on sturdy tweeds; there were some double collars too. He thought the look was Austrian and didn't fancy spending a small fortune on a jacket he might not wear again. Neither did a suit seem necessary; the expensive sweater, shirt and tie would suffice. He'd like shoes, but definitely trousers.

Now with a plan, and once muffled up against the heave of pedestrians shifting along ice-packed sidewalks, he ventured out into the weakening gloom to join them. He paused to take in his surroundings. The lights

246

he'd noticed in the trees on his journey into the city ran up everywhere, he now saw, over buildings and statues, along the facades of shops, around the market stalls, and were reflected in the new fall of snow. It was a glittering fairyland. The twins would love it. Everyone would love it. He took some shots, swivelling around on his heels, careful not to slip or obstruct other shoppers as he used the video on his phone. Then, gloves back on, hat pulled well down, he started along Nevsky Prospekt to look out for Gostiny Dvor, the much admired, not-to-be-missed department store, according to the hotel's reception. Then a fleeting thought occurred: was a backhander involved at the hotel to direct tourists to an agreed shop? He felt a boot sliding from under him, and concentrating more on his foot placement, he proceeded more carefully along the sidewalk, trying to take in some of the sights he was passing. In spite of the history of Communism, it seemed that many churches had survived. There was one in particular he was to look out for, but for now he was concentrating on shopping.

Once he'd pushed through into Gostiny Dvor, he was assailed by heat, perfume and piped Cossack music. After pausing to remove his hat and undo his coat, he braced himself before the store guide, which was written in multiple languages. As he found the shoe department first, he changed his priorities and, after scanning the display, pointed to black lace-ups with a toecap. Quite retro, he thought, pleased how comfortable they felt. He disregarded the price. Then he wandered into Men's Fashion and was guided to a row of trousers. There were some big sizes. He thought of Steppes Man, but couldn't picture him in this setting. He found some trousers in fine black wool, fully lined, and good and narrow. They were a bit long but he bought them, thinking he could tuck under the hems until he got home. Ah, home! He suddenly stopped in the middle of the transaction. The assistant looked at him uncertainly. 'Cash, sir, or card?' The accent was thick. Wow, he thought, did he look English? More to the point, who would carry this amount in roubles? He pulled himself together and entered his card. So carried away had he been, he'd totally forgotten the twins. He asked for the toy department, but having taken the lift as directed, and seen the display of complicated, very expensive, bulky items – more like oligarch territory, he'd thought – he decided to leave.

In one of the excellent markets he purchased some Russian dolls and fur hats for the twins and then, after hesitating, decided on a hat for Clara. After accepting the gift-wrapped items, he was suddenly very thirsty. There was a stall where coffee laced with Armenian brandy spurred him on to explore in his diminishing time window. Now daylight had won, but the air was misty and remained bitterly cold.

Still guided by advice from reception, he found the Church of the Saviour on Spilled Blood near to the hotel. Justin, curious as to what that name might reveal, stood before this building, reminiscent of St Basil's onion-domed cathedral in Red Square. He stood amongst hoar-breathed tourists, all booted and hatted, staring up, snapping and filming, taking in the colourfully decorated building. Although he'd seen pictures in his guide book, he was momentarily overwhelmed. Bottom-lit as this hefty edifice was, it had, contrarily, an ethereal look as if the whole thing might slip up into the atmosphere and be lost in the blue misty light. He left his bags with an attendant at the entrance and, accepting headphones, switched to English. This strange, overly ornate building had been constructed on the order of Tsar Alexander III after the murder of his father, Alexander II, in 1881. Justin paused to take in the exotic interior, built to memorialise an assassinated Tsar, the voice in his headphones told him, as he pondered what the Tsar might have been like. He followed the few other tourists as they paused to admire the grandeur around them. Looking at his watch, he cut away and hurried back to retrieve his parcels, thanking the attendant, then made his way on to the hotel.

Frustrated at having so little time now that his exploring appetite had been whetted, he determined to return. St Petersburg really wasn't the place to rush things. He dismissed the Hermitage Museum for another time. He would come back, but in warm weather with good daylight. He wondered who would be with him, if anyone. He'd like to see the ballet, to see everything.

Once back in his room, the poor daylight outside was already losing its grip to murky dusk, as he quickly unpacked his shopping. He'd been tempted by Cossack trousers with coordinating waistcoat for New Year's Eve, just for fun, but in the end he was glad he'd stuck to his plan. His credit card had already suffered considerably and he didn't expect anyone to meet him from Norwich when he landed, which could mean a long, expensive taxi ride, if he couldn't hire a car.

Checking his watch, he considered he just had time to order from room service and chose spicy dumplings in gravy and a small samovar of black tea. Whilst he waited, he removed price tags, hesitated over having a shower, but after sniffing himself critically, decided it was not necessary and no time anyway, so changed into his new gear. He gave himself a cursory look in the wardrobe mirror, pushing his dark hair back. His hair was still a good colour, although a pity it was getting thinner, but pointless to dwell on that. His body shape had improved, he saw, standing sideways to reassure himself that his stomach really had gone down since he'd been in the gym after recovering from that grim accident.

The food arrived with the young bellhop, for whom he found another tip. He hungrily devoured the excellent dumplings, a large napkin tucked into his new shirt, then poured himself water for the tea. He checked his watch. Five minutes, just time to clean his teeth, then he needed to go. Justin hadn't had time to ponder at length on the events which had unfolded so far. But here he was in the lift to the penthouse executive suite, and the mysterious Mr Zhu, on his way to find out why he was here instead of settling in at home. Ling had said to agree to a meeting, if he was contacted, and had advised that as Justin was a natural linguist, and the right age, to follow through if he was curious. Well here he was: following through and curious.

He knocked on the oversized polished birch door, which swung inward immediately, held open by a rotund, gleamingly bald-headed middle-aged man, Chinese, as expected, wearing a beige suit, with a pale blue open-necked shirt. Justin couldn't resist checking the footwear. Oh dear, he thought, suede safari boots. Still, Justin noted the smart casual ethic.

'Thank you so much for taking the trouble, Mr Kerr,' Mr Zhu greeted him, as he was ushered in with an expansive gesture, a wide smile showing small, very white teeth, his narrow eyes disappearing into convivial slits.

'Not at all,' Justin murmured, stepping into the vast room, conscious of heavy, draped curtains, undrawn across blank windows across the far wall. Now it was completely dark, and Justin wondered why anyone would leave curtains open after dark. It looked so bleak. But his attention was immediately pulled back to the present and the reason why he was in this enormous room.

'I'll get straight to the point of this meeting, Mr Kerr, if I may, bearing in mind I've disrupted your holiday.' Mr Zhu had already observed that this Mr Kerr wasn't entirely concentrating. He was now watching him carefully. It had been a very convenient opportunity to get a look at this prospect, from the company's point of view. Mr Zhu was interested to see how this man's intelligence and apparent keenness recorded in the file before him, matched up to his physical presence and responses. He liked, no enjoyed, meeting potential trainees to his team out of their normal environment. Often he would glean considerable knowledge by practising this unconventional method.

'Please.' Justin smiled back from the easy chair he'd been ushered to. To Justin's astonishment, Mr Zhu immediately sidetracked to explain why he was in St Petersburg. Mr Zhu was a birdwatcher. He had spent years holidaying at salt marshes across the globe, which had led him to the vast lands adjacent to the north of St Petersburg. During one such trip, he'd met his Russian wife, Ludmilla – here Mr Zhu paused and smiled – hence the reason he now spent his Christmases here, when they would endeavour to escape to the snowy wastes to capture a sight of some rare bird passing through. Though, he hastened to add, May or June was the best time. There was a pause, and Justin waited.

'We've been to your Norfolk Broads. History very interesting!'

To which Justin nodded, commenting that the Broads were peaceful and that good sailing could be enjoyed there, as he tried to recall what the history was. It came to him: something to do with peat extraction. Fortunately, Mr Zhu continued at speed, as Justin continued to wait, smiling and nodding as he felt appropriate. He had relaxed a little, wondering if this was some ploy to catch him out. They had been speaking in English so far, following Mr Zhu's lead, so he decided to stay calm and await the moment when the subject might revert to the reason why they were both in this oversized room during his Christmas break. Just as he was beginning to think he was wasting his time, Mr Zhu caught him off guard.

'How's your Bantu, then, Mr Kerr? No, I don't need you to answer!' He rolled his head back, his eyes disappearing as he laughed heartily, enjoying Justin's efforts to look anything but nonplussed. 'No, really. But it will have a small bearing, eventually. No.' Mr Zhu steamed on. 'What we are in the process of is assembling and training up an extended team in Guangzhou to then be transferred to Nairobi, where we are expanding and developing our facilities to accommodate a Chinese clientele.' Now Justin was fully alert. Mr Zhu continued, nodding, 'There is the railroad and where there is no railway, roads are being financed, as you probably already know, by the Chinese. The official language in Kenya is English, as you will be aware. However, we expect our staff to be fluent in Cantonese or Mandarin for our clients.'

'I understand, sir.' Justin swallowed, drawing himself up in his seat. Was he to be part of this?

'Good, I'm glad you understand!' He chuckled. 'We've looked at your progress.' He tapped the slim file before him. 'This is an informal meeting, obviously. However, if you are interested in such a venture, I do expect you to give some indication today. Then, once home, discuss with your wife. I understand you have a young family? Everything will proceed with due haste in the new year, once we are all back at the office.'

'I am very interested, sir. This sounds an amazing opportunity.' He paused, 'Of course, I shall need to know the details. As you say, I do have a young family.' Justin hated having to mention this setback, as he saw it, but considered that other staff must have families too. Mr Zhu had placed rimless spectacles on the end of his nose to check his notes. He now looked over the rims.

'No family in Guangzhou, Mr Kerr. You will only be there for three months, then a fortnight's break, before being ensconced in a gated community on the outskirts of Nairobi.' He paused, scrutinising Justin carefully. The company would supply two-bedroom flats in Nairobi, fully serviced. This wasn't a family environment, although family could visit during holidays. Mr Zhu knew this worked well for some families, as the staff worked long hours and enjoyed long breaks back home as a compensation, if they wished. He added that obviously salary would be commensurate with the commitment. He waited to see if Justin had any questions about the situation.

To his consternation, Justin nodded immediately, exclaiming his acceptance, should he be considered a suitable applicant. He would discuss details with his wife, of course, but thought she wouldn't have any objections to such a proposition. Mr Zhu, having spent many years dealing with staff, sensed family was not top of Justin Kerr's priority list, or at least his wife probably wasn't, which both saddened him, reflecting on his own long and satisfying marriage, and at the same time reassured him. This Mr Kerr could well be an ideal member of the team.

Mr Zhu stood up and Justin quickly followed as Mr Zhu shook hands, calling the meeting over. Paperwork and more interviews would follow at Canary Wharf. Mr Zhu hoped they would meet in the spring in Guangzhou, ready to begin training.

Justin found the stairs. He didn't want to stand still in a lift. He bounced down the levels to his floor, deciding to go to the bar for a drink. His flight was early the next morning and he'd booked a place on the hotel bus. Steppes Man was not taking him back to the airport. He grinned to himself. What a twenty-four hours! When Mr Zhu had asked how the drive into St Petersburg had been, thankfully, he'd been non-committal. Steppes Man, it transpired, was a member of Ludmilla's extended family whom they tried to support as best they could. Justin couldn't help wondering if the extended family made a practice of using his services themselves.

Over a double brandy, he relived the main points of the interview. He couldn't dismiss out of hand the dangers which he might be faced with. Somalia, to the south-east of Kenya, was an ongoing problem. It was common knowledge that Al-Shabaab had caused mayhem and death on incursions into Nairobi. He had to smile, as Mr Zhu had mentioned a gated community. Justin knew that these were compounds, far more secure than the elegant gated communities seen in the UK. However, in spite of these thoughts, he knew he would love to be included. He would take a few shooting lessons from Tom, he thought. He'd need a licence too. Tom had a licence for game, which was useful in the forest. Mainly he took home rabbits. But he helped with the deer cull from time to time. Another hurdle, and probably just as dangerous, was how he was going to discuss this possible promotion with Clara. At least there was no expectation of her and the children moving with him.

That evening, he texted Clara to confirm his flight the next morning. Rather than get a taxi, he'd managed to book a rental car to pick up at Norwich Airport, which he'd leave at their Bury depot, if someone could pick him up. He paused at this point, hardly expecting any reply, or at best, something scathing. Still, he guessed it would fall in the end to Dad.

Clara read his message and, wordless, passed her phone to Den, who'd come over to help with supper. They'd already asked Liz to eat the following evening to share in their plans for New Year's Eve.

'Here, Den, could you please? I'll do supper tomorrow. We can all sit round and discuss New Year together. That'll be a first, sitting round together.' She sniffed into her drink.

Den immediately texted confirmation to Justin, watching as Clara took another gulp of wine. He was concerned to see Clara drinking so much, but didn't dare comment. He could imagine how she might raise her eyebrows at him, which could be very chilling. At least she seemed less angry than on their return flight, and her considerably nerve-racking, fast drive back from the airport. He took another look at her. If anything, she seemed to have reached a place of indifference, as she took another slurp.

Clara's apparent indifference to Justin was misread by Den. She had begun to form a plan, but had decided to hold it all in, until after the New Year celebrations, hence the need for alcohol to steady her nerves.

Den sighed heavily. He was going to have to broach the subject of his correspondence from the district council, which, he had to admit to himself, he had been tempted to ignore. Truth was, he'd slipped up in his registration procedure, when he'd applied for living accommodation when the planning applications and building regulations paperwork went in. At the time there was no confirmation and it had completely slipped his mind to pursue it. He now discovered that he owned an expensive holiday home, one which he had to vacate every January and February. To ignore this could incur a heavy fine. He wondered how Clara and Justin would react. He was going to fall on their mercy, grovel a bit, but certainly approach the authorities to review their decision for the future.

Another thing he'd been wondering about, fretting over a little, was the friendly, conspiratorial, relaxed manner in which Tom and Clara behaved towards one another. It was nothing he could actually mention, but a feeling he had. He'd noticed their heads together rather more than he'd have thought necessary when the new computers were installed, immediately prior to the family flights to Finland. Something to do with a special offer,

Tom had said, when Den queried the purchase so close to sale time. Clara and he had exchanged confiding looks, smiling at something to do with Black Friday or Monday. Den guessed it was at Justin's expense.

Chapter Twenty-Four

Justin was coming in to land again; this time it was Norwich Airport. Linda had answered his text, several times in fact. He'd given her plenty of wriggle room in his first reply, should she want to forget what had been, at least to him, an extraordinary night and day before Christmas. She really did want to meet up! He'd had to look at himself critically yet again. He would have to explain that his wife was still in his life – at least, they were still married – and he did still have feelings for her, although probably terminally blunted by the year's experiences. Ling was still to be faced. He already imagined Ling's perceptive, recriminating look, and sweated at the thought of it.

Linda wanted to meet at the houseboat. How bizarre, he thought. Although Clara had agreed to his purchase of Bertha, encouraged him in the end, she hated staying in the houseboat – what was, in fact, their second home. Ah, well. Linda said she loved Bertha and everything about her. Though pleasing, he was wise enough to take that comment with some reservation.

Once landed, he initially walked straight past the car-hire desk, distracted by inner turmoil, his meeting with Mr Zhu and possible selection interviews to come. It was difficult to know quite what the outcome might be. Once back at work, no doubt things would unfold pretty quickly. It really was quite difficult to imagine what the new year would bring. Driving to Bury, his thoughts ranged over other recent events. He grimaced, fearing Clara's possible discovery of his infidelity. He could hardly make the excuse that Linda had seduced him, although she certainly played a leading role! How strange life was turning out to be. Clara had always attracted men to her without effort and had always laughed it off. He was still bemused by how different Linda was from how he'd imagined her. Ling had never really said much about her, except that she liked to party, shaking his head, as if in disapproval. That didn't fit with his initial impression of her. He'd already acknowledged that he was a bad judge of character.

Suddenly, he'd reached Bury. Once at the car-hire company, he handed the keys over and Den came forward in the car park to greet him and stood back, his hands still gripping Justin's arms.

'Well, how did it go, Jus?'

'Dad, hi. Well, I don't know yet. More meetings at work. I'll tell you more as I find out. We'd better leave it for now.'

Den made a face in acknowledgement. Later, once they were under way, Den sounded out Justin's feelings about Liz. Justin got confused for a moment, before realising Dad was referring to his own plans to ask Liz to marry him, and if Justin thought it was a good idea. Somewhat challenged, he hoped he managed an appropriate response.

'Dad, if it's what you really want, then I think it could work. Liz is solid.'

'Thanks son, that's a relief, but I'm not sure she'd like to be called solid.' In the gathering dusk they both grinned, as the vehicle continued to cut the distance between them and Keeper's and the evening ahead. 'Mind, I'm just thinking about it for now.'

'I understand, Dad. Big step.'

Den nodded agreement. He'd shelved his imminent problem of having to move out of his lodge for two months. Even he knew it would be crass to ask Liz just now to marry him. It would look as if he'd asked just to move in with her for two months. He didn't fancy her cottage anyway. There were women he'd entertained on invitation in the village. They'd never discussed that time. But she must be aware of it. That bloody calendar! No, it had been fun. Be honest. After the hiccup he'd had with Liz over misunderstanding his reason for taking Mary and her son out, things had gone along very nicely. She was a reserved type, who enjoyed being part of an audience, rather than the one attracting attention. He was glad she liked working for Clara too. They were both quiet types, both gifted needlewomen.

'When're you going to ask her then?' Justin hoped he had disguised his surprise, his shock even. His heart went out to his mother, now long dead, which he knew was about his own continuing sense of loss. Why on earth did Dad need to marry? They weren't going to have children.

'What? Like I said, not just yet. I want to sound her out a bit for a while.'

'How're you going to do that, Dad?'

Den shook his head. He had no idea, except he'd just cleared the way with his son, which was the biggest hurdle in his own mind. Jus had always been so close to Lola. He could sense a tightening of Jus's body next to him, trying to deal with this news. Good boy, he thought, you're coming along nicely. Pity about the problems at home though.

Den, in character, tooted the horn of his new hybrid car as he screeched to a halt outside the cottage, sending gravel flying and causing Arthur to bark hysterically from the hall. Weird vehicle, Justin thought, almost no engine sound. Then the front door opened and Zoe, Carl and Arthur bounced out. Liz was there, Justin noted, alongside Clara. Clara looked ethereal, delicate, beautiful and distant. Her white-blonde hair was way down her back today.

She wore a loose sweater, which slipped off one smooth golden shoulder, and tight black jeans. Sadly, she already seemed not to be his. More disturbingly, he wondered fleetingly, how was it he didn't desperately want her, desire her in that moment? His thoughts were pushed aside as he was immediately mobbed by Arthur up around his shoulders and the twins around his middle, all vying for his immediate attention.

Supper time was saved by Clara and Liz sharing their enthusiasm for New Year's Eve. The men settled on their casserole, remarking how good it was. The twins argued over how many peas they each had. Den was still bemused by their ride from Bury and how well it had gone. Justin, through the main course and dessert, tried to absorb this news his father had imparted. The twins, once Justin's gifts to them were unwrapped, had insisted on wearing their new hats to supper. Clara had resisted, not trying hers on, but placing it carefully on the hall table.

'It'll be good if we get snow,' she said, somewhat dismissively. She noted how the children looked at her sharply, picking up on her tone. Well, what did he, they, expect? She affected a smile. Things moved on. She had already decided not to ask him about his interview. If he wanted to talk about it, she wouldn't make it easy.

Liz, carefully schooled earlier by Den, resisted asking Justin how he had got on in St Petersburg. Clara had also asked her not to mention the contract she was securing with a children's clothing boutique in the West End. It was proving difficult to understand her reasoning. Still, it wasn't her news, so Liz kept quiet.

After supper, Justin wandered into the sitting room, once they'd cleared up, glass in hand.

'Where are the presents then from your parents? I thought you said they were to stay under the tree till New Year's Eve?'

Clara shook her head irritably. 'That was Dad. D'you think two seven-year-olds could leave them alone? I've put them away until the event.'

Justin put his glass down on the side table near the sofa and slumped back. 'God, I feel knackered.' He stretched his legs out, and Arthur tried hard to squeeze behind them to lie down. Den and Liz were still in the kitchen, deciding when to get the firework cakes, how much to spend and who was safest to light them. 'Do we have to have fireworks? What if it rains? It's turned quite mild.' Justin poked at the fire, which now, sullen and smouldering dully, reflected the turn in the weather; it was always a telltale sign.

'You needn't get involved if you are above celebrating. Are you desperate to escape already, then? Den or Tom will set them and light them. Don't put yourself out, will you?' With that she got up and threw another log on the fire. A few desultory sparks flew out onto the hearth.

Justin turned to look at her, taking a deep breath. 'Sorry. Even so, have to say, these cakes always have lots of bangers. I'll have a word with Dad. They can get a couple with fewer perhaps. The kids can wear earplugs if they're very loud. You know what Carl's like with unexpected loud noises.' He paused, 'Just saying.'

'Well, thank you, Jus. Yes, I do know what my children are like. I'm probably more aware of their development than you are. But, if you recall, Carl has come out of his shell recently. It was particularly noticeable in Finland!'

Justin bit his tongue. He really was very tired. Just finish this drink, he thought, and risk going up to their bedroom. Double beds with Clara were becoming very problematic, but he needed a decent sleep. If anyone was going to go in the spare room and make up another bed, then sod it, it wouldn't be him tonight. Before that, he still had to see to the children.

There was an unexpected knock on the kitchen door. Tom appeared, grinning. Supper was cleared and Justin, after finishing his drink, had gone upstairs, having taken on the twins' bath and instructions to sort out clean pyjamas and towels, before he collapsed.

'Tom! Lovely to see you. How did your Christmas go?' Liz, normally reserved, reached out to touch his arm, still wrapped around the door.

She and Mary had become accustomed to Tom. He was considered a good IT friend for Clara and her business, therefore also good for her and Mary. She couldn't understand why he wanted to braid his hair, or cover his arms in tattoos, but both women appreciated his good-natured efficiency. To their mutual surprise, he was also artistic. Before Christmas he'd brought in some designs, which Clara was thinking about incorporating into outfits for slightly older children, and using the computers to print finished freestyle designs. They used Instagram, Pinterest and Etsy sites. If they offered a wider choice, Tom was sure they could increase sales and not need more staff. Both Mary and Liz agreed that Tom had improved their sales offer already. Liz continued to beam at his sudden appearance at the kitchen door.

'Well, it was okay. No, actually, it was good.' He grinned again, his braids bobbing about as he nodded confirmation. 'Just that Ed, you know my brother? Well he's fine out in the forest. Not so good indoors at the smaller stuff. You know, the details.'

'Heavens, what happened?'

'We had a tree situation, which is a bit ironic. Mum arrived as he was setting it up. Forgot what he was doing. Hadn't fixed the supports properly, which was okay until we'd finished decorating it. I came in with a cuppa and mince pies to celebrate. Suddenly it listed to starboard. Fortunately, I was out of the line of fire. Arthur had been dozing peacefully underneath, after we'd put his bed there.'

Justin reappeared in the doorway, arms full of towels for laundry, to see the engrossed audience of Den and Liz, but more noticeably Clara, whose expression was one of rapt attention, smiling, eyes following Tom's gesticulations as he recounted his tale. Tom waved across at him.

'What happened, Tom?' Den asked, curious to hear the worst.

'Arthur chased around the room, trying to disentangle himself from tinsel and decorations which had attached themselves to him. We put the tree back properly. Mum got Ed to help her put the decorations up. Those which weren't wrecked, that is.'

'Hmm. Hope it didn't spoil your Christmas, then. We'll need to reimburse you, Tom.'

Even Justin could hear the coolness in his voice. He blamed it on the children's enthusiasm for Tom, when they'd revealed plans to have a trip out in the spring. Tomtom was going to show them where to go foraging, with Mummy.

'Daddy, you will come too, won't you? Tomtom says his friend runs a restaurant and uses lots of local stuff.'

'Not sure if it's actually legal, darling, not for business use anyway.'

Carl came into the bedroom, pulling on his dressing gown, as Justin was about to remind him that it was actually bedtime. 'Daddy, you don't have to worry. Tomtom has got licences and stuff. He can even pick stuff called something like campfire, legally, along the seashore.'

'Samphire, sweetheart, samphire,' Justin muttered between clenched teeth.

Tom was everywhere. Was this the smart-arse dickhead he'd been wondering about? If it were, he'd quickly reassess Tom, whom he'd thought was hardly more than a kid, though obviously very useful. Clara'd never be able to keep him, he thought. Immediately, however, he had to rethink that, as Linda's image sprang before him. What in heaven's name was wrong with them both if he was correct? Did it mean they were both immature? Were they trying to put back the clock? Still, he reassured himself, Tom would have plenty of admirers of his own age. Clara would have her work cut out. Then he dismissed the whole idea as fantasy on his part. He needed to relax.

Tom was answering his offer to settle up for Arthur's most recent chaos. 'Nah, you're okay, Justin. We had loads too many anyway, and the crate of fancy beers you gave us for having Arthur more than covered everything, including bauble losses!' He chuckled. 'They are excellent beers by the way. Good choice. You could all come over before you go back, Justin, for a chilli and help us down a few.'

'Excellent idea!' Den enthused. 'You don't go back till the second, do you, Jus?'

Trust Dad to follow the booze, he thought. He pulled himself together. 'I'd like that, Tom, thanks.' He hoped he managed a convincing smile.

Den changed the subject to fireworks. 'Liz said you know some fireworks people over in Ipswich, Tom. Any chance of getting a selection rather than a cake? Some old-fashioned ones, not all of the explosive variety. Kids are a bit young for those.'

Justin nearly snorted. What a treasure Tom was turning out to be. Next he'd be offering to take the twins with him. Still, at least Dad was on the right track with the fireworks scenario.

Tom nodded. 'I'm off till New Year. Time owing. Perhaps you and Liz and the twins would like to come as well. They do special packs for young families, or those who live near livestock. Tomorrow morning, say. Ten any good?' He looked around, suddenly aware of some sort of atmosphere, but was unsure what. Clara and Justin were staring at one another. Oh well, he thought, whatever it was, they'd have a chance on their own to sort it out, with a break from the twins. He quickly went over what he'd just said. He was only trying to help after all, and was reassured by Den's hearty pat on the back, with Liz's nodding, smiling agreement to his idea.

'We could make a day of it. See the train at Woodbridge. Think the Tea Hut'll be open. Have some lunch there. Kids have a run along the sand. What d'you think, Tom?' Den was in full flow now.

'Okay for me, but what about you two?' He indicated to Clara and Justin. 'I think the Hut closes for New Year's Eve. Still, there'll be other places.'

'I need to get food sorted for tomorrow evening, but thank you for all you're doing. By the way, can Ed and your mum come across tomorrow evening?'

'Mum's gone back, thanks Clara. Ed was going to his girlfriend's. I'll check with him. Is it okay if I bring a friend?'

There was a pause and Justin broke in too heartily, 'Of course, Tom, more the merrier. Did we say Mary's coming? I hear Mary's trialling a chap she met online. I think her son's at home with his girl, so they'll be along. Oh, then the Hodges from top of the lane. No, that'll be grand.' He heard himself. Grand? Where did that come from? He sounded an idiot.

Everyone was now talking about food offerings: drinks, what to bring, where to site the fireworks, how many buckets of water. Would there be a bonfire? And what about sand to stand rockets in and other safety issues? By now, Clara had lost track of more or less everything. She shrugged inwardly. Somehow it would all work out.

Den drifted off, thinking of earlier memories of Woodbridge, Lola's last year. Her illness had taken a swift and firm grip on her, but they'd had one last trip up to visit Clara and Justin. The twins were babies. Lola had cuddled them and got to know them. Then he and Lola had had a day trip out. It was early summer, the skies enormous in their Suffolky blue, as Lola called it, with gossamer wisps of cloud drifting along, reminding them it wasn't quite yet midsummer. They'd parked up and made their way towards the Tea Hut alongside the estuary. As they reached the bridge, Den realised he had forgotten the car rug. Lola leaned against the bridge and Den went back to the car. On his return, he observed Lola, unaware of his approach, weeping into tissues, though actually, he recalled, it would have been a handkerchief. His heart smote him. He had hurried to her, dropping the rug to take her in his arms. A few people were around, but he paid no attention to them. He embraced her, folded her to him as she gave way to deep sobs. They had nothing to say; there was nothing to say. Eventually, as her sobbing subsided, he stepped back a little to kiss her eyelids, taking in the saltiness of her tears, wiping them gently with his handkerchief. It was a nostalgia thing all of its own – the handkerchief thing, Lola's thing. He recalled that she became calm and smiled at him. He'd retrieved the rug, put his arm through hers as they walked on together to the café. What Den remembered most of that day was how precious it had been. They'd lived for that day. There were no more days like it. As he gave a deep sigh, Liz turned to him, questioningly.

'Okay there?'

'Okay here.' He grinned, then asked, 'Do you ever use handkerchiefs, Liz? No, daft question, everyone uses tissues. Me, I use them too, man-size of course.'

Liz shook her head, mystified. With Den, you never knew quite what to expect, or where his mind was taking him.

The thirty-first dawned with an air frost and colder than it had been for days. Tom's borrowed truck swung onto the gravel on time. He hopped down to open the passenger doors, assisting the twins up the step to the back bench seat, behind the mesh divider, with Arthur lying on the floor down the middle. He'd become attached to rides out with Tom and Ed over Christmas and assumed his rights. Liz and Den joined Tom on the front bench seat.

Clara and Justin waved them off, having loaded them up with wellingtons, cartons of drinks and a large thermos of coffee, a bottle of water for Arthur and towels against mud and water. They lingered in the cold as if unsure what to do next. Clara shivered.

'Think I'll check on emails and any orders. Need to keep an eye on them. We were really busy before Christmas.' She started to walk towards the workshop.

Justin looked after her thoughtfully. 'D'you need any help? Are you up to date with finishes?'

Caught out by this offer, she halted, a puzzled smile almost reaching her eyes. 'Jussy, I've never seen you thread a needle. What d'you mean?'

'I can press and pack things. I've seen that done often enough.'

She gave a hollow laugh. 'Thanks, but if you really want to help, there are veg to prep for the chilli and potatoes to wash ready for baking. We need to pull out extra plates and cutlery from the back of the cupboard too, to check on.'

'Oh, okay. I thought we were going to use disposables and save on clearing up.'

'If you remember, I've hardly had any chance to go shopping.'

Justin silently waved aside her excuses, wondering what was wrong with online ordering, but bit his lip, keeping his counsel. 'Fine, I'll go and get started.'

He watched her stride off towards the workshop, her breath in a haze around her. Now he was here, she was keeping him in his place, he thought. Only fit for kitchen duties. The day went quickly enough with random phone calls, a quick dash to the village for ice cream and extra milk and to post several orders. He thought there was a contract now for carriers to take orders, but Clara insisted it was quicker to post them over New Year.

Mission accomplished: there were plates stacked near the cooker, mugs and glasses on the table next to dishes to be piled with coleslaws and tomatoes, grated cheese, chutneys and butter for the jacket potatoes. Booze was to go in chill boxes on the floor.

As soon as the day trippers returned, Clara fed the children and sent them off for a lie-down with their books for an hour. Justin was impressed by how they seemed not to mind. Den and Liz brought in the fireworks. Tom suggested siting everything in the field, for safety's sake, as agreed the previous evening, along with buckets of sand to support the rockets and buckets of water, in case of need.

Justin continued to be directed by Clara, fortified by numerous coffees. Busy working on his own, he tried not to think about how he was going to face Ling in a couple of days. What if Linda had talked to Ling? Everything was in a state of flux. He had no idea what might happen next, although, if accepted, he was probably going to work abroad for the foreseeable future. Occasionally, he looked at Clara to gauge whether he could talk to her, but she had that closed look which daunted him. He'd tell her before he went back. He had still got almost a couple of days.

Den and Liz were dispatched to put their feet up before the evening celebrations. Den was initially miffed at being dismissed like an old fogey by Clara. Liz was grateful. But Den, as ever, neither in need of a rest nor wanting one, once back at the lodge, occupied himself and Liz happily on his king-sized bed, until they then migrated to the shower, to return to the cottage later.

Justin thought of Alice and Edie, now in Cape Town. They'd sent numerous postcards, which the twins had stuck on the fridge. This evening was going to be small fry in comparison to one of Alice and Edie's celebrations, but they were ready now, and Mary was the first to arrive, with her new man – a tall, rather gaunt, fifty-plus divorcé called Harold – who was anxious to pass over the pavlova he had carried through the woods on their walk from the village. Mary's son and girlfriend had dropped out to go off to one of his friend's parties. Liz and Den arrived next, bringing across a large bowl of savoury rice for the chilli and two bottles of wine, which Den immediately opened to get the celebrations started. Tom arrived with a male friend, a rather beautiful dark-haired man, probably about the same age as Tom. He was tall, slender, certainly well over six feet, Justin thought. They were obviously close. Tom placed his arm affectionately behind Neville's back, as he introduced him to Clara, then the others. The twins were initially shy but soon became confident enough to approach Tomtom's friend. Justin quickly reassessed his thoughts of Tom and Clara: now he hadn't expected that. He'd got that so wrong! He couldn't help wondering how much Clara knew about Tom's friend. Tom's brother Ed was a giant of a man and his girlfriend was petite, a vivid redhead, her skin alabaster. She obviously felt the cold; she seemed to be wearing several sweaters under her coat.

'Corinne works with me, sort of. She deals more with publicity and promoting forest walks. And stuff,' he added rather lamely, looking uncomfortable in a confined space.

Den liked him immediately. Corinne's brown eyes sparkled with laughter as she shoved Ed.

'What are you like? There's a lot more to it than that.' Ed looked down at her, slightly desperate. 'But that'll do.' She took his hand to reassure him it didn't matter.

It became clear before people had started to arrive why the twins had been happy to go upstairs to read and rest. This hadn't worked very well, for whilst Clara and Justin were busy finishing off preparations and discussing with Den and Liz the finer details of the fireworks with Tom, the twins had gone on a treasure hunt and discovered the presents hidden under Clara and Justin's bed in carrier bags, behind a box of vacuum-packed summer clothes. They very quietly pulled the presents out and crept back to Zoe's bedroom. Once they'd unwrapped their own presents, it was necessary then to see what Mummy had, then what Daddy and Grandad were given. Even Liz was included. Everything was now laid out on the floor and they weren't sure what to do.

This problem was resolved, however, when Justin went upstairs to get them up from their nap and found them looking very sheepish amongst a considerable amount of wrapping paper. Justin was privately amused by their resourcefulness. There wasn't time to sort everything out, so he sent them downstairs, and stuffed everything back into the carrier bags and returned them to his and Clara's bedroom. Really Clara's bedroom, he thought, though he had slept there the previous night as a concession but no more than that.

After they saw in the New Year with "Auld Lang Syne", Tom and Neville volunteered to look after the fireworks. Unlike at Alice and Edie's, there was no lake for added drama, but with the dry, clear air, there were no failures. Carl, Zoe and Sybil were wrapped up well, standing by the edge of the field with the older children. The neighbour's son, Frank, who'd brought a silent, rather sullen-looking girl from his class, stood silently. Mark, his younger brother, gifted with an easy-going manner, looked after the younger ones. The last explosion of light and colour signalled almost the end of the evening.

It was now freezing. Clara ushered everyone indoors again to warm up with glogg – traditional Finnish mulled wine. The children were given a similar non-alcoholic drink. Gradually, people began to disperse. First to leave were Mary and Harold, Harold clutching the glass dish the pavlova had arrived in. Justin wondered how they would make out. Harold had been very quiet, but had managed to divulge he was planning to return to Cambridge in the next day or so. Once they'd left, it wasn't long before everyone else made a move. Tom helped Neville into his coat, covertly watched by Justin. Then Tom patted Neville's scarf into place, as they smiled at each other, somewhat foolishly, thought Justin. But he envied them their obvious closeness. Clara was helping Sybil into her coat and fetching a blanket to wrap her in. He doubted she had seen Tom and Neville's intimacy. Corinne now reappeared from the utility behind Ed's mountainous coat, having already slipped hers on. Gathered by the porch door, kisses and thanks were exchanged in the frosted air, as they made to depart in Ed's truck. The Hodges were last, leaving to wander up the lane, James carrying a sleepy Sybil in the blanket. Clara and Justin then found themselves in the kitchen in the sudden silence, staring at the debris and the pile of glasses and dishes. The twins were attempting to be invisible.

'D'you fancy a nightcap?' Justin helped himself to a whisky, holding an empty glass up for Clara to choose from the remaining drinks.

'Okay. A whisky too, please, but I'll take the twins up first.'

Justin started to load the dishwasher, then set to, washing up glasses. Clara gathered up the now sleepy twins and ushered them towards the stairs and bed. Den and Liz had disappeared to the lodge.

Justin, occupied at the sink, with the sudden quiet around him, except for the swish of the dishwasher, paused with a glass in mid-air. He felt a strong sense of things finishing. Of course it was just a feeling that wouldn't last. As soon as the year started up again, he wouldn't give it another thought.

Chapter Twenty-Five

New Year's Day was clear, cold and bright. Justin and Clara had a slow start. The distance between them remained unchanged, but as they were both tired from the previous night's celebrations, they lingered over toast and coffee. The twins were still in bed, playing with some of their new toys. Den suddenly appeared, far too early, Justin thought. Den drew himself to his full height.

'Gotta ask you, son. Clara too, in fact.'

'What, Dad, something wrong?' His stomach twisted.

'Course not, no not all. No, no.'

'Dad, please!'

'Yes, yes. Well, can I move back in for two months? Only two months – I won't be any trouble. No, no trouble. Can do all the suppers. Sleep in the box room. I'll get onto the council straight away.'

Clara was listening from the doorway, having wandered off to get more bread from the freezer for later, and picked up the end of the conversation. 'Den, what's happened?'

After he'd repeated his problem, Clara looked to Justin, who answered, 'Yes, of course, Dad, as long as it's okay with Clara.'

She just shrugged and nodded. Her reaction seemed surprisingly calm. Much relieved and hardly believing his luck, Den thanked them profusely. Clara commented that he needn't overdo it. Thanking them both again, he backed out of the kitchen, turned and went back to inform Liz, intensely relieved he wouldn't need to take her up on her offer of hospitality at her cottage. He was far happier, more comfortable, out of the village, after all, but needed to sound regretful at the same time.

His plan was that if he did follow through with asking Liz to marry him, once he was back in his lodge permanently, he was sure he could convince her that the lodge would be preferable to live in. Then perhaps rent out her cottage.

Clara suggested they get the twins up and take them somewhere. They decided on a garden centre, which had a play area for various age groups. There was a cafe next to it, where they could keep an eye on the twins. It wasn't straightforward however.

'Can Sybil come as well, Daddy? You like Sybil too, don't you, Zoe?'

'I'd rather ask Deidre. Can they both come, Mummy?'

'Deidre? Sybil? Well, Sybil has her granny coming today. I'll find out if Deidre's free though.'

There was no reply from Deidre's number, so they set off, neither children now interested in going anywhere, in spite of Clara's encouraging comments on how good the rope walk was, and how grown-ups liked it too. This led to Justin and Clara with the twins between them, going along the rope walk, gripping the sides as the suspended walk slewed gently, but enough to require hands on both sides.

'Can we have a drink now we've done what you wanted, Mummy?'

Clara and Justin grinned. Zoe had a point, so they bought drinks and sat and watched other families making their ungainly way along the rope walk, with the occasional squeal, as balance was threatened.

Den invited them to the lodge for supper. His Last Supper, he called it. He had to pack and move back to the cottage; he should already have moved out. There was a slight frisson of anxiety from Liz, who was sure that the council would be banging on the door at any minute. They drank to the new year again, avoiding anything to do with Justin's job. It seemed fine to raise a glass to Clara's business and Den's lodge. Justin couldn't be bothered to make the point that the elephant in the room, his job, could possibly be the most eventful to drink to.

Clara remained cool towards him through to the next morning, although she did offer to drive him to Bury for the train, which surprised him. He fully expected Dad to be handed the honour; he'd moved back to the box room again for two months. Liz had returned to the village, a little sullen, Den thought, mystified, as he busily stashed a few bottles. Justin was packing to take the train back to London. He wondered at what point, if ever, he should mention the possibilities of his job to Clara, but decided not to risk another outburst as he was leaving. He'd wait until he knew what was planned for him.

He'd book a week off in February at half-term, as he'd suggested earlier. Of course, he told himself, come home before then for the odd weekend. But there were snags to planning anything. He wanted promotion and knew that if he were offered a place on this new team, everything else would come second. After all, it would help to secure all their futures financially.

Their drive in to Bury was subdued. Clara chose the direction of the conversation, suggesting how pleased they should be that the twins were beginning to make friends away from home. Only half listening, Justin agreed. He had this weird experience that he had already left her and was travelling away. He was busy trying to work out how he would cope with the new circumstances he found himself in with Ling and Linda, once he was back in London.

Suddenly, they'd arrived at the station. Clara surprised him as she leant across to kiss his cheek: no lips then, he thought. Justin reciprocated, feeling the softness of her cheek, turned, stepped down, nodding to her as he shoved the door closed and went to the rear to pull his case and bag out. They'd left the twins and Arthur at home with Den. He waved as she swung the Land Rover round and drove away, ignoring him. Justin shrugged to himself. Well then, better get the train.

He got a taxi to the boatyard from St Pancras. Distracted, he forgot his extra bag with overflow presents. The taxi driver tooted him back. For a moment, he was confused. He knew he'd paid. The driver got out, holding up the bag for him. Justin smiled apologetically and leaving his case on the path, he strode back and took the bag from the driver, thanked him and made his way to Bertha, pulling along his case with one hand with Dad's borrowed sports bag over his shoulder.

As he unlocked the door to Bertha, he caught a glimpse of a gaunt reflection in the glass of the door. He looked wretched: hardly surprising, was it? He had stuff to try and sort out now. He dumped his bag and case on the bed. The stove was banked up, so he opened the flue a little. Very quickly there was flame. The cabin was warm from Phil's conscientious care. Before he did anything, he needed to pop over and thank him for keeping Bertha warm. But when he went across, he could see there was only the hall light on, and there was no reply when he rang the bell.

Back in Bertha, Justin realised he needed to do shopping. There were no coffee pods for the machine, so he put the kettle on for an instant and messaged home to say he'd arrived. Clara rang him back, asking him to open his computer. She wanted to Skype. He was tired and couldn't think what wouldn't wait, but he huffed and complied.

'I think you should sit down, Justin.'

'Where are the twins?'

'In bed. Den's in the box room, reading.'

'Okay, fire away then.'

'Sit down please, Jussy. I've got things to talk about.'

Justin, sensing Clara had worked herself up to something serious, sat down.

Clara had planned everything, but now, in a state of high nerves, blurted out. 'Justin, I wanted a legal separation, to start with.'

'Oka-ay, what does that mean, to start with?'

'It meant that it wasn't as final as a divorce, but I wanted our finances separated and a maintenance allowance for the children. Oh yes, and I'm really sorry, but my share of your pension. Then, afterwards, I thought about it.'

'You thought about it? You've lost me now. D'you mean you've changed your mind?'

'Well, yes. I've decided a divorce would be best for both of us and gives us both our freedom.'

'Dear God, woman, make your mind up!' Exasperated and unsure what a legal separation might have been, his tone was frighteningly cold.

She pushed herself away from the computer, as if that small extra space might make her more comfortable. 'Sorry, I forgot. You can't live here either.'

'That would appear to be obvious. Is it fashionable these days to finish a marriage by Skyping, then? Not cool to do it face to face?' She blew her nose, sniffing. He couldn't help wondering if she had her eye on someone, someone near. Didn't look like Tom, after all, though they were obviously friends. So this was it – this thing which had been a few steps behind him for months. When so often he'd turned round quickly, there'd been nothing there, nothing real. Now there was no need to turn round; his future had been decided for him. Strangely enough, all he felt was the cold chill he could hear in his voice. 'How will you manage to keep the cottage, Clara? I'm really very interested to know. Even with all of the above, you'll need a mortgage. I assume you will be financed by outside interests?' Clara had the grace to flush. She looked a bit sweaty, he thought. Good. She wouldn't have an easy divorce or legal separation if he had anything to do with it. Even so, he knew he'd be financing the mortgage, more likely than not. He allowed himself the luxury of feeling bitter.

'Well actually, Justin, in spite of what you may think, I can look after some things. A boutique off Carnaby Street, specialising in high-end children's clothes have signed up for a one-year contract with us, me, I mean, guaranteeing to take specific stock during that time. That will help stabilise the company turnover and give me the opportunity to branch out as well.'

'Well, good for you! How will that affect my considerable outgoings, then?'

'Well, I've spoken to our solicitor in the village. She can't act for us, but put me on to Geefes & Co in Bury. Mr Geefes advised me that the boat can be signed over to you. Also, I want to try to pay the mortgage on the cottage while the children remain minors, so long as the business can take the cost. We can decide how to balance the value of the cottage, once the children have left education, so we'd need to have a charge on the cottage so neither of us could sell it without mutual agreement.'

Shocked at her unexpected organisational skills and, after all, apparently not planning to take him to the cleaners, he was still harbouring cold fury. 'It may not have occurred to you, Clara, but this situation is not entirely my fault, although no doubt your parents have been influencing you to the contrary.' Now she was in tears. Strange how he didn't care. All this and she didn't even know he'd been unfaithful! He let out a dry laugh. Well, he wouldn't give her that satisfaction.

A new thought emerged. Dad had just moved in for two months. He was very unsure how Dad would feel now. Then there was Dad's friend from his youth, the mysterious Constanza. He wondered when she might make an appearance, just to add to the mix. Dad mentioned she was visiting as soon as he got back to his lodge.

There was now an element of uncertainty around Liz, whose invitation to move in with her for his enforced vacation from his lodge for two months, had been turned down in favour of moving back to the cottage with Clara and the children. Dad had mentioned, regretfully, that she'd treated it as a slight. His earlier keenness to settle with Liz seemed to have slipped off the front page, for now at least.

Clara was speaking again, tears streaming down her face now. God, he thought, she still looks amazing, but I don't love her. I really don't love her.

'You'll be able to stay in the lodge with Den any time you want to see the children,' she was still talking, saying something else, sounding apologetic, but he broke in.

'Am I the last one to hear about your plans, then?'

'No, of course not. I'm assuming Den will welcome you.'

He cut her short. He'd been keeping an eye on his phone. It was vibrating. He picked it up to see that Ling had texted to meet up before they went back to work. Immediately there was another text, this time from Linda, who wanted to meet up urgently to speak to him. He made his excuses to Clara. 'I've got to go. I haven't eaten and I'm tired. I'll come up to Suffolk as soon as I can to discuss details. Goodnight!' He closed his computer, wondering if Clara was still staring at her screen.

He really was tired, but now he stared at his phone screen, thinking, how surreal, what a night! He wondered if it would be ridiculous to get whatever needed to be said between him, Linda and Ling, done. Grimacing at the very thought, he texted Ling, grabbed his coat and left. They met at the Bulkhead along the Cut. There were two beers on the table, and Ling was already seated, but he stood as soon as he saw Justin enter the pub. Justin worried momentarily if Ling was feeling violent, or, more likely, in view of the purchased drinks, ready to exchange a New Year's handshake.

Justin, humbled by Ling's polite reserve, slid into the old polished seat opposite and raised his glass. How to start? Justin wondered what to say first. He took a deep breath. But Ling beat him to it. New Year greetings played no part now in his opening salvo.

'I collected the antlers, Justin. You know, the antlers Linda forgot.' He left that in the air, watching with interest whilst Justin struggled to absorb this information and almost felt sorry for him, so startled did he look. Then he caught sadness, and guilt too. *Shadows Across the Moon* came to mind in the long pause. Bastard, he thought, but kept a slight smile ready for Justin's explanation. He knew his cousin, of course. He knew what she could be like when cocaine and alcohol were involved. Bottom line though, she was unattached. Justin was not. Both he and Linda were in their twenties; Justin was forty.

'Antlers? Oh God, Ling.' He took a few moments to process this news.

'Hasn't Linda spoken to you? She's pretty annoyed with me you know, getting involved.' Ling shrugged his excuse. 'We've always looked out for each other. It's just hard to step back.'

'Does Phil know as well?' Justin wiped a hand across a moist forehead, annoyed with himself. Why hadn't he actually spoken to Linda, only texting her, fielding her requests to speak, until he got back? Now he had to get to grips with a new problem. So Ling had got Phil to let him in. Justin had a high regard for Phil and his friendship and he tried not to explore how that would play out now.

'Phil thought I had loaned you the antlers. He didn't question it. I said I needed them for a party.' Ling continued to watch Justin's discomfort. He wasn't making it easy for him, but why should he? He wondered if Justin would be tempted to try and have a pop at him, though doubted he'd risk it. Ling, though slight, had black belts in most well-known martial arts and a few less well known. Not only that, he was confident he could read Justin. It would be out of character.

'Have to ask, Ling. Where are you coming from exactly? After all, Linda is an adult.'

'Okay, so what d'you think your relationship is with Linda?'

'What? What d'you think? If we're being honest here, then, well, I was flattered. You may not believe it, but I did attempt to send her home to begin with. As I said, I was flattered and she, well, she was quite determined.' He paused. 'Determined not to go, in fact. No excuse, I know. In case you think I'm just a callous bastard, I do think Linda is very special.' He took a deep breath. He needed to let Ling know how things had fallen apart completely at home to an even greater extent than before Christmas, but immediately knew he mustn't use that, so stopped himself.

Ling, somehow picking up something in the silence, looked ruefully at Justin. 'I'm so sorry that your domestic life is so fraught, from what you've confided in me.'

Justin snorted. 'I'll tell you everything next time, although probably not when we're at work. You don't know the half of it. Well, I couldn't even tell Clara about my meeting in St Petersburg. She cut me dead. I mentioned that, didn't I?'

'No. What happened?'

'I had to divert to meet a Mr Zhu. Interesting. I may get sent to Guangzhou for an initial course as part of a team, then Nairobi. May not happen, but I think it probably will. Clara said, at the Kuopio house, when I told her I was going to the meeting, that she'd be sure to make me pay, meaning, suffer. When I got back to Suffolk she was cold and distant over New Year celebrations. It did feel weird. Dad is settled there and they seem to sort of get on okay. Dad loves being around the kids too. God knows how it'll all pan out. Actually, sod it, Ling, I know how it pans out. Just before I left to meet you, Clara actually had the nerve to Skype. She waited until I'd left home and got here, then announced she wants a divorce. Why she didn't confront me at home is a mystery. Perhaps it's the fashion now. Her parents are somewhere in the mix, I can smell it. I thought they might have encouraged her to take me to the cleaners and get her to go after everything, but it seems I was wrong.'

'So you don't actually think she's got someone else at present?'

'Who knows? Dad hasn't said anything. I did wonder about Tom, you know, the guy who keeps her computers together, but he came to our New Year do with another chap. They seemed fairly keen on each other to tell you the truth. I suppose he may like Clara as well, it's perfectly possible. By the way, she doesn't know about Linda. In effect, Linda and I, well, we've only just started to see each other and it may have only been for that one time. Sorry, had to say.'

Ling listened, fiddled with his glass, thinking of Clara and how she had melted him, seemingly unaware of her allure, or of her effect on him and, he guessed, on other men. There was no possible reason to think he should or could explore any relationship with her, and he felt guilty for even letting that thought pass across his mind. He was settled in the city; she was rooted in Suffolk, which, in effect, was the trouble with her marriage. He'd been seeing a girl from work for a few weeks, but they were both half-hearted about this arrangement – but were both slightly lonely, he guessed.

Where Linda was concerned, he decided to leave it. He felt sorry for Justin, thinking that not everything he was confronting now had actually been his fault. They came out of their meeting as friends. After all, Justin and Linda were right. They were both adults. The next few months would test Justin in every area, he guessed. He sighed. Linda was not the demure figure she tended to portray. Ah well, he'd try to keep out of it.

'How are the finances going to work, then?'

'Got to give her her due, Ling. I expected to be wiped out financially. But she agrees the boat should be signed over to me, and now she's got some fancy West End contract for children's things, she says she wants to pay the mortgage. Of course I'm paying for the children and she wants her share of my pension, that's if the court agrees, when we get down to the nitty-gritty. And she wants ownership of her business. She says she would like a clean break, but the reality is she needs help with the children and I want to do that for them in any case. She says she can keep herself and won't seek maintenance. If I was an outsider and not personally involved, I'd have to hand it to her you know. It could be a lot worse.'

Thoroughly exhausted now, having been propped up by a thick ham sandwich and another beer, Justin eventually made his way back to Bertha, shaking hands again with Ling, considering himself fortunate in that regard, and glad he'd told Ling about the divorce he was going to be one half of.

He needed to speak to Linda. He guessed, sober, Linda might be distant, like she'd been before that fateful night, which would be very odd indeed, considering the numerous very clear, later memories he had of her. But once they met again, well, who knew? The other thing he knew he would have to do, would be to look into what a divorce entailed as soon as he'd had some sleep.

The next morning he was back at work, almost expecting a call to the top of the building, but his day advanced in the normal routine of a first day back after a break. He'd had no time to check out divorce procedures on Google, so decided to deal with that back at Bertha. He also needed to speak to Phil, explain what had happened and, if he could, rent one of his outbuildings for all the stuff he was worried might suddenly arrive from Suffolk without warning, should Clara suddenly become eager to dispatch his possessions. He'd have to go home again at the weekend to try and clarify exactly what was happening. He needed to reassure the twins, if he could, too. Then there was Dad, stuck between them all, having just had a new home erected. If he'd had time, he'd feel sick.

Chapter Twenty-Six

He did manage to arrange to meet Linda. They met after work in a Spanish restaurant he'd booked at Canary Wharf, nervous of choosing Chinese. He was there first, sat near the window. He saw her walking across the square, swinging along at a pace. Watching her, something dangerous and unrecognisable surged in his chest. As it wasn't a heart attack, it was, he was sure, terror and delight in equal measure. She stepped inside. An assistant took her coat as she slipped it from her shoulders, then made her way towards him. He rose as a waiter ensured her seat was pulled out for her, sliding her chair back into place. They exchanged a brief kiss, chose cocktails and were left with menus.

Linda smiled innocently at him. 'How are you? Did your Christmas go well?'

He burst out laughing. How, he wondered, how could he behave normally, when this was truly bizarre? Still, he managed a nominal reply, expecting her to rant at him for ignoring her texts over Christmas, but she behaved as if nothing untoward had occurred. He couldn't remember what he ate, what she chose. They finished and, having retrieved their coats, already knew they were going to go to bed, going to Bertha. Of course it was dark, so Justin hoped Phil would be settled for the night. He had yet to see him since his return and felt guilty when he had time to think.

When he asked about her bombardment of texts over Christmas, she smiled and shrugged. Boredom had taken over. Everyone was with their families. Everyone? He found her light-hearted dismissal odd. Ling's words came back to haunt him. She was a law unto herself. He'd endeavour to modify his expectations.

It seemed cocaine was to be their recreational choice once again. This time the only alcohol involved was the earlier cocktails, and their night was without setbacks. They both woke early. Justin made them instant coffee, black, with sugar. They'd talked about Ling, whom Linda was annoyed with and Justin defended. Then Justin told her about Clara and Clara's pronouncement, quickly adding that obviously he and Clara were over, but that didn't mean that there was any tie between him and Linda, unless they wanted there to be in due course. He raised an eyebrow, quizzically.

Linda giggled. 'I'm not looking to settle down, if that's what you mean. Fun is good. You'll be off somewhere or other anyway, quite soon, no doubt. Ling's calmed down now and accepts things as they are. I was worried over Christmas for you, as I wasn't sure how your friendship would go.'

Justin was unused to someone worrying about his welfare. It was a pleasant experience. This arrangement with Linda, if that's what it was, was very appealing to him. She was right; he might be working abroad soon. He guessed she might sleep with other men. The thing was, not to ask questions and to wear a condom. He was surprised that regarding Linda as a revelation didn't stop him from thinking of self-preservation. Ling had hinted that she was a bit wild. Justin, still mesmerised by her, hadn't asked for details. She left before light and Justin forced himself to settle down to text Dad. He told him he'd come up at the weekend and to give the twins his love. Then he texted Clara, repeating the message, saying he'd sleep downstairs.

There were texts back. Dad was not really shocked, apparently, but totally saddened. He was very supportive and ready to keep a careful eye on the twins, whom he'd bring to see him very soon. In the one from Clara, she was amazed that he could manage to come to Suffolk so soon after returning to London, when it suited him. She had told the twins, she added. They were upset of course. Den had promised to bring them to Bertha as soon as he could arrange it with Phil, where he'd cadge a bed. These texts triggered Justin's next move.

He still needed to speak to Phil. It was just getting light. He didn't need to leave for another fifteen minutes. On looking out of a porthole window, he saw Phil's lights were on.

Phil nearly undid him by being unexpectedly tender, giving him a bear hug in sympathy. There wasn't time to get into details, but it was clear that Phil was intending to be supportive. As he left, Phil rubbed Justin's back.

'Lad, you know I'm only across the yard. Any time.' His voice was gruff.

Justin gulped his appreciation, ran down the stairs across to Bertha, where he turned down the stove, locked up, unlocked his bike from the roof and set off for another day at work.

Clara had sat the children down. 'Carl, Zoe, I have to talk to you about Mummy and Daddy. Before I say anything, I want you both to know that we love you very much.'

Two small faces looked at her across the kitchen table.

'Are you ill?' Zoe burst out.

'I don't think it's like that,' Carl whispered.

'How d'you know anything I don't? It's not fair!' Zoe tried pushing her chair back to run off.

'Children, children, please. Neither of you knows what I'm going to tell you, so calm down, Zoe.'

Zoe huffed, but settled back in her chair.

'Daddy and I have decided, that…' She faltered, before making another attempt. 'Daddy and I are living separate lives now.' Before either of the children could add anything, she galloped on. 'We've decided to have a divorce. But not much will change. We shall still live here. Grandad will still be in his lodge. It'll just mean Daddy will stay at Grandad's when he comes to visit.'

This time it was Carl who moved. 'Well, I think it's very unfair! Daddy should be able to stay with us!' With that he shot off, out of the kitchen into the garden. Arthur was keen to follow. It was raining hard, but Carl was so full with how he felt, he hardly noticed and didn't stop until he got to the bottom shed, where someone had left the door open. He went inside, pulling the door to, with Arthur squeezed in next to him.

Zoe sat observing Clara. 'I think it was your idea, Mummy, or Daddy would have told us. We can still go and see Daddy on Bertha, can't we? We love Daddy and Bertha.'

Clara was totally unnerved. She had known it would be difficult, but it had felt much, much worse. Perhaps in a day or two everything would calm down. Now she'd better go and find Carl. She wondered if anything would comfort them and decided on eggy bread, where the twins helped to soak the liquid by squidging it down with wooden spoons. At least it would be an activity, and she might use Den to help lift their spirits. He did have a knack.

Later, Carl and Zoe sat on Zoe's bed, holding hands.

'I found a door in Sybil's garden wall.'

'What's that got to do with all this? Your silly friend gets on my nerves.' If they'd been on Carl's bed she'd have flounced off, but it was her bed, so she just shoved him.

Carl ignored her. 'I pushed it,' he whispered, his eyes big as saucers.

Carl had her attention now. 'What? And?'

'And it opened to a big shed.'

'Now you're boring. Not exactly exciting, is it?'

'We could run away is what I'm getting at. It's dry, you see, and not too cold. Only Sybie knows I found it. It's quite overgrown, their garden.'

'Sybie! Ha! She couldn't keep a secret.' In spite of scoffing, Zoe was beginning to get the idea.

'We could leave a note to say we've gone to live with Daddy. That'd make Mummy think, wouldn't it? We'd only have to disappear just for one night and stay in the shed. She'd be so sorry she'd change her mind about the divorce. It would have to be cancelled.'

The decision made, they got out their rucksacks in readiness and waited until they thought Mummy, Grandad and Arthur were asleep. Then they decided that they'd have to take Arthur, because he'd never let them leave without him.

Eventually, the house was quiet. They'd gone to bed as normal, had bedtime stories with Grandad and made as if to settle. Mummy came in to tuck them up much later, when they'd pretended to be asleep, fully dressed under their pyjamas. They'd agreed that they should wait until midnight, then, using their watch torches, they crept downstairs, avoiding the middle of the fourth stair, which creaked.

The utility room held the store cupboards. They took juice, baked bean pots, spoons for the beans, chocolate biscuit bars, two satsumas, an old plastic bottle with water for Arthur and some kibble in a bag. They'd agreed to wear their old slightly small coats under their new bigger ones, gloves and beanies. Now they could scarcely move. They'd bribed Arthur with chews as soon as they'd got in the kitchen. All they had to do was unlock the old kitchen door, which could squeak in cold weather. Very carefully Carl undertook this chore, as Zoe occupied Arthur by tickling his tummy. Finally, they were outside and, keeping to the side of the cottage, crept out where the five-bar gate was always propped open, and into the lane. Once they were clear of the cottage, they strapped an old satchel round Arthur's neck. He stood willingly whilst they adjusted it, so it wasn't too tight, like a St Bernard, Carl said. Zoe had argued it was unfair that he had to carry food right under his nose. Carl said that it was an emergency. Suddenly, Zoe stumbled and stifled a cry.

'Zoe!'

'It's very dark,' she grumbled, her breath rising in a cloud above her. There was no moon, which was good and bad, she thought, as she crunched along, past Grandad's lodge and on towards the Hodges' property.

'Hold on to Arthur. He'll follow me,' Carl answered.

They reached the top of the lane without any mishap. Zoe suddenly stopped, but Arthur pulled her on, as Zoe hissed that she thought the neighbours had a cat.

Carl stopped mid-step, whispering urgently, 'I forgot! They've got two. Think they're in at night, so we may be okay.'

What they couldn't have known, which suddenly became evident, was that an approach light had been fitted by Mr Hodges and they were now in the middle of its beam, which startled Arthur. He barked his deep throaty bark, very loudly. Zoe and Carl were too startled to move, now bathed in a cold white light; they were unable to stop Arthur, either. If he had a viewpoint, and later they decided he certainly did, then it would be that he was their guardian. Much later, they awarded him a homemade rescue medal for his noble efforts. But now, right now, they were petrified.

Arthur couldn't be calmed. The light started to blink, which made him more frantic. A window was thrown open and Mr Hodges appeared, his hair standing up in a strange way. As the twins tried to get away from the blinking, a new, full glare was triggered.

'What's going on? What's happened?'

Carl gathered himself to his full height. This was important. 'We're running away to stop Mummy from having a divorce, only it's sort of gone wrong...' His speech faded as he lost courage.

'Actually, we want Mummy to think we've gone to live with Daddy. We didn't know you had approach lights,' Zoe added, now defiant.

Mr Hodges, bewildered and not fully awake, called, 'Stay there, I'm coming down.'

They were in no mood to run back home. And Arthur, now calm, sat down. All they had to do was to remove his satchel and he'd be comfortable.

Mr and Mrs Hodges took them into the kitchen. Zoe noticed that Mrs Hodges had a dressing gown made of teddy bear material and she decided immediately that she'd ask for one just like it for her birthday, if she lived that long. Thoughts of their parents' anger had not escaped her. Mr Hodges offered them hot chocolate and seats at the table. He suggested they remove Arthur's satchel as he didn't look comfortable and he took up enough room anyway, but wasn't going to risk approaching him himself. Arthur had been first through the door to the kitchen and Mr Hodges, a cat person, was overwhelmed by his presence and hadn't attempted to stop him. The cats had escaped to the landing, ruffled by this untoward intrusion to their night's sleep by the warm Aga. Mrs Hodges said she was very sorry, but that they would need to ring home and report that Zoe and Carl were safe. She was discreet enough not to test their reasons for wanting to run away, or why they had decided that their route would take them through the wildness that was their garden. She resolved, however, that as soon as the frost lifted, they'd get cracking on sorting out the mess they'd inherited there.

Clara hadn't been sleeping well. She was tormented by the enormity of her actions and had gone downstairs to make a hot drink, hoping to calm down. She filled the kettle, pulled down a mug, then thought that she'd like some toast and, reaching across the table to take out some bread from the bin, saw the note. She sat down. The kettle boiled unnoticed. Looking around, she realised Arthur was missing. Grabbing a coat from the utility, she dashed outside, calling the twins and Arthur.

Den was a heavy sleeper normally, but the last few days had disturbed his sleeping pattern. He sat up, sure he'd heard something outside and pulled a curtain back, only to see a shadow moving around waving its arms about and calling. It was Clara: something was up. He pulled on his dressing gown, scrabbled for his slippers and, hurrying downstairs, tied his dressing-gown belt. Clara had left the door open and he rushed outside to discover how cold it had become, gasping in the freezing air. 'Whatever is it? What's happened, Clara?'

'They've run away, in this cold. They'll freeze to death and they've let Arthur out. I'm getting the Land Rover to drive towards the main road. They can't have got far.'

'I'll come with you. We should put on warmer things and ring the police too. What about Justin?'

'What about him?'

Den, stunned, thought that in shock, Clara could be forgiven for dismissing Justin. But he'd bring it up again very soon, although he earnestly hoped it wouldn't be necessary. It was about one in the morning now, and they didn't know when the twins had set off.

Isla Hodges was worried that no one was answering the Kerrs' telephone. It was hard to believe that Clara and Den were out at this time of night, leaving the children to their own devices. Admittedly, Arthur was quite an intimidating animal, but she would never leave children alone at night with a dog as childminder. Then she heard next door's Land Rover in the lane. Well, they must be home. She'd give them time to get indoors and try again in a minute or two.

Den drove, as Clara reported the children's disappearance to the police, driving slowly towards the main road. They were instructed to return home to await the police who would be there within half an hour. Clara said that it was mad to just go home and wait.

'We might see them walking along if they're making for Bury. If not, we can turn round when we see the police car coming.'

Den didn't bother to comment that they wouldn't know which direction the police car would come from. He knew they needed to do something, even if it proved futile, which it did ultimately. After moving fairly slowly, searching each side of the road into the trees as they went, they saw nothing, except once, when Den had to almost stop as a fox sauntered across the road in the glare of their headlights. Eventually, they decided to give up and go back. The twins couldn't possibly have walked all these miles, Clara was sure, although there was no sign of a police car yet, either.

James Hodges decided he'd walk down the lane to the Kerrs' cottage to see if there was any sign of life. He couldn't understand how there appeared to be no one at home in the early hours of a weekday night. They'd tried phoning again, after hearing the vehicle pass by. He took a crowbar with him. When Isla Hodges raised an eyebrow, he just shook his head. She didn't say anything, not wanting to draw attention to the weapon. Obviously, he was concerned there may have been something more going on than just two children and their dog leaving in the night.

As Den turned into the drive, they saw James Hodges by the kitchen door, holding what looked like a crowbar. He waved at them frantically, dropping the crowbar, just as a police car screeched in behind the Land Rover, scattering gravel. Den parked up as Clara jumped out and marched over to James. They were talking animatedly over each other. Den got between them with the idea of calming both parties, but James, regretting already his family's move to the top of the lane next to these maniacs, pushed Den aside, which caused him to fall backwards into the arms of a surprised constable.

'Whoa, whoa. Okay, everyone. I'm Constable Makejoy and this is Constable Reeves. We've answered a call for two missing children and possibly a dog. I take it we are at the correct address?'

Constable Reeves fetched out her notebook to check. Constable Makejoy carefully stood Den up against the kitchen wall.

'Okay, sir? Shall we go inside? This cold could bring on pneumonia.'

If Den hadn't been suffering from some sort of shock, he would have defended his sturdy health. But they all shuffled inside, James leaving his crowbar propped up in the porch.

Once inside, Clara turned on him, 'James, why were you here? What was the crowbar for?'

James, used to the suburbs, where nobody got involved with their neighbours, was out of his depth in this rural madhouse and almost forgot why he was in Clara and Justin's kitchen. 'The twins,' he managed.

'Yes?' came back from Clara and Den in unison.

He took a deep breath, feeling cornered. 'They're with us. They were apparently running away. Somehow got into our garden with that nightmare dog.'

Den huffed. Clara, hysterical with relief and totally out of character, shoved James in the chest.

'Why didn't you bring them back?'

'We rang you immediately, but you were out. Hence why I came down on my own. We couldn't understand what was wrong here.'

Den looked at Clara, shook his head in irritation, and pointed at James. 'What d'you think? We were out looking for them!'

James wanted to feel sorry for these people, but it wasn't proving easy. Still, it wasn't his problem. He'd be diplomatic. 'They did explain what it's all about. But I think they're very tired now.' He'd been tempted, so tempted, to blurt out the divorce revelation. Glad he'd resisted. After all, they were neighbours, but he did wonder for how long. Clara, grudgingly thought James, considering the seriousness of events, thanked him and Isla for taking the children in, but she didn't even mention that small donkey, Arthur, who'd frightened Babs and Sniffy out of the kitchen, not to mention terrifying him.

Constable Makejoy insisted that he and Constable Reeves drive up the lane with James and his crowbar to collect the twins. Den offered to go with them to walk Arthur back. Constable Makejoy, observing James collecting his crowbar, was curious as to why a neighbour would carry a crowbar to the Kerrs' establishment.

'Didn't know what lay ahead of me, is all.'

The constable grimaced, but it seemed to satisfy him and they set off, with Clara left behind, making up hot-water bottles, then preparing hot drinks and toast ready for them all. She looked up at the clock on the wall. It was almost four. It would hardly be worth going to bed by the time everyone was back. She'd keep the twins home from school, obviously. But, once back home and seated around the kitchen table, Zoe and Carl insisted they weren't a bit tired. Den looked across at them, on their second rounds of toast, as he sipped his whisky between gulps of coffee. He thought they'd all come out of it rather well, considering. He still couldn't grasp why the children had gone into the Hodges' garden, but that had been a blessing. It could have been so much worse. Strangely enough, Zoe and Carl seemed to have forgotten why they'd run away and were enthusing over the police car ride back down the lane. They considered Constable Makejoy the hero of the night, along with Arthur – Arthur for protecting them when the lights blazed on and he thought there was danger, then the red and blue flashing lights Constable Makejoy employed on the short drive back minus the siren.

Eventually, Clara got the twins to go to bed. When she came back, Den had come up with a plan, which he hoped she'd agree to.

'It's like this Clara – although it saddens me, more than I can say, I accept that you and Justin are following different paths.' He paused for a moment, gathering the right words, as Clara looked at him speculatively, wondering what gem might be coming next. 'Justin mentioned he'd come up at the weekend to discuss things, but how about, instead, I take the twins to London? Sort of begin as we mean to go on? I'm happy to take them regularly if you both agree.'

Clara couldn't think straight just then, but didn't turn the idea down out of hand. She suggested they get their heads down for a couple of hours, then have a rethink, after they'd let Justin know. Aha, Den thought, she's going to tell him after all. With that he took the last drop of whisky and climbed the stairs to the bed with the flat mattress.

It was agreed. Justin, initially horrified at the twins' attempt to run away, was then reassured by the idea that they would come to him at the weekend, just a day away now. Dad would bring down more of his clothes and some books he'd requested. He could see that it made sense to start up some sort of routine for them as soon as possible, and Dad seemed keen to take on the chore, which in fairness it would be. Phil was now in on all the latest. He had been concerned about the children's efforts to reverse their mother's decision, then relieved at the safe outcome. Almost all the latest, but not quite, Justin thought, guilt causing his face to flush in discomfort for not being upfront with Phil, who had shown nothing but kindness towards him. It didn't help, either, that Linda was still a question mark in every sense. His head filled with images of her, not least her light-hearted, evasive quality. He sighed in defeat. She remained a fascinating enigma.

Phil welcomed the idea of the twins' visit, and insisted that Den stay with him, as it was a bit tight on the boat, which of course it would be, and Justin didn't fancy sleeping with his dad in the double bed if he didn't have to. Clara seemed relaxed about Justin delaying his next visit to Suffolk under the circumstances. He hadn't really talked to her since her announcement of wanting a divorce, but Justin hadn't been idle, and had spoken to the legal team at work for guidance. He'd been given the name of divorce solicitors in the city. He needed offices somewhere within reach, and although he didn't want to find himself left without anything, the fees did give him pause.

*

Den arrived with the twins in Justin and Clara's old Land Rover instead of his new hybrid. Phil had warned that hybrids' catalytic converters were being stolen all across London, causing huge bills to put right, so Den's new silent car remained safely in Suffolk at Clara's disposal.

Justin worked late but got back to Bertha, strapped up his bike, got inside and checked the slow-cooker casserole, ready for them all. He'd invited Phil, selfishly hoping another body would help with what he was concerned might be an emotional time. Phil accepted his role, saying he'd bring Harvey too and they came over just before Den tooted from the end of the lane. Justin and Phil went out to help with baggage and to welcome the twins with a hug. Harvey made straight for the twins who knelt down on the frosting ground to fuss him; then, on Den's instruction, they took their rucksacks from him, and Justin took more bags as Den emptied the rear of the Land Rover. He and Phil came up last, as Harvey scampered between them all, jubilant at having something to do.

Once inside Bertha, they peeled off coats in the warm cabin as Justin placed the casserole on the table. Everyone squeezed around the small space, as he ladled out helpings.

Initially, the twins were subdued, until Zoe, squirming in her seat, spoke up. 'Daddy, when are you coming home?' She looked at Justin very carefully, watchfully. Carl stared at his casserole; the other two froze.

'Probably next weekend, sweetheart. Mummy and I need to talk. You understand that this is really my home now, although I shall come and stay with Grandad a lot, I'm sure, to see you all.' Justin could hear how he'd fumbled his explanation.

'Sybil said you're going to have a proper divorce. Is that true?' Carl was staring now.

Justin sensed that Sybil's parents had been discussing the Kerrs' predicament. Understandable under the circumstances, he thought, but he hadn't talked to Clara yet. He sidestepped Carl's question by getting up to pour more drinks, eyes following him in the awkward silence. Phil collected the finished plates and cutlery, placing them at the side for Den to put in the sink. Then, as a surprise, Phil produced ice creams in different flavours as his contribution, providing cones, waving an ice cream scoop in one hand, hopefully distracting further from a need to answer questions. Immediately, there were discussions on which flavour was going to be best. When they'd finished their cones, Phil said he wanted to make a toast.

'Are our glasses charged, everyone?' Phil looked around.

'Charged? What's charged, Uncle Phil?' Carl was aware it must be something special, as he and Zoe watched Daddy pass Grandad another beer and then fill their small glasses with juice.

Justin would have liked a whisky himself, but there wasn't time. He didn't want to break this temporary spell.

'Are we ready everyone?' Phil looked around the table. 'Okay, I'd like us to raise our glasses, all of us, to how lucky we all are to love and be loved, regardless of where we live and where our loved ones live. You know it makes sense. Glasses up, everyone!'

Too astonished to object, they all raised their glasses.

'Have to clink or it doesn't count!' Phil added.

Somewhat mollified, Zoe insisted they then clinked with Harvey's water bowl. Thanks mainly to Phil, the evening ended on a light note. Phil and Den eventually left with Harvey, Phil having previously discussed with Justin booking the twins for a ride on his motorboat in the morning to get supplies.

Later, much later, nursing the much-needed whisky, the stove almost out, risking his socks on its rather beautifully embossed top, toes toasting pleasantly, Justin listened to the children's steady breathing. Tonight, he thought, the children had passed a hurdle. It would all have to be endured many times, no doubt in different ways and in different environments, but they had begun a new journey. They're going to be okay, he thought.

His thoughts drifted to Clara at Keeper's Cottage, staking her claim to country living, being where she wanted to be almost more than anywhere, except perhaps Finland. He could afford to be generous enough, to acknowledge the cost to her in initiating their divorce, and her undoubted current suffering. Then there was Dad, having discovered where he wanted to live as well. Justin hoped Dad could stay; he flourished around the twins, without doubt.

Lastly, he considered himself. He saw himself in a rather unfavourable light overall. It was clear he could have tried harder with his marriage (but not very much in reality) and he was saddened by that truth. He'd chosen work over redundancy and there lay new responsibilities, which he'd found, to his surprise, he'd enjoyed, savoured even, but at very considerable cost to them all. But then, in fairness, they'd both wanted different things.

He was very tired now. He stood, waiting for the kettle to heat for his hot-water bottles. His ankle still troubled him. He allowed himself a wry smile. The ankle would always be a physical reminder, if nothing else, of Clara and her determination not to budge and of Dad's equal determination to keep him in the loop at the Suffolk end in those early days. The kettle boiled. He filled his bottles, checking the twins were snug under their duvets, before making his way to the bulkhead. At last in bed, he found he still was wide awake, one bottle near his ankle, the other against his back. He wriggled his feet in simple pleasure.

So, then, he thought, those he loved, had loved, were on their own various paths, with the year still before them, the year waiting for them. In spite of the shock of recent events and, he had to admit, an anger he still felt lurking beneath the surface, sitting uncomfortably alongside grief, the grief of loss he couldn't deny, he would be hopeful, was hopeful, that eventually they were all going to be okay and, turning out the light, he attempted to settle down.

Lightning Source UK Ltd.
Milton Keynes UK
UKHW012046031220
374578UK00001B/152